"Good friends are like stars. You don't always see them, but you know they're always there."

– Christy Evans

SPELLBORN

BOOK ONE:
THE HIDDEN STAR

Y. KAYDIN

ILLUSTRATED BY PATIGONART

Grosvenor House
Publishing Limited

This book is published by
Grosvenor House Publishing Ltd
Link House
140 The Broadway, Tolworth, Surrey, KT6 7HT.
www.grosvenorhousepublishing.co.uk

A CIP record for this book
is available from the British Library

Paperback ISBN 978-1-80381-050-8
Hardback ISBN 978-1-80381-051-5
eBook ISBN 978-1-80381-052-2

DEDICATION

This book is for my beautiful mother, for always filling my childhood with love, magic, and imagination, no matter how dark life seemed. You have always been and always will be my shining star. And my sister, for being the first person I shared my story with. Thank you for all your support. I couldn't have made it without you both.

ACKNOWLEDGEMENTS

Thank you to GHP for turning my book into a reality.

CONTENTS

PROLOGUE

The night was pleasantly warm but with a cooling, gentle breeze that softly whispered through the long slender branches of the pink and green willow trees. Fireflies danced, flickering beneath a blanket of burning stars that stretched to infinity. The beaming glow of the full moon reflected upon a ribbon-like body of water that twinkled under the moons mighty presence and gently streamed into the river below. Where a gold towering bridge shielded the river mermaids from its bright light that disturbed their sleep. The mermaids were huddled closely together, dreaming blissfully with the odd toroidal bubble escaping their mouths each time they snored.

But sadly, not all was blissful in the lands of Grazia that evening.

Searching deep into the stars, behind a line of brass telescopes stood work bunnies, writing reports, taking notes, working their usual routine. As one of the optics slowly panned across the sky, with terror it quickly shifted back to what was once a perfect chain of aligned stars, which now was rapidly distorting out of place. The bunnies ran around in chaos, with their notes flying around the room. Panic-stricken, one of them struggled to pull a large lever, so five more hopped on, finally managing to sound the alarm. Large, deeply carved wooden doors with great gold bolts instantly burst open, revealing a tall, thin mystical man with a long white beard.

"What's wrong?" the old man said. He limped towards the bunnies, using his sceptre as a walking stick. The bunnies ran towards the telescope, jumping up and down on the spot, making gestures and grunting noises, indicating something was wrong. The old man lowered his head and calmly took a glance with one eye.

"Good god!" he cried, swiftly pacing across the marbled floors to the middle of the room where a large crystal ball sat in a stand made from oak wood. The bunnies chaotically followed behind him. He picked up his sceptre and gently tapped the crystal ball with it. The whole room was instantly swallowed by darkness, surrounded only by stars, almost if they had teleported into space itself. The bunnies' ears pressed back as their little noses twitched, some standing on their hind legs, gazing at the false stars' with wonder. The old man, with his hands clasped behind his back, strolled over to the disturbing image that had him flustered. Inspecting the misshapen stars that were once perfectly aligned left a fearful look on his face. He sternly turned his head to one of the bunnies.

"Spread the word and warn the others." The bunny immediately hopped away, doing as it was told. Unclutching his hands, the old man gently stroked his silky white beard all the way down to the tip with a look of dismay in his eyes.

"So... it *begins.*"

LAKESHORE
SPELLENBORG
HEALERS TOWN
GRAZIA
ORO CITY

S LANDS
COLD MOUNTAIN
STORMVILLE
VINE CITY
THE GLASS CASTLE
CRAVING WOODS
SPELLBORN
SOMBRA

LAKESHORE
CHAPTER ONE

Large pillows of ominous clouds were slowly closing in, until they completely blocked out what little of the sun was left. The cold autumn sky darkened like a nightmare. Then came the first drops of rain emerging like bullets from the deathly clouds above, lashing down violently onto the school's roof. A gloomy young girl with a look of despair sat by one of the windows. With her pale hand pressed against her soft cheek, she daydreamed, watching the rain drizzle down the sides of the stained glass like teardrops.

"Ruya... Ruya Lakely!" Miss Gumberg violently whipped her cane onto the girl's desk, startling her enough to jump out of her pale skin. "What have I told you about daydreaming in my class, girl? Any more of that nonsense, you'll get extra work. I'd hate to have to give you toilet duty again!" Miss Gumberg sneered. The rest of the girls silently hid their giggles in the palms of their hands.

"Sorry, Miss Gumberg, it won't happen again," Ruya quietly replied with her head down, sighing as she continued to watch the rain beating down on the classroom window near where she always sat.

She was 16 years old, and unlike most girls her age, Ruya was a very shy and respectful young lady. She was petite and possessed beautiful, long chocolate brown hair that waved past her ribcage and dark eyes that complemented her pasty, fair skin. She was an orphan; nobody knew who she was or where she had come from. When she was just a babe, she was left by the foot of the door at Lakeshore, an old boarding school for girls that sat upon a hill in the middle of the woods surrounded by tall pine trees. She was wrapped in a blanket made from velvet as dark as the night sky embroidered with shimmering silver stars, bundled in a poorly made basket of sticks. She was taken in by the women of Lakeshore and had been raised and given a name.

Ruya wasn't like the other girls; while they spent their time fixing their hair and obsessing over boys, she would be in a corner somewhere with her nose buried in a fairy-tale book. Ruya was full of imagination and had always hoped someday something interesting and exciting would happen to her, to save her from her dull, boring life. Little did she know, today was the day her life was about to change forever.

The lunch bell rang. "Off you go now, girls," said Miss Gumberg, impatiently clapping her hands, shooing away the students out of her classroom like flies.

Ruya was the last to leave, but before she made it out, Miss Gumberg threw her large arm across with force, taking up the doorway. Every time Ruya gazed at her, she would fall into another one of her daydreams. She imagined she was a princess and Miss Gumberg was an ogre keeping her captive and making her life a misery, only there was no Prince Charming to save her. Not that she needed one. Ruya had always been independent and only relied on herself because she knew she only had herself to rely on. "You know, Ruya, I've noticed you daydreaming quite a lot in my class, and frankly I'm quite sick of it," said Gumberg.

"I'm sor—"

"Ah ah ah," she tutted, moving her chubby pink finger from side to side, not letting her get a word in edgeways. "You think you're special, is that it? So, while the other girls are working hard, you think you get to wander off into your own world with your silly imagination and not get any work done. Well not in my class! Get your act together."

Ruya just stood there and nodded like every other time Miss Gumberg gave her a scolding.

"Now be gone with you!" she grunted, harshly slamming the classroom door in her face without any remorse whatsoever. Ruya sighed, nodding her head from side to side, for she was sick and tired of constantly being picked on for the silliest things. She was making her way to the library where she'd often go when the lunch bell rang, the only place she felt free and safe. She had no friends; the other girls often addressed her as 'Basket Girl.'

The only friends she had were the ones she read in books.

"Where you off to, Basket Girl?"

Just when she had escaped Miss Gumberg, she had another encounter with an even more vile human being. Ruya, not paying any attention, continued to walk by with her head down. "I asked you a question!" the girl snapped viciously, grabbing Ruya by the arm.

"You off to the library again to spend time with your imaginary friends on the pages of a dusty old book? How pathetic." Lucinda and her friends laughed and brushed by Ruya's shoulder, giggling spitefully as they walked off, but not before slapping her book out of her hands.

Meanwhile, Miss Gumberg hid in the shadows, watching from afar with a hateful grin on her horrid face, like she always did whenever a student she didn't like was being bullied.

Ruya put up with a lot of spiteful girls in the school, but none compared to Lucinda Dowling. She was a nasty piece of work who thought very highly of herself and looked down on anyone who wasn't her. She was the complete opposite to Ruya. She had big gleaming blue eyes and perfect golden locks that were nicely held together with a huge pink bow. And her dress was always so perfect; it was sickening.

Ruya felt her nose burning; it made her eyes water. "*Don't cry... don't cry,*" she argued with herself, kneeling down to pick her book up off the floor. Dusting it off, she sat on the bottom step of a wooden staircase, taking a deep breath in, desperately trying to convince herself not to cry. "Come on, Ruya. Stop letting them get to you." She held her book tightly to her chest like a mother protecting her infant. Just when she thought she was OK, she suddenly began sobbing in her hands like a little child. She was sobbing so much that she hadn't noticed a strange scruffy girl on top of the staircase watching her with great curiosity.

The girl, intrigued, didn't speak a word. Chewing away, she continued to watch Ruya cry for a few seconds longer while eating a piece of stale bread she had stolen from Cook Fumble's kitchen earlier that day. Finally taking a large gulp, the girl decided to speak. "Oos upset you then?" she casually asked.

Ruya quickly raised her head and looked behind her. A boyish-looking girl with short black scruffy hair and eyes black as coal leaned over the wooden banisters. With one hand pressed against her dirty cheek and the other holding a loath of bread, the girl smiled.

"Who are you?" said Ruya, shooting up from the step, wiping her wet cheek.

With her legs dangling to one side, the girl slid down the banisters using one hand. Reaching the bottom of the stairs with a big jump, she readjusted her oversized hat and held out her hand in a friendly gesture. "Name's Drew Button." She coughed after taking another big bite of her bread, wiping the crumbs from her mouth with her sleeve.

Drew was a daredevil, not afraid of anything or anyone. She had a sharp tongue with a heart of gold. She wasn't the prettiest of girls, she knew that but wasn't fazed by it in the slightest, for she wasn't one for vanity, and she certainly didn't care what people thought about her. She was extremely scruffy, and her clothes were far too big for her; she would often roll up her sleeves because they were so long. Her hands were constantly dirty, but she hid them well with her fingerless gloves. And like Ruya, she had no friends and only depended on herself. Clasping hands, the girls shook.

"I'm Ruya Lakely."

"So, *Ruya Lakely*, why were you crying then?" she said, curiously scratching her chin.

"Oh... it's nothing really. Honestly, I'm just being silly," Ruya chuckled, wiping away her last tear that sparkled like a dewdrop in sunlight.

"Didn't look like nothing... are you a liar, Ruya?"

"What, no!" Ruya answered, looking slightly confused.

"'Coz I can't be friends with a liar, and nobody cries like that for no good reason."

"You... you want to be my friend?" Ruya asked, very suspiciously. For all the years living in Lakeshore, no one has ever attempted to talk to her, let alone be her friend.

"Of course, why wouldn't I?" she casually answered, not understanding why she would find such a thing strange.

Ruya suddenly felt a twinge of happiness, for she had made her very first friend and had never known what that felt like.

"So... you going to tell me why you were so upset then or what?"

Ruya hesitated. "Just some girls. Do you know Lucinda?"

"*Dowling*?" Drew responded, not looking surprised at all.

"Yes," Ruya sniffled.

"Of course. The girl's a pain in the backside," Drew tutted, rolling her dark eyes.

"That she is, so are her friends," Ruya continued, wiping her wet cheek with the back of her sleeve.

"Listen, Ruya... pay no mind to girls like that; they don't deserve your tears, especially someone like *Lucinda Dowling*. Never let them know that they got the better of you. You gotta be strong in any situation life throws at you cause there will be a time when you're gonna have to be. Sometimes you have to stand up to bullies no matter how big or scary they seem. Cause there will always be someone or something bigger than you, but just because they're bigger doesn't necessarily mean they're stronger. Always stand up for yourself... Got it!"

Ruya smiled and nodded at her kind words. "Wow, you're pretty wise, aren't you?"

"Far from it," Drew chuckled. "But I know in life, you've got to stand up for what you believe in no matter the cost, or else what's the point?"

Ruya paused and stared at her for a few seconds with a soft, bashful smile. "Why are you being so nice to me? We just met; you barely know me," she said.

"But I know Lucinda... *unfortunately*, and I really hate bullies. They make me sick."

The girls both paused. Ruya, still tightly gripping onto her book that was pressed against her warm body, awkwardly swished the tip of her shoe from side to side and opened her mouth to try to make conversation. But never being spoken to by anyone in the school, she didn't know how.

"I'm hungry. Are you hungry? I'm hungry," Drew huffed, rubbing her belly, finally breaking the silence.

"Sure, I could do with a bite," agreed Ruya, not realising she was hungry until she was asked.

"Before we go and eat, mind if I make a quick stop?"

"No, of course not." Ruya smiled, as she was happy to go anywhere with her new friend.

"C'mon then." Drew began leading the way up the stairs and down a wide hall cluttered with old painted portraits and dorm rooms on each side. With every blazer they passed, hung up on little brass hooks just outside the students' rooms, Drew carefully placed her hand in each pocket, hoping she would find something good. She had managed very early on in life to master the craft of being the best pickpocket in the whole of Lakeshore.

They continued their journey to another passageway to what seemed to lead to more stairs, which eventually led them to a small landing with a battered door made from rusty rotten wood. Drew placed her hand on the door and gave it a push.

As it creaked open, the crumbling ceiling dispelled dust over them, sending a tingling sensation to the back of their throats, leading them into a fit of coughs. "Hate when that happens," Drew moaned, waving her hand about, feeling slightly annoyed.

The dust cleared, and it revealed a little attic room. Ruya put one foot through the door.

"Watch your head!" Drew warned, quickly reaching out her hand. "Doorway's a little low. I still somehow always manage to bump mine," she chuckled.

"Is this your room?" asked Ruya, stepping further into the dusty old attic.

"Yeah, never did like sharing with the other girls."

The room was small but cosy in a strange sense. There were cobwebs settling in the corners of the wooden beams, and the floors creaked and cracked with every step they took.

"Wow, what a view! You can almost see the whole forest from up here. You're so lucky," Ruya gasped, excitedly leaning out of a little round window while trying to shield herself from the pouring rain that slightly sprayed its way through, leaving specks of water splattered on her face. But Ruya didn't mind; in fact, she loved being in the rain.

"The view's okay, I guess." Drew shrugged, not paying much attention to her.

Ruya finally turned away from the window to find Drew counting buttons that were neatly laid out on her bed. "Twenty-six… twenty-seven… twenty-eight. Damn, nearly made it. Oh well, next time," she tutted, angry at herself for not reaching thirty.

"What are you doing?" Ruya curiously asked.

"Counting buttons," Drew replied.

"I can see that," she laughed. "Where did you get them?"

"Stole 'em," she casually answered, sniffling her leaky nose. She gently collected the buttons with one hand, sliding them into the other, being careful not to drop them. She walked across the creaking floorboards to the other side of her room to a dusty bookshelf where she pulled out a little jar of buttons and added the 28 more she had stolen that day to her collection.

"It's getting there," she smiled proudly with both hands placed on her hips.

Although Drew was sometimes wise with her words and the same age as Ruya, she had a more childlike sense about her, whereas Ruya was quite mature for her age and tended to act more like a sensible adult. But that was mainly because she had no one to be childish with, until now.

"Right then… let's go for that lunch," said Drew, clapping her two filthy hands together, feeling rather pleased with herself. Ruya, not asking any questions about the buttons, just smiled as usual and went along with her new friend. Once again, they found themselves walking through yet another large hallway smothered with portraits. Some of the students brushed by them, walking in and out of their dorm rooms giggling, gossiping very loudly over one another like a bunch of cackling witches. They passed one room with a girl sitting on her bed in agony, struggling to brush the locks out of her knotty hair with a bristly brush. The next room they passed was four girls secretly gossiping among themselves. "Did you see her hideous—" one of the girls noticed Drew and Ruya walking by and slammed the door shut in their faces.

"Don't flatter yourselves," Drew yelled. "Thank god I don't share a room with any of these trolls."

"The headmistress must like you to let you have your own room. I hate sharing with the other girls. No one ever talks to me," Ruya sighed.

"Hence why I hate sharing. As for the headmistress, I've actually never met her," Drew replied.

"Neither have I," said Ruya. Lowering both her eyebrows, she curiously thought about it. "Don't you think that's a bit strange?" she continued.

"What?"

"Never meeting the headmistress?"

"Not really." Drew shrugged. "I heard she travels a lot, and she's only just returned from her latest trip. God, I could eat a horse! I'm starving!" she complained, too busy thinking about food and nothing else.

"Where are we going?" Ruya asked with a rumbling belly.

"Off to that old fart, Cook Fumble's kitchen."

Ruya's face looked unsure. "But students aren't allowed in the kitchen?"

"Oh, I'm not just a student," Drew smirked, leading the way down an unstable staircase that spiralled its way towards the kitchen, which was down in the basement.

Listening to the rumbles in her belly, Ruya followed without question. Reaching the large oak doors to the kitchen, they snuck in on all fours, crawling past Cook Fumble's legs while she was beating dough in a cloud of flour and humming a cheerful tune. Cook Fumble was a large, wobbly woman with a huge mole on the side of her chin that would put the girls off their food and was often the butt of cruel jokes. As the girls crawled through the aisles on all fours, Ruya, for the first time, gazed upon the kitchen, a room she had never entered before.

She looked upon the arched brick wall which concealed a large cauldron bubbling and boiling above the stove containing freshly sliced vegetables sown and reaped in the school greenhouse. The smell made their mouths water. It was a mixture of freshly baked bread, croissants with a hint of honey and a slight touch of the sugar-coated walnuts that were sometimes added to the porridge as a treat, although the students never had any, mostly the teachers ate all the good stuff. As Ruya looked up above her, brass pots and pans dangled and clattered, fine chipped china lined the old wooden dresser along with jars of herbs and spices. Drew snapped Ruya out of her daze, waving her hand impatiently, trying to grab her attention and pointing at the edge of a cheeseboard sitting on a wooden worktop garnished with a bunch of juicy, mouth-watering red grapes. As the girls made a grab for the cheeseboard, they hadn't seen the jug of warm milk, which was knocked over in the process, shattering to pieces, leaving a large puddle.

"OOS THAT?!"

Cook Fumble stopped what she was doing. The girls looked at each other in a sudden panic but still managed to grab the cheeseboard in time. They crawled as quick as they could under a nearby table. As they hid, Cook Fumble stomped about with her large feet and stopped at the table the girls were hiding under. Ruya felt her heart racing, while Drew, wide-eyed, slowly took a bite of cheese with a frightful look on her face.

"Come aat! I know you're in 'ere!" Suddenly, she bent down – "AHA! Gotcha!" – to see only a hunk of cheese with a large bite mark. Cook Fumble looked on curiously with her hand on her chin, scratching her mole. "Odd... rats are acting queer lately."

The door behind Cook Fumble swung shut as she reached for the mop, cleaning up the mess none the wiser. Out of breath, the girls were laughing with relief, pacing down the hallway. "Ang on... dropped my cheese. Bloody hell."

"Here, have half of mine." Ruya smiled, breaking the cheese in half.

Continuing to laugh, they ate their cheese and grapes on the way to the library.

"Basket Girl." A couple of girls giggled in passing.

"Basket Girl?" Drew raised an eyebrow, looking back at the girls, confused. "Who's she calling Basket Girl?" Thinking nothing of it, she swung her head back and caught another grape in her mouth.

Nibbling delicately on a piece of cheese, Ruya spoke. "I'm Basket Girl."

"Huh? What do you mean?"

"Well... I was left in a battered old basket made from sticks, so I was told, at the school door when I was just a baby. Hence the nickname Basket Girl." Ruya's face saddened as she explained the story. "I hate it when they call me that." She sniffled with a gentle tear appearing down her cheek.

Rolling up her sleeves, Drew stopped. "Should I go and give those girls what for?" she asked, angrily turning back in their direction.

"No, no," Ruya laughed, trying to stop her.

"You sure? Cause I'll be more than happy to. Who do they think they are?"

"Positive," she giggled.

Continuing their way to the library, Drew decided to share her story. "I'm an orphan too, you know. I was found in a button factory when I was five years old, just wandering about stealing buttons."

"Is that why your last name is Button?"

"Would you believe me if I said no, and it was just a funny coincidence?"

"No, not really," Ruya laughed

"Neither would I." Drew smirked, continuing to eat what was left of the grapes she held in her hand. "Nah, the factory owner caught me and put me to work counting buttons. The other workers would either call me 'Girl' or 'Button'. I didn't have a last name, and I was tired of people addressing me as Girl. So Button seemed more fitting, I guess," she explained, scratching her nose that was cute and round like a little button itself.

"Well, I can see now where your obsession with buttons comes from." Ruya smiled. "So, you were working at the age of five?" she asked curiously.

"Yep, until one day, I was being chased in the village because I went and got caught stealing bread. I stopped running when a loading carriage caught my eye. It was getting ready to take off, so I jumped in the back and hid in a hamper. I don't know what it was, but something was pulling me towards that carriage… like a strange energy." Drew's gaze wandered off suspiciously in the distance. "Anyway, glad it did; that's how I came to be here. Decided I liked the place, and the women seemed nice enough, said I could stay – so I did."

"Is that what you meant earlier when you said you weren't just a student? You live here?"

"It's a boarding school; all the girls live here," Drew laughed.

"Yes, but I mean permanently, this is your actual home where you grew up?" Ruya paused, then opened her mouth to speak again. "So… if you were raised here, and I was raised here, how come I've never seen you before? I think I would remember you. I mean, it's a big school but it's not that big."

Opening the library doors, Drew shrugged her shoulders, thinking nothing of it. Entering the library, Drew put both hands in her pockets and whistled in an impressive manner.

"So, this is what it looks like," she said, walking around blowing and wiping dust and cobwebs off the old books.

"You're joking, aren't you? You've honestly never been in the library before?" Ruya asked, looking shocked and slightly confused.

"Unless it's a kitchen, no point in bothering with the other rooms."

"God, I don't think I can make it a day without my books, I wouldn't survive. It's the only thing that keeps me going."

"Ten buttons sez you can," Drew challenged with a big grin.

BANG!

The storm grew more violent; a downpour of heavy rain lashed down. The raindrops were so strong, it sounded as if the stained-glass windows were going to shatter into a million pieces and bring down the whole school. The wind whistled to the dancing trees that violently swished from side to side like ballerinas swaying their elegant arms in the air.

"Woah, it's really coming down hard out there." Drew shivered, standing by a window with both arms wrapped around her body. "Love a good old storm, me. I liked to listen to the rain at the factory, it really helped me sleep. In some strange way, it gave me comfort."

"Me too!" Ruya jumped excitedly with a pile of books in her hands. "Finally, someone else that sees the beauty in what most people consider dreadful."

"Aww, how sweet," came a voice from behind a bookshelf. Lucinda stepped out of a shadow in the corner. "Basket Girl and the button scrounger. Must say, you two make a lovely couple. So what are you two losers getting up to in here anyway, hiding?"

"Why don't you just do one, Lucinda? You're not welcome here!" Drew spat, gritting her teeth tightly together.

"Well," she huffed, straightening out her dress. "No need to be rude." She walked further towards them. "Gotta admit, I'm surprised you two weirdos haven't associated sooner," she continued with a grin.

Drew felt a twinge of anger. Rolling up her sleeves, she began bolting towards Lucinda in a threatening manner.

"Go ahead, give me an excuse to go crying to that fat troll Gumberg."

Drew stopped.

"Thought so," she smirked with a cocky attitude, brushing by Drews's shoulder, flicking her perfect locks in her face, which made Drew's eyes flicker.

"God… what is your problem? Why can't you just leave us alone? Why do you have to be so nasty," Ruya shouted, the first time in her life to have ever raised her voice.

"I don't believe it; Basket Girl has a tongue. What, you think hanging around with this misfit suddenly gives you the right to talk back to me? Remember who you're talking to!" Lucinda threatened before giving Ruya a small unfriendly nudge on the shoulder.

"Oi!" Drew forcefully grabbed Lucinda with both hands on each side of her arms. "Don't you ever touch her like that again. Do you hear me?" she warned, shaking her with anger.

Unfazed by her threats, Lucinda sarcastically smirked and took no notice. Not taking her seriously at all, she just laughed it off, like she laughed off most things she didn't respect.

Until… something caught the side of her eye. Shifting her gaze towards one of the wet, foggy windows, Lucinda continued to pay no attention to Drew, who was extremely angry, shouting directly in her face. Lucinda was certain she had seen a rather unusual dark figure lurking in the trees outside in the rain, but when she looked again, it was mysteriously gone.

"Are you listening to me! Put your hand on her again, and I'll—"

"Yeah, yeah, whatever," she giggled, finally breaking free from Drew's grip.

"I think you should just leave," Ruya spoke quietly with her head down.

"I don't think so. I quite like it here," disagreed Lucinda, wiping a dusty shelf with her index finger and blowing the remains of the dust into Ruya's face.

Which was Drew's last straw. She leapt forward, striking her in the face. Lucinda fell to the ground and let out a dramatic cry.

"You made my nose bleed!" Lucinda gasped, looking up at Drew in complete shock. Never in a million years did she expect Drew would actually hit her.

"I didn't hit you that hard. You're being a drama queen." Drew glanced over towards Ruya with a childish smirk. "God, I could do that again."

Lucinda fiercely got back up off the ground, holding her bloody nose, when suddenly another student walked into the library, interrupting the girls' quarrel.

"GET GUMBERG!!" Lucinda commanded. The girl nervously pushed up her glasses with her index finger and ran back out of the library as quick as she could, clumsily bumping into other students, yelling down the hall and calling out for Miss Gumberg.

"You're in for it now. Just you wait."

"You provoked us first," Drew argued.

"Who do you think that fat dolt is going to believe? It's two against one, and I'm the one who's bleeding!" The two girls began to squabble among themselves with raised voices and hand gestures waving in the air. Suddenly, the doors burst open with no warning, startling them both to stop arguing.

"What's going on here?" Miss Gumberg barged in, waddling her way over to the commotion.

"She broke my nose!" Lucinda cried, stamping her foot like a spoilt child.

"Oh please. If I wanted to break your nose, I would have, believe me!"

"That's enough!" Miss Gumberg grunted, handing Lucinda a little handkerchief for her nose.

"Would somebody like to tell me what's going on?"

"What's the point? You're just gonna take her side anyway; you always bloody do," Drew spat, feeling annoyed, not giving Gumberg any eye contact whatsoever, staring across the other side of the room.

"Watch your mouth, girl," Miss Gumberg snorted, wide-eyed with a furious quiver to her lip.

"Well, miss," Lucinda politely interrupted. "I was quietly reading in the corner over there when I overheard them in an unpleasant conversation about you and the other teachers. I heard them calling you—" Lucinda hesitated. "A fat troll and all sorts of other unpleasant words I wouldn't dare repeat. A lady should never be heard repeating such vulgar language. It's absolutely disgusting and disgraceful. So, I felt like I had to come to your defence and put a stop to it, and that's when they both attacked me."

"LIAR!!" Drew jumped furiously with burning cheeks.

Once again, Drew, enraged, pounced for Lucinda. Miss Gumberg tried to stop her but slipped out of control and fell backwards, smacking into one of the bookshelves, which led her crashing down to the floor, along with a mountain of books that piled up on top of her like sprinkles on a cupcake. The girls immediately stopped in panic. The situation quickly became extremely uncomfortable and intense. Lucinda tried to suppress a giggle, while Ruya felt anxiety building up as she tried her best to pluck up the courage to speak.

"M... Mi... Miss Gumberg. Are you okay?" Ruya hesitantly asked, gingerly walking closer to her with sweaty hands, nervously gripping onto her books. Miss Gumberg rapidly jumped back up on her two feet with such rage you could almost see the steam coming out of her ears. Flared nostrils, clenched jaw, she balled her hands into fists as she glared at the girls gnashing her teeth from side to side with a face as red as a beetroot.

"YOU TWO!" She pointed her chubby finger towards Drew and Ruya. "With me. NOW!"

Not giving either of the girls a chance to explain or defend themselves, she grabbed them, holding on to each of their collars and pulled them out of the library. Lucinda, as usual, got away with it, giving them a smug little wave as they were brutally dragged away.

As the library doors shut behind them, all was silent, and Lucinda found herself all alone with an eerie feeling. Suddenly remembering what she had thought she saw earlier, she curiously skipped over to the window and wiped away the fog from the glass with her sleeve so she could get a clearer look, assuring herself she wasn't seeing things. She was certain she had seen something lurking outside in the trees. It didn't look human, she remembered thinking at the time. Was she going mad? Maybe she *was* seeing things, she thought with a strange look upon her face. Either way, she felt uneasy. Something wasn't right, that much she knew. Something was out there.

SCREAMERS
CHAPTER TWO

The girls stood to one side and laughed. With amusement they watched Miss Gumberg roughly drag and pull Drew and Ruya through the corridors like a couple of ragdolls. Although Gumberg was extremely rough with them, rushing by a wave of giggles, Drew still managed to stick out her tongue to the other students who took pleasure in watching them being manhandled. They continued to stand by and laugh, pointing and whispering into each other's ears. They loved it when someone was in trouble; it was the most exciting thing to ever happen in Lakeshore.

"So, you think it's funny, do you? Calling people names. Let's see what the headmistress has to say about this." Miss Gumberg grunted, dragging them through another long corridor with rolls of bookcases and stacks of empty wooded crates.

The girls had never met the headmistress but had heard she was regarded as a bit of an oddity. Being dragged through more corridors and passageways, they stopped at a wonky, dusty, spiral staircase, a bit like the one that led them to the kitchen, only this one was far more unstable. Proceeding with their journey, the girls wobbled from side to side in perfect rhythm with the stairs, making a racket as they walked up. It was an old building, and Gumberg was a heavy woman, and the stairs creaked and cracked with every step dispelling dust.

They had reached the highest room in the school. Miss Gumberg threw the two girls violently against the wall that had old wallpaper strips and large cracks going all the way down.

"Right. Wait here, the pair of you," Gumberg coughed, trying to catch her breath, holding her chest with one hand while the other supported her lower back.

"No!"

With a red, sweaty face, Gumberg slowly turned back around. "Excuse me? What did you just say?"

"I said no. We didn't do anything wrong. Why isn't Lucinda here? You know she's a bully and yet you do nothing about it," Drew forcefully spoke.

"I'll have you both scrubbing toilets. How dare you talk to me like that," Gumberg sneered, eyes wide open with fury.

"How dare I? How dare you! Just because you're a teacher, you think you have some authority over us, and you use that to belittle your students and treat us like we have no feelings. You're nothing but a pathetic bully, and you don't scare me, you miserable old wretch!" As usual, Drew's sharp tongue had run away with her.

Shocked, Gumberg stood silently squeezing her hands tightly together in rage, for no student had ever dared to speak back to her in such a manner. An awkward silence occurred as they felt the tension growing very quickly. Ruya, with both hands behind her back, stared down at her once-clean shoes that were now covered in a blanket of dust, too terrified to look up at Miss Gumberg's horrifying face.

"I've just about had it with you," she sneered with hatred

"Why? What have I ever done to you? You've had it in for me since I first arrived here," Drew argued.

"You don't think I haven't noticed all the buttons missing on most of the uniforms or food missing from the kitchen? You're a thief and a liar. I warned the headmistress; we should have never taken you in. Always knew it was a mistake taking in filthy little orphans. I could tell straight away that you were going to be a nuisance. You're no good... neither of you," Gumberg sneered, shifting her eyes over to Ruya, who was still awkwardly staring down at her feet. "If I had things my way, I would have left you both to the wolves the moment you arrived at Lakeshore."

The girls exchanged a look of shock.

Gumberg finally walked over to the headmistress's office, knocked on the door and entered.

The lanterns flickered on and off as they waited in a narrow hallway, listening to the muffled voices coming from the headmistress's office.

"Don't worry, Ruya, I'll tell her it was all my fault. I was the one who punched Lucinda. I should be punished, not you."

"Are you crazy? You wouldn't have even touched her if you weren't sticking up for me. We're in this together." Ruya sweetly smiled.

"To be fair," Drew grinned. "I probably would have found another reason to punch her anyway. It's been a long time coming with that one."

The girls waited anxiously for a while until Gumberg finally came back out.

"Right, the headmistress is ready to see you now," Gumberg smirked, looking rather pleased.

"Come in," a soft voice spoke.

Ruya took the first step cautiously into the room. Drew tumbled behind her, tripping over her feet from the small, but rough nudge Miss Gumberg had given her.

"Shut the door, please," said the headmistress.

The girls didn't know what to expect. They stood side by side and saw a woman with her hands clasped behind her back staring out of a balcony watching the rain. The room was intensely silent, with only the sound of the rain heavily tapping on the rooftop while the fire crackled in the corner of the room. The girls just stood still with anxiety, fearing how much trouble they were in. Drew was used to it, being in trouble practically half her life, but for Ruya, it was the first time.

"Miss Gumberg," the headmistress finally spoke. "Would you be so kind as to recite the rules on bullying, please?"

"Certainly, miss," she said with a smile. "Students shall not bull—"

"No. Not that one," said the headmistress, raising her hand in the air.

Miss Gumberg looked confused but continued anyway. "If we see a sad unwanted other, we, the women of Lakeshore, must treat them as if we were their mother."

"And have you?" said the headmistress.

"Have I what, miss?" Gumberg replied.

Miss Mabel finally turned away from the window and faced them.

"Been treating bullied students as if you were their mother? Giving them comfort?"

"Of course, miss. I keep a very sharp eye on all my students. No bullying gets past me," she replied, winking at the girls and putting on a fake smile, playfully nudging Drew on the arm.

"Good, you may leave now... Oh, and Miss Gumberg, in the future, keep that spiteful tongue in your mouth when speaking to my students. I'd hate to have you fired after all these years. Or better yet, feed you to the wolves."

The girls gave each other a sideways glance. Ruya tried to hide her smile, but not Drew; she wanted Gumberg to see just how much she was enjoying watching her get a scolding for once.

"Yes... miss, of course." Gumberg blushed with embarrassment, slowly making her way over to the exit.

"Don't let the door hit you on your way out now," Drew quietly laughed.

As she shut the door behind her, the room once again fell uncomfortably silent. The girls found themselves all alone with the headmistress. She was a wrinkly old woman with a very unusual taste in clothing, nothing like they had ever seen... well, not in Lakeshore anyway. She wore what looked like a long purple robe that draped down to her feet made from velvet, with gold embroidered roses and thorns, and a strange feathered hat that had the odd bird wing sticking out from each side. She had a slight rose tint in her cheeks, for the rest of her skin was extremely pale like freshly fallen snow.

At first, she just stared and smiled at the girls as if they had met before. She finally walked over to her desk. "Please, take a seat," she said, reaching out her hand. "Can I offer you some tea, milk?"

They hesitated to say yes but accepted anyway. Miss Mabel whipped out her best china. It was a soft pink porcelain tea set with golden handles shaped like swans. She picked up the fancy rich handle and poured the girls a cup of steaming hot tea.

"We haven't met before, girls, have we?"

"No," they both answered.

"Strange, don't you think? I thought I'd met all my students," said Miss Mabel, taking a sip from her cup with her pinkie in the air.

Drew arose from her chair, wandering about the room as the headmistress continued to speak. She had noticed this room was unlike any other in the dull grey building; it had colour and character. As she gazed up with her hands in her pockets, she noticed the ceiling was covered in star charts, some even making their way down the walls with the edges curled at the tips touching the floor. But what really caught her eye was a large golden telescope that pointed out of the fancy doors that led to a balcony where Miss Mabel kept an array of exotic plants. She walked along a beautifully carved bookcase, brushing her index finger along every book she passed, collecting a clump of dust on her fingertip. She stopped at one of the shelves, standing on tiptoes, trying to get a better look at the different shapes and sizes of globes of all different planets that Miss Mabel had collected from her travels. The room was full of shelves containing unusual gadgets and knick-knacks that would pique anyone's interest.

"Where did you get all this stuff?" she asked, curiously picking up an emerald gem shaped like a dragon's egg.

"Here and there." The Headmistress smiled. "Now please, child, do sit; we have much to discuss."

Drew did what she was told and finally sat down to drink her tea. Mabel was the first, and only person in Drew's life who hadn't asked her to do something twice.

Miss Mabel, pouring herself another batch of milky tea, grabbed her fancy teaspoon, stirred, then clanked it on the side of her cup until it was dry.

"Ruya, you were found on our doorstep when you were just a baby, no?"

"Yes, miss, that's right," Ruya sweetly replied, taking a gentle sip of her tea.

"And, Drew, you just happened to find your way to us when you were five years of age, correct?"

"That's right," she coughed, lifting one leg up, cupping her knee with both hands, and swinging the other leg back and forth like a little child.

"So, you both grew up here then? And yet neither of you have crossed paths until this very day."

"How did you know?" said Ruya, slightly confused as to how she would have known that.

"I'm sorry but aren't you going to talk about what happened in the library? I thought that's why we were here," said Drew

"What's there to talk about? You defended yourself against a nasty bully. That little brat had it coming."

"*Headmistress*," Drew laughed falling back into her chair, feeling slightly impressed.

"Hope you don't mind me saying, miss, but you're not at all what I was expecting," said Ruya.

Miss Mabel said nothing and just smiled.

"As I was saying before, the pair of you haven't met, even though you were both raised here... Why is that?" the headmistress said, leaning back in her chair, twiddling her thumbs and staring at the girls in turn.

"Just a really big school, I guess," said Drew, leaning over the headmistress's desk and helping herself to a cookie that wasn't offered. Miss Mabel paused, staring as Drew shoved the cookie whole into her mouth, chewing very loudly and spilling crumbs on her fancy rug.

"Follow me."

Walking over towards the balcony, she made a gesture with her hand, and the girls followed behind her. She opened a large fancy umbrella and hovered it over herself and the girls. "Look to the stars and tell me what you see," said Miss Mabel, pointing towards her large telescope.

"But... it's not dark yet. I thought stars only appeared at night?"

"Not these stars." Mabel winked

"Well, it's going to be hard to see through all this heavy rain, the lens is all wet," Drew complained, wiping it with her baggy sleeve.

"Stop your moaning and tell me what you see, child."

"I see... I see... stars. Huh, that's strange," she said, raising her head back up.

"And are they aligned?" asked Mabel.

"No," Drew answered.

"So, I wasn't seeing things, it really has begun," Mabel whispered to herself with a strange look on her face. Folding her umbrella back up, she walked away from the balcony and they returned to their seats.

"You see, children, those stars may be the very beginning to the end... it has begun." The girls looked at each other confused while Mabel drifted off into a strange daze. A few seconds went by and she still hadn't snapped out of it; she didn't even notice Drew doing crazy gestures with her finger, making Ruya suppress a giggle with her hand over her mouth, whispering to her to stop.

"Well, okey-doke, it's been... fun, but we best be off, lots to do n' all that," said Drew, as she slowly rose from her chair, quickly managing to sneak a couple of cookies in her pocket.

"Oh, indeed you do, girls, you have much to do, I'm afraid, and it's not going to be easy," she said, finally snapping out of her daydream.

"Sorry, what's not going to be easy?" asked Ruya.

"Your journey ahead of you, of course."

"Journey?" both girls gasped at the same time, looking slightly confused.

"Drew, please sit back down, child," said Mabel impatiently. Drew hesitated before sitting down but did what she was told.

Miss Mabel leaned over her desk with her fingers clasped together, mysteriously staring at the girls once again with a twinkle in her eye. "What if I told you there was another world beyond the school gates? A bit like the ones you read about in your books." She smiled, shifting her eyes to the book Ruya held in her lap.

"Oh, what a load of bull," Drew laughed, nudging Ruya on the arm, expecting her to laugh along with her.

"What's bull, young lady, is the both of you growing up in the same bloody building and never crossing paths. Would you like to know why that is?" Miss Mabel asked, leaning back in her chair.

"Then I'll tell you, shall I? Now open your ears, girls, because I'm not going to repeat myself. The reason you two haven't met, or I for that matter, is because we were under a spell. A very powerful spell, blinding us to the truth, and therefore to each other, for our protection. In fact, the whole of Lakeshore is under a spell, blinded to what's really going on out there in the real world beyond the woods. A world of magic and great danger."

The girls looked bewildered as they didn't quite understand what she was trying to tell them. Ruya opened her mouth to speak. "Wha—"

"Please let me finish without interruptions, dear," said Mabel, raising her hand. "A voice in my dreams came to me many moons ago and spoke of two babies that were going to be delivered to Lakeshore. Only the three of us would not be able to see each other for our own safety. Our eyes would only open to the truth when the time was right, and now that time has come and it's time for you to leave." Miss Mabel froze and drifted off again, staring at the girls for a few seconds, leaving Drew and Ruya feeling uncomfortable.

Suddenly she broke out of her gaze. "Right, any questions?" she casually asked, calmly taking a sip from her teacup.

"Wait a minute. Who told you we were gonna be delivered?" said Drew.

"A voice from the past… an old friend," she softly smiled.

"What voice? I don't understand." Drew coughed, left feeling slightly confused, scratching the back of her head.

"An old friend came to me in a dream. She spoke of two children who were extremely special and that I needed to hide them both. Keep you safe until the day came when the stars began to shift out of line. And that day has come. And I must send you on your way."

"On our way, on our way where? Where are you sending us?" Ruya asked with a shake in her voice.

"To the unimaginable, my dear."

Miss Mabel stood up and walked around from her desk over to the girls and pressed her pale hands onto each of their cheeks.

"My dear sweet children, we finally see one another and now we're saying goodbye. I wish you all the luck on your journey, god knows you're going to need it." A tear appeared, slowly running down her pink fuzzy cheek. She wrapped her arms tight around the girls and whispered in their ear. "Remember, the power lies within."

"EEEEEEEEK!"

Without any warning a loud piecing scream, almost like something was in extreme pain, had torn through the girls' ears like a shard of glass. The deathly cry had come from the dark forest. "What was that?" said the girls, frightened, jumping up from out their chairs.

"They're here," Mabel whispered with each hand pressed against her cheeks.

"Who?" Drew shouted in fear.

The colour flushed from Miss Mabel's face as if she had seen a ghost from the past.

"Well, who? Who?"

"*Screamers*," she replied wide-eyed with horror and anxiety in her voice. "Girls! You must leave now they know you're here!

Go, hurry! You must not let them find you!" She quickly ran over to an exceptionally large painting on the wall to reveal a secret door.

"Hurry, take the corridor to the left. You'll come to a staircase; it will lead you to a back door. Run into the woods and hide." The Screamers were getting louder. Their cries were getting closer. The heavy rain didn't muffle their invasive screams.

"Miss Mabel, come with us!" the girls cried in fear.

"Please! You can't stay here," a trembling Ruya pleaded.

"I can't; there's no time," she yelled, shoving them through the secret door, accidentally knocking over a lantern in panic. Mabel suddenly grabbed Drew by the arm. "You must find Oba. Now go... Go! I said run! Run!"

The Screamers were clawing their way along the rooftop trying to find a way in while letting out a horrible demon-like cry. Screamers were large and tall, almost ten-foot standing on their hind legs. They were thin, black, vicious, monstrous creatures with extremely long fingers, retracting their sharp claws that could cut you like a blade when ready for a kill. They had a mouth full of razor-sharp teeth along with 10 deathly black eyes and huge pointed ears that stood up straight that was sometimes mistaken for horns.

They could climb walls on all fours at a pace so fast you couldn't even see them coming, and when you do, it's too late. They were natural predators, born to hunt, born to kill. The girls ran, taking the route Miss Mabel instructed. They had made it through the secret tunnel and into the thunderstorm and climbed over the school gates. They headed towards the woods, pacing through the orange and brown autumn leaves.

They could still hear the vicious screams of the vile creatures clashing with the screams and cries of the other students. They didn't realise just how fast they had been running. Though the school was at a distance, they stopped to catch their breath and looked back. Lakeshore was on fire; they could see the flames licking the building and were horrified at the sight of what they once called home.

"What do we do now?" Ruya cried.

"let's find shelter. Miss Mabel told us to hide so that's what we're gonna do," Drew coughed, still trying to catch her breath from running so fast. The girls in panic looked about hysterically. "Look! Over there." Drew pointed to a large pine tree that tilted to one side with giant roots. They ran over and desperately searched for an opening. They finally found one and struggled to squeeze through the vines that were all tangled. It was almost like a cave. It kept them out of the rain and out of sight.

"What's going on," Drew spat, pacing up and down with her hands placed on her hips.

"Miss Mabel? Do you think she's okay? What the hell were those things?"

Ruya couldn't answer, she was still in shock at what had just happened. For a minute she thought she was still in class, sitting by the window and daydreaming, imagining the whole thing. But unfortunately, it was all so very real.

"Maybe we should go back for her," said Drew.

"Don't leave me alone!" came an alarmed voice from the shadows, startling both the girls. Ruya and Drew both screamed and jumped up, tightly holding on to each other.

"Lucinda!" both girls gasped in shock.

"What the hell you doing here?" said Drew, wondering how she managed to escape.

"Those creepy tall monsters were everywhere! I panicked, so I ran out before they made it to my dorm. I've never run so fast in my life. Their screams terrified me... I knew it; I knew I saw something outside in the trees when we were in the library." Lucinda began sobbing into her hands like a helpless little girl.

Ruya looked over to Drew, completely ignoring her sobbing like a mess. "If you're serious about going back for Miss Mabel, I'm coming with you."

"What!? Are you two completely mad?" an alarmed Lucinda cried. "Didn't you see the size of those bloody things? Honestly. What can you two do? Miss Mabel is probably dead already."

"Shut up!" Drew shouted and pounced for Lucinda.

Ruya quickly wedged her way in between them. "Now is not the time for this. What is wrong with you two? We're all in shock and we need to stick together, not fight."

"You're right, you're right. I'm sorry," Drew apologised, trying to keep her cool. Taking deep breaths in and out, she sat down on a large toadstool growing from inside the root of the tree.

"We're going to die. Those things are going to kill us, aren't they? AREN'T THEY?!" Lucinda cried, sitting with her arms wrapped around her legs, rocking back and forth, chomping on her nails.

"Not if I kill you first," Drew mumbled under her breath.

Being kind, Ruya kneeled and put her hand on Lucinda's knee, trying to comfort her.

"You need to calm down. If you panic, they might hear us, okay."

"Okay," she gently squeaked, wiping her eyes and sniffling her snotty nose. Suddenly, lightning struck, then came a loud, aggressive bang of thunder that rumbled through the whole forest, making all the trees rattle in fear.

"AAHHH!"

"Shut her up!" Drew snapped irately.

"Lucinda! Please. I know you're afraid, but so are we. You're going to get us all killed!" Ruya yelled, finally losing her patience, shaking her from side to side with frustration.

"Sshhh... listen."

They all fell silent. The only sound was the rain tapping on the branches.

"I think they found us," Drew whispered. Her whole body trembled in fear. The girls gently moved closer towards the entrance they came from and peeped through a tiny gap in the veins. During a split second of lightning, a dark shadowy figure with bright eyes was revealed.

Holding their breaths, terrified, they quickly stood back, shut their eyes tight, waiting for the worst to happen. A few seconds went by... and nothing. The shadow was mysteriously gone as suddenly as it appeared.

"I didn't hear a scream; maybe it didn't find us," Lucinda sighed with relief.

"Do you think it left?" Ruya whispered, tightly gripping Drew's arm.

"I hope so," Drew softly sighed.

IGOR AND THE LAST WITCH
CHAPTER THREE

It was morning, and the girls were tightly huddled together. Frosted air forced its way into Ruya's lungs and stung her eyes. She was the first to wake, frozen to the bone and breathing into her hands for warmth. It didn't feel like your average winter's day; there was an evil presence about the coldness that surrounded them.

"Guys, wake up," she whispered with clouds of smoke puffing out from her mouth with every word she spoke. She continuously nudged them both until they woke up. Drew and Lucinda slowly opened their eyes only to find themselves in an embrace, then immediately separated when they finally came to their senses. They both shot up quicker than lightning and brushed themselves off like they were covered in dirt.

"Oow, it's freezing," Drew complained, rubbing her hands together then cracking her back in pain.

"Yeah, I know, look outside; the whole forest is covered in snow," replied Ruya, popping her little head through an opening of the tree, making the snow crunch all around her.

Drew looked confused. "How can winter be here already? It's as if winter has swallowed autumn whole," she said, rubbing her tired eyes.

"If it snows anymore, we might get caved in and freeze to death. We've got to look for new shelter," said Ruya.

"I agree with you, Ruya, but if we go out there and don't find shelter, we're still going to freeze to death. Better we freeze in here than out there," said Lucinda in an unhappy tone, rubbing her puffy swollen eyes with her pretty hair bow bent out of place.

"Why don't we go back to Lakeshore? You never know, Miss Mabel might still be alive," said Drew with hope, looking up at the others with enthusiasm to see if they agreed.

"Okay. Let's go back," Ruya sighed after a few seconds of thinking about it.

"Let's not!" Lucinda snapped. "Are you two forgetting those *things* are still out there."

"Miss Mabel and the others may still be alive," Ruya argued.

"Yeah, and if we risk our lives looking for them, we won't be!"

"Fine. Stay here. We don't care," Ruya huffed, walking over to the clearest entrance of the tree. Lucinda finally got to her feet with rage. "Stupid Basket Girl! Have you lost your—"

Drew bolted towards Lucinda, pressing one hand against her shoulder. "We're not in Lakeshore anymore; there's no Gumberg to go crying to out here, remember that. Call us names again, you're on your own. You should be lucky we're even letting you stick with us after what you pulled."

Lucinda slowly sat back down, scolded like a little child that hadn't got their own way. With her arms tightly crossed against her chest, she pouted her lips and didn't dare utter another word.

The woods grew colder by the minute. The snow fell silently like a soft melody.

"Come on, let's go back," Drew sighed, fixing her hat. As the girls climbed out of the tree, they found themselves almost knee-deep in snow as they stood.

"How long were we asleep to not have noticed it snowing this much?" asked Ruya, with her arms tightly wrapped around her body, bouncing up and down, trying to keep warm.

"Well, almost being murdered by strange creatures can tire a girl out," Lucinda sighed, trembling, breathing down her top then rubbing her frozen hands together as they made their way crunching through the pure, untouched snow.

"Back at Lakeshore, Miss Mabel said to find Oba," said Drew.

"What's an Oba?" asked Lucinda.

"Let's just concentrate on finding the school first," said Ruya.

"So which way is it then?" Lucinda huffed unhappily, with every inch of her fragile body shivering.

"Well, it's this way... or was it that way?" Drew wasn't sure. It had been snowing so much that everything looked the same, and the girls couldn't remember which way they had come from.

"This is just great," cried Ruya. "We'll never find our way home now."

"What home? The last I saw it went up in flames," Lucinda grunted.

"Let's just keep moving straight and we'll see where we end up," said Drew, trying her best to stay positive like always.

Once again, the girls trekked through the snow trying to find their way back to Lakeshore. As they walked, Ruya looked like she was in deep thought.

"You know, I just realised something. I've never been outside Lakeshore, never been beyond the school gates."

"Neither have I come to think of it, you know, besides the button factory in town. But I was just a kid. I don't really remember what's out there. Only knew life in the factory for a short time then ended up at Lakeshore," Drew replied, struggling to walk through the thick snow, desperately trying to catch her breath.

"What about you?" asked Ruya, looking over to Lucinda.

"Bet you've been *everywhere*," Drew muttered beneath her breath, sarcastically rolling her eyes. Just as Lucinda opened her mouth to speak, it stopped snowing and the forest fell completely still with an ominous silence.

"Shh, listen."

The girls stood close to each other, still as a rock, not daring to breathe. Suddenly they heard the sound of footsteps crunching in the snow approaching eerily towards them. The footsteps got closer and closer; the girls leaned into each other in a panic with their backs pressed against one another. They knew they weren't alone. Something had been following them.

Once again, the forest fell silent, and the footsteps ceased. They all turned their heads, looking around anxiously with heavy breath puffing out of their mouths like little clouds.

"There's something out there," Drew whispered with little crinkles in between her eyebrows, making them lower down closer towards her eyes. She balled up her hands into a fist, ready for whatever it was. Lucinda held tight onto Drew's arm. The girls stood still for a few seconds shifting their eyes from side to side, scanning the woods.

"I think we should keep mov—" Lunging out of nowhere, a Screamer jumped out from behind a tall tree.

"AHHHH!"

The girls were paralysed with fear, too frightened to move; they just stood still, tightly gripping on to one another.

The Screamer's deathly black figure against the pure ghostly snow left the girls terrified and helpless like they were stuck in a nightmare they couldn't wake up from.

The creature stood up on its hind legs and aggressively ran towards them, then continued on all fours in attack position, retracting its claws and letting out a terrifying cry as it rushed closer towards them.

BANG!

Something exploded, filling the forest with a green fog that managed to frighten the Screamer away. The girls screamed, falling to the ground, still holding on to each other for dear life with their eyes shut tight. Once the green fog faded away, the sound of footsteps crunched towards them.

"You can open your eyes now," came a strange gruff voice. The girls slowly opened their eyes, and as their sight got into focus, they saw what seemed to be an odd little creature standing before them. It was half their size with huge ears pointing outwards, its skin murky green with shades of brown and a lumpy texture, with big bright yellow eyes that gleamed like torchlights. It was wearing a little velvet waistcoat the colour of burgundy that didn't quite cover its large plump belly and a long droopy hat that almost touched the floor. With his big feet, he hopped over to them in a friendly manner. In panic, the girls crawled back on their hands and feet, shuffling into each other.

"Calm down. I'm not going to hurt you... but the Screamers will if we don't get a move on, so we better hurry. Soon night will be upon us," he said, cautiously shifting his large eyes from side to side. The girls eventually stood on their feet and just stared with curiosity at this funny-looking creature. What was it, they wondered.

"Well, come on then, come on!" he complained, hopping off. The girls followed, taking their time, dragging their feet cautiously behind him.

"Do you think that's what we saw standing in the rain last night?" Ruya spoke quietly.

"What in god's name is it?" Lucinda whispered with disgust.

"I don't know. Whatever it is, we can't trust it," Drew replied.

"I can hear you, you know," he said, hopping back over to them. The girls just stared at him every time he spoke, exchanging glances of confusion.

"I'm sure you have a lot of questions, and they will be answered in time, but we really must pick up the pace. The Screamers are still out there hunting you. So, either you trust me, or you don't... your choice."

"Well, he's not a Screamer, and he did just save our lives, so I'll take my chances," said Drew. The girls nodded in agreement.

"Good... let's go. Follow me."

Slowly they continued with their journey. "So, if we're going to be travelling companions, let's exchange names. I'm Igor," he said, with his peculiar gruff voice.

"Drew's the name."

"*Drew?*" Igor repeated with a chuckle.

"Oi! What's so funny?" she said, not amused at being made fun of.

Igor ignoring Drew, turned his attention to the others. "And you are?"

"My name is Ruya."

"That's a nice name," he said.

"Thank you." She smiled politely.

"And you?" leaving Lucinda to last.

"I'm Lu—"

"That's nice," he said, hopping away. Drew glanced over to Ruya and they both giggled.

"What are you supposed to be anyway!?" Lucinda sneered, irritated she had been rudely cut off.

"I'm a hobgoblin," he answered with pride.

"A hob what? Sounds vile... and where are you taking us?!" she snapped.

"To the last witch, Mother Oba. She will explain everything."

"Oba?" Drew whispered to herself with wide eyes, hearing Miss Mabel's last words in her head. The girls looked scared. Who was this woman he was taking them to?

Nevertheless, they continued to follow him anyway, not having any other choice. The snow came down heavily, and night had fallen upon them. They had been walking through the deep freezing snow for what seemed like forever, turning their lips blue. They felt like giving up until they finally reached what appeared to be a little cottage with clouds of smoke puffing out of the crooked chimney. It looked warm and inviting. Igor struggled to open the rusty gate covered in thick snow that led to the front door. He hopped on the steppingstones and looked back at the girls. "Well, come on. Don't be afraid; she's one of the good ones."

The trio followed gingerly, making their way to the front door.

"Who is this old hag anyway?" Lucinda rudely whispered.

"SSHHH!" Hushing Lucinda, Igor knocked, tapping the worn-out, old door knocker shaped like an owl's head. The door creaked, slowly opening.

"Come in," a thick voice responded.

Igor turned to them, nodding, suggesting they enter. Following behind the girls, he closed the door behind him. The cottage was warm and cosy. They had forgotten what warmth felt like after walking in the bitter cold for so long. The ceiling was low and lined with old wooden beams with dried up herbs, plants and cloves of garlic hanging from brass hooks.

"Children, come. Sit by me," the voice said, coming from behind a large brown armchair facing the fireplace. They walked over and saw an alarmingly large, robust old woman in a long black dress and a handsewn coif bonnet. She sat there like she had been waiting for their arrival. "Come, warm yourselves. We have much to discuss."

The girls walked over and sat by the crackling fire. "Igor, bring us some pie from the kitchen. You hungry? I bet you are, being out in the cold for so long," said the witch.

"Famished," Drew and Lucinda answered at the same time, giving each other a sideways glance as it was the first and only thing they had ever agreed on.

The girls and the old woman sat in awkward silence for a few minutes listening to Igor make a racket in the kitchen. With the sound of plates smashing and cutlery clanging, Igor finally came out, wobbling about trying to balance five plates of freshly made pumpkin pie.

"Do you know why you're here?" asked the witch, watching the girls stuff their faces with pie.

"Back at Lakeshore, Miss Mabel tried to tell us, but by the time she could explain any further we were attacked," Ruya answered.

"I'm sure she told you you're both incredibly special," the witch said, cutting the girls another slice of pie each.

"Special? Them? Pfff," Lucinda muttered under her breath before taking another large bite.

"Yes, she did," said Ruya, accepting the second helping of pie from the witch's hand.

"Tell me, have you heard the story of the three Queens?" the witch asked.

"No," all three girls responded with their mouths full of pie.

"Then I shall tell you. There are many queens to the unknown world, but only one can truly rule."

The witch began her story, making everybody look through her crystal ball that sat on a little wooden table placed between them, which glowed brighter than an evening star.

"A long time ago, there was a premonition of something, something that would change things forever. Every century the Great Star God, Zivot, bursts, shedding his greatness upon our world into a thousand pieces, falling from the heavens above like fallen angels. Those falling pieces were indeed his own children. Some say it was a test, that he had sent out his children to our world and many others to distinguish if we were worthy enough for the gift of life the Gods had bestowed upon us. The offspring of Zivot spread out across the universe, showering us with a bright light. A few pieces landed on our world, but only one piece would contain great cosmic power to unlock the universe and be one with their father and return home. For years people were driven insane searching for the real fallen Star that maintained true power. Many thought they had found it, but were deceived, for as soon as they came in contact with the Star, the light would dim and turn to dust.

"The real piece ended up on what we witches like to call The Valley of The Fallen Stars, where most objects had landed from the world above. One day a blacksmith had been strolling by when suddenly a blinding light had caught his eye. He had found the fallen child of Zivot and thought it was the most beautiful thing he had ever seen, so beautiful in fact he decided to mould the Star into a crown fit for a queen. Discovering the Star possessed starlight, an unstoppable force only the Gods consume way above in the never-ending sea of darkness, the blacksmith had fled with his family in fear, leaving the Star behind.

"Word spread quickly throughout the kingdoms of what the blacksmith had found. Many tried to take the Star for themselves but died a quick death, for mortals were not strong enough to contain the power of the cosmic, for they would burst instantly into dust. Only someone who already possessed strength and strong blood would be able to consume the Star for themselves. All were desperately hungry for the taste of omnipotent power that would define their place as the one and only ruler of all, for eternity, bearing them the gift of immortality and strength against their enemies. The war had begun.

"Hungry and desperate to become Queen of all queens and the one and only ruler of all worlds, born from black magic, was the mighty and wicked, Queen Ates. The lady of the underworld. She who manipulates fire to her every command and moves as one with the flames from hell. Backed up by her ruthless army of Gors and Screamers, who hunted down her enemies one by one and obliterated anyone who stood in their queen's way. Word had reached her ear. Together they began seeking the one Star to destroy her two rivals, who were also in pursuit of the object of power. And she would stop at nothing to get it.

"On the other side of the magic realm, also seeking the fallen Star, was Queen Lumi. Ruler of the Icy Mountains. She ruled her kingdom with her siren-like cry that echoed throughout the ice world, sending shivers down the peoples' spines where her castle stood solid, crystallised upon the silent cold, deathly mountains. Where trespassers were frozen into ice sculptures that would one day be reborn and join her army. The ghostly cold mountains lacked any sign of life, caressed with sharp, blinding flakes covering the castle like a blanket. Every snowflake that fell from the cold misty sky and every blade of icicle was under her control and her control only.

"The third lady of power who sought the Star was Vapour, Queen of the swamp and ruler to all foul creatures who lived there. But looks can be deceiving, for she was once an unbelievably beautiful woman and unusual being and went by the name of Vidalia. She was a princess of very a poor kingdom. She lived high up in her castle, where only her most trusted servants could go near her. She was kind and a just princess, for she did try to do her best for the people as much as she could, although they never saw her in person. Until one day there was a gathering in the town square. The villagers went on a rampage complaining about the lack of food while the princess sat on her throne.

"One villager who had been a former servant in her presence spoke of the princess; he told the people she possessed a golden shell on her back that grew from her flesh. Almost like a giant human snail. They decided that they would kill her and rip the shell from her mortal body, so they could possess the most valuable gold that was known and be wealthy men and women. The villagers went insane and forced their way into the castle, aggressively waving about their torches and weapons. They attacked the guards protecting the castle gates and stormed in fighting. A group of them made their way to the highest tower, where they gazed upon the princess and were stunned to see that for once the rumours had been true, that a beautiful woman who possessed a shell made from gold, growing from her flesh was all so very real.

"She cried and begged. 'Have I not been good to you?' but the people were not interested in her cries for mercy. They held her down and hacked away, removing the shell entirely from her soft mortal bleeding flesh as her screams and cries echoed throughout the castle halls. They dumped her body in the swamp for her to drown in the murky waters, for they were now taking over her lands and residency in her castle.

"Outraged with hate, anger, and betrayal, she swore she would seek vengeance. She was no longer Princess Vidalia but Queen of the Waste Lands, for the murky green waters did not kill her but consumed her body and soul, making her toxic with hate as she rose again, reborn from the swamp. She executed every last villager who entered her castle that day, even those who didn't. Her taste for revenge wasn't enough; she wanted more. She wanted the Star. And her army of swamp creatures swore to serve their new queen and help her get it. News spread, Ates and Lumi had heard about their new rival, neither of the element queens feared Vapour as they feared each other, for she did not possess the power they had.

"Vapour envied both women, for they had the power of fire and ice, where she had neither of their gifts of the elements on her side to use against her enemies. Our world grew dark.

Because of all the hate, desperation, and greed the three evil women desperately craved for power, the Star had vanished into thin air, leaving the queens tormented. Outraged by what they deemed as deception; evil had spread deeper into the lands. Desperately seeking the Star, they each sent out their armies, murdering, invading homes, burning every last city, village, and farm to find it. But still they found nothing, and time had gotten the best of them. Slowly their powers were fading, and they grew weak. They, too, had mysteriously vanished along with their dark armies."

The light dimmed from the crystal ball as the witch's story came to an end.

"You see, the queens' armies have already woken, and the queens themselves will be next, waking from their dark slumbers now that the Star has returned from hiding."

"The Star was hiding?" said Ruya.

"Yes, when the Dark Queens sent out their armies, spreading their evil like a plague taking innocent lives, us good witches from all over the lands gathered together. We wanted to hide the Star so the queens would never find it. You see, the Star never really vanished; it was here all along, hiding in plain sight, invisible to those seeking it. We hid the Star in the form of a child. We performed such a powerful spell making the object invisible to all evil, and it worked, but like any powerful magic, it too can have some minor hiccups along the way."

"Like what?" said Drew.

"The spell had split the Star into two pieces, taking the form of not one, but two human babies."

"What happened to them?" said the girls, both intensely staring at the witch for an answer.

The room fell completely silent, with only the sound of the fire crackling in the corner of the room. Oba sat still, glaring back at the girls with not even a blink. Slightly shifting her body down her armchair, she leant forwards and finally spoke. "One of the babies was taken to a girls' boarding school and was left outside the front door, bundled in a basket made from sticks."

"NO! No, no." Ruya got up with her hands shielding both ears, not wanting to hear another word the witch had to say.

"I don't want to hear this... I don't believe you!" she cried.

"I'm afraid it's true. Why do you think the Screamers were hunting you? And why winter had come so early. Evil has awakened."

"This is impossible," Ruya cried.

"Why hide the Star in human form?" said Drew, looking extremely flushed.

"That way no one would ever suspect. You both are very desirable objects that evil desperately seeks. You have starlight coursing through your veins. Starlight is not from our world but way beyond, deep into the galaxy where the stars never sleep."

"What exactly is starlight?" the girls asked with a shake in their voices.

"Starlight is particles and atoms of a very unusual star, the Great Star God himself, Zivot. The King of all Gods. He's been around since time itself; Zivot was the first form of life ever to exist and creator of all worlds. He cannot be killed."

"Immortality," Ruya whispered.

"Correct," said Oba. "Therefore, whoever consumes the Star, they too will be immortal and become one with Zivot and control not just our world but the universe itself."

"What makes this Zivot so special? I thought all stars lived forever?" Lucinda interrupted.

"My girl, just like any other life, stars too eventually burn away. Zivot is a God, and unlike any other star you have ever seen, he is the almighty father."

"So let me get this straight... you mean to tell me, anyone who takes the Star for themselves would have god-like powers?" Lucinda continued, leaning forward with her finger pressed against her pale cheek, looking very curious and interested for once in her life.

"No. Mortals cannot... they are easily seduced by power; they just can't help themselves. They're a weak race. That kind of power would be far too much for them to process, and eventually they would burst and be nothing but a pile of stardust. A Spellborn, on the other hand, may be able to contain it, but not for too long, for their blood is far stronger than the mortals but not stronger than the Gods," Oba answered.

"Spellborn?" said Drew, raising one eyebrow with a hint of curiosity.

"We did our absolute best to hide the Star as long as possible, but unfortunately the spell would eventually break once the stars fell out of line. The first star to fall was the invisibility spell; that is why you were able to finally see each other for the first time in all those years. The second star that shifted out of place was a protection spell, which is why the Screamers were able to enter your school and attack. The protection spell that kept them and all things evil away for all these years had finally broken."

"Keeping all things evil from entering the school? Well, clearly that didn't work with Gumberg and Lucinda lurking about," Drew muttered under her breath.

"And the third star?" Ruya gently gulped, feeling terribly anxious.

"The banishing spell," the witch sighed, lowering her head. "That was the last and only thing keeping the Dark Queens away. Evil has begun to wake. The third star is why we must get a move on before it falls out of line because once that happens, the fight for survival begins."

"So... are we safe or not?" said Drew, shrugging her shoulders.

"Weren't you listening? You both had a protection spell over you, but that would only last for as long as the stars were aligned, which unfortunately they are no more, so you are no longer safe. The queens' armies have already woken, and we are running out of time."

"I don't like this; I want to go home," said Ruya with a tear in her eye.

"My girl, that was not your home. The world you knew was merely a distraction, an illusion from keeping you all from knowing the truth. Lakeshore was created by those who wanted to live in peace, a world without magic and war... a different time. The whole of Lakeshore was under a deep spell keeping the new generation from ever knowing the truth. The creator of this new world had listened to what we witches had to say and was kind enough to hide you both."

The room was silent until Drew began to laugh hysterically. Everybody turned their heads to Drew and just stared at her like she was insane.

"What a joke," she chuckled beneath her breath.

"It's not funny," Ruya gasped, unamused.

"No... but it is when you think about it. We just saw the only home we ever knew go up in flames. We're going to be caught up in some 'war' we had absolutely no knowledge about until a few minutes ago. We were living under a spell in a world that didn't really exist... Oh, and we're not even human; we're 'stars' apparently. Everything we thought we knew about our lives has been one big fat lie, not to mention Evil Queens are out hunting us down cause they want to murder us, and not just one queen... three! How is that not something to laugh about."

"Of course, you're real. But the world you knew wasn't. You're not those lonely orphans you both grew up to believe," said Oba. "But what you must understand is you did not come from mortals; you were conceived by magic. You're Spellborns. Unlike any other Spellborn ever to exist in our world, for you do not have red blood like the mortals or blue blood like the Spellborns, but silver blood like the star you have always been. You have the power of the universe beating through your hearts. You are the daughters of Zivot, the King of Gods."

"All this talk of stars and the universe, that would explain all the star charts in Miss Mabel's office," Ruya gasped. "Wait... it was you. You were the voice she heard in her dream, a voice of an old friend." Ruya paused in deep thought then spoke again. "Mabel, she was the creator of Lakeshore, wasn't she?"

"Yes. It was I who came to her in a dream, and it was she who created Lakeshore, a world without magic. Mabel and I go way back. She's a very dear friend of mine, I knew she would keep the secret safe, and when the time came, she would send you on your way."

"There's something I still don't quite understand. If we really are a star in human form, how would the queens 'consume' us, or whatever, to… you know, take our powers?" Drew asked suspiciously with a deeply concerned tone, raising one eyebrow and staring at the witch, hoping the answer wasn't something she would regret hearing.

"The power lies inside you both. You have starlight, silver blood running through your veins and the cosmic power pumping through your hearts. No matter what form you're in, crown or human, you've only ever been one thing… a Star. And only you can stop them. When the spell split you into two babies, it also split your heart. They need both pieces of your hearts to consume the full power you each contain within, and if they do… we're all lost. There will be no more light in our world or any other world for that matter, only pure darkness."

Once again, all three girls just sat in complete silence, each with a different terrified expression. They looked confused, scared, and unsure if what they had just heard was true.

"OUR HEARTS!" the girls cried.

"All this time I've been living with half a heart?" Drew shrieked, holding tightly to her chest, feeling confused and terrified more than ever.

"I know it's a lot to take in, but we must move on with our journey. Igor! Bring me my sceptre, child," the witch said, slowly rising up from her large armchair. "We must make haste."

"Right away, Mother Oba," said Igor, quickly rushing across to the other side of the room.

"Did she really just say our hearts?" Drew continued to whisper to Ruya, who looked pale as a ghost.

"Where's your wand?" asked Lucinda, eyeing up the witch with her hand pressed on her hip.

"I beg your pardon?" exclaimed Oba.

"Your wand. Don't witches have wands?"

"Oh. I see… because witches couldn't possibly own a sceptre, they're just an object only wizards can handle, I suppose. Maybe I should fly around the room with a broomstick and a pointy hat too!"

"No, what I meant wa—"

"Gather around!" the witch yelled, cutting Lucinda short with irritation in her thick voice.

She made everyone in the room hold hands. Igor brought out the sceptre which was made from an old tree bark. It had two crooked edges on top and pointing out between the crooked edges was a crimson stone shaped like an eye. As they held hands and formed a circle, the witch, with all her strength, hit the sceptre to the ground with force, making a loud thunderous bang. And just like that, they vanished.

HOUSE OF GRAZIA
CHAPTER FOUR

"Welcome to the real world." Oba smiled, raising her sceptre high in the air.

Slowly opening their eyes, the girls found themselves on top of a lush, green hill concealed in the shadows of a weeping willow's majestic pink leaves. Sun streaks gleamed through the willow branches as the girls pulled them to one side like curtains, letting in the sunlight.

"Where are we?" Lucinda muttered. She sat herself up rubbing the back of her head, grimacing at the throbbing pain.

"The Lands of Grazia," said the witch.

"The lands of what?" she answered with an attitude. Feeling a horrible migraine coming on, she continued to sooth the back of her head with the palm of her hand.

"The Lands of Grace, miss," said Igor, kindly helping her back on her feet. They were surrounded by lush trees, green hills, and slopes with rocky, snow-capped mountains in the far distance. A flock of blue, red, and green birds of otherworldly beauty with large, pointed beaks that curved at the tips and long skinny feathery tails fluttered by – dancing around one another in perfect harmony and making magical patterns in the sky. Drew and Ruya's eyes welled up, watching the birds with happiness.

"Let's not dawdle. Best not keep them waiting any longer. Come on," said Oba, walking ahead. The girls looked at each other. Who was she talking about, they wondered? Not asking any questions, they continued to follow her. As far as their eyes could see, they saw nothing but pure, unimaginable beauty.

It made a huge difference from Lakeshore; all they ever saw there were boring pine trees. Taking in a deep breath, inhaling the fresh pure air, they followed the witch down a hill with tall grass and the occasional flower.

"Come on, keep up," she yelled, way ahead of them using her sceptre as a walking stick.

They reached the bottom of the hill and walked through a wide, open field with little farmhouses, crops, and old windmills.

Great chubby creatures with four short tree-trunk-like legs and beady little eyes pulled on huge wheelbarrows filled with hay. Almost every farmer had a Worker Beast helping them on their farm. They were slow, simple creatures but got the job done, and they were more than happy to be paid in apples. The farmers all stopped their chores and watched the girls as they passed by. The men made hand gestures in conversation while the women giggled and whispered into each other's ears. A little girl ran towards Ruya, handing her a yellow flower, smiled, then ran back into her fathers arms, continuing to stare at the girls with hope and happiness.

"Who are these people?" said Ruya.

"Simple farmers," Oba replied.

"Why are they staring at us like that?" said Drew.

"It's been a long time since the people had any hope for the future, until now of course."

"They know who we are?" said Drew, trying to catch up with the witch who was extremely fast for someone with a limp.

"No," Oba laughed, "but the people are not dim; they know a good thing when they see it." They had reached the end of the farmer's field. In the distance they couldn't help but see a beautiful mansion sitting on a giant hill that looked like an island surrounded by sparkling waterfalls, rivers, and spectacular willow trees, bearing gold and pink leaves that left the pathway shimmering like stardust. It seemed more like a palace than a mansion. Its beauty was elegant and astonishing, with green mountains in the far distance. In order to reach it, they had to make their way across an elegant bridge made of white gold, towering over a gleaming river that snaked its way around the House of Grace.

"LOOK!" Drew gasped with amazement. All three girls stood still like statues, gobsmacked as they watched a couple of river mermaids swimming beneath them. Transfixed by their unusual beauty they continued to watch the sun reflect from their tails beneath the water that twinkled. As the mermaids emerged to the surface, the girls got a better look. They each had green skin; one was the colour of sage and the other moss green. Their eyes were large, round, and gleaming blue, resembling bright pebbles. Their hair was silky silver that twinkled just as bright as their scaly fishtails, which were a darker shade of green than their skin. The mermaids giggled as they watched the girls with curiosity, then eventually swam off, leaving the trio speechless. They continued to walk across the river. Each side of the bridge had carvings of men in armour, ready to protect.

As they continued to walk across the bridge, they witnessed another phenomenal creature, something that looked familiar yet they had never seen before... it almost looked like a fish but had wings with rainbow gills that were metallic. Little soft pink frogs hopped by with transparent wings that sparkled as they air-hopped by them, leaving little trails of dust that glittered in the sunlight. The girls just stood there in awe, admiring all the magic that surrounded them. As Lucinda stood in disbelief, she hadn't noticed a firefly dancing around her. 'Slurp!' suddenly one of the flying frogs reached out its tongue quicker than a blink of an eye, gulping the firefly leaving specs of fresh saliva splattered all over her face. "ERRR!" Lucinda squeaked, wiping her cheek with the back of her hand in disgust. Reaching the entrance, they approached large solid doors of carved wood and golden vines that slowly squeaked open as they moved closer.

"Welcome to the House of Grazia, home of the Protectors, defenders against all things evil," said a thick stern voice. A little fat man waddled from behind the door with huge ears that pointed upwards and an unusually large nose. "Straight ahead," the funny-looking little man instructed. They entered the house and stood in a large entrance with shiny marbled floors and stone walls surrounded by exotic plants.

"Look," Drew whispered, pointing over to the plants. "Miss Mabel had the exact same ones on her terrace." But Ruya was far too busy admiring the painted muraled ceiling covered with dragons and warriors that loomed above them, finished with an exquisite candlelit chandelier that glistened, lighting up the main entrance.

"Come on," Oba continued. "This way," she said, leading them to a lavish elevator made from gold vines, operated by one of the help. A very stern, uptight frog half the size of a man, wearing a mediaeval red velvet butler's uniform with gold buttons. His name was Gustav Scrivener, the last of his family to serve the House of Grazia. "Going up?" he said sternly.

"Yes, thank you, Gustav," Oba answered as they made their way into the elevator. The grumpy frog pulled the lever in his high maintenance manner with his nose still high up in the air after closing the golden gates. The ascent, which only took a few minutes, seemed to last forever in an awkward silence while they squeezed tightly together. Gustav gave the girls a sideways glance with one raised eyebrow like they were peasants. Finally, they had reached their floor.

They made their way out of the elevator in an orderly fashion. Once again, the golden gates closed, and the frog, after pulling the lever, noticed a button missing on his uniform. Exasperated, as the elevator slowly descended, he looked up only to see Drew flipping a button up and down in the air, smirking and giving him a cheeky little wave as he went back down. Just as it dawned on him what had happened, Drew was out of sight.

"What do you look so smug about?" sneered Lucinda.

"Oh, nothing," Drew laughed, flipping Gustav's gold button safely into her pocket.

"Really? Did you just steal that attendant's button?" said Ruya.

"Well, if he hadn't had his nose so high up in the air, maybe he would have noticed me taking his stupid button. Besides, I've never had a gold one before." She smiled.

"Oh, Drew," said Ruya shaking her head disapprovingly. They continued to follow behind Oba, walking through a never-ending hallway plastered with old painted portraits filling the entire walls all the way down. They found themselves at the foot of a tiny door, disguised as one of the paintings that led them into a dark cave-like tunnel where the walls were encrusted with crystals and gems, blinking as it lit the way to a second door. Oba knocked.

"Enter," came a voice.

As Oba entered, the girls anxiously followed, taking that first step into a secret study. Oba ushered them towards a table that stretched out across the room. Around the table sat unusual humanesque creatures, whose stares seemed to bore through the girls, which left them feeling uneasy and intimidated. One of the creatures that sat at the table just glared at the girls with his huge eyes. He had a very long, thin moustache that drooped all the way down to his hips, along with long pointy antennae's sticking out from his head while little gold moths hovered over him.

"Is this them?" a grumpy old man spoke. He was wearing a robe made of thick satin in the colour of royal blue, very similar to what Miss Mabel had been wearing. He also wore a hat with two golden angel-like wings attached to each side with a long white beard that draped down to his feet.

"I thought you said there were only two. I see three young ladies standing before me," he said, confused and a bit irritated.

"There are only two. Lucinda here managed to escape the Screamers when they attacked Lakeshore."

"In other words, she isn't special? Just a tag-along," said the old man.

"Yes," answered Oba.

Lucinda looked over to the others and folded her arms, tutting her teeth, not taking too kindly to the old man's blunt comment.

"Right then, let's get on with it, shall we. My name is Sir Abner Aldrich, but you may call me Sir Abner. I presume you all know why you're here?"

"Yes." The two girls nodded, not wanting to be reminded.

"Everyone you see around this table are Protectors or Wisemen. We protect the lands from all forms of evil and destruction. This here is Sir Arkin." He turned around and looked over to an old oriental man that had a black beard twice as long as his own. Like Sir Abner, he had wings attached to each side of his hat, but they were not gold or angel-like, but black raven wings. "He is my oldest and dearest friend; you'll show him the same respect as you will to me."

The girls looked over to Sir Arkin and gave him an awkward smile but did not receive one back, for Sir Arkin was twice as serious as Abner.

"All creatures look to us for help. Igor here, for example... his family's lives were taken many years ago by the Swamp Queen's Lurkers when she took over the swamps that surrounded his homeland, Goblin Ville. He came to us for help, now he serves the House of Grazia. He will be accompanying you on your journey." He then turned his head to Oba.

"Have you told them?" he asked.

Oba slowly turned her head towards the girls and let out a sigh. "I'm afraid you'll be taking separate roads," said the witch, failing to mention this vital detail before. The girls gasped.

"But why? We want to stick together," pleaded Ruya.

"I know, dear, but you must understand, it is dangerous times, and we must keep you safe. Separating you is the only way to do that. If the Dark Queens find out, they will hunt you both down. We need to make it harder for them by keeping you as far away from each other as possible. They don't know the spell hiding you from them was split into two. Only that the Star hides in human form as a young girl. Ates will send out her Screamers to seek you out. She will be on the hunt for one of you, the one she thinks is the Star... they all will."

"How do they know the Star could be one of us? I thought you said they would never suspect the Star was hiding in human form." Drew forcefully spoke, feeling rather annoyed.

"Before the Fire Queen was banished, she found out the witches had cast a spell, hiding the Star from her. In a rage, she managed to kill nearly every last witch, incinerating them all alive. Until one of the witches had finally cracked and spoke of the Star hiding in the form of a human child... only Ates had killed her before she could finish telling the Evil Queen that the spell had split into two. I managed to escape and flee here, where we all pledged an oath to protect the lands once the queens had awoken and the Star had returned. And here you are," she softly smiled.

"You won't be alone," the old man interrupted. "You will all be accompanied by Protectors. This here is Grazox Landa; he'll be with you all the way." They turned their heads to a big stocky man with reddish-brown hair, bushy eyebrows, and two little plaits hanging down from each side of his big scruffy beard. The House of Grazia contained only the strongest of heroes and warriors from all over the land. "And remember, no one outside this house knows who and what you really are, tell no one... trust no one!" He walked towards the girls. "There will be no goodbyes, for now. I'm sure you young ladies are hungry and very tired. You'll be staying here for just a couple of nights. In your short time here, you may wander in the library and the gardens; anywhere else is off limits, understood?"

All three girls quickly nodded. "Now, Igor here will take you to the kitchen. You have been through a great ordeal, and I'm sure you would like some supper before bed."

"Thought you said we were only allowed in the gardens and library?" Drew cheekily grinned. Sir Abner, not amused at all, just stared at her with a blunt, stern look that terrified her.

"Kitchen sounds great, I'm famished... Igor, shall we," Drew nervously chuckled, nudging the hobgoblin towards the exit. The girls quickly scurried along, following Igor out the door.

"Are you sure you brought me the right girls?" said Sir Abner, straightening out his beard as he watched them quickly leave the room.

"Of course, sir," said Oba.

"That scruffy one, with the sharp tongue, have her train with Grazox. She'll make a good fighter, I can tell."

"Yes, sir. I have already prepared which group will accompany the girls."

"Good, because when they set off on their journey, things will never be the same for them again. They need to be ready for what's to come."

"Yes, sir."

As the girls were exploring the halls that were lit with a thousand candles leading the way to the kitchen, they couldn't help but wonder at the fancy furniture that seemed fit for a king. They thought they had seen it all when they entered Miss Mabel's office, but nothing could compare to the elegance and splendour of this house.

"This place is huge and look... you can almost see your reflection on the floor. I've never walked on floors like this before," Drew spat with excitement as if all the awful things she had heard before didn't matter.

"Oh, yes, miss. The House of Grazia is a very extraordinary place. Only the best of the best live here and have walked these halls," said Igor.

"The best of the best?" said Lucinda in a snide manner. "What like those miserable, sad old freaks sat around that table? Please. They looked like a bunch of weirdos to me."

"Oh, no, miss. They are the High Council; if it weren't for them, the House of Grazia wouldn't be here today, then where would folk go to for help? Besides, you shouldn't even be here. You ought to be grateful standing before the Great Sir Abner."

"Well, I'm not grateful! That old goat called me a tag-along," Lucinda snapped, strutting off with a huff.

"That *old goat* happens to be the wisest wizard to ever live," Igor yelled across the hall, defending Sir Abner's honour. As they continued shuffling their feet through the long corridors, Ruya couldn't help but notice a beautifully hand-carved door that was slightly open, almost inviting her in. She stopped while the others walked ahead with their mutters echoing down the long hall. Feeling very curious, she slowly pushed the door open, making a creaking sound and stuck her head through the gap before entering. It was like walking into one of her dreams. You couldn't see the walls for books; the shelves were so high she couldn't even see the top.

Dust mites danced in the sunlight. She was so amazed she just stood there in awe, taking in the smell of books old and new alike. She couldn't help but walk further into the library when suddenly she noticed some of the books on the shelves were mysteriously moving. Each shelf filled with books rattled, almost as if they were coming to life. Frightened, she ran out of the room so fast she began tripping over her own feet until she finally caught up with the others out of breath and gasping for air.

"Igor. The books... in the library, they're moving!"

"Oh, that's just work bunnies."

"Work bunnies?" she coughed, out of breath with her head between her knees.

"Yes, they work in the library mainly; who else do you think keeps all the books in alphabetical order and dust-free? A library that big doesn't keep itself clean. They're awfully hard workers, you know."

"Work bunnies sound very adorable 'n all, but seriously, where's this bloody kitchen? I'm starving! I feel like I've been walking forever in this place," Drew complained, holding her rumbling belly in pain.

"We're here, it's just beyond these doors. Are you all ready?" he said, teasing the girls.

"Yes!" they answered eagerly.

"Are you sure?" he continued to tease.

"OPEN THE DOOR!" they shouted, losing their patience with the hobgoblin.

"Oki-dokey, try to contain yourselves." Igor leaned his back against the doors and finally pushed them open. As they entered, their mouths immediately watered.

"I think I just died and went to heaven," said Drew with what looked like a tear in her eye. The girls were so overwhelmed they didn't know where to start; they all were licking their lips in anticipation. The kitchen was huge, with big windows towering over them, casting golden sunlight. Hanging from the ceiling were fancy pots and pans, along with herbs and spices and legs of venison. Every cabinet was full of delicious goodies they couldn't wait to dig into, from honey cakes to lemon tarts and roasted sugared walnuts. The room filled their noses with a warm baked aroma, coming from the large, bricked stove, where mouth-watering bread loaves were being baked next to cauldrons and pots, bubbling soup and stews.

Right in the centre of the kitchen was a long oak dining table that seemed never-ending with chairs carved into the shape of bunnies. The table was heavenly spread with divine appetisers that looked fit for a royal family. The girls couldn't stand there any longer. With their mouths watering, they ran into the kitchen, each going their separate ways.

Typical Drew headed straight for dessert; she had never seen or inhaled such sugary sweet, lip-smacking goodness in her wildest dreams. Stacks of pancakes, platters of sugar-coated pastries, rainbow sugar balls that change the colour of your tongue for each flavour you had, ice cream and jelly mountains, honey-dipped sugar sticks and candy apples. Jugs of warm sweet milk sat next to a plate of rich golden cookies. Drew quickly snatched up a sugared pastry and dipped it in a bowl of syrup and began her sweet feast. Meanwhile, on the other side of the large kitchen, Ruya was mesmerised by the fancy mountain of fruit that glistened and sparkled like gold at the end of a rainbow. Sugared plums and dragon fruit, gold pineapples to crimson apples, blood oranges that looked ready to burst, and an array of juicy berries next to a bowl of fresh cream. Ruya took her time sampling each fruit, savouring the tangy tastes.

As the two girls were enjoying themselves, Lucinda was being extremely picky; nothing was to her fancy. She wasn't amused at what the kitchen had to offer. Not impressed, she eyed up the roasted suckling goose, seasoned and garnished with the finest herbs, taking the smallest nibble.

"Taste this, my lady," said Igor, holding up a crispy toad's leg to her face. Lucinda gave a girly dramatic gasp.

"Get that disgusting thing away from me, you filthy little cretin!" she shrieked, slapping the leg from his hand.

"Suit yourself." He smiled, picking the crispy toad leg off the floor, devouring it whole, then hopping off without a care. Lucinda looking distraught, heard laughter coming from across the kitchen. She saw Drew chuckling in a mocking tone.

"And what may I ask is so funny?" snapped Lucinda.

"Oh, nothing, your highness," she replied, grinning, ripping into a turkey leg. Lucinda, who liked to mock, not be mocked, took a handful of creamy mashed potato and, without hesitation, slung it towards Drew. Being one step ahead, Drew ducked while Igor took the blow to the back of the head, making Drew laugh even louder.

Ruya walked over with her hands on the side of her hips, scolding the girls in an authoritative tone. "You'll make a mess, stop this nonsense before you get us all into troub—"

Igor threw a bowl of wobbly green jelly, hitting Ruya full in the face. They all froze, waiting for her reaction.

"So sorry, my lady, I was aiming for Lu—"

SMACK!

A creamy custard pie masked his face. Ruya calmly stood there, straightening out her clothes and adjusting her hair. "Now I'm not usually one for impulsive behaviour and violence, but you had that com—"

WACK! A piece of cake splattered into her face once again.

"FOOD FIGHT!" Drew hollered from the top of her lungs, standing on a chair. Chaos and carnage erupted in the kitchen.

Drew used pots and pans to shield the blows that came her way, sending some crashing back, having the most fun. The girls went completely wild. The kitchen was in an utter state, but none of them thought about the consequences of their reckless behaviour, not even Igor. They just laughed and enjoyed themselves in that moment, forgetting where they were. The kitchen door forcefully swung open, catching the girls off guard; they all immediately stopped as Sir Abner aggressively entered the room, followed by Oba.

"What the devil is going on in here?" Sir Abner paused with absolute shock as he entered, completely disgusted by the mess they had made. "This is not a playground! In all my years, nobody has ever shown the House of Grace such disrespect... AND YOU!" Sir Abner roared in fury with his eyes boring through Igor. "You should have known better... Get out of my sight, the four of you!"

Covered in all sorts of mouth-watering delights, the girls slowly made their way out of the kitchen with what seemed like shame and embarrassment slapped upon their faces.

As they walked by with their heads down, not daring to give any eye contact, Sir Abner grunted, staring at the mess they had made in disgust. Unexpectedly, Drew popped her head back through the kitchen door.

"We didn't actually finish eating." She cheekily grinned.

Sir Abner, in outrage, turned his head around so fast as if it were about to pop off. He stared at her with his eyes wide open. Frightened, she quickly caught up with the others.

"Just look at this mess. I haven't seen this much destruction on a battlefield. Sooner they leave, the better."

"Don't be too hard on them, sir. They will not get another chance to laugh and have fun in a long time; they are still very young after all," said Oba.

"Well, it's time they grew up," he replied with attitude. "See to this mess."

"Yes, sir." As he left the room, Oba very loudly clapped her hands together three times. The floors rumbled, pots and pans were shaking, clanging together, cutlery on the tables were wobbling out of control. An army of work bunnies came rushing into the kitchen, flooding the room. "You know what to do, now get to work!" the witch demanded.

Without any further instructions, they all began to clean. Work bunnies were extremely fast workers; they liked to keep things organised and presentable at all times. They lived for cleanliness.

"I'm still hungry," Drew complained. "I need food to function," she continued with frustration.

"Well, you should have thought about that before you started flinging it everywhere," hissed Lucinda, picking bits of food out of her golden locks.

"You what? Excuse me, but you threw it first. You started it!" Drew argued.

"Whatever," she huffed, rolling her eyes with an attitude.

"We should have never had made that mess; I should have never retaliated. It's all my fault," said Ruya with shame in her voice.

"Oh, do shut up! Little miss perfect," snapped Lucinda with irritation.

"Oi, don't talk to her like that!" Drew yelled, coming to Ruya's defence.

"Make me!"

All three girls began squabbling with their voices loudly echoing through the halls of the large house. "My ladies, please," Igor pleaded. But still, they continued to argue.

"MY LADIES!"

Silence.

"Do you three have absolutely no respect at all?"

"We're sorry, Igor," said Ruya.

"Good, now follow me, please." They continued walking through the never-ending halls of the elaborate structure.

"Wow, these are amazing." Ruya smiled, stopping to stare at one of the painted portraits framed in fancy gold decoration filling the walls all the way down. "They look just like those strange human-like creatures that were sitting in Sir Abner's study," she continued.

"Who are they?" asked Drew.

"Generations of Protectors and Wisemen from the past and present. It's a great honour to have your portrait hung on the walls of grace," he explained. "One day, my portrait too will be up there, among the Heroes and Wisemen," he said with a tear in his eye.

"Isn't there a height requirement to be a hero?" Lucinda spitefully laughed.

Scrunching his face, Igor stuck out his bright pink tongue in a childlike manner. "Right, here we are, your room, my ladies."

Igor opened the door to reveal a huge room of grand structure, where their eyes immediately gazed upon three king-sized beds, perfectly aligned in a row with thick quilted bedding and large plump feathered pillows.

"Middle bed's mine!" Drew ran as fast as she could into the room towards the large fluffy bed, jumping up and down with excitement like a child. The others ran in after her, jumping up and down from one bed to another.

Meanwhile, on the other side of the house, a heavy discussion was taking place.

"Ates's armies have spread throughout the lands like wildfire, their numbers are growing larger. They are preparing for her awakening," Sir Arkin explained.

"The House of Grazia is no longer safe for them; this will be the first place they will come looking," said Oba.

"Then they may have to leave sooner than we thought, have the Protectors ready. They leave tomorrow." Night had fallen upon the House of Grazia and the girls were in bed.

"I'm starving," Drew moaned, sadly listening to the rumbles in her belly.

"Me too," the others complained.

"All that glorious food right in front of us... wasted! We had the opportunity of stuffing our faces, and we blew it. We probably won't come by food like that again, I'll tell ya," she continued to moan, feeling sorry for herself. They all huffed with sadness, feeling depressed.

Even Lucinda had great regret for being so fussy.

"If only we knew someone who could lead us back to the kitchen," Drew grinned, tipping her head towards Igor, who was lying on the other end of the large bed.

"Me? oh, I don't think so. It's after dark. If Sir Abner were to catch us again, I'll—"

"Please," Drew and the others begged.

"We won't make a mess, I promise," said Drew.

"We will have a quick snack and come straight back to bed." Ruya smiled.

"Oh... fine." He wasn't happy, but Igor finally agreed. Leaving their room, they quickly snuck into the hallways, sneakily passing the night guards. Once again, they found themselves in the kitchen, and Drew wasn't happy at all.

"Oi! Where's all the mountains of food that were lying around before?" she said, with her hands in the air, feeling frustrated.

"Wow, the work bunnies don't mess about," Igor laughed, scratching the back of his head. Taking Ruya by the hand, he made her and the others take a seat while he warmed them up a bowl of honey porridge. He then handed them each little wooden carved bowls that he had poured the porridge into. "Good enough for her majesty?" he sarcastically smirked, handing Lucinda a bowl. Not saying a word, she just rolled her eyes and nodded, she knew not to be fussy this time or she might not get another chance to eat. All three girls went at their bowls like savages.

"My lady," Igor gasped, staring at Ruya slurping at her bowl with her head tilted back.

"Sorry," she giggled with her hand over her mouth. "Really hungry." She continued to smile. Drew was licking her bowl, trying not to miss anything out, while Lucinda was scraping her spoon around the bowl, trying to get all the last bits of porridge that were left over. Finishing, emptying their bowls squeaky clean, they all leaned back on their chairs and sighed with full bellies, licking their lips with satisfaction and contentment.

"Thank you, Igor," said Ruya.

"Now I can get a good night's sleep," said a happy Drew, wiping her dirty mouth on one of the fancy tea towels before letting out a belch.

"I don't like porridge, it's a poor man's dish, and I certainly don't like honey, but thanks anyway," said Lucinda, barely giving Igor any eye contact, finding it extremely difficult for she never said thank you to anyone.

"I'm glad to be at your service," he said, bowing, looking very pleased with himself.

The girls found themselves once again tucked up in their warm beds with only a flickering lantern that Drew kept beside her so she could see Ruya's face while they whispered through the silent night.

"What do you think happened to Miss Mabel and the others? Do you think they're alive?"

"I really don't know, I hope so. I still can't believe any of this is real. What do you think is going to happen to us?" Drew whispered, trying not to wake Lucinda and Igor, who were fast asleep snoring away like pigs.

"Who knows what's going to happen to us," Ruya replied, worried, fiddling with a loose lock of hair.

"You know, Ruya, that day I found you crying on the step, something pulled me to you. I don't know what it was but... something did. I don't make friends that easily, and I've never tried to befriend any of the other girls before, but I wanted to be yours. In a strange way, I felt connected to you. Guess now it all makes sense" Drew laughed, itching the tip of her round nose.

Ruya smiled. "These last few days have been crazy, sure we might go to war, and Evil Queens are out hunting us down to eat our hearts, but if there is any good that came from all this, it's gaining a sister. I've always wanted a family. I can't tell you how happy I am that we found each other, despite the circumstances.

And if we are really going to be separated, we will find each other again. I promise."

"You read too many fairy tales. They don't all end well, you know."

"Ours will," Ruya whispered, giving her a soft little smile of assurance. Drew suddenly felt herself getting all emotional, which rarely ever happened to her. She quickly tried to change the subject, clearing her throat, she spoke. "So, what about Lucinda? Think you've gained a sister there?"

"I wouldn't go that far, maybe an evil stepsister." They both turned their heads in Lucinda's direction, and as they did, she let out a loud snort that made them both giggle.

Covering their mouths under the covers, trying their utmost not to wake her up, they laughed all the way through the night.

PROTECTORS
CHAPTER FIVE

Magical golden rays peeked through the bedroom windows, filling the air with warmth as dust modes floated, suspended in the air. The morning sun in the House of Grazia was heavenly and captivating, almost as if an angel had come to visit. It was dazzling, to say the least. Too bright to look at, yet too enchanting to look away.

"Rise and shine, my ladies." Igor came bursting through the large bedroom doors with great energy and excitement in his gruff voice.

"Good morning, Igor," said Ruya, rubbing her puffy eyes, slowly raising herself from the warm cosy covers with a friendly smile.

"Today is a big day." He grinned.

"What is he babbling on about?" an unhappy Lucinda moaned, pulling the covers back over her head, not interested in what he had to say that early in the morning.

"What's so special about today?" Drew yawned, with her eyes closed, still half asleep.

"You all finally get to meet your Protectors," he continued.

"Can we have 10 more minutes; I still haven't quite woken up yet," Drew coughed, cosying back down into her soft duvet.

"No. Now make sure you come down for breakfast, don't keep them waiting. After the kitchen incident, you don't want to get on Sir Abner's bad side any more than you already have."

"He has a good side?" Drew laughed, popping her head back up from the covers.

"Just be on time," Igor demanded, closing the door behind him.

At last, the girls found themselves once again in the kitchen sitting in front of a pleasant breakfast that was elegantly laid out. Just when they began to feast on their scrummy eggs, Mother Oba walked through the door, leaning onto her sceptre for support.

"Good morning, girls. I trust you slept well?" She paused. "Judging by the state of your hair, I'll say you slept very well," she laughed, staring at their tattered hair in turn.

"What idiot's idea was it to stuff the bloody pillows with sharp feathers?" said Lucinda.

"Excuse me?" Oba replied, not amused.

"I hardly got any sleep last night, too busy being stabbed to death by those ghastly pillows in the guest bedroom," she continued, unamused.

"Well, I hardly got any sleep cause of all your poxy snoring!" Drew argued.

"How dare you, I've never snored in my life. A lady never snores," Lucinda argued back.

"You do, too," said Ruya jumping into the conversation.

"I do not!" Once again, they began to squabble among themselves as usual.

"Hush! Sir Abner is coming," Oba whispered very seriously.

"Ah, young ladies, I was about to send someone to wake you, but I'm glad to see you're up and about. Finish your breakfast, then make your way to the courtyard; that's where you'll be introduced to your Protectors. Time we got a move on, but before we do, Igor has put fresh clothes on your bed, can't have anyone meeting you looking like that." Not saying another word, he left the girls to finish their breakfast and engaged in conversation with Sir Arkin, walking off with their hands behind their backs.

"The cheek of it. Somebody needs to look in the mirror... old fart," Lucinda sneered, scoffing on an egg. Finishing their breakfast, they made their way back to their room and found themselves standing in front of their new outfits that had been neatly laid out on their beds.

"I'm not wearing that. It's not ladylike at all, I mean... look at it for heaven sake, it's disgusting." Lucinda complained, sickened at the sight of the clothes she held up to her body and stared at it up and down with a horrible frown.

"Well, I like it; looks like something a strong woman would wear," said Ruya, changing into them without any hesitation.

"Well, I wouldn't wear it to a funeral," Lucinda hissed, throwing the clothes back onto her bed, folding her arms disappointedly like a spoiled brat.

On the other hand, Drew was extremely excited, for she was the first to change, admiring her new clothes in the mirror. "Look, it even has a belt for your weapons. Do you think they will give me a dagger, or a bow and arrow... or maybe a sword?" Drew bounced on one spot with eagerness and passion as she continued to admire her new outfit.

"Calm down," Ruya laughed.

"Knock, knock. May I come in?" Oba entered the room. "They are waiting," she said.

"We're ready." Ruya smiled. "Well... not all of us." Shifting her eyes over to Lucinda.

"Why aren't you dressed?" said Oba.

"Because she thinks it's beneath her, just like everything else." Drew rolled her eyes, adjusting her belt.

Oba looked over to Lucinda. "I understand. Maybe I'll call for Sir Abner, and you can explain to him just how the clothes the House of Grace has kindly provided you with is beneath you."

"NO!" she snapped. "I'll change; there is no need to call him," she continued, quickly undressing out of her old clothes and into her new ones. Oba turned to the others and gave them a little wink.

Groomed and polished, the girls were finally ready and found themselves standing in front of a tall, gold, vine-covered gate. It opened, and they didn't know what to expect on the other side. Anxiously dragging their feet along the pebbled pathway, the girls knew this was it, the beginning of their journey, which made them feel nauseous. As they drew closer, they heard muttering ahead that sounded like a group of people talking and whispering over each other. The whispers had gotten louder with each step they took, then suddenly stopped when the girls approached. The silence made them nervous.

"I'm scared," whispered Ruya. Drew took her arm into her own and smiled, assuring her things were going to be okay, as long as they had each other.

"Ah, finally, we thought you were never going to be ready," said Sir Abner impatiently, as if they'd kept him waiting for hours.

"Well, let's get on with it then, we have no more time to waste." The group of Protectors stood in a line while Sir Abner began introducing the girls to them one by one.

"You remember Grazox Landa; you met him in the study," said Abner.

Of course the girls remembered him; how could they forget such a serious face. "He is one of our bravest men, a real war hero," he continued. With no expression on his face, he just stared at them as they were being introduced, looking profoundly serious and uptight.

"This here is Tobin Landa," said Abner, moving on to the next person. "Grazox's nephew, who is still in training to become a Protector himself."

Tobin, just like his uncle, looked far too serious. He was a handsome young man, just a few years older than the girls. He had dark hair, almost black and fair skin and hazel, honey eyes. He kept his head down, rudely not giving the girls any eye contact as he was being introduced. Unbothered, he finally decided to look up, remembering he had to be professional. As his bright eyes took a quick glimpse, he was suddenly mesmerised by her beauty. Speechless, his face lit up, locking eyes with Drew. Of course, she hadn't noticed. She thought maybe he was staring at some leftover breakfast on her face. When it came to boys, the girls were clueless, being raised in an all-girls school their whole lives. Tobin quickly cleared his throat; suddenly realising he was staring at her, shifting his eyes that blinked uncontrollably, he turned his face away and went back to being all grumpy and serious – even more than before.

"And this here is Zyra Ray and Zyron Ray, twins, both children of war," Sir Abner continued as they moved along to the next Protector. The twins were in their early twenties and extremely rough-looking, they each looked like they could take on a whole army and win.

"And here you have Kruze Hanley; he has won more sword fights than any living man."

Kruze ran his fingers through his thick, black silky hair with pride as he told them that, he always did love the title of being the best swordsman. He loved the celebrity status, and he loved the ladies even more.

"And finally, this here is Ludlow," he said, moving onto the last Protector. The girls gasped as they stared up at this large man-like being looming above them. "His family are the last of War Giants to roam our realms. You'll all be travelling together. Now—"

"AND ME!" screamed a voice from a distance, getting closer towards them.

"Ah, yes. I almost forgot you… the stable boy," Abner huffed, not bothering to give him a proper introduction.

With his head between his knees, the boy stopped, desperately trying to catch his breath. "Fen Scully, it's nice to meet yo—" lifting his head up, he had forgotten how to speak. He found himself dumbfounded by the site of Lucinda, instantly falling in love with her.

"You could learn more about each other on your travels since we have no time left." Sir Abner turned to Drew and Ruya. "And this, young ladies, is where we say goodbye. We won't see each other for what I imagine will be quite a long time. You're in good hands, so don't worry. And soon, you'll both be taking separate roads to prepare for the war to come."

The girls quickly exchanged a shocked look. "I thought the whole going to war thing was a bad joke; they don't actually expect us to go to fight, do they?" said Drew, leaning in closer towards Ruya, raising one eyebrow.

"I wish you all a safe journey, and remember, no one knows who you are; it must remain a secret. If it gets out, the Queens of Darkness won't be the only ones seeking you, there will be others. Stay close to your Protectors." After his goodbye, he finally walked off, not once looking back.

"Goodbye, girls," said Oba.

"You're staying too?" Ruya sighed, disappointed.

"Yes, I'm afraid I'm needed here. I am the last surviving witch after all; Sir Abner needs me close by. But we will meet again, that I can promise... now come here." She opened her large arms to embrace the girls. Ruya and Drew leapt towards her; Lucinda hesitated at first but eventually joined the group hug. Oba was a large, rounded woman and managed to wrap her arms around all three girls. Finally letting go of each other, wiping away their tears, Oba called Igor over by her side.

"Now, Igor, I'm trusting you to watch over the girls for me. Can you do that?"

"I will, Mother." Igor hopped up into Oba's lap and hugged her tight like it was the last time they would ever see each other.

"Let's get this show on the road!" Grazox shouted, waving them over impatiently from where he sat on his horse.

"Well, I guess this is it then," said Drew.

"WAIT, WAIT!"

As they were about to leave, they all turned around and saw the elevator operator, Gustav, hopping towards them, carrying fancy luggage in each hand.

"Isn't that the frog you stole that button from?" Ruya asked Drew.

"Gustav, what are you doing here?" said Oba.

"Sir Abner agreed to let me join this expedition. All my life I have waited for an adventure like this. It is my dream to one day become a Protector and live among the warriors." With confidence, he rudely brushed by the girls with his luggage.

"Looks like you've got competition," Drew laughed, nudging Igor on the shoulder. Flinging their bags at the back of an open-top carriage, the girls gave the witch one final goodbye, waving their hands high up in the air as Oba watched them from a distance. Settled in the carriage, Igor and Gustav squeezed between the girls who found themselves sitting opposite the twins and Fen, the stable boy. Tobin rode in front of the carriage with his uncle and Kruze, while Ludlow the Giant rode at the back with Gloob. Gloob was a bunyip, the only creature big and strong enough to carry a giant and other heavy loads at the same time. Bunyips were like horses for Giants. Flying above them, leading the way was Aero, Tobin's pet eagle. Aero was like Tobin's shadow, always nearby. The carriage began to move, making its way down Grace Hill. The beginning of the journey was rather uncomfortable; the girls sat in awkward silence while the carriage bounced up and down on the bumpy path. The twins and Fen just stared at the girls, not saying a word making them feel quite uneasy. The twins both looked rough; they had scruffy brown hair, with matching headbands that kept their fringes out of their eyes, along with matching daggers and crossbows that they always carried around. The only thing they didn't share was a scar that the boy had going down his left eye.

Fen, on the other hand, was an extremely cheerful and friendly young man. He was scrawny, with tattered blonde hair that looked like hay and shiny blue eyes that he couldn't seem to keep off Lucinda. He carried no weapon, only being the stable boy.

"What's your name?" he said, smiling at Lucinda. "I'm Fen Scully," he continued politely. Lucinda, not amused at all, just rolled her eyes like she always did whenever something got on her nerves and rudely ignored him.

"You're a shy one, I see. That's okay," he laughed. "All in good time." He continued to smile.

"That's Lucinda, I'm Ruya and this is Drew."

"Nice to meet you," he happily replied.

"So, children of war, eh? Sounds exciting," said Drew staring at the twins.

"Have you ever been to war? Not so exciting when a man or beast is running towards you, ready to kill," Zyra answered, very seriously, intimidatingly shining her dagger as she spoke.

"Oh, no... I just meant—"

"It's okay," she smirked.

"How did you become children of war anyway?" said Ruya.

"We were abandoned at the age of five. Our parents wanted us to learn to fend for ourselves, so they left us in the forest until Grazox found us and took us to the House of Grazia when he saw our potential. That's where we began our training."

"Abandoned in a forest? You didn't come by a gingerbread house, did ya?" Drew laughed.

"What?"

"You know, Hansel and Gretel?"

The twins looked confused.

"Never mind, carry on," she said. Drew hated when someone didn't get her jokes, made her feel stupid.

"We had our first battle at the age of eight, the House of Grazia's youngest warriors, children of war. And that's how we got our name," Zyron finished explaining.

"What about the others? What's their story?"

"Tobin is still in training, he's a good fighter, but he still has a lot to learn. He's eager to be the best and please his uncle. You see, his parents were murdered by Kang, the Fire Queen's general, many years ago. Grazox is the only family he has left."

No wonder he looked so miserable, Drew thought.

"As for Kruze," she huffed unamused. "He was named one of the best swordsmen in the House of Grazia, giving him a really big ego, as if it weren't big enough already. And the ladies just *love* him," she explained, rolling her eyes.

"What about that guy?" Drew said, pointing over to Grazox.

"Grazox is a completely different story. He's an enormously proud and humble man. He never has been amused by fancy gold armour or fancy swords like Kruze, just give him an axe and he's ready for war."

"He seems a bit too serious," said Drew.

"You would be too, if you saw your wife and only daughter murdered in front of your eyes by a pack of Screamers."

Everyone fell silent with awkwardness; for a while, the only sound was of the carriage bouncing up and down on the rough, rocky path.

I'm sorry... I didn't mean anything by it," said Drew, feeling embarrassed.

"Just don't ever mention it to him, okay."

"Okay," Drew softly spoke, scratching her chin.

After the awkwardness had passed, Ruya decided to speak again to break the ice. "What about him?" she said, excitedly turning her head around to have a good look at Ludlow, who was still riding at the back. "I've only read about Giants; never thought I'd be on a journey with one."

"He's a complicated story," the twins replied.

"Was he abandoned too?"

"No, not exactly. He decided to leave Skala and join us."

"Skala?" said Ruya.

"Home of the War Giants. You see, his family always made him feel worthless. Far as War Giants go, Ludlow's a bit on the small side and can be quite a softy, which is embarrassing for Giants, especially for War Giants who are known for being fearless and brutal."

"Bless him, that's horrible," said Ruya.

"Yes, how very sad," Lucinda muttered beneath her breath, picking at her nails as if she couldn't care less. After a while, the girls had fallen asleep, travelling for such a long time.

Suddenly the carriage wheel drove over a large pothole making the carriage violently bounce up and down, startling the girls, Igor, and Gustav from their sleep.

"Oh, for god's sake, are we there yet? I'm going to be sick!" Lucinda impatiently complained.

"Where are we going anyway?" said Drew.

"Healers Town. We're almost there," said Grazox, riding his horse close to the carriage, then galloping off to the front to ride beside his nephew.

HEALERS TOWN
CHAPTER SIX

They journeyed continuously for a great while, but at last they had finally reached their destination, Healers Town. A place where folk travelled to from all over the land for the famous medicines, potions, and other elixirs. The backstreets were filled with an aroma of herbs and other strange botanical scents that they couldn't quite identify. The town was built on an old hill that was once a nesting ground for Dragons' thousands of years ago when they still roamed the skies. Some say if you searched deep enough, you may still find a Dragons egg, but it was impossible. Healers Town was so high that some of the rooftops found their way into the clouds. Cobbled stairs spiralled around the hill, leading to different levels, where you would find some of the locals residing in their cosy homes made from old bricks, stones, and oak wood with round stain-glass windows. Most of the houses had crooked straw rooftops; some of them looked like they had been set on fire with little clouds of smoke puffing through the chimney tops.

The girls couldn't believe that such a town existed, every corner to every alley they drove by looked enchanted, as if in a dream. Even the locals looked unusual, some were human, and others clearly weren't. They wore funny little hats and had small antennas on each side of their bizarrely pointed ears, and great bulgy eyes that looked ready to burst out from their sockets. The women wore huge frocks and large bonnets and fancy gable hoods. They looked exactly like the High Council that sat in Sir Abner's study and the portraits that hung on the walls of Grazia.

"Fairy dust! Get your fairy dust!" a two-headed salesmen kept hollering from the top of their lungs, strolling by pushing a wooden cart of crates that contained little glass jars filled to the top with colourful glittery dust.

"Fairy dust?" the girls gasped with curiosity.

"Rubbish!" Fen spat. "Fairy dust won't help you on a battlefield, I'll tell you that much; it's just a waste of your coins. Doesn't actually do anything useful," he continued.

The girls finally jumped off the carriage, grabbing their bags. Suddenly Ruya felt something moving around in hers. She opened her bag to take a look and, kicking its back legs, out hopped a work bunny jumping right into her arms. "Where on earth did you come from?" she whispered.

"A stowaway, hah? Well, that's your problem now," said Grazox, swinging a heavy bag over his shoulder.

Drew was completely fascinated by the wonders around her. She bolted off the carriage quicker than lighting; she couldn't wait to explore. "Can we look in there?" she asked, pointing to one of the potion shops in a childlike manner.

"No," said Grazox.

"How about there," she said, pointing to another.

"NO! We only came here for things we need; we have no time to waste."

"Boor-ing," Drew huffed, rolling her eyes.

"You four with me," said Grazox, pointing towards Fen and the three girls. "The rest of you will meet us at the Sky Docks shortly." Fen and the girls followed behind him through the town, pacing along the cobbled floors.

"Stay close, and don't go wandering off. Nobody knows who or what you are; best we keep it that way... Now, keep up," said Grazox.

"Where we going?" said Ruya.

"To pay old Healer Higgles a visit."

"Healer Higgles, who's that?" they asked.

"His real name is Helix Higgles. He's the best healer and potion maker to ever live. He can cure almost anything, but death, of course," Fen explained.

They continued walking through the noisy town of people rushing about chaotically, talking over each other while salesmen hollered from the top of their lungs, standing by their stools selling herbs and fruit. They turned around a little corner that took them deeper through the back alleys. The girls had noticed a drastic change in scenery, things seemed dark and eerie, and the sound of the townspeople seemed to dim until it was completely silent. Grazox finally stopped and looked up at a little battered sign which read Beggars Hollow.

"There are a lot of unfriendly folk wandering about these parts of town; stay close and speak to on one," said Grazox.

"Unfriendly folk?" said a worried Ruya, looking to Fen for an answer.

"Gypsies," said Fen. "God help you if you even look at one in a funny way; they'll put a hex on you without any hesitation."

"So, what in god's name are we doing walking through these parts of town," responded a petrified Lucinda.

"Helix Higgles potion shop is through here." Fen casually smiled.

"COME ON!" Grazox shouted, growing restless of the others taking their time at the back.

They continued to follow Grazox cautiously through Beggars Hollow. Shifty looking characters cloaked in unwashed rags brushed past the girls, coughing and suspiciously, but not so discreetly, staring at them. Walking by one of the back doors to a creepy little inn, a wrinkly old woman in filthy rags held a rusty tin bucket. Emptying out the dirty water, she splashed Lucinda's legs. Lucinda gagged with revulsion, seeing all the filth dripping from her leg. Quickly trotting off, she pushed ahead of the others to get away.

"Spare change," came a croaky voice. Drew looked down to see an old gypsy woman that appeared to be missing a nose and only had one eye, grabbing tightly onto her leg.

Drew felt bad for the old woman. "Sorry, I don't have any," she replied, pulling out her empty pockets, with the odd button falling out. But before the gypsy could say another word, Drew suddenly felt someone grab her arm. It was Grazox, pulling her away from the old woman.

"Keep moving… I told you not to talk to anyone"

"She was just asking for some spare change," Drew argued.

"I don't care what she was asking for. You don't talk to anyone here, am I clear!"

"Yes," she huffed, removing his hand from her arm with a frown. Grazox stormed off once again with an attitude, continuing to lead the way.

"He just wants you to be safe," said Fen.

"She was just an old lady," said Ruya.

"Don't let looks mislead you. It's always the ones that look harmless that are usually the most dangerous."

"I don't like this place. Not one bit," an uneasy Lucinda whispered, alert with every step she took, covering her nose from the stench. With no warning, a creepy man jumped out from behind a wall, startling Lucinda by leaping in front of her.

"Would the lady like to buy a necklace?" he said, holding a ruby necklace close to her.

"It matches those pretty blue eyes of yours." He creepily grinned, moving the necklace closer to her face. Lucinda looking distraught, just froze, not responding to the man's offer, for she couldn't speak out of fear.

But luckily, Fen wedged his way in-between them. "She's not interested!" he snapped, slapping the necklace from out of Lucinda's face, taking her by the arm and pulling her away.

"It's a fake anyway!" Fen shouted behind him. "Don't worry, I'll keep you safe." He smiled, looking pleased with himself. Lucinda, still too frightened to speak, just went along with him arm-in-arm. At long last, they had come to the dead-end of Beggars Hollow.

"We're here," said Grazox, pointing towards a little crooked shop that slightly tilted to one side like it was going to fall over. They all looked up to a rusted wooden sign hanging to one side with some of the letters faded away, which read Potions, with purple clouds of smoke puffing from the chimney. They all gathered outside the door while Grazox heavily knocked twice with his strong fist.

"Yes! Yes! Hold your horses. I'm coming," complained a croaky voice. A little secret door unlocked, revealing two beady eyes gawking at them.

"Reveal yourself," said the croaky voice.

"Helix, it's me," said Grazox.

"Just do it!" said the mysterious grumpy old potion maker.

"Grazox Landa," he replied, rolling his eyes and scratching his head, tired of revealing his name every time he paid him a visit, even though he knew who he was. The little door hatch suddenly shut. They all stood there with anticipation, not sure if he was going to let them in. The main door unlocked. Grazox was the first to enter the potion shop, the others followed shortly after.

"Don't take all day about it, you coming in or what? And shut the door behind you!"

Helix Higgles was incredibly famous for his cures and potions, but even more notorious for his ill-mannered behaviour, he was extremely impolite, even by gnome standards. Just like most gnomes, he had a fluffy white beard and bushy eyebrows that made him look even more grumpy than he already was. He wore a little hat that made his long-pointed ears stick out from the sides; his ears were almost as long and pointy as his shoes.

"Blasted beasts!" Helix pounced and caught something in a little glass jar.

"What's that?" Drew asked, staring at what the potion maker had just caught with curiosity.

"Ember flies," said Grazox.

"Little rascals destroy everything they touch," Helix complained. "Nobody can have straw rooftops anymore because of these blasted beasts... raising blazes!" he continued to moan.

"Ember flies are full of mischief. They love deliberately setting fire to folks rooftops; they're like naughty little children, only smaller and made of fire," Fen quietly explained to the girls.

It suddenly came to mind, remembering some of the rooftops in passing; they looked like they had been set on fire, now they knew why. Helix walked over to a tall shelf made from worn-down wood, full of glowing jars that lit up like lanterns filled with ember flies and added the one he had newly caught to his collection.

"Is this a bad time?" asked Grazox.

"It's always a bad time. What do you want, Landa?" Helix snapped

"I hear you have information for me?"

"Shhhh!" Helix quickly silenced him from speaking another word, shifting his beady eyes from side to side suspiciously and hurried over to the window, tiptoeing to see if anyone was out there listening.

"Not here." He quickly scurried over to a little stoned fireplace covered in cobwebs and pulled a secret lever. The fireplace slowly shifted to one side.

"In here... quickly now!" he said, pushing them in one by one. They all squeezed through, and the fireplace slowly moved back into its original place, as if it hadn't moved at all.

"AAHHHH!!"

Without any warning, they found themselves rapidly dropping.

"WE'RE GOING TO DIE!" Fen screamed like a little boy calling for his mother, tightly holding onto Lucinda. They were dropping so fast, then they all slowly floated, levitating up in the air. Then just like that, the feeling of falling out of the sky stopped, and they crash-landed back onto their feet.

"Ah, here we are," said Helix, casually walking out while the rest of the group struggled to squeeze out of the fireplace at the same time, getting awkwardly stuck in the process.

"Get off!" hissed Lucinda, slapping Fen's arms off, which were clinging onto her like a leech.

"Where are we?" asked Ruya.

"This is where I keep all the good stuff, my rarest potions and medicines that I do not sell to the locals – unless they meet my price, of course."

"What's in there?" Fen curiously pointed towards a large door, bolted, and sealed with chains.

"Nothing, there is nothing in there. Mind your own business," he yelled anxiously.

"But I just heard something move around in there"

"I said mind your own business boy!" Helix snapped.

"About that information you have for me?" Grazox interrupted.

"Yes, about that. How many times have I told you not to talk business in the front shop? There are eyes and ears everywhere, especially in these parts of town, you know that. You must always be cautious. You can never be too careful. There are enemies everywhere."

"Helix, I apricate the advice, but I have no time. We're on a tight schedule, our transportation will be leaving soon. Do you have info or not?"

Helix reached up, tiptoeing, grabbed Grazox by the arm and led him away from the others so they could have their conversation privately.

"Don't touch anything!" warned the grouchy old gnome, addressing everyone in the room, walking away with Grazox to get some privacy. Even though he had warned them not to touch anything, Fen and the girls saw this as an opportunity to go exploring through his unusual belongings like naughty little children alone in a sweetshop. There were mountains of books everywhere, potion books, spell books, books about medicines and herbs and all sorts of other elixirs. Bottles of bubbling potions that boiled out of control. Mixtures of herbs and plants crushed up in a brew boiling on a little brick stove. Onions and dried up garlic dangling from the ceiling along with charms that sparkled and chimed, making a tingly melody in the air.

Lucinda felt a tap on her shoulder. She turned around and found herself face to face with a skull, practically kissing it.

"AAHHH!" she screamed with a girly squeal. Fen laughed like a little child, holding the skull in his hand.

"You stupid idiot!" Lucinda embarrassedly snapped with pink cheeks.

"Bahahaha, I'm sorry, but you should have seen your face," he laughed, hysterically bending over, slapping his scrawny knees.

"Get that thing away from me!" she ordered, slapping the skull in his hand.

"Oh, come on, give us a kiss," he laughed, continuing to make the skull's mouth move closer towards her, which made her even angrier.

"Ruya, look at this," said Drew, calling Ruya over to her to look at something she had found.

"Looks like a... fairy?" she said.

Drew had come across a little glass case concealing a deceased fairy with its wings pinned up, next to a pile of drawings and stacks of notes about fairy anatomy.

"You're right; it is a fairy. That's horrible," Ruya gasped with horror.

"Why?" Fen replied casually.

"Why? What do you mean, that was a sweet little fairy."

"Sweet?" he laughed. "Fairies are crazy and incredibly vicious," he continued.

"But I've read about fairies, they're kind and pleasant," she argued.

Fen couldn't help but laugh. "Well, I don't know what books you've been reading but fairies are far from kind. They're notorious for their temper, and they have sharp teeth that feel like needles; they attack for absolutely no reason at all. One almost took my cousin's eye out. Let me tell you about the time when..." Fen continued to explain and teach Ruya about fairy behaviour. Meanwhile, Helix and Grazox were in a serious discussion of their own.

"And you're sure about this?" said Grazox with tension in his stern voice, running his plump fingers through his thick beard, lost in a daze, looking very serious.

"Absolutely, you don't live in these parts of town without hearing a thing or two," Helix replied. "The Wise Shroom knows all. He has answers that could help end the war before it even begins. You must find him."

"Thank you, Helix. This is useful information," said Grazox, patting the old gnome on the shoulder.

"All this nonsense over some poor fool who happened to find the Star. I mean, what idiot moulds a star into a crown anyway, honestly."

"Evil needs no excuse. None of this is happening because some blacksmith made a crown from the fallen Star; the queens would have found another reason for war. This was always going to happen whether the Star had fallen on our world or not... it was only a matter of time," Grazox responded.

"True, true," Helix huffed, scratching the back of his pointy ear. "Trust a woman to want to take over the world," he tutted, rolling his eyes. "So, any word on where the Star may be?" he continued.

"No luck yet, but we're still searching," answered Grazox, trying his best to hide the truth from the old gnome.

"Best you find it before those vile queens do... never trust a woman," he said, shaking his head disapprovingly.

"Don't let anyone hear you say that, Helix," Grazox laughed. "Some of the finest warriors, leaders and heroes are women. We would be lost without them fighting by our side. Someday you might just have your life saved by one."

"A woman? Save me. HA!" he laughed. "Pfff... please," he continued, flinging his wrinkly hand in the air, dismissing the idea entirely.

"I'd be careful if I were you. You might end up eating your own words someday," said Grazox, shamefully nodding his head.

Meanwhile, the girls were still exploring through Helix's mysterious magical belongings. The work bunny once again hopped out of Ruya's backpack.

"Where did that come from?" asked Drew, not noticing the first time it jumped out of her bag.

"I don't know, it must have snuck into my bag back at Grazia." The work bunny excitedly began hopping about, knocking over bottles of potions that blew up in colourful clouds of smoke, puffing about in madness like rainbow bombs.

"Make it stop!" the others snapped at Ruya.

"It's not my fault," she argued, feeling pressured to put a stop to the chaos.

"Well, it jumped out from *your* bag, so it's your problem," Lucinda insisted.

"Come here, little bunny." Ruya quickly tried to grab the work bunny but failed for it was way too fast, quickly jumping away. This led Ruya to accidentally crash into glass jars filled with eyeballs, making them roll all over the creaking wooden floors.

"What in god's name is going on?!" Helix came rushing back into the room, quickly followed by Grazox.

"My potions! Everything is a mess!" he yelled, tightly grabbing, and pulling onto his hair with both hands in distress.

"We're sorry, it was an accident," said Fen.

"You're an accident!!" Helix viciously snapped back at the boy.

"Ruya, are you okay?" said Drew, helping her clean off the broken glass that was embedded in her sleeve.

"I'm fine, I just cut myself."

Drew went to take a look. She gently pulled up Ruya's sleeve when suddenly she stopped and gasped. She was stunned.

"Oh my god... Ruya."

"What... what is it?" she answered worriedly.

"Your blood... it's... it's silver."

"What?" she gasped.

Ruya looked down at her arm and was astonished to see her wound dripping out silver liquid. The others fell silent while Helix continued to moan like the miserable old git he was.

"Clumsy fools," he complained on his hands and knees, picking the eyeballs back off the ground and carefully placing them back into a glass jar.

"That's the last time I—"

He stopped. Dropping the eyeballs on the ground once again. "Silver blood?" he whispered to himself, finally noticing Ruya's arm.

"Yes, she's a Spellborn," Fen nervously laughed.

"Mortals bleed red, Spellborns bleed blue, but in all my years, I have never come across anyone with silver blood running through their veins… Unless, of course…" He looked wide-eyed at Grazox in complete disbelief.

"You mustn't tell a living soul," Grazox demanded.

"So the whispers are true, the witches hid the Star, posing as a human."

"Yes," said Grazox.

"AH! Amazing," Helix chuckled. "A man finds a star, moulds it into a crown, the witches find the crown and give it life as a mortal… genius," he continued, intrigued.

"Well, they're not actually mortal, more like an extremely rare Spellborn," Fen interrupted.

"They?" said Helix with a confused expression.

"Yes, Drew too." Fen smiled.

"You mean there are two of them?" he spat, immediately turning his head to Drew with wide eyes, completely in shock.

"Yes… wait, oops," said Fen, throwing the back of his hand to his forehead, realising he had let a huge secret slip.

"Idiot," Grazox muttered beneath his breath, furiously shaking his head in disappointment.

"I don't understand. How is this possible?" said Helix, puzzled. "Answers," he snapped, impatiently clicking his wrinkly fingers in the air.

"The witches conjured a spell trying to hide the Star, making it invisible to those seeking it. But something went wrong. The spell was so strong that it split the Star. Instead of forming one child, it made two," Grazox quickly explained.

Helix stood there silently, then spoke. "Who else knows about this?" he asked.

"Only the House of Grazia, and we want to keep it that way. No one else must ever know."

"Of course, of course. I understand," he replied. "And what of the queens," he suspiciously asked, scratching the back of his wrinkly neck.

"If we're lucky, nothing. Their people may know that the Star hides in the form of a young girl, but we can't be certain how much they know."

"That's why we need to keep them apart; one is useless without the other. In order to unlock their full power, they need both Drew and Ruya together," Fen interrupted, once again sharing vital information, completely unaware of the raging look Grazox had given him.

"It's all very poetic, isn't it... Well then, young lady, let's see to that wound." Helix walked across the room; the others followed him to a little wooden cabinet with a large lock. He pulled out a key hanging from a chain that rested around his neck. Unlocking the cabinet door, he pulled out a jar that contained thick, slimy transparent liquid.

"What's that?" said Lucinda.

"Dragons' saliva," he answered.

"Dragons?" Drew spat with excitement.

"Don't get too excited, girl. Dragons have been instinct for centuries, that's why I keep this locked up. It's extremely rare and expensive."

"What does it do?" Drew curiously asked him, watching the jar carefully.

"Dragons' saliva is famously known for its antiseptic healing powers. It practically cures any wound, it's exceedingly rare and awfully expensive. The Higgles were the first to discover its potential when dragons still roamed the skies. Generations and generations of these jars have been passed on, not having to use a single drop, thank heavens," he explained as he carefully drizzled saliva onto Ruya's forearm.

"It stings," she cried, pulling her arm away.

"Hold still, god damn you!" Helix finally finished cleaning Ruya's wound. "Right then, that should be healed in just a few minutes."

"Thank you." She smiled in pain, carefully pulling her sleeve back down.

"Next time, control that hairball or else I might '*accidentally*' slip it a poisonous carrot, understood!"

"Yes, sir," she said, quickly nodding and holding the bunny safely in her arms.

"A bit selfish of you, Helix," said Grazox with a jar of saliva in his hands.

"What is?" said the old gnome.

"Keeping this all to yourself for all these years. Our wounded soldiers could have really done with this stuff when they were fighting for the land."

"Not my problem. Nobody told them to fight," he responded without a care in the world.

"We lost some good men and women out there fighting against the queens' armies, fighting to keep *you* and everyone else safe, so you could all live your lives peacefully without fear. How could you say it's not your problem."

The old gnome once again showed absolutely no interest in the conversation and didn't even bother to answer or continue to talk about the very sensitive subject that Grazox so clearly cared about. On the other side of the room, something caught Lucinda's eye. She picked up a round glass bottle that almost resembled a snow globe with a lid. Only she didn't have to shake it for the inside to move. Fascinated, she held the round bottle close to her face for a better look, then with the tip of her finger, she slowly began to twist the lid.

"STOP!!!" cried the old gnome.

Just in the nick of time, Helix quickly managed to stop Lucinda before she could finish twisting the lid off.

"You stupid girl! Do you know what you almost did? We could all have been blown away!!"

"What is it?" she asked.

"I call it... a stormball," he replied dramatically with wide eyes. "It's my best work yet."

"What does it do?" said Fen, holding it up. Everybody gathered around to stare at the strange little bottle with curiosity. The inside of the round jar was white.

"It's snowing?" a confused Ruya whispered.

"Yes, it's a blizzard storm trapped inside a bottle, very dangerous… and this twit almost unleashed it!" he grunted, furiously looking over his shoulder, eyeballing Lucinda up and down, scrunching his bushy eyebrows with a frown.

On the other side of the room, a little cauldron began bubbling up; bubbles popped out of control with red liquid rippling down the sides while the cauldron overflowed.

Helix quickly hurried over to the cauldron; climbing on a wooded chair, he grabbed the lid and waved it from side to side, clearing away the bubbles and red mist and began stirring the liquid with a large wooden spoon twice his size.

"What insane concoction are you brewing up this time, Helix?" said Grazox.

"A drink credited with magical powers. It can make the one who takes it love the one who gave it," he replied.

Nobody said anything, for they weren't quite sure what he was talking about.

"A love potion!" he snapped, annoyed that they didn't understand the first time.

Lucinda curiously leaned towards the cauldron. "Does it work?" she asked.

"Of course it works. Everything I do works, you silly girl… I mean, it's missing a few ingredients, but once I add them, it should be completed."

"I didn't take you as the love potion making kind of guy," said Grazox.

"I'm not, but this stuff is one of my best sellers, it's highly requested these days. They fly right off the shelves. Hmmff, can't see why… what's so great about love," he said, sniffling his nose.

"Just don't get yourself into any trouble. Love potions have been illegal for centuries; you'll be sent to the high court in Oro City if you're caught. And you know how they feel about magic."

"Don't worry, my old friend, us gnomes never get caught," Helix chuckled, tapping the tip of his pointy nose, looking rather confident and proud with his sneakiness. Almost taking a sip of the potion for a taste test, Helix quickly remembered and stopped just in the nick of time. "Whoops," he laughed, slapping his hand against his forehead.

Grazox just chuckled and nodded. "Best we get a move on; the others are waiting."

"Here, take this," said Helix, handing over a little satchel. "It's filled with some stuff that might be of use to you on your travels. I also took the liberty of putting a jar of dragons' saliva and a stormball in there for you, might come in handy. You could just pay me when you're back from your trip," he coughed.

"Of course, thank you," said Grazox, patting him on the shoulder with his large plump hand, tilting Helix to one side and making him fall over. Making their way back towards the fireplace, Lucinda sneakily shifted her eyes from side to side. She made sure no one was looking before secretly slipping a little bottle of love potion into her pocket.

"Good luck!" shouted Helix, bidding them farewell from a distance, then closing the door behind him.

"So, why are love potions illegal?" Drew curiously asked.

"Any form of magic that has control over someone's emotions against their free will is illegal. It's cruel to play with someone's feelings for your own selfish needs. Love is extremely powerful and it's not to be forced," Grazox answered.

At last, they were no longer in Beggars Hollow but found themselves on the edge of Healers Town. They saw the others standing by the Sky Docks, where a flotilla of huge ships just floated in the air, tied down by thick ropes.

"Wow!" Ruya excitedly jumped. "Flying ships, that's incredible," she continued with a wide smile.

"Which one's ours?" said Drew, running towards the edge to get a better look.

"None," Grazox answered.

"So... how will we be travelling?" she replied, disappointed.

"On that," he said, pointing, suggesting they turn around. They slowly turned to look and heard a huge moan that echoed through the sky. They were utterly speechless and gobsmacked to see a giant turtle with a wooden ship-like deck built onto its large shell. Its beautiful groans vibrated, streaming through the air, hitting the girls' ears that sent tingles down their spines.

"It's beautiful," said Drew with a tear in her eye.

"Breathtaking, isn't she? The old girl's still got it," said Kruze walking up from behind them, taking their bags and loading them up with the others.

"You can sit with me," said Fen, grinning at Lucinda with confidence.

"Thanks, but I'd rather be sitting with him," she replied, focusing her attention on Tobin, who was busy helping load up.

"What?" Fen huffed with a frown. About to follow her on board like a lost puppy, Grazox stopped him, placing his large hand on his scrawny shoulder.

"The secrets we learn from the House of Grazia stay in the House of Grazia. Keep that in mind the next time you decide to open your big mouth. You're just a stable boy, but we are Protectors, and it's our job to keep those girls safe. So in future, think before you speak to an outsider and let out important information that could possibly be used against us and jeopardise our mission. Or I'll have no choice but to send you back to Grazia." He finally let go of the boy's shoulder and stormed off.

One by one, they climbed up an unsteady rope bridge that wobbled from side to side. Hand in hand, Drew and Ruya being the last to board, took one final glance at Healers Town. Taking a deep breath in, they shared an expression of fear, knowing there was no turning back to the world they once knew and that nothing would ever be the same for them ever again. This was it, and there was no turning back.

SKY RIDE

CHAPTER SEVEN

"Prepare for take-off!!"

The giant turtle steadily swayed from side to side while the ropes were released.

"Hold on tight!" Fen yelled, holding on firmly to one of the ropes tied onto the side of the deck.

"Everybody, hold on!" Grazox howled. For take-off could be quite rough sometimes. They all slowly rose up off their feet; the gravity was pulling them high up, almost floating off the deck while the final rope was released. And just like that, they had taken off and at last found themselves flying through the silky blue sky.

"Whoa," Fen laughed in relief. "That was nerve-racking," he chuckled, wiping the sweat from his forehead. "Thought I was going to fall off and plunge to my death," he continued to laugh.

Drew and Ruya didn't waste any time; they ran, darting towards the side of the deck and leaned forwards, gasping in amazement as they flew over Healers Town. A little boy strolling along eating a pastry snack looked up and saw the huge silhouette hovering over the clouds flying above the town. "Look, Mama... look," he spat with enthusiasm as he tugged on his mother's thick gown with his little sticky finger pointing towards the sky. They were so high above, everything looked like a map.

"Amazing, isn't it," said Igor, squeezing his way in between the two girls, trying to get a better view. "Can you believe this is my first sky ride," he continued.

"Still can't believe any of this is real, to be honest. I feel like I'm stuck in a dream," Drew sighed with her head resting in her arms, staring deep into the blue sky, drifting off into a deep daydream. As she did, the sound of Igor's voice slowly faded away. After a while, the sun began to set, layers of puffy pink clouds spread across the blushing sky. Ruya reached out her hand and managed to catch a chunk of pink cloud that sparkled in her hands like magic. She smeared the cloud onto the work bunny's face, shaping it into a little beard.

The bunny, not bothered at all, just twitched her little nose from side to side and sneezed, blowing the sparkly pink cloud away like fairy dust. Ruya giggled, taking the bunny into her arms.

"You know, you almost got me into a lot of trouble back there with Mr Higgles. He was furious, you destroyed most of his potions," Which reminded her of the cure Helix had given her. She quickly pulled up her sleeve only to see her wound had vanished like it never existed. "Saliva, who would have thought," she laughed, amazed by Helix's work. "Now," she said, holding the bunny close to her face. "We need to give you a name." She thought about it, then it hit her. "I've got it," she said, snapping her fingers. "Potion, I'll call you Potion." The bunny looked up at Ruya, twitching her little nose approvingly.

Once again, Fen found himself sighing in and out continuously, hopelessly staring at Lucinda, who was settled on the other side of the deck trying to win Tobin's attention.

"She's not worth the trouble, boy," said Kruze, patting him on the shoulder.

"Do you believe in love at first sight?" said Fen with bright eyes.

"Personally... no," Kruze answered, admiring himself and stroking a loose lock of hair away from his face, gently pushing it back to blend in with the rest of his sleek hair.

"You're good with the ladies, Kruze. What can I do to get her attention and win her over?" Fen pleaded.

"Well, I've never been in your situation before… being rejected, that is. Usually, the ladies just fall right into my arms, I don't have to do a thing. But you know, being the greatest swordsman to ever live can do that sometimes. Not to mention my great set of hair." He smiled, running his fingers through his thick raven hair, once again admiring himself in a little gold hand mirror.

"Hmm, amazing swordsmanship and silky black hair, two things I haven't got. Thanks, Kruze, you're a great help," Fen replied sulkily, resting his face in-between both hands like a little boy.

"I can't help being blessed with hair by the Gods. If I'm honest with you, it can get quite tiring being a celebrity and having so many women throw themselves at you. Sometimes I wished I were an average joe myself. Life would be a lot easier. Count yourself lucky, boy, women are a hassle."

"Don't listen to that show offing arrogant fool," interrupted Zyra, who had overheard their conversation. "Believe me, not every girl cares about meaningless things like fancy hair and a fancy title. You're funny, loyal, and caring. And if she can't see that, then maybe her attention isn't worth fighting for. Just keep being you, and the right girl will come along and love you for who you are," she continued.

"Thank you, Zyra." Fen smiled, raising his head up and feeling a little more light-hearted.

"Rubbish," Kruze laughed.

"Rubbish?" she repeated, annoyed.

"Of course women care about those things, don't be filling the boys head with garbage… 'Keep being you', huh, don't make me laugh," he chuckled.

Zyra paused; her cheeks boiled in anger. "In all my life, I have never met such a vain, arrogant arse as you," she spat with disgust.

"Oh, you love it, really." He grinned, deliberately trying to get a reaction out of her. He loved making her angry because it was so easy to do, which he often thought was quite amusing.

Meanwhile, on the other side of the deck, Ludlow wasn't quite feeling himself.

"You're looking a bit green there, Ludlow, not a good colour," said Grazox.

At that exact moment, Gustav was strolling by and had overheard his comment. "Well, I say." Finding his comment offensive, he huffed, sticking his nose in the air with an attitude and continued strutting on by.

"Is he okay?" said Ruya, showing concern for the giant.

"He's fine, just a bit sky sick. He's not so good with heights," Grazox replied.

"May I sit with him?" she asked.

"Be my guest, don't think he'll do much talking, though." He smiled before walking off. Ruya slowly walked over to the giant and sat by his side.

"Hello, we didn't have the chance to speak before, I'm Ruya, and this is Potion," she said, holding the bunny in her lap. "May I sit with you?"

Ludlow, who could sometimes be painfully shy with strangers, just nodded.

"Would you like to hold her?" she said, catching the giant staring at Potion. Ludlow said nothing but took Potion into his large hands; she popped her little head through his ginormous fingers. He smiled and finally introduced himself.

"Ludlow," he said with his deep voice, followed by a bashful smile.

"It's very nice to meet you, Ludlow." She smiled back. The sun eventually set, and the soft salmon-pink clouds slowly began to fade away. Everyone grew restless as the sky dimmed, getting darker for night had come quickly.

***

"And that's how I came to be here," said Lucinda, explaining to an unimpressed Tobin about her journey. "Did I mention how I managed to escape the Screamers all on my own," she proudly continued.

"Yeah... you did, twice," he replied, not showing any interest whatsoever.

"And did I also mention—"

"Oh, please do shut up!" Gustav moaned angrily.

Lucinda, shocked, quickly turned her head around. "Do you mind? I'm trying to have a conversation," she snapped back.

"And do *you* mind. I'm trying to get some sleep! If I have to listen to another word of your pathetic rambling, I'm going to jump off the edge. The boy is clearly not interested, so take a hint and be off with you!" he continued to yell, right before pulling his silky eye mask back down and going back to bed.

"But—"

"Shhh!" Igor interrupted. Silencing her from speaking another word, then pulled his covers over his head and went back to sleep.

"How rude," Lucinda muttered under her breath. "As I was saying..." She turned back around only to realise she was talking to herself, for Tobin had already left, and she was standing all alone.

It was now midnight, and the gang were fast asleep making a musical melody with their snores that whistled through the creaking deck, except for Ludlow, whose snore sounded like thunder. It was a long night. The turtle's moan echoed through the silent breezy night sky. All were asleep but one. Drew sat up with a blanket wrapped around her, pulled out a little pin from her pocket and pricked her finger and just stared at the blob of silver blood, feeling low-spirited. She glanced up to the stars scattered above her like diamond dust that glittered like beacons of hope in a never-ending sea of darkness.

"Can't sleep?" said Grazox.

"No, I was just..."

"I know, it's a lot to take in, but you'll get there," he said. After a long pause, he decided to speak once more. "I didn't mean to grab your arm before," he continued.

Drew looked up at him. "That's fine, you was just trying to keep me safe, right?"

"Right." He smiled, settling down beside her.

"So, when do I get separated from Ruya?"

"When we land, we will take it from there," he answered.

Without another word, she put her head back down, continuing to stare at her finger.

"It's funny, I always felt different from all the other girls, like I didn't belong, until I met Ruya. I didn't think I needed a friend before I met her. The first time I saw her, I felt connected, like we were the same person. She was all alone like me."

"You'll see her again, don't worry," Grazox replied.

Drew just huffed, shaking her head in disbelief.

"You will. Never give up hope; you hear me? Take my nephew, my brother's son, Tobin, for example. Poor lad's parents, my brother, were murdered by the Fire Queen's general. He was ready to give up on life at such a young age, he was a very lost soul for some time, but I made sure he never gave up. I took him to the House of Grazia and made him train hard every day, gave him something to release his anger on. It gave him a new outlook on life, it made him strong, it made him into the man he is today. I helped him, and now together, we help others. There is nothing more powerful than hope if you believe enough." Grazox continued explaining about his nephew's troubles, unaware Tobin had been listening to the conversation the whole time.

"Your nephew, Tobin... is he a Protector?"

"No, not yet. The lad's strong but still has a lot to learn."

"Thought he looked a bit too serious, guess now I know why," she said.

"Nah, he's a good lad, he has a heart of gold deep down, he always was such a happy little thing. I think he's just afraid to love again. His parents dying was a massive blow; it changed him." They both paused, gazing up at the stars. "Right, little lady, best you get some sleep. Goodnight," he said, gently patting her on the head.

"Goodnight," she softly whispered.

Once again, Drew was all alone with only her haunting thoughts. She eventually closed her eyes and fell into a deep sleep like the rest of the gang.

The dark velvet sky was still, with only a cold whisper that danced through the silent breeze under a glow of the full moon. Deep in a blissful sleep, Ruya was abruptly awakened by the sound of grunting. She slowly opened her eyes. Potion sat above her chest and twitched her little nose against hers, grinding her teeth from side to side. Ruya looked around the deck to see if anyone else had woken up, but everybody was fast asleep in dreamland.

"What are you doing?" she whispered. Potion began hopping up and down out of control.

"What. What's wrong?"

Potion hopped up on the edge of the deck and twitched her little nose. Her ears pressed back, staring towards a blanket of stars.

"Yes, they're beautiful," she said, feeling exhausted. "But I'm very tired, and we really must get some sleep," she continued to whisper, trying not to wake the others. Gently taking Potion back into her arms, ready to go back to bed, she suspiciously turned her head back around. She couldn't help but notice the stars; they looked much closer than usual. She squinted her eyes to try and get a clearer look when suddenly a little glowing light speedily rushed towards her, making a silvery sound and violently attacking her face.

"OUCH!"

Zyron, who was the first and only one to be woken by Ruya's scream, immediately got up and ran over to her rescue. "What's wrong?"

"Up there," she said, holding her eye in pain, pointing towards where the little aggressive ball of light came from. Quickly shifting his eyes upwards towards the stars, his face suddenly dropped with dread.

"SKY SPRITES!!" he hollered and yelled from the top of his lungs. Waking everybody from their sleep, they all immediately jumped up on their feet in shock, wondering what was happening.

"What is it?" Grazox yelled.

"Up there!" Zyron answered, pointing to the sky. Grazox looked up to see a cluster of Sky Sprites rapidly hurtling towards them. Sky Sprites were vicious little balls of light that disguised themselves as stars in the night, tricking the eye. They were famously known for taking down large ships that roamed the skies.

"HELP!" Lucinda screamed, running around like a crazy person trying to grab the vicious little balls of light that clutched onto her hair, lighting her up like a Christmas tree. Fen quickly ran to her rescue but failed to help her, for the sprites didn't give him a chance, grabbing hold of him too.

"I say, let me go. I demand you release me at once!" Gustav yelled, being pulled up into the air by a bunch of sprites, dangling him upside down, holding onto his webbed feet and trying to throw him over the edge.

Luckily, Ludlow reached over, grabbing Gustav to safety, holding him tight in his large hand just in the nick of time. His heart rapidly pounded out of control while trying to catch his breath.

"I say, thank you, old chap," huffed Gustav, dropping his arms and sighing with relief as the green completely flushed away from his entire body.

"Oh no you don't... get back here!!" Kruze snapped, quickly grabbing onto one of the sprites trying to fly away with his pocket mirror.

Chaos struck, everybody began swirling around in complete madness, fighting off the Sky Sprites.

"MY LADY... MY LADY, HELP ME!" a panicked Igor yelled from a distance from the top of his lungs. Drew looked over to where Igor's voice was calling from and saw him being dragged away by sprites. She ran across the deck as fast as she could. Quickly leaping towards him, she managed to grab his large droopy feet with both hands. She suddenly found herself in a tug of war with the sprites as they held on tight to Igor's arms.

"HELP!" he continued to yell in pain, being pulled from each side like a ragdoll.

"Hang on, Igor… Let him go!!" she shouted, but the sprites were far too strong and Drew was outnumbered. She began to be carried away along with Igor, her feet slowly rising off the ground.

"You have to let me go!" he pleaded.

"NO! I won't let them take you!"

In that moment, Drew found herself dangling in the air, holding on tightly to Igor's large feet. Nobody had noticed them being pulled away, being too busy battling with the sprites themselves.

"I'm sorry, my lady," Igor cried as he was taken higher and higher into the air, feeling completely helpless. Just as they lost all hope, suddenly Drew felt something grabbing her. She looked down and saw Tobin clinging onto both her legs, pulling her back down.

"Tobin. Help us!" she yelled.

He tugged onto her legs even harder, pulling them both closer down, but a bunch of sprites rushed towards him, attacking viciously. Losing his focus, holding onto Drew with one hand and fighting off the sprites with the other, he almost let go of them, but Aero, Tobin's pet eagle, came swooping to his side, fighting them off. But still there were too many of them.

Suddenly something hit the sprites clenched onto Igor's arm, scattering them all one by one. Drew and Igor came crashing back down onto the deck, landing on top of Tobin. Drew quickly looked up and saw Zyra holding a wooden slingshot that she used to dash a rock into the sprites, scaring them away. Drew smiled as if to say thank you, Zyra returned a little nod and went back to slinging more rocks, continuing with the battle. Drew looked back down and came face to face with Tobin with their eyes locked onto each other like the first time he had seen her.

"I'm sorry," she said, quickly jumping to her feet, awkwardly brushing herself off. "Thanks for saving us," she continued, reaching out her hand offering to help him back up.

"Just be more careful," he seriously replied, ignoring her kind gesture and helping himself up. They watched him strut off with an attitude.

"I know I should be grateful, him trying to save us and all, but that boy seriously needs to crack a smile now and then," said Igor.

More and more sprites attacked from all sides, causing damage to the woodwork. Everybody grew tired of fighting them off, for more and more just kept coming, growing in numbers. A bunch of them ambushed the gigantic turtle, striking her huge sad eyes, leaving her extremely angry and restless. She let out the biggest deafening cry anybody had ever heard. The sound of her cry was so ear-piercing that everybody fell to their knees, protecting their ears, shielding them with their hands. Her thunderous wail swept every last Sky Sprite away, scattering them in different directions, blasting them into infinity until they were no longer in sight. The turtle's cry came to a stop, the sound faded away, and everybody slowly rose, removing their hands from shielding their ears. They all stood silently, suspiciously shifting their eyes about, looking for more Sky Sprites, but thankfully there wasn't one to be seen.

"YESS!" Fen yelled with victory, leaping up into the air and balling his hand into a fist. Everybody laughed and cheered with relief once they realised the sprites weren't coming back and that it was all over.

"If only every battle was this easy," Grazox chuckled, wiping away the sweat from his forehead.

"And that, my boy, is why we ride turtles instead of ships," Kruze laughed, throwing his arms over Fen's scrawny shoulders.

A NEVER-ENDING STORM
CHAPTER EIGHT

A thunderous boom erupted in the gloomy morning sky; a single raindrop splattered onto Drew's face, awakening her from a deep sleep. Slowly raising her head, she shifted her eyes towards Grazox. He was awake. With a gold spyglass in his hand, he stared through the harsh fog.

"What is it?" she said, rubbing her eyes, fighting to keep them open. She was still feeling extremely exhausted from last night's event.

"It's stormy up ahead... We're getting close."

"Close to what?" Drew curiously asked, walking over to stand by his side to see for herself.

"Stormville," he said, handing her the spyglass. With one eye squinted, she carefully peeped through the wet lens. But she couldn't see a city. It was very well hidden, enclosed by green trees as big as mountains huddled together surrounded by mist and fog. The dark smoky clouds seemed to only hover above the forest like a vortex of darkness, pelting down large droplets of cold rain and bolts of lightning flashing viciously around it.

"That's where we're going?" she said, raising one eyebrow with concern.

"Yes. Now wake the others, it's going to get bumpy."

Drew immediately did what she was told and woke everyone one by one, nudging them each on the shoulder until they opened their eyes.

"Wha... what's going on?" yawned Ruya with her hand over her mouth.

"I'm not sure, but you need to get up now. I think this is the end of our skyride."

Finally, everybody was up on their feet.

"Zyron, Tobin… prepare the canopy," Grazox instructed, clicking his fingers impatiently towards the ropes with his gaze fixed through his spyglass. The boys quickly ran over, each pulling on the ropes. The canopy slowly began to rise up, ready to shield them from the harsh rain up ahead.

"Where are we going now?" said Ruya, shielding Potion from the harsh rain they were about to enter.

"Stormville," Grazox answered.

"The only place where you would find Spellborns and mortals living together among other folk," Zyra shouted, helping the boys tie down the canopy.

"Other folk?"

"You know, goblins, gnomes, frogs… such as yourself." She turned her head to Gustav. "Even fairies, despite their reputation," she continued to yell across the deck.

Ruya looked slightly confused. "But I thought mortals and Spellborns already lived together?"

"Once upon a time, they did, but that was a long time ago. Most mortals are very suspicious of anyone who was born from magic; they tend to keep their distance and stick with their own kind. Most mortals see magic as a sickness or a curse," said Zyron.

As they flew closer to Stormville, deathly black clouds moved fast towards them. A heavy downpour of rain came crashing down, spitting out large beads of water. The rain was so strong, the canopy struggled to stay up.

"HOLD IT DOWN!!" Grazox roared.

They all hurried over to each side of the canopy with their hands forcefully clinging onto the ropes, trying their utmost to help.

"The rains too heavy!" said Drew, struggling to help hold it down.

"What do we do?!" Fen yelled from the other side.

"I've never seen the storm this violent before. It's not safe to fly through... We have to jump."

"JUMP!" Fen and Lucinda cried together, letting go of the ropes in shock.

"Uncle, are you sure about this?" said Tobin, concerned that his uncle wasn't thinking straight.

"Of course, lad, it's been done before, don't worry, it's the only safe option we have at this point. We can't fly any deeper through the storm; the gates to Vine City are just below us, trust me." Giving his nephew a pat on the back, he handed him a parachute made from an enormous rhubarb leaf that was big enough to wrap around two ogres. He gathered everyone together, handing out the rest of the parachutes.

"Right, listen up. Everybody will be jumping in pairs; it will be a lot safer if you go with a Protector. The storm is getting stronger, so let's get a move on before it gets any closer."

Ludlow, as the largest of the 12, was the first to jump with an even bigger parachute than everyone else, holding onto Gustav, who was safely tucked in the giant's hands.

"Right, who's next?" said Grazox, staring at the others.

"Come on, boy, let's show the ladies how a real hero jumps," Kruze smirked, winking at Zyra just before leaping off the edge with his arms wrapped around Fen. Rolling her eyes, she was next to jump with Ruya. They were followed shortly after by Zyron and Igor. The fourth pair to jump was Tobin and Lucinda. "Thanks for letting me be your partner," she said, blushing as she held on tight to his arm.

"I didn't really have a choice, you clinging onto me so quick the way you did," Tobin replied, with not an ounce of bother in his tone of voice. They both stood on the edge, ready to jump.

"Now, be very careful. I'm quite delica— AHHH!"

Before she could explain just how fragile she was, Tobin jumped with no warning, leaving Lucinda screaming for her life, while Aero followed swiftly behind them, fluttering his wings chaotically in the rainy wind.

"Looks like we're the only ones left," said Grazox.

Drew shifted her eyes to the side. "What about her?" she said with her hand in the air, worried for the flying turtle.

"Who... Anga? She will be fine. The old girl's seen more adventures than any living thing. Trust me, she's been in far worse situations. She knows her way home... Now, are you ready?"

"Let's do it." She grinned, feeling scared and excited at the same time.

Grazox held onto her with both arms and leapt off the edge.

"HANG ON!" Grazox yelled.

Meanwhile, Tobin and Lucinda finally made it to the ground, where the others were shielding themselves from the rain. As they hid under their parachutes, they watched Tobin and Lucinda safely land. Lucinda untied herself from Tobin and shrieked, buckling over a large rock.

KERPLUNK!

She fell face down and plopped into a deep muddy puddle.

"HA-HA-HA"

Everyone burst out laughing hysterically. On the other hand, Fen was the only one to show some concern, quickly rushing by her side. But the corners of his lips slowly curled, his cheeks swelled from pressure holding it in, but it was no use. His laughter erupted like a volcano, and he bent over, slapping his knee repeatedly in a fit of laughter. Even Ludlow, who barely smiled, couldn't control himself. His face crinkled in laughter, making him appear a hundred years older.

Wiping the wet soggy mud from her face, she got back up with rage. "IDIOTS! STOP LAUGHING!" she screamed, stamping her foot like a spoiled child. "I said stop!"

But they couldn't control their laughter. The more she tried to silence them, the more they laughed.

Before Lucinda could shout again, Tobin raised his hand, stopping her. "Be quiet!"

"What's wrong?" said Zyra with concern.

"They should have made it down by now; something's wrong."

Still struggling to make it down, Grazox and Drew were battling against the gusting wind that blew harder, carrying them deeper towards the storm.

"Aero, find them!" Tobin yelled, lifting his eagle towards the sky.

"I'm going to cut you loose," Grazox shouted with heavy rain drizzling down his face.

"WHAT... No, we're too high up, you can't!" she cried.

Finally, Aero had managed to find them in all the chaos. Flapping his white wings around their parachute, he immediately flew back down to Tobin, squawking repeatedly, fluttering his wings, indicating something was wrong.

"I have to cut us loose. We don't have any other choice; the storm is sucking us in!"

Grazox managed to pull out his dagger and began to cut the ropes, detaching them from the parachute.

"NO... wait, wait!" Drew pleaded. But it was too late, he had already cut the last rope that kept them holding on together, each going their separate ways. In fear, Drew yelled from the top of her lungs while the heavy wind violently blew into her face, almost choking her. She thought of nothing but the very painful landing she was about to experience when suddenly she felt two bulky arms tightly clutching onto her. She looked up and saw Grazox.

They were falling closer and closer towards the ground.

This is it, Drew thought. She closed her eyes tight and emptied her mind. Everything went blank. She was ready to accept her fate. Just when she thought it was the end and all hope was lost, she felt a huge thud as they landed. She slowly opened her eyes; everything was dark. A tiny spike of light touched her face. The light got stronger, then she saw the others standing there with panic in their worried faces. Seeing that both Drew and Grazox were okay, they all cheered and laughed with relief. Ludlow managed to catch them both safely, clasping them into his large palms, saving them from the terrifying landing they were about to endure.

"I knew I could count on you," Grazox laughed.

"Drew. Drew, are you okay?" Ruya immediately rushed over to her side, helping her leap out from the giant's hands.

"I'm fine." She smiled, bending down with both hands on her knees. "Well, I will be once the feeling in my legs come back," she continued to laugh.

"I was so scared for you." Not giving Drew a chance to catch her breath, Ruya grabbed her, slinging her arms tightly over her shoulders.

"I'm glad you both made it down alive, but can we please get out of this rain," Kruze complained, holding the giant leaf above his head.

"Oh no, we can't have your hair getting ruined," Zyra smirked in a mocking tone.

"You're right. We need to move. Follow me," agreed Grazox. Slinging their belongings over their shoulders. One by one, they followed behind him.

"What happened to you?" Drew laughed, staring Lucinda up and down, who was filthy with mud smeared all over her clothes.

"None of your business," she snapped, storming off, marching through the soggy mud with a huff.

"She fell into a puddle," Ruya softly giggled with her hand over her mouth.

"Argh, I missed it, would have given my button collection to have seen that," Drew huffed disappointedly.

"It was the funniest thing, my lady, her face when she got back up… priceless," Igor laughed with enthusiasm. Cold and exhausted, being dragged down by their heavy wet clothes, they were relieved to have finally made it. They stopped at a large wooden sign, reading Stormville and an even smaller one beneath it, which read Vine City.

Beside the signs stood a tall pole with a flag, half red, half blue with a dagger plunged into a black heart in the centre that fluttered in the wet wind.

"What does that flag stand for?" said Ruya.

"Red bloods and blue bloods live as one. The black heart represents evil; the dagger going through it shows the bond between mortals and Spellborns."

Lucinda heard something approaching. "What's that?" she said.

"Sounds like hooves," said Gustav.

Two cloaked figures on horses greeted them. "Grazox Landa?" said one of the men.

"Yes," Grazox answered.

"Follow me," the man continued. They followed the mysterious men over to a huge wooden gate.

"OPEN UP!" he shouted to the gate-keepers. On each side of the gates above, two men with large hoods holding onto firelit torches began to pull on the levers on each side. They stood back while the rain heavily drizzled down their hoods, the wooden gates slowly opened. "This way," the man instructed.

He led them to an awfully long green river that seemed to go on for days. There were three large and thick boat-like lily pads waiting for them. They got into groups of four, and one by one they all carefully hopped onto a pad, all but one. Ludlow was far too big to sit on a lily pad without it sinking like a rock. A few men pulling on thick ropes dragged out a huge hollow turtle's shell, large enough for him to sit comfortably in.

All settled in, the man began to lead, controlling the way down the river by holding onto a long wooden stick, while the other two groups of four followed behind him, and Ludlow behind them. Little drops of rain pitter-pattered in the river.

"How come it isn't raining as much in here as it is out there?" said Drew, confused.

"Well, isn't it obvious? The trees block out most of the rain. Why anyone would want to live here is beyond me," Gustav answered in his usual snobby manner, shivering and cosying deeper into the collar of his cloak.

The river took them deeper and deeper into the rainforest. The deeper they got, the smell of earth and condensed moisture grew stronger. Potion hopped to the edge of the pad, gazing into the river. Her wobbly reflection stared back at her as she twitched her little wet nose from side to side. But the twitching soon stopped, her beady eyes focused on something skulking in the water. A shadowy black silhouette lurked beneath them.

"What's that!" a panicked Lucinda squeaked, with one arm clutched onto Tobin and the other pointing towards the large shadow swimming beneath them.

"Don't panic," the man yelled behind him. "Loogers are peaceful creatures; you don't cause trouble for them; they won't cause trouble for you. Just don't go starting mischief in their river and things will be fine," the man continued. The river curved gently, lightly splashing against the rocks as it moved through the large worn-out tree trunks. Fluttering butterflies hovered above their heads, flicking dewdrops from their colourful wings. The atmosphere was quiet and calm.

But what seemed like an easy and pleasant ride was about to become a very harsh and bumpy one.

"Everybody hold tight, we're heading for a steep drop!" the man yelled.

"WHAT!!!" everyone cried together in panic.

Ruya immediately reached out for Potion, holding her tight in her arms, while Drew and Gustav clung onto each side of Ruya. Igor, Fen, and the twins did the same on the pad behind them, and on the third lily pad, Lucinda, as usual, quickly grabbed onto Tobin, sticking to him like glue. Grazox and Kruze, on the other hand, gazed at one another. Kruze hesitated before opening both arms with an awkward grin, suggesting they cuddle.

"I'm good, lad," Grazox awkwardly responded in a manly way with his hand in the air. "You okay back there, Ludlow?" Grazox yelled over his shoulder. Poor Ludlow, who sat at the back, had no one to hold onto. The giant put his hand up, suggesting he was okay.

The soft, rippling flow of the river began to take a violent turn, brutally crashing onto rocks and branches. Their eyes fixed upon two large boulders on either side of the terrifying drop ahead.

"THIS IS IT... HOLD ON!"

They all closed their eyes tightly, and just like that, one by one, their lily pads had leapt off the edge into the air, falling into a misty plunge pool.

VINE CITY
CHAPTER NINE

Silence.

All was still, with the sound of the stream burbling over rocks and branches and the water that trickled down the cliff while the mist filled the air. The water that was once gentle began bubbling up. Emerging from the cold water, Ludlow was the first to rise. As he stood on his two large feet, the water rushed down his body and beneath his droopy hat. Shortly after, everyone else quickly rushed up to the surface.

"POTION... POTION!" Ruya cried, splashing around in a panic.

"She's over here," came a voice of misery.

Ruya looked over to see Potion was alive and well, firmly gripping her claws onto Kruze's thick black hair that he adored so much.

"You alright there?" said Grazox, helping Drew, who looked like she was struggling to climb back onto her lily pad. She tried to get on herself, but her wet clothes were so heavy, dragging her down, so she couldn't even manage to get one leg over.

"I'm fine. But dropping like that twice in one day can really tire a girl out. Hope there aren't any more unexpected surprises waiting for us," she sighed.

Grazox laughed. "You and I both know there are going to be plenty more surprises coming our way."

"Hope they're good surprises, don't think my heart can take any more of this," she chuckled, feeling out of breath.

"If only," he sighed, still trying to catch his own breath.

"Is everyone okay? Is everybody here?" their guide man shouted.

"Yes," they all answered, feeling rather miserable.

"Good, follow me."

Once again they were on the move. They reached another wooden gate, only this one was a lot smaller than the one they had entered earlier; this gate hovered over the river while the water flowed beneath it.

"OPEN UP!" he yelled to the second gate-keepers. Two men on each side pulled on ropes, swinging the gate's open.

"Welcome... to Vine City."

Drew, Ruya, Lucinda, Fen, Igor, and Gustav's mouths had opened so wide their bottom lips almost touched their knees.

Drews face lit up. "Wow... it's, it's..."

"Breath-taking," Ruya sighed with a twinkle in her eyes.

Vine City, was the most majestic and enchanting city of all time. The only place where you would find all species and races living among one another, together as one. Their lily pads continued to slowly flow through the silky jewel-blue stream as it curved gently through the tree homes and toadstool houses.

Warm yellow lights flickered through cosy little windows; wooden bridges towered their way over the river, each going in different directions like a maze. Tall trees growing from the river were embedded with glowing mushrooms that twirled their way around their large trunks that just kept going higher and higher like a magical luminous staircase. With their heads tilted all the way back, mouths agape, they looked up and saw little fairies flying in and out of their tiny fairy homes. The city sparkled with hundreds and thousands of glowing lanterns that hung from the trees and bridges. It was a city of tree homes and bridges made from vines and thick ropes, with railway tracks that spiralled throughout. The locals would pass each other baskets of food, pulling on ropes, sending them up and down.

"I take back what I said before. I can now see why somebody would want to make a home here; it's absolutely enchanting,"

Gustav gasped with amazement. On the riverside was a row of toadstool houses; most of them had giant leaf canopies above them to keep the rain from lashing down on their roofs. Passing through the river, they had witnessed one of the inhabitants, a little bearded gnome. He was trying to fix his battered canopy, and while doing so, he lifted the giant leaf and a large amount of water splashed down, leaving the poor gnome completely drenched from head to toe.

"Blasted thing!" he snapped.

The girls couldn't help but giggle as they passed by.

"Here we are." They had finally come to an end of their river journey, they stopped at a wooden pier, and one by one the man helped them climb out from their wobbly lily pads.

"I trust you know where you are going?" the man asked.

"Yes, I can take it from here," said Grazox.

"You can't go any further, I'm afraid," he said, addressing Ludlow. "The bridges won't be able to handle your weight; you're far too big. You must continue your journey on foot."

"Go, I'll be fine," said the giant in his deep low voice.

Puddles on the ground began plinking, the rain had started up again.

"Where are we going?" asked Drew, wiping her wet face with her sleeves.

"To visit one of the greatest men I have ever known," Grazox replied.

They all walked to the start point of the railway and climbed into a wooden cart that would drive them through the city. It started off smoothly and slow, then suddenly, their pleasant ride turned into a heart-pounding experience. The cart started to move faster, zooming through the trees, with the railway taking them under and over as they twirled upside down, making their stomachs turn. Everybody rushed around the bridges in a hurry, the city was huge and hectic, there were so many bridges they had almost forgotten which way they had come from.

"Which way now?" said Fen, wet and exhausted.

"If my memory serves me well, we are looking for the tree with the largest branches and leaves in the city, which should be right... over there," said Grazox. With the railway coming to an end, the cart slowed down and stopped at their destination.

Finally finding the right house, Grazox knocked on the door three times. They stood back in silence, listening to the muffled voices arguing inside.

"Someone get that!" a woman shouted.

"I got it last time!" another replied.

"Well, it's not my turn to get it!" argued the third voice.

"I'll bloody get it!" complained the fourth person.

The door swung open; a large man stood in the doorway with an expression of excitement like a little boy when he saw a familiar face.

"GRAZOX!" he yelled.

"TIBBOT!"

They both embraced in a rough manly hug. Tibbot Baxter was twice as stocky as Grazox. He had a short brown beard with two little braids dangling from each side, bushy eyebrows and a droopy hat, and he spoke with a strong Scottish accent. Although one of the toughest and bravest men, he was also extremely cheerful at most times. Always cracking a joke, no matter what dark and dangerous situation he found himself in. He always found a reason to laugh. "My old friend, I wondered when I'll be seeing you again." Tibbot smiled.

"Sorry it took so long," Grazox huffed, wiping his wet forehead with the back of his hand.

"Well, don't just stand there in the rain. Come in," he said, patting Grazox on the back, roughly nudging him through the doorway.

"Love, look who's here."

Martha, Tibbot's wife, came rushing into the room. "Do my eyes deceive me, come here you!" Once again, Grazox found himself in another rough embrace. Martha Baxter, who was also a large woman, wore her heart on her sleeve; she never was too shy to show her love and affection. The Baxters were an extremely loving and warm family that made anyone feel welcome in their home.

"Oh my goodness, you're all soaked to the bone. Sit by the fire and I'll go and fetch you all some warm towels and blankets. Won't be a tick," Martha smiled.

"Come and relax, warm yourselves up. Leave all your belongings over there," said Tibbot.

They all sat down, shivering, rubbing their hands together, trying to get nice and warm by the fireplace.

"You know why we're here?" said Grazox.

"Of course I do, but we'll talk business later. Let's get everybody warmed up, then have some grub, then we'll get down to the nitty-gritty," he laughed before slapping him again on the shoulder.

"UNCLE GRAZOX!"

"Girls!"

Four plumpy girls came charging down the stairs like a stampede rushing towards him, roughly gripping their arms around his neck, and clinging onto him like leeches.

"Wow, I haven't seen you since you were smaller. Where have those little girls disappeared to?" He smiled.

Celia, Greta, Ida, and Matilda Baxter were quadruplets. They all had scruffy curly ginger hair and freckles you could count for days.

"Girls, leave the poor man to catch his breath," said Martha, walking back into the room and handing everybody warm blankets and towels.

"You remember my youngest," said Tibbot, pointing over to his son, Huxley Baxter, who was standing in the doorway too shy to talk.

Unlike the rest of his family, Huxley wasn't stocky or plump at all but quite on the scrawny side and was very shy, which his family always thought was strange, seeing how extremely loud and outspoken they all were.

"Of course I do. You have grown into a fine young lad," he said, shaking the boy's hand.

"Right, is everybody nice and dry yet?" said Martha clapping her hands together. She then looked at Gustav, who seemed to be struggling, for the towel was a little too big to dry himself with.

"You okay there, love. Need any help?"

"I'm fine, thank you," he replied, still having a hard time.

"Don't be silly. I'm more than happy to help," she laughed.

Not taking no for an answer, she grabbed the towel off Gustav and wrapped it around his entire body. "Right, let's give you a good wipe down, shall we? Get you all nice and dry."

"Really, there is no need, I'm quite alrig—"

Not giving him a chance to speak, she got his head in the towel and roughly shook him from side to side, all the way down his body.

"MADAM! Please, that is quite enough," Gustav gasped.

"Well, when you're done, dinner's on the table," she giggled, happily waddling off back into the kitchen.

Once they dried themselves, they all gathered around the dinner table. As there was not enough room for them all, Martha pulled out another little wooden table for the rest to sit at. On the table lay bowls of shroom soup, toad pie and slices of warm baked bread. Martha handed Gustav a bowl of frog stew. His mouth fell to the table in horror when a little webbed foot stuck out from his bowl.

"Oops, sorry, love. I forgot." She awkwardly smiled, taking the bowl back.

As they ate their dinner, a loud bang of thunder startled them.

"Does it always rain this much here?" said Fen.

"It's not called Stormville for nothing, lad; you get used to it eventually," said Tibbot.

They all settled down and filled their plates.

"I feel bad eating all this food knowing Ludlow's by himself down there," said Ruya.

"Don't worry, sweety, I've already sent some down to him," winked Martha, always being one step ahead.

"So, how do you two know each other then?" said Drew, taking a huge unladylike bite of bread then slurping down some soup, forgetting her table manners as a guest. Not that there was any need for manners around the Baxters.

"Let me tell you about this fella right here," Tibbot laughed. "This man has saved my life more than I've blown my nose." In the middle of his story, he let out a huge belch.

"Charming," Gustav sniggered beneath his breath with disgust, taking small gentle sips of soup.

"Ooh, aren't we proper," grinned a sarcastic Greta, overhearing Gustav's sly comment.

"You know, you wouldn't have that snobbish accent of yours or even be able to talk at all for that matter if it wasn't for the clumsy witch," said Matilda, licking her spoon clean.

"Not being able to talk? What are you babbling on about?" Gustav coughed, unamused.

"A long time ago, a young witch in training was sent out on a task by her mistress. Strolling through the woods with a sack of potions, she stopped at a large frog pond that prevented her crossing over to the other side. Too lazy to go around, she thought she could just freeze the pond and walk across. Reaching into her sack of magic potions, she hadn't realised she grabbed the wrong one; instead of liquid freeze, she picked out a potion of intelligence. She slipped, and the whole bottle fell into the pond, making all the frogs grow larger and smarter. So you have the clumsy witch to thank. She's the only reason you're sat here at this table."

"Yeah, if it hadn't been for the clumsy witch you'll still be stuck in that filthy pond with the rest of the scum," Ida laughed.

Gustav paused with his mouth wide open, feeling deeply offended.

"How dare you! I've never heard about this; it's complete and utter nonsense. I've never been so insulted in my life," he said, folding his arms with a huff like he always did whenever he was offended.

"No, I'm afraid it's true, lad," Tibbot mumbled with a mouth full of pie.

"Who was the clumsy witch?" said Ruya.

"You know her as Mother Oba." Martha smiled.

"No," Ruya laughed. "Oba, really?"

"Yep, that's how she got the title of 'Mother'. She has given life to so many creatures. Who would have thought that clumsy little girl would grow up to be one of the most powerful witches ever known? She's a good woman," said Martha, laying more food out on the table.

"Yes, she is." Igor smiled with tears in his eyes, missing her deeply.

"What other creatures?" Drew asked curiously, slurping on her soup.

"What, love?" Martha coughed.

"You said she gave so many creatures life. What other creatures?" Drew repeated.

"Oh, would you just listen to that rain," Martha giggled, deliberately avoiding her question. Just as Drew was about to ask her question for the third time, Greta let out a huge belch, followed by Matilda.

"That's my girls," Tibbot laughed like a proud father, throwing his fist in the air.

"This is all very fun, but there are serious matters we need to discuss," said Grazox, feeling a little frustrated.

"Of course, of course. What's on your mind, old friend?" said Tibbot.

"I need your help. As you know, war is coming, and we need to recruit as many men as possible to join our army, or else we don't stand a chance in defeating the enemy. Queen Lumi has her soldiers of Akulls and Snow Beasts, and god knows what else. The Fire Queen, with her large army of Gors and Screamers, not to mention Vapour, who has an entire army of goblins and swamp creatures that could possibly get in the way of the real threat. We need help to build a stronger army; the queen's soldiers have already begun building theirs."

"What do you need me to do, my friend?" said Tibbot.

"I need you to travel to Cold Mountain. Nobody knows their way around the snow mountains better than the Vorst people. They will come in handy. Get them to join us."

"Whatever you say, my friend, I'll do my very best." Tibbot nodded.

"All this talk of war just brings tears to my eyes; whatever happened to peace, eh?" Martha sighed, looking out of the window, watching the violent rain drizzling down the branches.

"Was there ever peace?" Fen replied, grabbing another loaf of bread from the middle of the table.

"Once upon a time there was, love. But it all changed when the two kings went to war."

Everybody around the table fell silent, listening to Martha tell the story.

"You see, mortals were once ruled by the mortal king, King Linus and the Spellborns by the Spellborn king, King Saiyan. Together the two races lived as one in peace; they were so close they were almost like brothers. One night, King Linus held a ball in honour of his new-born child; he longed for a son but instead the Gods decided to bless him with another daughter. Princess Vidalia. Sadly, the queen had passed away giving birth, something the king couldn't quite get over. But as time passed, his sadness slowly faded away. On the princess's sixth birthday, King Saiyan wanted to bless the child with a gift, a spell of beauty. The next morning just like every other, the child woke from her sleep, only this time she opened her eyes and felt great discomfort; she had a shell made of gold growing on her back from her flesh. King Linus was furious and ashamed by this, for not only did he not have any sons to be the next heir, but two daughters, one of whom was now permanently deformed, and in the king's eyes, that meant weakness. And for this he blamed the Spellborn king, claiming his kind gesture wasn't a gift at all but a curse... 'black magic'. And for this reason, he had banned all magic. Scrolls were hung all over the realm, forbidding any form of life conjured by magic, which would be treason, and if caught committing such crimes, you would be punished and put to death by hanging.

"Going behind the Spellborn king's back with these new rules created horrible tension, and the feud between the two grew more intense, for magic was the way of the Spellborns. After all, that is how they came to be. The feud carried on for years until things took a turn for the worse. Mortals and Spellborns began murdering each other; they were now on the brink of war, red bloods vs blue bloods. The two kings forced other folk to choose a side, or they too would die. Not having any choice in the matter, they were now involved in the kings' war. Giants, wizards, witches, fairies, gnomes, dwarfs, trolls, and goblins had no choice but to fight in a war they didn't believe in. Everyone was now a part of this madness, everyone except two young wizards and a young witch. You know them as Sir Abner, Sir Arkin, and Mother Oba.

"Abner was King Linus's apprentice, soon to be his advisor, and Sir Arkin had already finished his training and had become the Spellborn king's advisor immediately. Oba was just a young witch in training who had moved to Spellenborg, a Spellborn city, to study magic, but her skills were far beyond expectations for a witch of her age. All three had a very disturbing premonition of something extremely dark heading their way, something much bigger than the kings' silly feud. But when they tried to warn them, nobody listened. Not the people, not the lords and certainly not the kings. They saw there was no hope, so they left and created the House of Grazia, a safe haven for all, and began to prepare an army for the future war to come."

"What happened to Princess Vidalia?" asked Ruya.

"Her father banished her at a very young age to be raised in a poor kingdom where she grew into a beautiful young woman, then sadly was murdered for the gold on her back."

"Vapour," whispered Ruya. "Mother Oba told us this story, about a beautiful princess who possessed a rare golden shell, who turned evil," she continued.

"Yes, she wasn't always evil, and it was very sad and unfortunate what happened to her, but once she rises again, she'll be thirsty for blood once more."

"Just like the rest of 'em. We have enemies everywhere," said Grazox.

"What about the king? What happened to him?" said Drew.

"He and King Saiyan were both incinerated alive by the Fire Queen at a ball," said Martha.

"A ball?" said the girls.

"Yes, usually before a war, the two parties would set aside their differences for one night. The fancy folk would throw a grand ball and a magnificent feast. The fools were warned something dark was coming, but, nope, neither of them wanted to listen. They were so caught up in their own silly feud they hadn't seen the real threat heading their way. They were both warned years in advance, but their stubbornness got them both killed. They had so much time to prepare themselves for what was coming. They had a fair warning of the future seen by Oba and the others in their premonition if only they had listened to them. Who knows, maybe we wouldn't be dealing with all this madness now," said Martha, shaking her head in disappointment.

"Why did she kill them?" said Lucinda.

"Well, because she wanted both kingdoms for herself. She was the dark premonition the three youngsters saw, but little did they know another premonition was yet to come true. The prophecy of the fallen Star."

In that moment, Drew and Ruya secretly exchanged a little fearful look.

"Of course, when word got out, she made it her mission to find the Star and keep it for herself. I mean, could you imagine what someone like that would do with that kind of power. I get the willies just thinking about it," said Martha, shaking her body.

"And the king's first daughter, whatever happened to her?" Lucinda interrupted.

"Princess Milo… nobody knows what happened to her. When her father went insane going to war with the Spellborns, she just vanished and was never seen again. She could be dead for all we know. It was a very long time ago. I hardly remember, love, being just a child myself at the time."

"So, there's no royals left at all on both sides?" said Ruya.

"Nope." Martha nodded.

"So, who rules the kingdoms now then?"

"The High Council of Lords."

"A bunch of stuck-up, no-good-for-nothing pompous twits," Tibbot grunted.

"The law says if there is no royal bloodline left, then the kingdoms fall to the lords of the city," Martha continued.

"But if there was still someone out there like the missing princess, would she still have a claim to the throne?" said Ruya.

"Well, to the mortal throne, of course she would. She is, after all, the king's firstborn."

"Wonder whatever happened to her," Ruya sighed, daydreaming in deep thought, gazing off into the distance.

"God knows," Tibbot huffed, taking a huge chunk of chicken in his mouth.

"There was something else," said Grazox. "Back in Healers Town, Helix Higgles had told me abou—"

"Helix Higgles… that old imbecile," came a croaky old voice. They all turned their heads to a little old gnome standing in the doorway, hanging his coat up that was dripping wet, leaving a small puddle on the floor. He looked just like Helix, only his beard was brown and longer. He wore a pointed hat, sharp as a blade, with matching pointy shoes and a blue button waistcoat. "What poxy potions has that silly old fool been brewing up this time?" he continued to complain.

"Sorry, who is this?" said Grazox impatiently, being rudely interrupted.

"Oh, sorry," said Tibbot, wiping his mouth. "This is Berwin Whitby, our neighbour from downstairs. He lives in one of the toadstools by the river… well, he used to until Ida here," he paused, nudging his daughter on the shoulder, "accidentally landed on his house," he continued. "I was teaching her some moves; she almost had that backflip," he said with his eyes wandering off. "Anyway, now he's staying with us until we fix him a new home."

"Don't make it sound like you're doing me any favours, seeing that it's your family's fault I no longer have a home," Berwin snapped. "My poor house," he continued. He turned his head to Martha. "I don't know what you've been feeding them girls, but it needs to stop before they land on someone else's home and kill them. They're too damn big!" he continued to complain, losing his temper with flaming red cheeks.

A huge commotion broke out, for the girls and their mother did not take too kindly to his rude, offensive comment.

"THAT'S ENOUGH!" Tibbot shouted authoritatively, flinging his fists onto the table, making the bowls and spoons bounce high in the air. "Grazox was trying to tell me something... Please continue, my friend."

"As I was saying," Grazox coughed, clearing his throat. "Helix spoke of the Wise Shroom."

"The Wise Shroom? Isn't he supposed to be like some kind of oracle that's been around for centuries and has answers for things that haven't even happened yet," Fen excitedly interrupted Grazox once again. "Sorry, please continue." He awkwardly smiled.

Grazox cleared his throat for the second time then finally spoke, feeling rather annoyed. "He told me to find the Wise Shroom; he may have answers on how to destroy the queens. We could end this war."

"So what are we waiting for!" said Tibbot, slamming his wide-open palms onto the table.

"Let's go and find the old fungus!"

"Anyone for dessert?" Martha walked over, holding a large tray of pudding and custard tarts.

"Right after dessert." He smiled, quickly seating himself back down.

It was getting dark, and Vine City lit up like a giant Christmas tree. The lanterns and glowing mushrooms shone ten times brighter than when they had first entered the city. It was like being inside a dream, one you never wanted to wake up from.

"What is it, love?" said Tibbot, tenderly grabbing his wife from behind, kissing the back of her neck while she did the washing up. He could tell something was on her mind and making her sad.

"Cold Mountain," she answered with a tut.

"Don't worry, I'll be fine. I've been on tons of quests before, and you've never worried."

"Yes, I know, but something feels different about this time," she said.

He held his wife closer and smiled. "I'll be back before you know it. I need to help Grazox. After all, what sort of man, husband and father would I be if I didn't try and help to make this world a safer place for our children."

"A man I wouldn't want to be married to. You're right," Martha sighed. "Well, you're not going anywhere without warm blankets and mittens. I'll pack some up for you and the others. Can't have you catching a cold and leaving all the hard work to Grazox now, can we."

He smiled. "I love you, Mrs Baxter."

"I love you more, Mr Baxter," she giggled, snuggling up closer to her husband.

"Get a room," Greta yelled from across the room.

Drew took a step outside for some fresh air while the others helped Martha clean up. Sitting with her chin pressed on her arms, she let her legs dangle off the edge of one of the balconies made from old wood and vines. Taking a deep breath of the fresh earthy smell the rain had left behind, she listened to the pitter-patter of the dewdrops softly falling through the leaves of the city. Frogs croaked from the river below while the crickets chirped; she watched the local residents in their cosy little homes minding their own business. It was a perfect night, calm and peaceful... Well, it was until she heard someone pass gas from inside the house.

"Alright… who did that?"

"Argh… that's disgusting!" complained Zyra.

Drew heard the door open; Huxley came out and sat beside her. "Mind if I join you?" he said.

"Nah, of course not." She smiled. "I like your family; they seem fun, my kind of people," she laughed.

"Yeah, they are," he replied, scratching the back of his head. "A little too fun. Sometimes I think I'm a Spellborn."

"What makes you think that?"

"Dad, Dad! Listen to this one… *brrrrrp.*" said one of the girls proudly from inside the house.

"Does that answer your question?" he said, turning his head away from where the belch had come from.

"Not really." She smiled, even though she was really thinking the same thing.

"Oh, come on, you've seen my family, we're nothing alike," he moaned.

"You should be thankful. I'd kill to have a family like yours. I've always wondered what it would be like to have a sibling to argue with, to have a father pat you on the head, or what it felt like to have a mother hold you in her arms and feel her soft hands pressed against your face and have her kiss you… You know, to be loved." She gazed off with sadness, then continued to speak. "Sure, they burp and fart a lot, but they seem like good people, and they won't be around forever, so try to appreciate them while you can and don't take them for granted, or you'll be sorry. If these past few days have taught me anything, it's in this life we'll never know what's waiting for us around the corner… anything could happen."

As he listened to his family's laughter coming from the inside of the house, his eyes wandered off with her words stuck in his head, knowing deep down he was wrong. "You're right… they're irritating and disgusting most of the time, but I'd be lost without them."

"Of course you would; they're your family." She smiled.

"Hey, listen to this." Huxley lifted his arm and made fart noises with his armpits to lighten the mood. After seeing how sad she had gotten talking about family, he wanted to make her laugh. It worked. They laughed so much that they hadn't noticed Tobin watching them looking down from the balcony above. His face was serious, almost angry as jealousy coursed through his blood, making his face turn red as he listened to them laugh and joke.

"We better go back in, the rains starting up again," said Drew, reaching out her hand, helping Huxley get back to his feet.

"And then... I plunged my sword right into the beast!"

Walking back into the house, Drew and Huxley had just managed to catch the ending to one of Tibbot's adventurous stories while he explained to the others.

"That's my man," Martha giggled.

"You're so brave, Dad." All three girls jumped up and slung their arms around their father.

"My little beauties, I was brave cause I had my family to come home to. What would I do without you crazy bunch, eh?" he said with a little sniffle, giving each of his daughters a kiss on the head.

A sudden sadness had come over Grazox as he watched them from a distance. Seeing Tibbot with his family brought back memories of his own, remembering the times when he once kissed his own daughter gently on the head and held his wife safe in his arms, and that warm feeling of having a family to come home to. Martha noticed the distant look of sadness in his face. He got up and left the room to be alone. He just stood silently on one of the balconies and listened to the rain fall.

"You okay there?" said Martha, following behind him.

"Being here brings back so many memories," he said with no expression, then placed his face into both hands, trying to hide the tears that he could no longer hold back.

"I miss them so much," he muttered from under his hands.

"I know you do, love. There's not a minute of the day when I don't think about them too. My sister was a lucky woman, having you by her side, always protecting her."

"But I didn't protect her. I failed them both as a father and a husband. I should have been there for them."

"Now, you listen to me." Martha sternly spoke. "You can't keep blaming yourself for what happened; she wouldn't want you to."

"I should have saved them!" he said with anger, slamming his fist against the wood.

"There were too many Screamers. There was nothing you could have done."

Grazox finally looked up at Martha. Holding his face in her soft, caring hands, she slowly wiped away his tears. "Someday, you'll be together again," she whispered with a soft smile.

"How you doing, Ludlow?" said Tobin, checking up on the giant, who had to walk to the Baxter's and patiently wait by himself this whole time, sitting underneath a ginormous toadstool that shielded him from the miserable rain.

"Mind if I sit with you?" Tobin handed the giant some leftovers from dinner.

"Why aren't you up there with the others?" Ludlow asked, tossing his head back then throwing the bag of leftovers into his large mouth like a snack.

"Too hectic, I couldn't listen to another one of Tibbot's stories, needed some fresh air."

"Oh... I see." The giant grinned.

"What?"

"Nothing," Ludlow chuckled.

"No, tell me," Tobin huffed.

"I know why you really look miserable." Tobin looked at Ludlow, confused. "It's that girl, the scruffy one. You're in love with her," he cheekily grinned.

"WHAT!"

"You don't hide it very well; you stare at her all the time. The only one who hasn't noticed is her," the giant laughed.

"That's ridiculous. I'm not in love, especially with her!" he said, rolling his eyes.

"Why, what's wrong with her?"

"You've seen her manners; she's worse than a Dwarf. How can I love a girl like that?"

"Maybe that's why you secretly like her, because she's different from all the other girls you've met."

"She's different alright," Tobin muttered sarcastically.

"Put it this way, would you rather be with someone like that snobby little blonde one, you know the one that likes bragging about herself constantly."

"Who... Lucinda? God no, that girl is driving me mad; she won't leave me alone. She's always finding an excuse to cling onto my arm." They both laughed.

As they continued to gossip and make fun of Lucinda, one of the guards walked by doing his usual rounds, checking the perimeters. "All clear here!" the guard said to another as they crossed each other's paths.

"How's it looking over there!" the watchmen shouted with his hands clasped around his mouth to the guard on the other side.

"All clea—" the guard stopped when he heard a strange grunting noise coming from one of the trees. Holding on tightly to his fiery torch, he cautiously walked over to where the suspicious noise was coming from. The heavy rain drizzled down his pale face. As he held his torch closer to the tree, he thought he saw something move but was uncertain, for it was far too rainy to tell. Trying to get a better look, he held his torch higher and squinted his eyes.

BANG!

Thunder aggressively echoed through Vine City, startling the guard to quickly turn around in panic. Relieved nothing was there, he once again turned back, facing the tree. A flash of lightning struck, revealing a Screamer, and he was face to face with the beast. Its wide-open jaw watered, dripping wet with both disgusting salvia and rain, drizzling down its deathly sharp teeth. Being paralysed with fear, the guard's legs had turned to jelly, he tried to run, but it was too late. The Screamer had already sunk his sharp razorblade teeth into him, dragging him away into the bushes.

"AAHHHH!"

"What was that?"

Tobin and Ludlow stuck their heads out from beneath the toadstool into the rain, wondering what that yelling was about.

"Probably Lucinda, calling out for her Prince Charming," Ludlow chuckled.

"Shut up," Tobin laughed, playfully nudging the giant.

A panicked bunch of guards holding out their weapons rushed by them, blowing on whistles.

"What's going on?" said Tobin, quickly grabbing one of the guards that ran by.

"We're under attack. One of our men has been killed," the guard replied, then immediately ran back, joining the other men that rushed towards the screams.

"Screamers?" Tobin gasped. "I've got to warn the others!" he said with panic in his voice.

Meanwhile, back at the Baxters house, everybody was warm and comfortable with no clue what was going on down below.

"You sure you're okay, love?" said Martha, continuing to comfort her brother-in-law.

"I'm fine, Martha, thank you," he said, resting his head on his arms that were folded against the wood of the balcony.

SCEEEEEECH!

Grazox lifted his head up with a fearful frown. His ears buzzed with the memories of a disturbingly familiar sound that sent shivers down his entire body.

"They've found us."

I'll SEE YOU SOON
CHAPTER TEN

"Rain, rain... bloody rain," Lucinda huffed. "Don't you ever get sick of living here?" she moaned, sluggishly turning away from the window, all depressed in a dismal gloom.

"Not really. We were born here, so we're kinda used to it. Living someplace where it didn't rain, now that would be weird," said Celia, eating some leftover pie.

"Well, I couldn't live here. It's horrid."

Celia opened her mouth to speak, but before she could say another word, the front door violently swung open.

"THEY'VE FOUND US!" Grazox hollered, rushing back into the house with Martha behind him.

"What's going on?" the girls gasped in panic while the others rushed into the room.

"Screamers... they're here!"

"What do we do?" Lucinda squeaked in a high pitch, jumping up and biting her perfect nails.

"We need to leave immediately."

Once again, the Screamers had managed to hunt down their prey. Vine City, the most peaceful place throughout the whole kingdom, was now under attack by the Fire Queen's Hunters.

"We can take the Mini Skyriders. They're just below us under the river caves," suggested Tibbot.

"Good man," said Grazox patting him on the shoulder. "Let's go!" Suddenly Grazox's expression had changed, realising someone was missing from the group.

"Where is my nephew?"

Tobin and Ludlow were still on the ground, observing the Screamers from a distance while they hid. Ready to make a run for it, Tobin quickly ducked, not seeing one of the Screamers lurking close by, dragging its knuckles across the soggy muddy ground with its back hunched, salivating from the mouth.

"We need to stop them. We can't let them reach the others," Tobin whispered. "On the count of five, we go." He paused, waiting for his moment. "One... two... three... four...."

Suddenly a pack of Screamers ran by on all fours, jumping up and sinking their killer claws into the trunks of the trees. As they climbed, they viciously gnashed their teeth from side to side, thirsty for blood.

"NOW!" he yelled. "We can't let them reach the others!" Tobin pulled out his bow, quickly loading it up with three arrows; using three fingers to lightly hold the arrows on the string, he pulled the bow's drawstring back towards his face and let go. Hitting the target, three Screamers came crashing back down to the ground, but still some managed to get away, continuing to climb up and getting closer towards the others.

"WHAT DO WE DO! WHAT DO WE DO!" Gustav cried, hopping about in chaos, panicking for his life.

"We need to get to the caves!" said Tibbot.

"I'm not leaving without my nephew! I'll be damned if I let one of those things take another person I love!" Grazox roared with fury with his blood boiling, turning his entire face red.

"Shhh... listen," whispered Ruya.

Everyone stood still, staring up at the ceiling, silently listening to the pitter-patter of rain falling through the leaves down to the rooftop.

"What's happening? It's too quiet," said Kruze, suspiciously reaching for his sword.

"Do you think they're up there?" Fen whispered, trembling with sweaty palms. A thunderous boom erupted as one of the Screamers clawed through the roof, making twigs and leaves fall through the ceiling into the living room. The Protectors quickly reached for their weapons, while the others in fear scattered around the room in panic. One of the Screamers finally broke through, crashing down onto the floor, followed by two more.

"RUN!!" shouted Tibbot to his family. Chaos broke out as they battled with the monstrous creatures. With rage, Grazox violently swung his axe from side to side, fighting off the larger Screamer, while the rest of the gang battled it out with the other two. Igor, Gustav and Berwin hid behind one of Mrs Baxter's wooden dressers, assuming that would keep them out of sight and out of harm's way. Cold icky slime drizzled down the back of their heads; they slowly looked up and were distraught to lock eyes with one of the Screamers looming over them.

"AAHHH!"

In a sudden panic, they scattered, each running in different directions, desperately trying to get away from the monstrous beast.

"HELP... HELP... HELP!" yelled Gustav in fear, hopping out of control like a headless chicken. Everybody was far too busy battling with the creatures themselves, so they hadn't noticed poor Gustav being cornered by one of the Screamers. He thought this would be the end of his adventure, and his portrait would never be hung in the halls of Grazia. He shut his eyes tightly and took a deep breath, convinced it would be his last. Ready to kill in attack position, the Screamer creepily moved closer and closer towards Gustav and pounced.

SMACK!

Luckily, Something hit the Screamer on the back of its head, distracting its gaze away from Gustav. Ruya was standing there with a pile of books in her arms. She quickly picked up another one and threw it even harder towards its face. The Screamer was extremely angry; it turned away from Gustav, focusing its attention on Ruya. With one ginormous leap, it made its way over to her, making her slip backwards onto the ground. The Screamer stood above her, slowly opening its mouth and revealing its killer teeth, spitting out saliva that sprinkled into her face as it cried in rage. Just when Ruya thought this was the end, out jumped Potion to the rescue, clawing at the Screamer's eyes and trying to protect her. The Screamer, trying to shield its eyes from Potion's little but very sharp claws, screamed in anguish and fury but still tried to attack, and once again leapt towards Ruya, who was still helplessly lying flat on her back.

WHACK!

Martha hit the Screamer with a pan right in the face before it could attack, sending the creature crashing out of the window and plunging into the river below.

"AND STAY OUT!" she shouted. But unfortunately a hit with a pan wasn't enough to keep the beast away. With rage, the Screamer splashed back up out from the water and ran towards Tobin, who was still fighting off the others on the ground. Just when it was about to attack the boy, a Looger jumped out from the river, snatching the Screamer into its large wide-open jaw with a killer grip, dragging the creature back into the water with it. Wiping his forehead, Tobin sighed in relief that the Looger had saved him, for he wasn't prepared and hadn't seen the Screamer coming.

"AIIEEEE! HELP!" Lucinda shrieked from the top of her lungs from above the trees.

"Ludlow... give me a boost!"

Ludlow kneeled down with his hands on the ground, and Tobin ran towards him as fast as he could and jumped into the giant's large hands. Ludlow lifted his arms towards the sky, throwing him high into the air. The city was in utter chaos. Tobin hurried, trying to make his way higher through Vine City, rushing across bridges, desperately trying to get to the others. Meanwhile, back at the treehouse, there was one Screamer left to fight off. It had Huxley trapped in a tight spot. Trying to be brave, he stupidly thought he could take on the beast himself and make his father proud. But unfortunately Celia, Greta and Matilda had once again beaten him to it and stolen his chance of trying to be brave and save the day. They ambushed the beast that had their brother cornered.

"I'm coming!" Ida yelled from the top of her lungs, pouncing from the balcony, flattering the Screamer to the ground. Their father came rushing over and plunged his axe through the beast, finishing the Screamer off.

"What would you do without us," the four sisters laughed, grabbing their baby brother into their arms, barely giving him space to breathe.

"We need to leave now!" yelled Zyra.

"There will be more coming," said Kruze.

"Not without my nephew!" Grazox howled furiously.

"UNCLE!" the doors burst open with a gust of wind; Tobin stood in the doorway dripping wet.

"BOY! Where have you been?" Grazox sighed with relief grabbing his nephew tightly in his arms.

"I was down below fighting. The Screamers have found us. They run in large packs, so you know there will be more coming."

"We need to go!" insisted Kruze, swinging his belongings around his shoulder.

"Come on, we need to get to those caves," said Tibbot. "But we must hurry." Ready to move on with their journey again, everyone quickly grabbed their bags and hurried to the back door. "Wait... what about Ludlow? We can't just leave without him," said Ruya, being the only one to show some concern for the poor giant.

"Ludlow is a Protector; trust me, he will know what to do," said Grazox.

"Don't worry, love, he'll be fine," said Martha.

Tibbot grabbed his wife into his arms, followed by a passionate kiss.

"Take care of the kids."

"Oh please," she chuckled. "It's going to take a lot more than stinking Screamers to take down the Baxters."

He smiled, then gave her one last kiss and gave all five of his children a hug and quickly slipped out the back door with the others. "This way," he said, scurrying down a secret bridge that even some of the locals were unaware of, that led them to an underground tunnel. They almost made it. But a pack of Screamers rushed by, making horrible grunting sounds that made your skin crawl.

"Duck," Tibbot whispered, pushing Fen's head down, but luckily the Screamers hadn't seen them and continued running by.

"Will your family be okay?" Grazox expressed his concern, watching the pack of Screamers aggressively making their way to the Baxters house.

"It's not them I'm concerned for; it's those poor Screamers," he chuckled. Meanwhile, Vine City in mayhem led folk to gather together and fight off the Screamers. Gnomes, goblins, elves, mortals and Spellborns rushed out of their homes, protecting one another, fighting side by side to keep their homes that they had worked so hard for peace, free from the queens' destruction.

"CHARGE!" The Baxter family ran towards a pack of Screamers and fought with passion to save their home. A swarm of fairies came swooping down from above the trees, viciously attacking with their tiny, razor-sharp, needle-like teeth, overwhelming the Screamers, which fell off the swing bridges. The gang had safely made it through the cities chaos, jumping into a wooden boat that would take them through a dark narrow stream leading them into a cave. Things seemed gloomy for a while. The girls breathed heavily in the dark with anxiety, afraid Screamers would be waiting for them on the other end. They had been through so much already in such a short space of time that they didn't know what to expect anymore.

"I can't see," cried Lucinda.

"It's too damn dark!" complained Berwin with his croaky voice echoing through the cave.

"Keep your beard, on old man, we're almost there," Tibbot laughed, leading the way.

Berwin, not happy as usual, opened his mouth to complain once again but stopped when he noticed a little light flickering in the distance. The stream spread out, growing wider as they got further into the cave.

"I see light," said the old gnome, pointing towards the small bright speck.

"Finally," Fen sighed with relief, for he had always had a fear of the dark. Everybody moved closer to the front of the boat, realising the speck of light wasn't the end of the tunnel at all. Drew and Ruya gasped; the whole cave suddenly lit up, filled with hundreds and thousands of glow-worms. The dreamlike stream glittered and sparkled like a huge trail of fairy dust.

"Unbelievable." Ruya smiled, managing to gently catch one in her palm.

"Isn't it magical, my lady?" Igor grinned, staring at the glow-worm she had caught in her hand.

"I could stay down here forever, it's so peaceful," she replied, letting the glow-worm go.

Drew leaned over the edge of the boat and gently touched the sparkly water, leaving a trail of magical ripples behind. She was so mesmerised that she hadn't noticed Tobin staring at her. His eyes brightened as he watched her, being mesmerised himself.

"Right then, here we are," said Tibbot, stopping the boat. The sun hit their faces as they came to the end of the tunnel. They hopped off and found themselves on a cliff, which was the end of Vine City.

"How are we getting down?" asked Drew.

"We'll fly, on Skyriders," Tibbot answered.

They turned their heads over to a row of three turtles, just like the ones back at Healers Town, only they weren't nearly as big as Anga. Anga was a beast of a turtle, bigger than any ship, unlike Mini Skyriders. They were much smaller, only managing to fit five people at the most. They each had thick, secure leathery saddles placed upon their shells.

"Say your goodbye, girls. This is where you part," said Grazox.

Was this it? Were they really about to be separated? After only just finding one another? Drew and Ruya gazed at each other with their eyes welling up with tears.

"Do we have to go our own ways?" Ruya pleaded emotionally, sniffling her nose and wiping away her tears.

"You know why we need to keep you apart. Now please don't make this any harder than it has to be, you'll see each other again, I promise. Now say goodbye it's time to go."

"I'm going to miss you." Drew smiled, playfully nudging her on the shoulder.

Ruya grabbed hold of her. They both squeezed tightly for a good few seconds before finally letting go.

"Stay safe," whispered Ruya with a tear in her eye.

"You too." Drew smiled, trying not to cry.

"Okay, girls, that's enough. We can't waste any more time, not with Screamers lurking this close by," said Grazox.

Giving one last final squeeze, they let go of one another, smiling with tears in their eyes as if it would be the last time they would be together.

"Drew, you're with me," said Grazox, snapping his fingers and taking her by the arm.

"The others will stick together, but we have other plans," he continued. The time had come for the gang to finally depart as they settled into their own groups. Drew and Igor sat between Grazox and Tobin. As they took to the sky, Drew looked back at Ruya, waving her arm in the air with one final goodbye.

"I'LL SEE YOU SOON!" she yelled, with the wind blowing away her very last tear.

"BYE!" Ruya yelled, feeling choked up, jumping up and waving until she could no longer see her.

"GOOD LUCK, MY FRIEND!" Tibbot hollered, waving his large hands about. "Now, remember," said Tibbot, "there are strong winds ahead of us. Try and stay as close to us as possible."

"Roger that," Kruze replied, climbing onto his Skyrider.

The second group climbed aboard the shell. Tibbot sat at the front while Ruya, with Potion on her lap, sat in the middle of Berwin and Zyron.

"Let's ride!"

Behind them followed the third Skyrider. Kruze, Zyra, Lucinda, Fen and Gustav would meet Tibbot's team once they had landed.

They all took to the sky once again, flying towards what they hoped would help them in the war to come.

LORDS OF ORO CITY
CHAPTER ELEVEN

It was another glorious morning in the House of Grazia. The sun rose up like an angel, shedding its pure light upon the home of Protectors.

But inside the house, the mood wasn't quite as bright.

"Sir, we just got word from our Watchers. Queen Ates's army is growing in great numbers. They're preparing for her arrival; they were spotted moving down south," Oba stressfully explained. She watched Sir Abner pacing up and down with his hands behind his back, breathing heavily through his nose, making his nostrils expand each time he breathed in.

"Sir..."

"I'm thinking!" he snapped angrily.

"But, sir, we have no time. War is practically on our doorstep, and we are not ready. It won't be long now before the Akulls start preparing for Queen Lumi's awakening. Our army of Protectors is not enough to defeat one queen's army, let alone two. We need help; we need more men."

"We've sent out our best Protectors; they will find us more allies. I trust Grazox will keep the girls safe; that's the most important thing. We must stick to the plan and keep the Star away from those seeking it, or else game over."

"Yes, sir, you're absolutely right. But we ourselves must try and recruit more allies. We can't leave it all to Grazox and the others."

Sir Abner walked over to the window, intensely staring out with his hands clasped behind his back like he always did every time he was in deep thought.

"Then there is only one thing we can do."

"What is that, sir?"

He slowly turned away from the window with a stern frown. "We need to go back to Oro City."

***

Clouds stretched across the pale blue sky while the wind sounded its mighty roar, making all the tall trees that surrounded it shake in fear. Even the birds fled in terror. The salty gusting wind whipped their hair into their faces that stung their eyes. Their clothes flapped uncontrollably in the air like birds soaring in the sky. Tibbot and the others flying behind him desperately tried to fight against the wind that blew powerfully with passion. But they were not the only ones trying to flee against the harsh wind's fury. With no warning, a flock of geese chaotically flew into them, flapping their large wings about, causing both groups to fall off their Skyriders down deep into the woods.

***

The carriage bounced up and down as they sat still in silence, not saying a word to one another. Everything they wanted to say showed on their faces as they exchanged glances of concern while making their way down a familiar road, a road they never intended going down ever again. Never in a hundred years did they think they would be back where it all began. Sir Abner was the first to climb out of the carriage, Sir Arkin and Oba hesitantly followed behind. Their faces drained as they stood outside the gates to Oro City. The world of royals and lords, the wealthiest grounds of all the lands, where only the social elite resided. Mortal grounds.

All three of them stood there, taking in deep breaths as the mighty gates opened.

"Ready?" said Sir Abner. They both nodded and entered. The gates opened to Oro City, a place where jewels were plentiful, and golden coins were in abundance. Poverty was non-existent to the people of the Golden City. The structures were encrusted with iridescent crystals that were blinding in the sun and twinkled in the moonlight. Carriages of rose gold rattled along, being pulled by silky Unicorns, the only place where you would find them, for no poor man has ever seen one in person. Women strolled along with elegant gowns made from material of the most superior quality and headwear of the rarest gems and jewels custom made by the hands of dwarfs.

"Well, I see nothing has changed," said Oba, spotting a fancy uptight couple strutting by with their noses in the air, glaring at her as if she didn't belong there.

"Sooner we get this over with, the sooner we can leave," Abner huffed. At long last, they had reached the palace of the fallen mortal King Linus, where a council of lords and wealthy men sat in a row of high golden chairs, looking down on the people as if they were Gods. For they were the voice of the kingdom. Large doors echoed as they slowly opened. Sir Abner and the others walked into the great hall. The floors were brightly polished with the sparkling reflection of the jewel-encrusted ceiling that looked like a cluster of stars twinkling at night, and great golden carved pillars on each end of the hall. They walked closer and found themselves standing before the king's council.

"Well... well... well. If it isn't the amazing Sir Abner Aldrich and his pets. Isn't this a surprise," a thick voice echoed through the hall.

Sir Abner looked up to an unsettling familiar face. Lord Genzo was sat in the middle of the council, his throne slightly higher than the rest. It was the throne of the late king and where he once sat. He held the stone of royalty in his stretched-out hand; he always thought himself supreme among all jewels and gems. His robe of blue silk glittered like radiant diamonds every time the sun's rays hit him and matched his cold blue eyes. He was wrinkly with a pale complexion and slick hair whiter than snow neatly tucked behind his slightly pointed ears.

"Surprised you're here after all these years. Very brave of you, I should have your head for treason."

"On what grounds?" Abner sternly replied.

"The crime of betraying one's king, of course."

"I betrayed no one. Especially the king."

"Oh, but you did. You were the king's advisor, were you not? And yet, you abandoned his side in the time of war and joined the enemy. A Spellborn, no less." His eyes glared down at Sir Arkin in disgust. "You're a traitor; you failed your duties to the king."

"Well, thank heavens you were here, fulfilling my duties for me. You certainly didn't waste any time filling the king's ear with your toxic hate towards the Spellborns. You always were so desperate to take my place as the king's advisor."

"I had the king's best interest at heart!" Lord Genzo snapped, loudly slamming his fist on his golden armrest.

"And I had the peoples! If you had everything your way, we would be at constant war with the Spellborns. Me and my men—"

"Your men? Ah yes... the House of Grazia. A safe haven for the people," he sarcastically chuckled.

"We gave the people hope and protection – more than the king ever did." Sir Abner looked up to everybody in the room. "My Lords, I'm afraid I bring distressing news. War is coming."

Lord Genzo tutted his teeth, rolling his eyes in disbelief.

"And whom may I ask is this war with? Hmmm?" he said.

"The queens are returning," announced Sir Abner. The room immediately filled with voices mumbling over each other.

"HA!" Lord Genzo laughed.

"It's true, My Lords," Oba interrupted. "The Fire Queen's general is building a large army for her arrival. Not to mention the Cold Queen, it won't be long now before her army is also on the move," she continued.

"Impossible. The queens are dead."

"No, my lord, they were banished by magic, thanks to the witches who paid for it with their lives. It was their spell that bought us more time, but that's all they got us… time. Which is now coming to an end. War is coming, and we need to be ready before the last star falls out of line."

"So what do you suggest we do?" Lord Genzo smirked, not taking the matter seriously at all but rather amusing.

"We reunite the two kingdoms."

Everyone gasped with disapproval, shaking their heads. Once again the room filled with the sound of mumbles. "You want us to reunite the two kingdoms?"

"Yes, my lord, if we do, we might stand a fighting chance against the queens' armies."

"If what you say is true, why not let the queens go to war with each other? What has it got to do with us? This isn't our fight," he laughed.

"This is no laughing matter, my lord," said Oba, feeling extremely frustrated.

"Oh, but it is. After the abandonment of your king, you come here after god knows how many years and demand we reunite two enemies who I remind you have been at war for decades, to fight beside you in some false war you've clearly made up for god knows what reason. Tell me, if the queens really are alive, then why haven't they attacked yet?"

"Because the spell that the witches conjured is still keeping them away… for now. But once the final star falls, nothing will stop them from attacking. That's why we need to join the two kingdoms before they awake from their sleep."

"I said it once, and I'll say it again. Why should we care? Let the queens fight among themselves; neither of them will ever get this throne."

Sir Abner shook his head from side to side with disappointment.

"You forget, Lord, the Fire Queen took the throne once before when she murdered our king. But luckily for you, it's not the throne she's after, but that doesn't mean you're safe from harm," said Oba.

"What could she possibly want more than this throne. There is nothing more powerful than being king of the Golden City." Genzo laughed, turning his head to the lords on each side of him while they laughed along with him.

"No, but being a God is," Sir Abner seriously replied.

The laughing ceased; the room fell completely silent.

"The Star has returned," said Oba.

The lords gasped, leaning in and whispering into each other's ears. Lord Genzo, for the first time in his life, was silent. "You're sure about this?" he said, with a strange look on his face.

"Yes. And before you get any funny ideas of claiming the Star for yourselves, know this. You could never handle such cosmic power, your mortal flesh was not built to contain elements of the Gods, and if you try doing so, you'll be nothing but stardust within seconds. That goes for every mortal man or woman with selfish intentions."

"And you've seen the Star?" he replied with great curiosity. Lord Genzo slid his body down his chair like a snake closer towards Abner. "Tell me... is it as beautiful as they say?" he asked with a twinkle in his bright blue eyes.

Sir Abner paused. "Even better." He softly smiled.

The room filled with whispers as the lords muttered their plans and ideas among themselves into each other's ears in turn, nodding their heads in agreement. Lord Genzo raised his hand, and the room fell silent. Clearing his throat, he finally spoke.

"If what you say is true, we must find the Star and prepare for war immediately."

Sir Abner and the others felt a twinge of relief. "We've already sent out our very best Protectors to find more allies. We won't be alone," said Abner. For the first time in a long time, he began to feel some sort of hope and achievement. He was finally on the verge of reuniting the two kingdoms after all these years.

"Once we have the Star, there will be no need for allies. We'll have all the power we need to be rid of the Spellborns once and for all, wiping them all out."

"What?" Confused, Sir Abner, Sir Arkin and Oba stared up at Lord Genzo in a muddle. "My Lord? I don't understand. You said we should prepare for war," said Oba.

"Yes. War with the Spellborns." He wickedly grinned.

"What are you talking about? Didn't you hear a word I said? Our war is not with the Spellborns; they are not our enemy. We need to fight together to defeat the real threat."

"THE SPELLBORNS ARE THE REAL THREAT!" Lord Genzo yelled, slamming his fists. "And with the Star, we could obliterate them all, removing their kind from our world once and for all. Making it pure once again, as the Gods intended."

Sir Abner and the others stood still, disgusted with what they were hearing from the lord's cruel mouth. "You will thank me someday," Genzo continued.

"Thank you for what?"

"For bringing order back into the world, how it used to be before magic was used to conjure life... It's unnatural and unholy, and we must be rid of the blue bloods. We will make the world a better place again... once you bring me the Star, of course." Genzo grinned, with his fingers pressed together.

Sir Abner looked up with such rage in his face, almost like he was about to burst.

"A man like you has absolutely no interest in making this world a better place, you never did then, and you never will now. You want rid of the Spellborns because you're afraid of them. They're the stronger race and you can't handle it; you never could. I came here today in good faith and hoped you would help, but now I realise just how selfish the mortals really are. You are just as blind as the king was, and he died because of his selfish stupidity. Don't make the same mistake."

"Enough of your blabbering! You are going to find the Star and bring it to me. THAT'S AN ORDER!"

"You are not the king. I do not take orders from you."

Lord Genzo blushed with embarrassment; his face burned up with rage. "How dare you. I am the head of the High Council."

"Yes. Still... not quite a king. People only follow you out of fear. A real king is followed out of love and respect. You're nothing but a cowardly worm, looking out for his own selfish interests."

The lords turned their heads on each side, waiting for Lord Genzo's response. With his thumb, he brushed his left eyebrow, neatly pushing it to one side and smirked, trying to keep his cool. "Well, it's obvious why you're really here," he said. "All this nonsense of the queens returning and the fallen Star is all just a trap."

"What?" Oba and the two Sirs replied, shocked.

"You're a spy for the Spellborns. Using the dead queens as a distraction while the real enemy is getting ready to attack."

"Have you completely lost your mind!" said Abner.

"GUARDS!" Genzo growled. The large doors forcefully burst open, a bunch of guards with armour and swords came crashing through the doors like a wave into the great hall.

"SEIZE THEM!"

"WE ARE NOT SPIES!" Oba argued with frustration.

"Maybe. But you are still traitors for abandoning your king all those years ago and for bringing a Spellborn into the great hall. And for such crimes, you must be punished, starting with the Spellborn," he said, glaring down at Sir Arkin with such hatred Arkin could feel his eyes burning through him like lava.

"What are you waiting for...TAKE THEM!" Lord Genzo ordered his guards once again, snapping his fingers impatiently.

"You're a fool, Genzo, the queens will return, and you'll all be sorry for this," said Abner.

The guards shifted closer towards them. Surrounding them, the guards formed a circle, closing them in like a cage.

There was no way out. It seemed hopeless for a while, then suddenly Sir Abner, Sir Arkin and Oba pulled out their sceptres. With force, they hit all three of them simultaneously on the ground, causing a thunderous bang and filling the entire hall with a bright light. The brightness was so intense it blinded the guards, who dropped to their knees. The lords sat tightly back in their high chairs, shielding their eyes from the blinding light. The light finally faded. Lord Genzo removed his arms from his face and looked down from his high chair.

"Where are they?" he said breathlessly, rubbing his eyes.

The guards got back to their feet. "They are gone, my lord. They just vanished," one of the guards answered.

"TRAITORS. FIND THEM, YOU FOOLS… FIND THEM!" Genzo yelled so loud his veins bulged out from the side of his temples, ready to burst like a balloon.

***

"Wake up." Zyra picked an acorn off the ground and slung it towards Kruze. Passed out, he continued to lie there until she threw an even bigger one.

"Ouch!" he groaned, slowly waking up, rubbing the side of his head in pain. "What happened?" he muttered, finally coming back to his senses.

"A flock of geese, that's what happened," she answered with a huff.

He slowly got to his feet, brushing the twigs and leaves off his clothes. "Where are we?" he coughed.

"I'm not sure, but we better find Tibbot and the others quick," said Zyra.

"Wait… Fen, Gustav, and the girl… they were flying with us. Where are they?" Kruze spat with worry.

Zyra looked around with her hands on her hips and nodded. "The wind was pretty strong; it must have carried them to the other side of the woods. We need to find them." Agreeing, he shook his head and followed behind her, slowly dragging his feet.

***

"Boy!" Tibbot grumbled loudly, lying flat on his back. "Help me up," he said, reaching out one of his arms. Zyron ran to his side and with all his strength pulled Tibbot up off the ground. "Thanks, lad," he sighed, patting Zyron on the back.

"That flock of geese really took us by surprise," he chuckled.

"Help! Help!" came a distressed voice whining from beneath a large pile of leaves and twigs. Tibbot, with one hand, reached down into the pile and pulled out Berwin.

"DAMN WIND! DAMN BIRDS!" he complained furiously, wiping the twigs off his clothes. He then began to irritably straighten out his bushy beard.

"Where's Ruya?" said Zyron, quickly shifting his eyes from side to side, searching behind every tree.

"RUYA! RUYA!" Tibbot hollered with his hands clasped around his mouth, calling for her in panic.

Zyron felt a sudden panic come over him. "We were supposed to keep her safe. We were her Protectors... if anything happens to her, I'll—"

"Calm down, lad, we'll find her. She can't be too far from here," Tibbot calmly replied, trying to keep his cool, running his plump fingers through his scruffy brown beard. "Who knows," he said, staring at Zyron, "maybe she's with your sister and the pretty boy. Best we go and find them."

After gathering themselves back up from the fall, they began their search for the others. "Keep up, Berwin," Tibbot chuckled, looking back at the miserable old gnome, whose face was all scrunched up and bitter as if he had just sucked on a lemon.

"I'm coming, you big oaf!" he answered in a very rude manner as usual.

Zyron turned to Tibbot. "Does that not bother you?" he asked.

"What?" answered Tibbot, cluelessly.

"The way he speaks to you, he should show a little more respect."

"The little fella has been living with me and my family for days. I'm used to his mood swings," he chuckled.

"Mood swings? Seems grumpy all the time," said Zyron, turning his head to Berwin, who was still complaining to himself about the geese, completely unaware of their conversation.

"Gnomes, lad, miserable little things, but what can you do? They were born with a bad attitude. It's in their nature."

A couple of hours went by, and neither of the two groups had found each other.

***

"Stop. I'm out of breath. Can we please sit for a little while?" Kruze pleaded breathlessly.

"Wow," Zyra grinned, "the greatest swordsman to ever live wants to take a break."

"I'm only human. And we've been walking forever. I'm thirsty," he moaned, sitting on a log for a rest.

"You're tired, you're thirsty… what next? You're a Protector, for god's sake, man up. This is part of what we do."

"Warriors get to have a rest sometimes too, you know."

"Just because you have some fancy title and you're good with the sword, it doesn't make you a warrior," she argued.

"And being tough and strict all the time doesn't make you one either," he argued back.

"What's that supposed to mean?" she snapped, quickly turning back in his direction.

"I'm just saying, you could do with a little fun now and then. It's like you're always looking for a fight. Lighten up a bit, will ya."

"We're on the verge of war, and you want me to lighten up and have fun?"

"Exactly." He grinned. "We could die at any moment. And before I do, I would love to have seen that pretty face of yours smile for once… Come to think of it, I've never seen you smile, not even once… Why is that?"

"We live in a toxic world. What's there to smile about," she answered seriously.

"Oh, it's not all bad. There's lots of things to smile and be happy about."

"Yeah, like what?" she grunted.

"Love." He smiled with a little twinkle in his eye.

"Love?" She paused. "What do you know about love?"

"Lots of things… What?" he said, catching her laughing to herself with her head down.

She put her head back up and just stared at him for a few intense seconds, then finally spoke. "Love is something you fight and die for… Love is something you live for. Love is a feeling deep inside you, a feeling words can't explain. A feeling that makes you petrified and happy at the same time. Love… is *not* fame and all the nonsense that comes with it. If that's your idea of love, then you know nothing of true heartache or what love can do. The only person you've ever loved is yourself."

The woods were silent as her speech came to an end. They both paused, once again staring at each other. "Now hang on a minute," he tutted, waggling his finger from side to side.

"Look, I've seen you with women. You're a ladies man. You love the fame and everything that comes with the title of being the 'greatest swordsman', and that's okay, but please don't ever talk to me about love like you have the first clue what it's about. Okay?"

He opened his mouth to speak, but once again he was silenced. "Shouldn't you be fixing your hair or admiring yourself in the mirror?" Not saying another word, she walked off, leaving him behind.

"Wait!" he breathlessly yelled, dragging his feet after her. Finally catching up, he placed his hand on her shoulder, trying to catch his breath. "You know what your problem is, don't you?"

"What?" she answered with a blank expression, removing his hand from her shoulder.

"You need a fella." He playfully grinned.

"Oh my god. Do you hear yourself?" she huffed with irritation.

"I know you say hurtful things cause you secretly like me. No point denying it," he continued to tease, deliberately trying to get a reaction, which he always did. Zyra was a hothead and was easily annoyed and very quick-tempered. They continued their journey through the woods, arguing all the way like an old married couple.

"Shhh!" she whispered, quickly placing her hand over his mouth, silencing him from speaking another word. "I heard something. There's someone over there." Slowly pulling out one of her arrows and placing it on the bow, they walked closer to where she heard the noise. Kruze quietly pulled out his sword, and together, they jumped out from behind the tree.

"AHHH!" cried a croaky voice.

"Berwin?" said Zyra, lowering her weapon. Berwin rolled up into a ball on the ground like a bug, slowly looked up and removed the arms shielding his face.

"You okay?" she said, showing some concern for the old gnome, holding out her hand.

"You fools. You halfwits. YOU ALMOST KILLED ME!"

"He's okay," Kruze sighed, rolling his eyes, and putting away his sword. Finally, the two teams had reunited, but unfortunately everybody wasn't there.

"Where are the others?" Zyron asked his sister.

"I think they might have fallen on the other side of the woods. We searched as far as we could."

"I feel bad for the others, but Ruya is our main priority. God knows what will happen if she falls into the wrong hands. Who knows what's lurking in these woods," said Tibbot with deep concern and worry.

"We must find her."

INTO THE WOODS
CHAPTER TWELVE

In the woods, the sky vanished almost completely, with only the occasional streak of sunlight that rarely touched the forest floor. The sound of the creaking branches and the crows hummed in Ruya's ear. The tree's cries whispered with emotion, almost as if they were alive.

"Ruya," a soft ghostly voice whispered, calling the girl's name.

Barely able to open her eyes, she just lay there, lifeless, flat on her back. All she could hear was the enchanting symphony of the leaves dancing, whispering their songs to the wind. Once again, the voice spoke, calling out her name. *"Ruya. Wake up."*

The darkness blurred away as she blinked repeatedly, slowly opening her eyes. A shadowy figure loomed over her.

"Wake up," the stranger's voice echoed, then vanished entirely into thin air like a dream. Ruya finally came to her senses. She slowly sat up, rubbing the back of her head in agony, while Potion comfortably sat on her chest with not a scratch.

"Ouch," she whispered, trying to stand on her two feet as she wobbled about.

"Thank god you're not hurt," she said, holding Potion in her arms, swaying her from side to side and smothering the little bunny with big soggy kisses.

"RUYA! RUYA!"

She heard a familiar voice calling out her name. She quickly jumped up and rushed towards the calls.

"I'M OVER HERE!" she yelled. Tibbot and the others had finally found her. Tibbot grabbed her and hugged her tightly. She could barely breathe but somehow managed to survive the famous Baxter hug. He held her in a fatherly way, just as he would his own children.

"Let me take a look at you, lass." Finally releasing her from his tight grip, he checked her from head to toe, making sure she wasn't too badly injured.

"I'm fine." She smiled, rubbing her eye.

"You sure you're not hurt?" he replied with concern. She nodded and smiled once more, assuring him she was okay.

"Okay then, good. We better move and find a way out of here."

"Wait." She paused and looked around. "Where is Lucinda... She was riding with you two, wasn't she?" she said, turning her head over to Kruze and Zyra for an answer.

"We think the wind must have carried her to the other side of the woods," said Zyron.

"Fen and Gustav?" she replied with concern.

"They're probably with her," said Zyra.

"Well, shouldn't we go and look for them? They could be hurt... or worse," Ruya voiced her concern.

"Lass, you must understand, we'll waste valuable time looking for them. I know that sounds bad, but we must stick to the plan and keep it moving. You're my responsibility and priority. You're the main person we need to keep safe. Grazox left me in charge to look after you. Fen's a bright lad. I'm sure they'll be fine."

"Well, I hope you're right," she sighed, not happy at all, feeling absolutely awful and guilty about leaving them behind.

"Right then, let's get a move on."

On the move once again, the others had walked ahead, but Tibbot stopped. Looking back, he noticed Kruze didn't follow behind but just stood still, staring at something.

"Kruze! What are you doing? We need to go," he yelled behind him.

Kruze didn't answer but continued to stare at whatever had him distracted.

"Pretty boy, did you hear me? We need to leave."

But once again, he didn't respond. Tibbot bolted towards him, feeling irritated that he had not listened to him, roughly grabbing his shoulder from behind. Kruze finally turned around, facing him with a strange look on his face.

"I was calling you. Why didn't you answer me?"

Kruze said nothing but handed him a piece of thick paper he was holding tightly onto with his nails gripping through.

"What's this?" Tibbot asked, snatching the paper from his hands.

Kruze handed him a poster. It was dry with age, and some of the words had faded away with the edges all crooked like a wild animal had been nibbling away at it. There was a blurry old portrait of a young boy, and above it in large writing: MISSING.

"A missing person poster?" said Tibbot, raising one bushy eyebrow.

"Yes," Kruze coughed, looking horrified. "They're everywhere; look around you. There's one pinned on almost every tree."

Tibbot looked confused. "So?" he said, shrugging his shoulders without the slightest concern.

"So? Don't you understand. Don't you know where we are?"

Once again, Tibbot looked puzzled, scratching his head like a little confused child. The others stopped walking and turned back when they realised Tibbot and Kruze hadn't been following behind them.

"Err, excuse me... What's the hold-up? I thought we needed to keep it moving," said Zyra with an attitude, turning back around.

"Don't ask me. Ask the pretty boy over here. He's the one with his knickers in a twist over a few missing posters."

"Wow. You really don't know where we are, do you?" Kruze gasped. "We're in the woods... there are missing person posters everywhere... Ring any bells?"

They all stood silent, exchanging glances with one another, still with no clue what he was on about.

"OH MY GOD! Have you not heard the stories of the cannibal who lives in Craving Woods?"

"No," they all answered at once.

"My mother used to tell me stories about the large woman who lived in the woods. Said she'd eat me if I misbehaved."

Thinking deeply, Tibbot began twirling his beard, when it suddenly hit him. "Oh, hang on... I think I have heard this story before," he laughed. "It's just a creepy old story mothers tell their wee ones to behave themselves. My missus used to tell our girls about the large hungry woman who lived in the woods when they were naughty. They never believed her, of course, except for Huxley, poor lad wet the bed. It's nothing but an old wives' tale."

"How do you explain these posters then? Huh?" He jumped, holding one up close to Tibbot's face. "I heard people from local villages kept going missing, and not just children, adults too. I'm telling you were in Craving Woods, and if we don't leave now, we're all going to end up in a pie!"

"Stop it!" Tibbot yelled. "You're scaring poor Berwin here," he coughed, awkwardly clearing his throat.

"No he's not!" Berwin snapped. "It's going to take a lot more than some fat old hag to scare me. Hmmff. I'd like to see her try to make me into a pie," he grunted.

"Can we just please leave. We really shouldn't be hanging around these woods," said Kruze with the sound of fright in his voice, shifting his eyes from side to side cautiously.

Tibbot chuckled, holding onto his round belly bouncing up and down. It gave him such pleasure to see the greatest, most famous swordsman who ever lived cower in terror like a toddler over a silly bedtime story.

"Alright, if this so-called 'cannibal' lives in these woods, that's all the more reason for us to get the hell out of here as fast as we can," said Tibbot. "We've already wasted valuable time just talking about this nonsense. Let's go."

Walking off, Kruze took one final glance at the poster and shivered like a scared little boy. "I just hope Fen and the others make it out of these woods safely," he quietly whispered to himself. Throwing the poster to the ground, he quickly followed behind the others as fast as he could.

****

It was silent, with not even the sound of the crows or the branches creaking. Fen, Lucinda, and Gustav had woken up all the way on the other side of Craving Woods.

"Where the devil are we?" Gustav moaned in pain, wiping dusty dry mud and twigs off his clothes.

"My leg," Lucinda groaned in pain. "It hurts," she continued to cry.

Fen immediately rushed to her side like the gentleman he was. "You okay, Lucinda?" he asked.

"Well... I was attacked by geese and fell off a turtle from god knows how high above and landed in the middle of nowhere with you two useless idiots to protect me. And my leg is in agony. So... no, I'm not okay," she harshly answered.

"How dare you," huffed Gustav.

"Well, it's the truth. What good is a stable boy and a slimy frog!"

"Slimy!" Gustav gasped, feeling incredibly offended.

"Jeez, I was just trying to be nice," Fen replied, feeling rather embarrassed and scratching the back of his head.

"Well don't, I didn't ask for your concern," she snapped with a scrunched-up face, rubbing her leg. "Stupid geese," she continued to huff.

"Well, look on the bright side, at least we have the satchel Helix gave to Grazox. Could come in handy."

"How did you get your hands on that?" said Gustav.

"Must have accidentally switched bags back at the Baxters. I mean, we did leave in a rush," he replied. He stood up, shifting his eyes from side to side, his hands on his hips.

"We need to find a way out of these woods; we can't stay here," he said, scratching his scruffy blonde hair.

"No," said Lucinda, "we should stay put, the others are probably looking for us. We shouldn't go wandering around by ourselves, there might be Screamers out there."

"I've been a stable boy in the House of Grazia long enough to know that the Protectors do not delay their plans or waste time on something unnecessary to them. We are not their mission or priority, so believe me when I say they're not looking for us," Fen sternly replied.

"What do you mean not their priority? They're Protectors aren't they, so shouldn't they be... protecting us?"

"Yes of course, but you don't understand there is a war coming, the greatest war we might ever face, and they need to do everything they can to stick to the plan and not delay. Ruya and Drew are the ones that need them the most, not us. If I was them, I'd do the same thing. It's hard being a hero. You've got to make tough decisions. And I have no hard feelings towards them for not searching for us. I knew what I was getting myself into when I came along on this journey."

"Well I didn't! I didn't sign up for any of this madness. I should have just stayed at Lakeshore," she whined.

"Well, you didn't, so stop complaining and help me figure out which way to go from here."

"You can't be serious. What about the Screamers?" she shrieked.

"Trust me, there are a lot more things out there to fear besides the Screamers."

"Like what?" she said, anxiously biting her nails.

"You don't want to know."

Gustav leapt towards what seemed like a bumpy pathway paved with sticks and stones.

"Over here!" he yelled, interrupting their conversation. "Do you think it could lead us out of here?" said Gustav.

"Maybe," said Fen. "Only one way to find out, eh?" No matter what tough situation Fen found himself in, he always somehow managed to stay in high hopes and continued to smile, even through the darkest of times.

After a very long while nagging, Lucinda finally got up and followed Fen and Gustav down the mysterious lane, limping on her bad leg. Too afraid to stay alone, she realised she didn't have any choice but to follow them, even though she complained all the way. Some time had passed, and the woods got slightly darker as they walked further and further down the path.

"Toilet break," Fen jumped, quickly rushing behind one of the bushes behind an old oak tree. "You guys need to go... guys?"

"AAHHH!"

"Guys?"

Hearing Gustav and Lucinda scream in distress, Fen immediately jumped from behind the bush, rushing to their side, but they were gone.

"Up here," Lucinda squeaked. He looked up only to see them panicked and helplessly caught, tangled in a net trap like wild animals.

"Don't worry, I'll get you down." He looked around cluelessly, hoping he would see a large stick to poke the net with or a sharp rock to try and cut the rope, but he found nothing of the sort, only small twigs and a few blunt stones.

"Fen... Fen, someone is coming. Hide," Gustav whispered. Fen speedily bolted back behind the bush and hid. The sound of wheels and hooves got louder and clearer the closer they approached.

"What do we have here?" a high-pitched voice giggled excitedly like a little child.

Two scrawny men jumped off a wagon and approached the trap, creepily grinning up towards Lucinda and Gustav. Their clothes were tattered and of poor quality. With their filthy hands, they pulled out their spears, poking up through the net and almost piercing them both.

"Stop!" Lucinda screamed.

"Release us at once!" said Gustav, with his voice calm and authoritative. The two men laughed, showing their crooked, discoloured teeth like a couple of naughty little boys.

"Looks like we've got ourselves a proper one here. Madame's never tasted frog before," the scrawny ragged man sarcastically grinned. Most of his teeth were missing.

"What did he mean by that?" Lucinda whispered, horrified.

The men pulled on the rope, lowering the trap down and dragging them along the rough pathway towards their wagon, and violently slung them in the back, still tangled and unable to escape. Fen, from a distance, watched and observed, trying to think of a rescue plan, but it was too late for that, for they were already on the move. He quickly and discreetly followed behind the wagon, trying to keep up and not be spotted.

"How much do you think we'll get this time?" said one of the men.

"They should be worth two coins each at least," the other answered excitedly, whipping his horse to move faster. After what seemed like a lifetime of running, Fen, exhausted from chasing the wagon on foot, stopped, catching his breath when he realised the wagon had slowed down and halted. He quickly hid behind the nearest tree.

Where had they taken them? he wondered suspiciously, feeling very uneasy with a bad feeling in the pit of his stomach. He secretly watched the scrawny men jump off the wagon from a distance. Wherever they were, it couldn't have been good, that much he knew. The wagon had stopped outside a small cottage that rested in the deepest parts of the woods. When Fen looked closer, it was much more than what meets the eye. He realised he had only been looking at the entrance of something far greater. Behind the small cottage and hidden, camouflaged with trees, stood a massive three-story castle-like mansion. The building was old, constructed with an abundance of bay windows that filled the old house from top to bottom, and on the side of the house was a large watermill turning slowly while the water flowed into a murky pond.

"What is this place?" he whispered to himself.

The men grabbed the net and dragged Lucinda and Gustav, who were kicking and screaming, desperately trying to break free from the trap. They hauled them over to the front door and knocked four times.

"LET US GO!!" cried Lucinda helplessly.

"Shut up! Be quiet, you stupid girl. And stop jiggingly about," said one of the men impatiently, kicking both her and Gustav, silencing them both.

The front door opened to reveal a well-dressed, pompous looking man in fine red velvet with golden embroidered cuffs. With his large pointy nose stuck high up in the air, his enormous nostrils flared, looking down at Lucinda and Gustav.

"What do you have for me?" he said in an eloquent manner. The man was clearly a toffee-nose.

"A beautiful young girl and a large..." Giggling, he stopped mid-sentence. "Frog," he continued.

"A frog?" the doorman replied, raising one of his eyebrows so high it looked as if it were about to come flying off his forehead. "Well now, Madame has never tasted frog before; this would certainly be a treat for her."

"That's exactly what I said," the scrawny man spat, excitedly nudging his friend on the shoulder.

Raising his eyebrow once again, he reached into his pocket and pulled out a little coin purse made from green silk. "Hold out your hands," said the doorman.

So the men did what they were told and happily reached out their hands, expecting payment of two shiny gold coins each, but only received one.

"Hang on a minute... what's this?" one of the men spat in anger. "They're worth at least two coins each. Pay us what we're owed or we'll take them elsewhere."

"I'm afraid you're mistaken; Madame does not dish out coins that easily. You get paid what you deserve and unfortunately bringing her a frog half the size of a man does not get you two coins. I suggest in future you bring her something more fulfilling if you want full payment."

"Well, we're not leaving until we get paid what we were promised." The two men grabbed the net, dragging Lucinda and Gustav away from the door. The doorman, without the slightest bother, calmly clicked his fingers and out rushed four guards who grabbed the two bandits without a struggle, dragging them both into the house along with Lucinda and Gustav. Before closing the door behind them, the doorman stopped and turned around when he heard the sound of a branch cracking in the distance. Standing there for a few seconds longer, he suspiciously shifted his eyes from side to side, then eventually closed the door behind him. Fen quietly crawled away from behind a tree, hid Grazox's satchel, and with a quick pace, tiptoed towards one of the windows and peeped inside.

"Lock them up in the dungeon," the doorman said, referring to the two scrawny men. "And take those two to the kitchen dungeon."

As he secretly watched, he saw the guards taking Lucinda and Gustav away, screaming and begging to be released.

"I have to help them," he whispered, desperately searching for a way in. He searched on the side of the house, hoping for a secret entrance but found and climbed up the old watermill instead and luckily squeezed through a window that had been left open halfway. Making it in the house without being spotted, he quickly ran to the other side of the long creaking corridor when he heard someone coming. Two maids walked by gossiping; the house was full of servants; it was going to be impossible to stay out of sight.

He had to think of a plan and quick. He followed the maids into the laundry room where there were piles of dirty uniforms that the servants wore and hid behind an old dusty shelf and overheard them talking.

"Looks like the chef's preparing another grand feast tonight," said one of the maids.

"Hmmff, if that fat old hag gets any larger, we'll have to build her a bigger house," the second maid giggled.

"Did you see what they brought in today? Some measly girl and a scrawny frog of all things. As if that's going to appease Madame's appetite."

"Well, it's been slim pickings lately since all the local villagers have moved away. Just got to make do with whatever we find in the woods."

"Well, if the bandits don't start bringing more to the table, it won't be long before the servants start disappearing."

After loading their baskets with dirty laundry, their voices got further away, and they closed the door behind them. Fen quietly crawled out from behind the shelf with the maids' strange conversation stuck in his head, leaving him feeling uneasy and frankly quite creeped out, even though he hadn't quite understood what he had just overheard.

Without a second thought, he grabbed one of the uniforms and quickly wore the attire over his own clothes, giving him the advantage to move freely among the others. He searched the house looking for the kitchen, knowing that was where Lucinda and Gustav had been held captive, but where was it? The house was very well proportioned, and he didn't have the first clue where to start. He found himself in a luxurious room filled with solid antiques and carved bookshelves that made their way around the entire room. In the middle lay a big swanky rug that covered the dark creaking wooden floorboards. The whole house was tasteful and incredibly spacious. Fen could tell just from the décor of this mansion the owner was disgustingly rich and clearly insane; from what he had seen and heard, no one normal owned this house, that's for certain. Not even kings have this many servants running around after them. *Who is this Madame they speak of?* But he had no time to waste trying to work that out. The only thing on his mind was finding the others and getting the hell out of there. Once again on the move, he swiftly moved through the halls trying his best to stay out of sight. Even though he wore a uniform, Fen knew that wasn't enough to keep him out of trouble; he needed to be cautious at all times.

Pressing his pale hands against one of the large carved doors, he was suddenly stopped.

"Boy!"

Fen hesitated before turning around. In panic he felt his heart pounding out of control, his forehand was clammy with sweat that lightly drizzled down his face. Wiping his sweaty head with trembling hands, he finally turned, facing the man that was calling.

"Yes… sir," he replied, with a shake in his voice.

"Servants are prohibited from wandering around the mansion," the man sneered seriously. "What were you doing?"

"I'm sorry. I got a bit lost… I'm new here."

"That's right, I heard talk of new servants joining us. Nevertheless, you should still know not to go poking your nose around where it doesn't belong. Your place is in the kitchen." The man roughly took Fen by the arm and led him away from the forbidden parts of the house.

"Girl!" he yelled from across the hall, snapping his fingers loudly at one of the servants wobbling by holding large pots and pans.

"This here is… boy, what did you say your name was?"

"Jasper," Fen sharply answered, not even thinking twice about it.

"Jasper here is one of the new ones, show him to the kitchen where he could be useful. I'm sure Chef is very busy this evening and needs all the helping hands he can get."

"Right away, sir," the maid politely replied. "This way," she said, leading Fen in the right direction. Walking down a large wooden staircase, the girl wobbled about trying to maintain her balance but managed to hand Fen a few of the pots. The man watched them for a while with his arms crossed, then eventually left and yelled at another servant that had been walking by, grabbing his attention.

"I'm Susie, by the way."

"Fe… Jasper," he replied nervously.

Susie was small and had a cute round face. She had short curly red hair with bangs, bright green eyes, freckles, rosy, pink cheeks and a tiny round button nose and the kindest smile.

"I know, you already told me your name," she giggled. "Listen, you had a lucky escape, if you wasn't a newbie, you would have been seriously punished wandering around the house like that."

"Sorry," he whispered with an awkward smile. "So… we're going to the kitchen, are we?" he suspiciously asked with a slight grin, thankful he didn't have to go wandering about looking for it himself.

"Yes… why?" she replied, wondering why he looked so optimistic about it.

"No reason, I was just curious about this big feast I keep hearing about, that's all."

She paused, almost like she knew he was hiding something. "Take my advice, newbie. If you don't want to end up as a dish on Madame's table, I suggest you stop acting so shady."

"What do you mean?" he said.

"I know you're not one of the new servants cause I was the one who showed them what's what around here, and I don't remember seeing you at all."

Fen took a large gulp, trying to wipe his forehead but struggled to do so with all the pots he was holding.

"I…"

"Relax. You don't need to explain." She smiled. "You're not the first one who's broken in here in disguise, you know, but things didn't end so well for those who did. You're curious what goes on in here. I understand that, but you really must leave; it's not safe."

"Believe me, I don't want to spend another second in this house, but I must find my friends. They were taken against their will and brought here. I need to get to that kitchen; I think that's where they're being held."

"Oh dear." Susie paused.

"What?"

"Were your friends a rude blonde girl and a stuck-up, well-spoken frog?"

"Yes, that's them. Will you help me get them out of here?"

Susie paused with fear in her eyes. She knew very well the consequences if she got caught helping him.

"Look, I could take you to them, but that's all I'm afraid," she whispered, shifting her eyes from side to side, making sure the other servants hadn't overheard them.

"That's good enough, thank you," Fen smiled with relief.

"But we better hurry, Chef works fast."

"Yes, about that. What is this great feast everyone keeps mentioning, and who is this Madame lady?"

"Wow," Susie gasped. "You really don't know where you are, do you?"

"Should I?" he replied, confused.

"Did your mother not ever tell you about the cannibal who lived in Craving Woods, who kidnapped local villagers and passers-by who got lost in the woods?"

Fen paused, thinking deeply about it, trying to remember. He knew what Susie was saying sounded familiar, but somehow he had forgotten the haunting tales of Madame Balina. His eyes widened, almost popping out of their sockets. His eyebrows raised so high they could have touched the ceiling. His face was flushed with fear, just like when his mother used to tell him the stories when he misbehaved as a young child.

"Oh my god!" he gasped, finally remembering. "She's going to eat Lucinda and Gustav, isn't she. That's what the others were talking about in the laundry room… I think I'm going to be sick," he gagged, turning green with one hand over his mouth and the other pressed against his stomach.

"Calm down, Jasper. We'll get them out before that happens, don't worry."

"Fen."

"Excuse me?" said Susie.

"My name's not Jasper, it's Fen."

"Well then, Fen, let's go save your friends."

MADAME
CHAPTER THIRTEEN

A large puff of smoke appeared in the halls of Grazia.

"What do we do now, sir?" said Oba, back from their visit from Oro City.

Sir Abner turned his head to Oba and Sir Arkin, and with his pale wrinkly hand, he straightened out his long white silky beard. And with his thumb, he pressed his bushy eyebrow to one side, something he often did when he was frustrated.

"I always knew deep down going back to Oro City would be a waste of time. Mortals are difficult creatures... too set in their hateful ways."

"Maybe we'll have better luck with the Spellborns," said Sir Arkin.

"I hope so, my old friend. We're going to need all the luck we can to raise an army large enough to overthrow the queens. I pray the Spellborns will see sense and join their forces with our own and not be so blinded by the past like that fool Genzo. But if not, then we'll just have to rely on Grazox and the others to find us strong allies to fight by our sides."

"Off to Spellenborg it is then," said Sir Arkin, grabbing his sceptre.

"Off to Spellenborg indeed," Abner sighed, setting out on their journey once again.

***

"Susie... Susie, where are you?" a panicky Fen cried out in fear for the housemaid.

"Over here, you twit," she whispered. Secretly lurking around a narrow corridor, she waved her hand about to grab his attention.

"Thought I lost you," he whispered, nervously taking a large breath, leaning on the wall with his hand pressed against his chest.

"Didn't I tell you not to leave my side? This house will swallow you like a black hole; it's very easy to get lost if you don't know your way around. Now for the love of god, stay close to me."

"Not a problem," he quickly responded, grabbing her by the arm. For a stable boy, Fen was usually quite brave and heroic, usually nothing ever scared him. But this time was different. Just the idea that a horrifying bedtime story once told to you as a child only to grow up to find out that it was all so very real scared the life out of him. It was like your worst nightmare coming to life. Not even the Screamers managed to strike this much fear into his heart.

Susie grabbed him by the arm. "Now, remember, stay close, try not to speak too much and do exactly what you're told."

He nodded, took a deep breath, and followed her down a steep wide stone staircase that led them into the kitchen.

"Susie! Where have you been? Hurry up with those pots and pans," said Chef, turning away from a large stove made from large bricks.

Chef was a tall, gangly man with long legs and wobbly knees. He wore a candy-striped apron smeared with food stains that draped over his plump pop belly. His large chef's hat covered most of his black oily hair that was shoulder length and neatly tucked behind his ears. It was the same colour as his imperial moustache that twitched every time he gave an order.

"Sorry, Chef." Susie smiled, bringing over the pots and pans, nodding over to Fen to follow behind her.

"Who's this?" Smearing his dirty hands onto his apron, he raised one eyebrow, suspiciously eyeballing Fen up and down.

"This is Jasper. He's one of the new ones. Just showing him the ropes."

Fen's efforts to look for Lucinda and Gustav in the kitchen were to no avail. While Chef and Susie were back and forth in conversation, Fen took the opportunity to gaze about and take in his surroundings. The kitchen was hectic, with workers rushing around like headless chickens and the sounds of silverware clanking onto plates. There were mountains of giant pots and pans with some hanging from the ceiling and others on large stone stoves, and on the other side of the room, a row of wooden dressers filled with jars of seasonings and pots of honey. Nothing seemed amiss; it looked like a regular kitchen to him until he heard familiar sounds of distress coming from another staircase in the corner of the kitchen.

"Those two haven't stopped yelling since they came here. Talk about a headache," Chef complained.

"Maybe I should go and check on them and show Jasper here where we keep the prisoners," suggested Susie.

"Good idea, but don't take too long. I need you both up here."

Susie grabbed Fen by the arm and pulled him towards the dungeon door, where he heard the sound of shrieking that curdled his blood. The dungeon stairs led down to a narrow passage with cobbled stone floors. It was where they kept the odd prisoner, trapped inside the cells and birdlike cages made from old wood with large rusty locks, and hung from the ceiling. Fen looked up and was aghast when he saw Lucinda and Gustav together, tightly crammed in one of the cages hanging from the ceiling.

"FEN!" they both cried out wide-eyed, making the cage rattle from side to side.

"Sshhh," both Fen and Susie whispered with their fingers pressed to their lips. "Be quiet. We can't let Chef hear us," said Susie. Fen looked up to the others and reassured them that he had a plan to get them out of there.

"Who's she?" said Lucinda.

"This is Susie. She's going to help us get out of here."

"Well, you better hurry. I have no idea what is going on, but I heard them say something about a frog being on the menu. What do you think they meant?"

"Gustav, there is no time to explain, but we are all in grave danger if I don't get you guys out of here."

"Why, where are we?" Gustav asked suspiciously, not sure he really wanted the answer.

"Does the name Madame Balina ring any bells"

Gustav thought about it for a second with his hand pressed against his chin. "Madame Bali… HHHH," he gasped mid-sentence. "OH MY GOD. GET ME OUT OF HERE!" he cried, grabbing onto the bars of the cage.

"Shut him up," Susie snapped.

"Would somebody like to explain to me what's going on? Who's Madame Balina?" said a confused Lucinda.

"Some things are better left unknown," Gustav responded with a trembly lower lip, feeling more green than ever.

"SUSIE!" Chef shouted impatiently.

"Were coming! Fen, we must leave now before he catches on what we're up to," she said, grabbing him by the arm, slowly pulling him away from the others.

As they were about to make their departure, the cages on the ceiling suddenly began to rattle, and dust dispersed from all the cracks. The sound of big, heavy footsteps slowly creaked along above them, with dust following every step. A look of terror came over Susie's face.

"She's awake."

They all paused in fear, then Fen quickly looked back up to the cage with alarm. "Don't worry, I'll come back for you and get you both out of here," he whispered.

"Promise?" Lucinda sniffled with a tear streaming down her pale cheek, along with apprehension in her eyes.

"Scullys always keep their promises," he smiled, trying to look positive, then quickly hurried behind Susie back up the dungeon stairs.

"Quick, quick," said Chef ordering the servants around, snapping his fingers in their faces. "Madame is hungry; best we don't keep her waiting... You, boy!" Chef snapped, staring at Fen. "Jasper, was it?"

"Yes, sir," Fen nervously answered.

"Take this dish here to Madame's table."

"Right away, sir... And where would that be exactly?"

"In the dining room," Chef snapped, impatiently fiddling with his moustache.

Meanwhile, Gustav had been filling in Lucinda with the horrifying tales of Madame Balina.

"We have to get out of here!" she cried, continuously grabbing hold of the cage, rattling it from side to side like a maniac. Making a series of clagging sounds as she rattled the cage, she immediately stopped when the dungeon doors opened. Two servants pulled out a couple of prisoners from their cells, kicking and screaming as they were being dragged away. As the door shut behind them, they could still hear the prisoners crying for their lives. The dungeon fell silent once again, once the screaming had finally faded away. Gustav and Lucinda began to yell, desperately trying to break free from their cage. But they stopped once they heard the sound of sarcastic laughter coming from another cage.

"You can keep shaking that all you like; it won't set you free," spoke a husky voice with a strange accent. They turned their heads over to the row of cells but saw no one and heard only a cough in the distance. Then from the darkness appeared two filthy hands, reaching out, holding onto the rusty bars. "If you think you're getting out of here, think again," the prisoner chuckled.

"Wh... who is that? Who are you? Show yourself," said Gustav.

With no intention of revealing himself, the man just continued to laugh with a dry cough.

"By this time tomorrow, we'll all be on the menu, nothing you can do to change that," the man spoke once again with his hands vanishing back into the darkness of his cell.

Gustav and Lucinda gave each other a look of concern and continued to rattle their cage more than ever.

Trying to blend in with the other servants, Fen followed behind as they made their way to the dining room.

"Just stay calm and try not to stare too much," Susie whispered into his ear, holding a large shiny silver platter with juicy appetisers while Fen held another. One by one, the servants entered the dining room and placed the platters onto Madame's large table. The time had come when Fen could finally put a face to the name that had haunted his childhood.

"You're up next," Susie whispered. "Try not to stare at her too much."

His entire body trembled from head to toe as he tried to keep his hands steady. The platter clanged and wobbled in his sweaty hands as he took his first step forwards. The dining hall was dim and warm, lit with a thousand candles flickering and dancing around the entire room. Before he took another step, he was stopped by the eerie sound of bones crunching. As he was about to turn the corner of one of the fancy carved pillars, he stopped and gazed upon a horrifying sight of an enormous shadow on the wall. The shadow of the beastly woman had her head tilted back, pulling out a large goose bone from her mouth, licking it clean then smacked her lips together with delight.

"Mmmm," a low, blood-curdling voice groaned with satisfaction. Being too afraid to walk any further, Susie pushed him ahead, making him stumble into Madame's grand hall.

"Bring me my pudding," the thick, creepy voice spoke impatiently, slamming her large fists onto the table, making all the plates jump.

Fen took a large gulp and finally walked further in. And there she was. The large lady who was notorious for her inhuman appetite. She was so large, some of the smaller servants would need little ladders to reach her when she was too lazy to feed herself. He couldn't quite believe what he was seeing. She was a beast of a woman, enormous to say the least. He hadn't seen anything quite like it. Her rolls of fat spread out and sagged from her wide body. She was monstrously obese; he wondered how she even managed to fit in her dress that was clearly made from only the best quality fabric imported from Oro City. She sat on a large throne made from dark wood with thick red quilted padding. Her never-ending dining table was laid out with mountains and platters of food that looked like a feast for a hundred kings, and above her hung a big luxurious candlelit chandelier. Fen slowly walked over and laid down the platter on the far end of the table, hoping to quickly leave.

"Boy," said Madame, "bring that platter to me."

Fen's heart dropped to his stomach when he was given the request. Biting his lower lip, he reluctantly turned around and walked back to the table and picked up the long silver platter that was filled with all sorts of pastries. His legs almost gave way as he got closer to her. She watched him intently with great big bulging green eyes that gleamed greedily, drooling from a wide mouth with sharp crooked teeth. She tapped her long shiny red nails against the dark wood, impatiently waiting for her food. The mighty fireplace spat out embers, startling Fen as he rested the platter in front of her. She took one of the pastries and devoured it whole with her eyes still observing Fen. While he stood there helplessly, he placed his hands behind his back and put his head down, not daring to look up.

"Mmmm," she moaned enthusiastically with pleasure in a low blood-curdling tone, smacking her lips once again as she salivated.

While Madame was busy feasting, Fen discreetly peeked up and immediately his eyes were drawn to her large chubby hands that could quite possibly crush him in one go. But the size of her hands wasn't what caught his attention; it was the jewels that twinkled brightly. Each of her fingers was adorned with diamonds, red rubies, emerald and blue-purple gems. One ring in particular caught his attention; his eyes widened when he noticed an object embedded in one of the rubies. He squinted to try and get a better look. As Madame reached her large hand for another pastry, Fen caught a glimpse of the object once again, only this time he had luckily caught it in the candlelight which revealed a golden key. Two more servants walked in, placing more platters of food onto Madame's great table, which was his cue to leave, for servants was not permitted to stand around gawping. The rules were once they had placed their platters of delicacies, they immediately had to leave for the next person to serve. The servants moved like clockwork, bringing the food in and out.

"Fen," Susie quietly called out, secretly waving him over. "You okay?"

Fen took a few minutes to breathe and come to terms with what he had just witnessed. "My god, Susie, she was so much worse than what I imagined her to be. She was beastly and creepy. I had no idea where to look, especially when she was staring at me with those big bulging eyes. My whole body turned to jelly," he replied with a dry throat.

"What... she looked at you?" Susie gasped in shock. "She has never given eye contact with any of the servants before, not even Chef."

Fen paused. "Oh god, what if she wants to eat me!" he said, shivering and chomping on his nails. "We've got to get the hell out of here. I refuse to end up on one of those platters. We need to save Lucinda and Gustav and run for our lives."

"Getting your friends out is the easy part, but leaving this house is going to be a lot harder than you think."

"We could just climb out of a window; that's how I got in here," he replied.

"Fen, if it were that easy, I would have run away a long time ago, but it's not that simple, you got lucky, that's all. You see, there is only one key for the whole house, even the servants are trapped here. We're all prisoners. I'm afraid I haven't got the first clue where it is, nobody does."

Fen clicked his fingers, he suddenly remembered Madame's large sparkling ruby ring. "Oh my god. I know where it is. Her ring... the key, it's inside her ring." He jumped up.

"Her ring... of course," she laughed.

"But how would we get it?" said Fen.

"After her feast, she always falls into a deep sleep. First, we'll rescue your friends, then wait for Madame to fall asleep and steal the key."

The idea made Fen feel nauseous. "I don't like the sound of that," he said, placing his pale hand on his belly.

"Believe me, neither do I, but what other choice do we have? We either try to take it or you and your friends stay stuck in this house and become delicacies."

Some time had passed, and the house grew silent by the hour.

With all the servants finally finishing their last chores, they made their way to their chambers for bedtime. Fen and Susie knew this was the only chance they had to free Lucinda and Gustav from the kitchen dungeon.

"This way," Susie whispered, calling him over with her finger. They snuck their way down the stone stairs that led to the kitchen, then eventually the dungeon.

"FEN!" both Gustav and Lucinda jumped up, reaching out their arms as far as they could.

"Shhh," Fen whispered with his finger over his mouth, quickly looking over his shoulder. "Be quiet." Fen held up a large candle, giving Susie some light while she pulled out a thin sharp pin-like object from her apron and managed to pick the lock while standing on a wooden chair and reaching her arms to their cage as high as she could. With luck, she managed to unlock their cage on the first try. With not a single moment to waste, Gustav and Lucinda jumped out as fast as they could, and both landed on their hands and feet.

"That was easy," Lucinda sighed, brushing off her clothes.

"Don't get too ahead of yourself there, Goldie. The hard part's just begun," Susie replied, leading the way back out the dungeon.

"Wait," said Gustav and hopped over to the cell where the mysterious stranger had spoken to them. "We have to set him free; we can't just leave him behind." The stranger stood from out of the dark corner of his cell and walked closer. He had big scruffy brown hair that stood up straight, a filthy, unkempt beard, and his face was hairy with great big thick sideburns and bushy eyebrows. He had one green eye and the other bright blue that glowed like a cool sapphire.

"Much obliged for your kindness, Mr Frog," he said, reaching out his filthy hand in a friendly gesture. "Clayton, but you can call me Clay."

Gustav paused before touching the man's dirty hands but didn't want to be impolite and hesitantly shook his hand. "I'm Gustav, and this here is—"

"There is no time for introductions. We have to leave now before one of the servants wakes up and catches us," Susie snapped, releasing the stranger from his cell. They all scarpered out of the dungeon and headed towards Madam's chambers. "After a big feast, she usually falls into a deep sleep sat on her throne. We need to be careful, and whatever you do... do not wake her," Susie whispered.

Standing outside Madam's chambers, they had to quickly decide who was going to be the one to retrieve the key. "It has to be someone who is light on their feet," Susie whispered.

"I agree," said Fen. "This someone should be small, too, and slippery," he continued, with his hand on his chin. They all turned their heads to Gustav, who was nodding in agreement, not realising he was the one that had been chosen for the frightening task. He let out a small gasp with both hands flying to his chest.

"ME?" he cried as his posture stiffened like a statue. The lump in his throat didn't allow him to continue to speak and decline the task, and before he knew it he was being shoved in the direction of Madam's chambers against his will.

"Remember, the ruby ring holds the key," said Fen.

"Go on... go," they all whispered, making hand gestures for him to move faster.

Gustav entered the chambers; it was tasteful and incredibly spacious with dark wooden floors and large beams across the ceiling with another candlelit chandelier slightly smaller than the one in the dining room. Gustav silently tiptoed on his round toe pads making his way further and further into the chamber.

He instantly froze when he heard the sound of snoring coming from a very large throne made from gold and thick quilted red velvet padding.

Madame Balina had fallen asleep in her chair with her insanely inhuman hands resting on the armrest of the throne by a large stone fireplace. Gustav seeing her for the first time was utterly and completely gobsmacked. With his bottom lip trembling out of control, he moved slightly closer to her. With each step he took, her snores got louder and more aggressive. She took deep breaths in, gasping for air, almost as if she were choking, then breathed out again, making her lips vibrate while her nose made snorting sounds like a giant pig. The whole room filled with the sound of her mighty snore. Her body slid slightly down into her chair, making her look even wider. Each roll of fat on her double chin collapsed on the next as if she had no neck. Rolls of fat filled out the sides of her throne.

Gustav took a deep breath and moved closer. He eyed up each hand, desperately searching for the ruby ring in a silent panic. At last, his eyes gazed upon the key as it once again revealed itself in candlelight. As he reached his slimy webbed hands over, the sound of the fire aggressively cracking startled him, and with a deep breath, wiping his forehead, he moved closer and tried again. Her hands were monstrously large; just one finger was the size of Gustav, which could quite possibly crush him whole. He carefully placed both hands onto the ruby and, with a big gulp, gently began pulling it down. He was already halfway there, almost completely sliding it off her chubby finger. The others watched from a distance giving him encouragement by silently throwing their fists in the air and cheering him on.

"He almost has it," jumped Lucinda, biting her nails.

"He's going to do it," Fen whispered with positivity, almost stopping the blood flow in his hands by squeezing them tightly together.

"Come on, Mr frog," said Clayton.

Gustav, rather pleased, felt like a hero in the making. Seeing his friends cheering him on like that gave him such courage he felt like he could do anything. He fantasised, envisioning his portrait hanging in the House of Grazia alongside the greatest heroes to ever live, just like he had always dreamt. Bowing down, thanking the others in silence, he finally turned around to continue to retrieve the key. Shocked, he had let out a huge croak when he saw a great big green eye staring directly into his. She had woken. In a moment of panic, Gustav grabbed the key, pulling it down her finger with force and hopped as fast as he could out of her chambers.

"COME ON, COME ON! HURRY!" the others yelled, waving their hands about, jumping up and down in one spot. Madame pulled hard on a thick rope beside her throne that sounded an alarm.

"AFTER THEM!" she hollered from the top of her lungs like thunder. Slowly taking her time, she finally managed to get up from her throne and stood on her two large feet. A bunch of guards came rushing to her aid.

"THEY'RE ESCAPING. AFTER THEM!" she demanded, pointing her large finger in the direction they had escaped.

"You did it, you did it!" Lucinda cried with happiness.

"Were not out the door yet, Goldie," Susie huffed, out of breath as they were still running through a long corridor for their lives.

"Which way now, Susie?" said Fen, finally reaching the end of the corridor and catching his breath.

"This way," she said, pointing towards a large staircase.

As they ran down the stairs, they could hear Madame's voice in the distance yelling, ordering her guards to catch them. With the sound of the guards' footsteps gaining on them, they had finally reached the large front door.

"Quick! Smash it," said Susie, pointing to the large ruby ring. Clayton grabbed the ring from Gustav, and with all his manly strength, he threw it towards the ground, smashing it into a hundred pieces. Fen grabbed the key from the floor and stuck it through the main keyhole, automatically unlocking the rest of the locks. The door opened.

"LET'S GO!" Fen yelled.

As they ran off into the night, one of the guards managed to grab Gustav, forcefully dragging him back towards the house.

"HELP. HELP ME!" he yelled to the others, but they were already out of sight, trying to get away as fast as they could themselves.

Almost reaching the front door, the guard had turned around when he heard a whistle. Clayton, standing behind him, managed to grab his sword and plunge it through his belly. As the guard fell to the ground, Gustav was free and thanked Clayton for saving his life. As more guards approached, Clayton quickly grabbed hold of Gustav and flung him over his shoulder and ran into the dark woods. They ran until they couldn't hear the guards behind them any longer.

"Thank you, good sir, you saved my life," said Gustav with gratitude as the man gently helped him climb down from his shoulders once they were at a safe distance.

"No need to thank me. You could have left me back there, but you didn't."

"Gustav... Gustav. Are you okay?" said Fen, grabbing him in a panic. "I'm so sorry; we didn't mean to leave you behind. Forgive me."

"That's quite alright. Clayton here saved me." He smiled.

"Thank you," said Fen, reaching out and firmly shaking Clayton's hand.

"I'm always there for those who help me," Clayton replied, finally releasing Fen's hand from his tight grip. "I better be going," he continued.

"Why don't you come with us?" said Fen.

"Thank you, but I have a family waiting for me," he replied in his foreign accent. He looked over to Gustav and pulled out a round gold thumb ring with a wolf carved in the centre. "If you ever get into a spot of trouble, this will help you," he said.

Handing the ring to Gustav, he patted him roughly on the shoulder. And just like that, he vanished into the darkness.

"Come on," said Fen. "We can't hang around here," he continued, slinging Grazox's satchel around his shoulders.

"What's that?" said Lucinda.

"Grazox's satchel," he answered.

"You mean the one we got from Healers Town. The one Helix gave us with the stormball inside?"

"Yeah." He casually smiled.

"You mean to tell me you had that on you the whole time?"

"Yes." He smiled once again.

"You idiot, you could have used that old goat's stormball to save us a long time ago," Lucinda furiously snapped.

"Of all the ungrateful," said Susie. "We just saved your life."

"Who's talking to you?" Lucinda hissed.

"First of all, I didn't have it on me the whole time. I hid it before I entered the house. If they found it, they would have taken it from me. Secondly, I couldn't have used the stormball with us still trapped inside the house; we all would have been caught in the blizzard and frozen to death. You have to be careful when dealing with sorcery. Anyway, best we save it for when we really need to use it, which I'm hoping is never," said Fen.

Lucinda just rolled her eyes and huffed, folding her arms, not looking at them. "What situation could we possibly get ourselves in that's worse than that back there? We almost became pies! If that wasn't a good enough excuse to use the stormball, what is?" she continued to complain.

"Where to now?" said Susie, ignoring Lucinda completely.

Fen looked unsure. "Let's just find a way out of these woods first. Let's go." They all followed behind him in a line; Gustav was the last. Admiring the ring Clayton had given him, he stared at the wolf carving in the centre, and at that exact moment, he lifted his head when he heard the howl of a wolf in the distance that echoed through the dark trees.

"*Clayton*?" he whispered as his eyes wandered towards the dark forest with a suspicious look upon his face.

"Hurry up!" yelled Susie, as he was taking his time at the back.

He placed the ring safely in his pocket then quickly caught up with the others as they vanished into the night.

THE GREAT HALL
CHAPTER FOURTEEN

The entire village was on fire, burning in a sea of red. They were under attack by the Fire Queen's army of Gors and Screamers. The cries of the villagers echoed into the night. Men, women, and children ran around in chaos, searching for their loved ones, desperately trying to escape the flames from hell. A young boy watched the blazing flames rip their way through his once happy home. Surrounded by black smoke, he coughed hard, his chest making a wheezing sound. He hid behind a forest tree away from the village, like his mother had told him to. From a distance, he watched his father and mother with all their strength trying to fight off the Gors and Screamers, preventing them from heading in the direction of their son. They were brave and fought hard to keep him safe. The boy's father stood strong and fearless as he took on the queen's army, fighting like a warrior. Suddenly the Gors suspiciously stopped fighting and backed away from the boy's father.

His face burned with rage. "COME ON, YOU COWARDS!" he yelled, fearlessly gripping tightly to his axe. But still the Gors did nothing. The boy's father looked over to his wife, who cried out his name in a high-pitched tone. Blood spat out from his mouth as a jagged black sword plunged clean through him. Kang, the Fire Queen's Henchman and Head Commander of the Gors, roared ruthlessly as he stood behind him, violently pulling his sword back out, kicking the boy's father's lifeless body to the ground. The man's wife cried in rage, grabbed a sword off the ground and bravely ran towards the Fire Queen's Henchman like a warrior on a battlefield, ready to defend her husband's honour. But it was no competition, for her strength was no match for the queen's henchman. She tried to plunge the sword through his armour but failed, for the general was far too quick. With his large rough spiky hand, he grabbed her by the neck, squeezing at the throat tightly. With amusement, he watched her gasp for air. Nevertheless, despite the agonising pain she was in, she tried to bravely raise the hand that was still tightly holding the sword. He grabbed it from her hand. Finally releasing her from his deathly grip, he roughly threw her to the ground. The Gors surrounding him held her down, forcing her to her knees. As he loomed over her like a dark shadow, he raised his sword to her head. Still not frighted, she spat in the general's direction with no sign of regret. With a vile smirk, he lifted the sword once again.

The boy in the distance watched on edge as his eyes welled up; he wanted to help his mother but also keep the promise he had made to her and hide, no matter what he saw. As the general raised his sword, the boy quickly looked away as he cried, burying his face deep into his arms, shielding himself from the horrifying sight that would haunt his thoughts forever. He took a few seconds before looking back up again. Finally when he did, he saw his mother's lifeless body on the ground alongside his father's. After all the destruction and chaos, General Kang and the Gors were on the move again, heading towards the next village.

Watching them leave, the boy peeped his little head from behind the tree. Then suddenly, Kang eerily turned back around. With a large blazing flame dancing in-between them, his eyes flared mercilessly as he watched the boy from a distance. He raised his jagged black sword high up in the air and pointed it towards the boy, warning him he would be next. The general's malicious sarcastic grin left chills down his spine, making him sweat and tremble in fear. The boy turned his head with the sound of a twig snapping behind him. A Screamer emerged from the darkness, grabbing him in his clutches, dragging him away into the shadows. Its scream was the last thing he heard.

Tobin's eyes snapped open from his dark nightmare. Covered in a cold sweat, he rapidly sat up, holding his chest tightly with his heart pounding out of control. Shaking with confusion and dizziness, he looked around, wondering where he was. His eyes shifted from side to side with suspicion and paranoia, thinking he was still trapped in his dark nightmare. His forehead dripped with sweat. He looked over and sighed with relief when he saw his uncle Grazox fast asleep beside him.

"Nightmare?"

Tobin turned his head to Drew. She was lying on her side with her head relaxed in the palm of her hand. Igor, fast asleep beside her, continued to snore. At first, he didn't respond and just ignored her, trying to get comfortable, punching the lumps out of his bag and trying to make a comfy pillow. Feeling the tension leave his body, he felt a lot more relaxed now he knew he wasn't still stuck in his horrid nightmare. He took a deep breath in and closed his eyes, trying to fall back to sleep, when suddenly, he opened one eye, feeling annoyed when Drew decided to speak once again.

"You know, you've been waking up in sweats almost every night now. Must be some nightmare," she said. He still continued to ignore her, but that didn't stop her from talking anyway. "I hate nightmares. It's funny I haven't had one since Lakeshore. Except that one night whe—"

"Look, I don't want to be rude, but I'm trying to get some sleep, and you talking doesn't really help," he replied, feeling a little frustrated.

"Sorry," she whispered, biting her lower lip, watching him once again turn his back to her.

It was a gentle night with only the sound of a soft breeze sweeping through the grassy cliff overlooking the dark ocean. She closed her eyes and listened to the stars whispering, almost as if they were trying to share their secrets with her. Drew fell into a deep daydream lying flat on her back with her head resting in her arms folded behind her head. She gazed up towards the dark velvet sky that sparkled and glittered with stars. Some were in clusters of faint and bold light. A shooting star shot across the sky, and in that moment, Oba's words replayed, echoing softly in her mind: '*You have the power of the universe beating through your heart; you are the daughters of Zivot. The King of Gods.*'

Tobin turned to his side and caught a quick glimpse of Drew staring off into space. He secretly watched her for a short while. Drew, who was completely unaware of her surroundings, still stuck in a deep daze, hadn't noticed him at all.

"What was it about?"

Finally snapping out of her stargazing, she turned her head to Tobin. "What?"

"Your nightmare. You said you hadn't had one since Lakeshore, except that one night. What was it about?" he asked, trying his best not to seem too curious.

"Wasn't so much a nightmare, more of a fear really," she replied.

"Which is?"

"Loneliness. In my nightmares, I'm always lonely."

"And that scares you?" he said, slightly lifting his head up and showing a little more interest in what she had to say.

"It used to; I mean I've always been alone. But after Ruya and finding out what I really am, I stopped having those dreams." She paused and continued to stare at the sea of stars above with admiration in her dark eyes. "I swear I can hear them whispering sometimes," she said with a soft sigh and a twinkle in her eyes. "I know we're in danger, but... ever since coming here to this place, I've never felt safer. I finally feel like I belong somewhere, and I have a family watching over me," she continued to address the stars above. She then turned to her side, and they both found themselves awkwardly face to face. With his cheeks blushing, he quickly cleared his throat and shifted his eyes away from hers.

"You were calling out for your parents. You have been almost every night now. I take it that's what wakes you up in a harsh sweat."

Tobin paused, unsure of how to respond. "I don't really want to talk about it," he said with sorrow in his broken voice.

"Of course, I understand," said Drew, scratching her little round nose, trying not to pressure him too much.

"Let's just say you're not the only one who fears ending up alone."

"At least you have your uncle," Drew replied, rolling from her side, staring back up towards the night sky once again.

"Yeah. My uncle is the strongest person I know, he's been more like a father than an uncle. He's always been my rock, always has my back. Don't know what I'd do without him."

"You're lucky." Drew smiled.

Grazox had overheard their conversation, which left a soft smile on his face.

"You look like her."

"Who?" said Drew, shifting her eyes towards Tobin.

"Raina. His daughter."

They both said nothing and continued to watch the stars twinkling above them. Grazox slowly opened his eyes; a tear drizzled down his pale face when he heard his daughter's name. The memory of his daughter was far too painful to bear. He couldn't even say her name, he would try, but no words would ever come out.

The soft, cold breeze gently blew through the night. All was still and fast asleep. Like a typical hobgoblin, Igor snored through the whole night while the Skyrider made a soft wailing sound that echoed through the night's breeze.

"Rise and shine. Come on, you lazy bunch!" Grazox clapped loudly, waking the others, for morning had come.

"On the move again," Igor yawned, stretching out his arms as wide as he could.

"Where to now?" said Drew, rubbing her tired eyes.

"We need to get to Zehir Island. There will be a large army there ready to fight alongside us in the war to come. It's also where you will start your training," he said, turning his head to her.

"Training?"

"Yes. You need to learn how to fight and defend yourself. We can't always rely on magic to save us. Non-magic folk can only rely on their wits and their strength."

"How do we get to the island?" said Tobin.

"We'll have to travel by sea, taking the Skyrider on such a long journey would be a far greater risk. There will be mighty winds ahead and a lot more Sky Sprites to deal with and believe me you don't want a repeat of that. We might not be so lucky next time."

"But we don't have a boat. How would we travel by sea?" said Drew.

"On that," he smirked, handing over his spyglass. Standing on the edge of the cliff, she took the spyglass from his hand and pointed it out towards the sea. At first she saw nothing but the blue ocean, shifting it slightly to the left, she spotted a gigantic old ship.

"Who are they?" she curiously asked, squinting, trying to get a closer look.

"Pirates," Tibbot answered.

"Can we trust them?" said Tobin.

"You can never fully trust a pirate, but they're our best bet for reaching Zehir Island. We're going to convince them to fight with us; the captain's men are fierce and have a high reputation for winning battles."

"It's going to take a lot of convincing. Pirates have a hard time trusting outsiders," said Igor.

"All we have to do is convince the captain, and the rest of the men will follow like a moth to a flame. Pirates are, and always will be loyal to their captain."

The salty sea air blew through the grassy cliff. They stood still and continued to watch the pirates from a distance while quickly conjuring up a plan to approach them.

***

The large doors to the great hall swung open. Two guards entered, each holding onto an arm of a scrawny man.

"What is his crime?" asked Lord Genzo, sneering down his nose at the man as he sat high up on his throne, impatiently tapping his fingers on the side of his gold armrest.

"He snuck into the city, my lord. He was trying to sell livestock."

"A farmer?" Genzo sneered angrily.

"Ye... yes, my lord," replied the farmer with regret in his sad eyes. "Ever since our village was burnt down, my family are not doing too well, my lord; things are very difficult at the moment. My little daughter is sick, so I thought... If I came here, I could—"

"You could what?" Genzo chuckled. "Sell your livestock?" he continued sarcastically.

"I just thought a place as wealthy as Oro City, I could maybe make a few—"

"Make a few what... money?" Genzo laughed, once again mocking the poor farmer. "My poor man, there is a reason why Oro City is so powerful and wealthy. It's keeping the likes of you and your kind on the other side of those gold walls. What did you think... hmm? That you could just show up as an outsider with your farm animals, and the men and women of this city would feel pity for you and reach out a helping hand. Pathetic. Oro City is not a charity, and you do NOT belong here. Take him away." Lord Genzo raised his hand and gently waved it effortlessly as he ordered his men to take away the poor and helpless farmer.

"PLEASE, MY LORD. I HAVE A FAMILY! THEY NEED ME," the farmer desperately begged as he was dragged away. "MY LORD... PLEASE." The large doors slammed shut, and as they did, the cries of the farmer faded away like a ghost.

"Who's next?" asked Genzo picking at his nail.

"His name is Helix Higgles, my lord."

"Higgles? The famous healer?"

"Yes, my lord."

"And what crime has Mr Higgles committed?"

"The making and selling of illegal potions, my lord."

"Send him in." Genzo nodded. Once again, the large doors opened, and within seconds the lords could already hear Helix complaining, yelling before he even entered the great hall, causing the guards great grief.

"Unhand me, you halfwits. Don't you know who I am? I'm the great Healer Higgles!"

"Ah, Mr Higgles, we finally meet. I must say your name travels far. I've heard rumours you're quite the potion maker, isn't that right?"

"That's right," he responded with an attitude, scrunching his bushy eyebrows.

"Well, as you know, Mr Higgles, you have been summoned to court for selling illegal substances. Love potions, to be exact," he continued to read a scroll. "We here in Oro City sneer upon any form of magic, including potion-making."

"Well, if that is the case, what am I doing here among mortals? I should have been summoned to the Great Hall of Spellenborg, where I could be judged by folks whose lives revolve around magic. Be around my own kind. It's my right."

"If it were under any other circumstances, you would have been sent to Spellenborg. But there are rules. Anyone using magic illegally in any form would be sent to Oro City for punishment. The kings signed a treaty in blood many years ago, making this rule very clear on both sides. It's our job to keep order. Clearly, the lords of Spellenborg are incapable of keeping a tight lid on things. Could you imagine if the mortals hadn't stepped in every time careless fools such as yourself behaved in a reckless manner? There would be chaos, and my people would be the ones paying the price. We need to punish those who disobey and break the rules; there must be order."

"Us Higgles never break the rules, you great big imbecile! How dare a mortal talk to me about magic? Me! The great Healer Higgles. You should be kissing my boots, you pompous twit."

Like most folk, Lord Genzo sat still and was taken back by the gnome's rudeness. Genzo's face changed from being still to being quite serious, for he did not take too well to Helix's rude behaviour. "I must say your reputation precedes you," Genzo responded unamused, twiddling his thumbs.

"I could say the same for you. I mean. Pmmff, I heard the Lords of Oro City liked to dress in ladies' gowns but to see it for myself, well... that's something else. Who knew mortal men had such a feminine side," he chuckled. The lords sitting high above tutted their teeth, shifting their heads from side to side, feeling incredibly disrespected.

"This is a robe made from one hundred present unicorn silk. Only those in power are allowed to wear such splendid quality. It is *not* a lady's gown!" Genzo replied, gritting his teeth and feeling the need to justify himself. Which he had never done before.

"Well if you say so," Helix chuckled under his breath with his tongue to one side.

"Do you know the penalty for selling love potions? Ten years imprisonment!"

"That's outrageous!" Helix snapped. "You should be worried about murderers and thieves and those that practise black magic. Why are you wasting your time on me? And besides, we all know you people are the biggest criminals here. It's you who should be locked up."

Lord Genzo chuckled at the gnome's sly comment. "I don't think you quite understand. You see, to mortals, all magic is black magic, and everybody knows love potions are extremely dangerous. As for the murderers and thieves, well... they can do as they please as long as it's on the other side of those walls. Illegal magic is my greatest and only concern, and we here in Oro City will not tolerate such crimes."

The time had finally come for a decision. The lords whispered among themselves, leaning into each other's ears as their jewels made jingling sounds every time they moved, while Helix waited, anxiously biting his lower lip for a verdict.

"Helix Higgles. We here from the High Court of Oro City find you guilty of your crimes. You will be stripped of your rights to sell potions and medicines. And will be sentenced to prison. You will serve a ten-year sentence at Black Rock."

"BLACK ROCK!" Helix spat, raising his large bushy eyebrows in shock. "I can't be sentenced there, there has to be a mistake. Black Rock is known for imprisoning some of the most dangerous men and beasts in all the lands. Only the most evil and vile get sent there. A little fellow like me would be eaten alive; I wouldn't survive a day. I only sold a few bottles of love potions for heaven's sake; this isn't fair!."

"Yes, well, life isn't fair, is it." Genzo raised his pale hand that sparkled with jewels. "Take him away," he ordered. The guards on each side lifted Helix off his feet and carried him away towards the large doors like he was a feather.

"WAIT! WAIT." He yelled as he was carried away.

"It's far too late, I'm afraid," Genzo sighed, unbothered and shining his thumb ring.

"THE STAR... THE STAR!"

Wide-eyed, Genzo immediately sat up and raised his hand. "WAIT." The guards were almost out the door, but before they could carry Helix away, Genzo had ordered them to stop.

"What did you say?" said Genzo, leaning forward in his chair.

"I can give you information about the Star," Helix replied.

"You have information about the Star?"

"That's right." Helix coughed with a sweaty forehead.

"Tell me!" Genzo demanded.

"Do I look like a brainless halfwit to you? This little birdie won't sing until he's released. Let me go, and I'll tell you everything I know."

Genzo nodded to his guards to release him. "That's what I thought," Helix smirked, sarcastically fixing his hat back into place once his hands were free.

"Just get on with it and tell me what you know, old man," said Genzo, already losing his patience with him.

"You're hardly a spring chicken yourself. Anyway... I'm sure you've heard by now the Star has returned."

"Yes, that fool Abner informed me."

"Did he also tell you there is a great war coming?"

"Yes, he did. He wants the mortals to join forces with the Spellborns. Ha!"

"Well, you might have to because the Star isn't the only thing that has returned. There's rumours of the Evil Queens waking from their dark slumbers. Apparently they already have a large army waiting for their arrival."

"So I've been told," Genzo sighed. "I did not set you free to talk about the queens, I want to know what you've heard about the Star."

"And if I tell you, you'll clear my sentence, and I won't be stripped of my rights to make potions and sell medicine?"

Genzo effortlessly raised his hand to his chest. "On the honour of the lords, I swear to clear your name and drop all charges," he replied, rolling his eyes. "Now, tell me what you've heard!" he snapped, slamming his palm on the side of his throne.

"It's not so much what I've heard... but what I've seen."

Genzo sat up with his back straight. "You've seen the Star?" he gasped.

"Yep," he smirked, feeling smug.

"What did it look like in person?" he asked curiously.

"Well, to be honest, not much. The Star hides in the form of a human girl."

"So the whispers are true?" Genzo smirked, scratching his chin with his thumb that held a bulky gold ring.

"Yep, and she travels with Grazox and his men. Abner sent out his Protectors to seek others to build their army." As Helix continued to share very vital information, Genzo had finally come down from his high chair and made his way over to him.

"We have certainly lots to discuss, my friend. Shall we continue this somewhere private?" he said, placing his hand on the old gnome's shoulder.

"I would prefer if we continued this conversation over dinner. All this information is making me hungry. Not to mention information like this doesn't come for free." Helix grinned, slowly rubbing his fingers to his thumb, with his beady eyes wandering around the room.

"Of course," Genzo smirked. "Hickman here will take good care of you," Genzo said, clicking his fingers to one of the servants to go with Helix. "I'll join you shortly." As Helix walked away with the servant, Genzo called over another worker and whispered in his ear.

"I want a list of all the Protectors Abner sent out and anyone travelling with them. Search the sea, search the sky. I want them found. I want posters and scrolls plastered all over every city, village, and farm in the realm. A hundred gold coins, dead or alive. Any young girl travelling with them is to be unharmed and brought to me. Do I make myself clear? Unharmed!"

"Yes, my lord." The servant nodded.

"Good. Now go!"

Genzo walked onto a large marbled, wide-open balcony overlooking the whole of Oro City that lit up in the sunlight. He stared off into the distance with his hands behind his back. The light hit his face, with streaks of gold rays lighting up his pale blue eyes. "So, Abner. Looks like you were telling the truth after all. Too bad your Protectors won't be able to build you that army. I'll make sure of it."

SEA RAIDERS
CHAPTER FIFTEEN

The day dawned crisp and clear. The seagulls danced around one another, squawking in the bright blue sky, fluttering their wings chaotically to the soft breeze that gently whispered through the cool salty air. It was a perfect day for sailing; Drew could almost taste the salty sea on her lips already. The time had come to contact the pirates. With no more precious time to waste, Grazox and the others quickly gathered their belongings after taking one final glance out to sea through the spyglass. "Let's move," said Grazox, climbing onto the Skyrider, reaching out his large hand and pulling Drew closer towards him, helping her climb aboard. "We need to be careful. The pirates mustn't see us before we board the ship. They will get suspicious and think we are a threat and try and bring us down before we even get close," he continued.

"How are we going to board the ship without being seen?" said Drew, with her arms tightly wrapped around Grazox's large waist.

"We'll fly low and sneakily climb aboard; it's the only way."

"Aero could fly ahead and make sure it's clear," said Tobin, while he and Igor climbed onto the Skyrider behind them.

"Sounds like a plan," his uncle replied as they took to the sky. Pirates were famously known for their fierce and reckless behaviour; they obeyed no one and trusted no one that wasn't their own. The rules of the sea were that anyone who wasn't a pirate was an enemy. As they moved closer towards them, Drew found herself completely enthralled with the unnatural, eerily magnificence of the ship's structure; it was nothing like what she had expected. At three storeys high, the ship was bulky, made from dark, worn wood with brass bolts, large, rusted cannons and black sails that resembled scaly dragon's wings. The sides of the ship were encrusted with skulls and bones that curved their way around to the figurehead, where an even larger skeleton of what seemed to be a beastly troll stuck out as the main attraction; it almost looked as if it was trying to escape. The image of this ship was enough to scare off any enemy. No one ever dared to approach.

As they flew closer, Drew felt her heart racing with fear and excitement, she wasn't sure which one she felt more. In danger of being spotted, they flew low, so low that the Skyrider's belly was skimming, touching the ocean below them as they kept to a safe distance, gliding behind the pirates. Igor grabbed onto Drew as if his life depended on it.

"You okay, Igor?" she said, slightly turning her head while a loose strand of her raven black hair flickered in her face, whipping her eye, and making it water.

"No," he gasped, choking on the wind, barely able to talk as he tightly gripped onto her waist while his large droopy ears fluttered back in the wind like wings.

"What's wrong?" she said.

"Didn't you know goblins hate water? Especially hobgoblins," said Tobin, who sat behind Igor.

"But, what about Stormville? You didn't seem to mind the river and the rain back then?"

"The ocean is different," Igor squeaked, with his eyes still shut tight. "It's full of danger. How could you compare it to a bit of rain?" he continued.

"I wouldn't have called that a bit of rain. I thought we were going to be washed away at one point," Drew chuckled with a boyish smirk.

"Be quiet, all of you," Grazox sternly muttered under his breath as they flew closer towards the ship. Grazox turned his head towards his nephew and gave a slight nod as a go-ahead.

Tobin whispered to Aero, who was clutched onto his shoulders. "Now," he said to his pet eagle. Aero fluttered away, flying high above, trapping the wind beneath his wings, gliding through the air, analysing the ship like a map. With his bright yellow eyes, he watched the pirates like a predator stalking its prey. Eventually, he came back down and squawked into Tobin's ear. "It's all clear. We need to board now," said Tobin.

"How do you know it's safe?" said Drew.

"Didn't you just hear him? He said it's clear."

"All I heard was a squawk," Drew replied with confusion, raising one eyebrow.

"That's because you don't listen. Don't expect you to understand," he seriously replied.

With her face burning with anger, Drew snapped. "I've just about had it with your attitude. Who do you think you ar—"

"Hush!" Grazox strictly commanded under his breath.

Grazox gently leaned forwards. "Take us higher," he whispered to the Skyrider. Discreetly, they stood and tiptoed onto the Skyrider's shell with their noses perfectly aligned with the quarterdeck as they watched the pirates who were at the far end of the ship. The coast was clear, and Grazox was the first to carefully climb aboard. Reaching out his hand, he helped Drew, who was up next. He pulled her onboard with his eyes cautiously shifting back and forth while helping the others after her.

The pirates looked far too busy exchanging gory stories, acting them out in a childish manner and spilling their rum all over the deck to even notice intruders boarding the ship. "This way," Grazox whispered, directing them with his finger as they headed towards the captain's cabin.

"What are you doing?" Drew whispered beneath her breath.

"We need to find the captain."

"Why?" she asked, discreetly shifting her eyes towards the pirates who got louder and louder with each battle story they told, laughing, and falling over themselves like drunk monkeys.

"The captain is the one we need to convince. Stop questioning me and do as you're told," he replied, growing restless with her questions.

Without another word, the others followed behind him. The wooden decked creaked through the wind, whispering, almost speaking to those who listened. Some say you could still hear the weeping souls of those who lost their lives at sea. There are even stories about the old ship, how at midnight the bones of the dead would come to life and get drunk beneath the stars. Some sea folk have even claimed to have had the pleasure of exchanging battle stories with the dead beneath the jewelled midnight sky.

Grazox and the others had secretly managed to find the captain's cabin without being spotted by the pirates, or so they thought. Before they could even approach the door that would have led them to the captain, a sudden darkness covered their eyes, like a great black cloud had fallen upon them. They were brutally dragged away, with each of them being roughly manhandled by the pirates. Drew tried to yell, but she couldn't. Through a tiny rip in the sack that was put over her head, she could only make out a few blurry faces. Through the darkness, she heard the pirates with their rough voices, laughing, speaking over one another like impatient children. Suddenly the sound of the pirates' mumbles had suspiciously stopped. All was silent. The only thing she could hear was the seagulls in the distance and her own fear, taking deep breaths in and out like they would be her last. But she wasn't fearful for herself, but for the others. If anything were to happen to Grazox, what would become of Tobin and Igor.

Even though she had never been in a situation like this before, she wasn't as afraid as she thought she would be. In some strange way she was even a bit excited. She had the same strange feeling when Miss Mabel had first told her she was special, and when Oba had spoken of the Great Star God and was told she was a Spellborn. Was she afraid because she was excited, or was she excited because she was afraid? Her emotions were all over the place, and she couldn't quite make sense of it. Since leaving Lakeshore, she couldn't make sense of anything anymore.

The pirates still remained silent until the sound of heavy boots slowly stomped across the deck, creaking, getting louder and closer with each step. Once again, Drew squinted her eyes to see who the other pirates were staring at, backing off as the mysterious figure approached. Roughly pulling the sacks off their heads, a man dressed in all black stood before them. He was bald and serious. He wore a black turban that covered most of his head, with a long braid pushed to one side with the odd gold coin dangling, decorating his braid all the way down. Black rags draped around his slender but strong body, and a large, pointed dagger in the shape of a snake was tucked to one side in his belt made from leather. And like all the other pirates on board dressed all in black, he had thick eyeliner smeared under his eyes that made its way down to his cheeks like tears of death. His name was Feroz, he was the most feared among pirates, and his name was known across the seven seas. In his eyes, anyone who wasn't a pirate was an enemy.

"I want to speak with your captain," said Grazox, tied and bound on his knees.

"You're speaking to him," Feroz replied, with a strong foreign accent.

"You and I both know you're not the captain."

Insulted, Feroz raised his hand and struck Grazox across the face. Tobin waddled about in a fit of raging anger. He wanted to help his uncle but couldn't speak or move, for he was still gagged and bound. Igor, on the other hand, kept his head down, shivering in fear.

"Oi!" Drew yelled fearlessly. "Why don't you untie him and do that, you coward! Go on, I dare you."

Feroz walked over to Drew, analysing her with his hazel eyes. Who was this young girl that spoke to him in such a fearless manner?

"Drew! Be quiet," coughed Grazox. "She didn't mean it," he continued, licking a little drip of blood from the side of his mouth with his tongue.

Feroz gazed upon Drew with his head cocked to the left, then looked back over at Grazox. He could tell he feared for her life but tried to hide it.

"You care for this girl. She is special to you," he said, pointing his dagger in her face.

"Just don't hurt her or the others. Do as you please with me but leave them out of it. They mean you and your men no harm. We only came here to speak to your captain. It's a matter of life and death."

"Nobody gets near the captain, nobody! Now you will all die for trespassing." Feroz was never the type for negotiating and wasted no time hearing what the enemy had to say. Without any hesitation, he pulled out an even larger dagger from the side of his belt and held it against Drew's soft neck.

"WAIT!" Grazox yelled. "You don't understand. We need to speak with your captain. It's important. You're going to want to hear what we have to say."

"I already told you, nobody gets near the captain." Feroz lifted his dagger high up in the air, swinging it closer to Drew's throat. Tobin and Igor watched in terror, mumbling, wriggling about helplessly. They wanted to save her, but it was impossible in the position they were in.

"WAIT! NOO!" Grazox yelled.

"What is going on here?"

Feroz immediately lowered his dagger and took a step back bowing his head out of respect. The rest of the pirates did the same as the captain approached.

Grazox, Drew, Tobin and Igor looked up and saw the captain standing before them. It was a woman. She wasn't young, nor was she old. She was dressed all in black like her men. And like Feroz, she wore a turban that was wrapped around her thick dark hair with a thin braid poking from the gaps of the fabric decorated with gold beads and one gold coin dangling at the tip. She also had tears of death smeared down her gold sun-kissed face, making her green eyes shine like emeralds in the sunlight.

"Who are you and why have you come?" she also spoke with a foreign accent.

"My name is Grazox Landa, and I have come here seeking your help."

"A bunch of trespassers coming onto my ship uninvited, and you're asking for my help. Why would I do that?" she said seriously.

"Because you and your men are in grave danger."

The captain paused, staring at the trespassers each in turn, then tutted her teeth as if to release them.

"Captain, you're letting them go?" Feroz sighed, looking frustrated, watching the men untie them.

"I want to hear what they have to say," she said curiously.

"It could be a trap."

"Feroz, my friend. Look at them. What harm could they possibly do to us, ha?" Without another word, he gritted his teeth in anger and obeyed his captain's orders. He didn't have a choice, but if he did, they would have been shark bait already.

"This way," she said, leading them to her cabin that was below deck. They entered the captain's cabin. It was made from old, dark wood that looked ready to fall apart. On her desk were maps made from leather and sacks of gold coins.

It was dim, and the only light was the odd streak of sunlight coming from a tiny round window and a few flickering candles. Out of the darkness appeared two bright gleaming yellow eyes to reveal a large panther with silky black fur. It hunched down, ivory teeth bared in attack position, as it watched Grazox and the others. Grazox moved in front of Drew, taking her by the arm and slowly pulling her behind him where she would be safe.

"Sshhh, Siyah... stay. Good girl," said the captain. "Don't worry about her, she only attacks when I tell her to. Please sit," she said, reaching out her hand.

"Forgive me," said Grazox, "but you're awfully young to be a captain of such a large crew." He finally sat down, with his eyes nervously observing every move the panther made.

"We blue bloods tend to take longer to age than most. That is why the mortals envy us."

"You're a Spellborn?" said Drew.

The captain nodded, giving a little smirk. "I must say I'm very impressed. I must congratulate you. No one has ever boarded my ship and survived to tell the tale. And believe me, there have been a few that have tried." She moved a small teacup close to her lips then took a sip.

"So, tell me. Why do you seek my help?" She shrugged, curiously leaning back in her chair, lifting her legs up, then crossing her feet on her desk. Her black boots left dirty smudges and prints on her maps.

"There will be a great war, and we need you and your men to fight alongside us. I know you have a connection with other raiders that sail the seven seas," said Grazox.

"And why would I do that, hmm? Why would I want to risk my men's lives to fight in your war?"

"It's not my war; it's *our* war. I'm sure you've heard of the Evil Queens; I'd be surprised if you haven't."

"I've heard them mentioned once or twice, yes. And what of it?" She shrugged without a care.

"Well, they will be returning soon. And everybody will be in great danger."

"We are sea folk. Whatever happens on dry land stays on dry land. It does not concern those born on the sea. This is not our war."

Grazox paused with frustration. "Do you honestly think you and your people will be safe? War will find its way to you; it will only be a matter of time. Is that what you want?"

"Let them try. They will be fighting on unknown territories. As sea folk, we have the greater advantage. They will never win," the captain laughed.

"Really?" Grazox huffed. "Then tell me, Captain, what will you do when the Cold Queen freezes over the seven seas. How will you and your men survive then? It will be a slaughter."

Lowering her legs from her desk, she leaned forward with her hands clasped together. "She could do that?" she spoke with concern, slowly raising one eyebrow.

"Haven't you heard the stories? Of course she could. That's why we need your help. We need as many men as we can get to fight alongside us. Send out a signal to your friends, call them to join us."

She leaned back in her chair and took a deep breath. "No," she huffed, feeling unconvinced.

"Fine," said Grazox, "I'm not going to waste any more time trying to convince you. But you will do something for me."

"Will I now," she smirked, with her arms folded, interested in what he had to say.

"Zehir Island, I need you to sail us there. Have you heard of it?"

"Have I heard of it?" she laughed. "There isn't an island us sea folk are not aware of. Why do you wish to go there?"

"There will be a large army waiting for us. I'm sure you've heard tha—"

"It's where the greatest warriors have trained, yes I've heard."

"Then you will take us?"

"What is in it for me," she replied, scratching her chin. "How will I benefit from taking you to the island?" she continued, making a hand gesture.

"If you take us to the island, I will show you the way to Oro City. A city made from mountains of gold and endless riches. Never again will you and your people go hungry. There will be no need for raiding other cities. You will all live like kings and queens for the rest of your days."

She was silent.

"Do we have a deal?" Grazox stared deep into her eyes with a certain sternness and held out his hand in hopes she would take it.

With a twinkle in her eye, she smiled, nodded, leaned over her desk, and shook his hand.

"Deal." She sat up from her chair. "What did you say your name was?"

"Grazox Landa."

"Yes," she said, waggling her finger in the air. "I thought your name sounded familiar. I've heard stories about the Protectors," she grinned. "I'm Io—"

"Iona," Grazox interrupted. "I've heard stories about you too. That's why I'm here. You and your men have quite the reputation."

She smiled and walked away from her desk towards the doorway and held out her hand. "Please, after you."

A couple of pirates on deck were busy wrestling each other while the others surrounded them in a circle, placing bets, yelling aggressively with their fists in the air with spit drizzling down their chins like animals. They hadn't noticed the captain standing behind them with Grazox and the others.

"Ahem," she coughed with her hands behind her back. But still they did not hear.

Feroz, with wide eyes, aggressively raised his voice at them to stop. "Captain Iona wishes to speak!"

And just like that, there was silence.

"Thank you, Feroz." The captain nodded.

"My brothers, I bring you good news. Our friend over here," she said, shifting her eyes over to Grazox, "informs me about a city. A city of dreams made from gold. And we will invade and take their riches for ourselves."

The men yelled ruthlessly, holding their swords, axes, and daggers high up in the air, eager and ready for invasion.

"TO ORO CITY!" the captain bellowed from the top of her lungs. The pirates gave one last shout, raising their weapons even higher, then scattered around the deck like rats ready to sail to the City of Gold.

"Wait a minute," said Grazox. "We had a deal. You were to take us to Zehir Island first, then we would show you the way to Oro City."

"Did I say that? Hmmff, I don't remember," she huffed, unbothered.

"Now wait a goddam minute!" Grazox growled with frustration, grabbing the captain by the arm.

Feroz immediately pulled out his dagger, but before he got any closer to Grazox, Captain Iona lifted a hand and tutted her teeth, raising her eyebrows. With his hazel eyes burning with anger, he stopped on the spot listening to her order and hesitantly put away his dagger.

"Here's the new deal," the captain spoke, calmly removing Grazox's hand from her arm. "You take us to the City of Gold, and if it is as you describe, then we will take you to Zehir Island."

Without another word, Grazox nodded. He knew there was no point in negotiating with pirates. You just had to take whatever they offered you. He was in no position to argue about it, for he had to reach Zehir Island, and the captain was the only one who could get him there. Grazox finally walked away.

"Uncle," said Tobin, "are we really going to show them the way to Oro City?"

"We have no other choice, lad."

"But won't that set us back?"

"If the captain decides to join us in the fight, it won't. But if we've done all this for nothing and they don't take us to the island, this whole journey was a waste of time, time we simply do not have."

"Feroz!" Iona yelled.

"Yes, Captain?"

"Who was supposed to be on watch?"

"Clem and Luka, Captain," Feroz sternly replied.

"Bring them to me."

Feroz followed the captain's order and came back with the two men who were supposed to be on watch.

"Ah, Luka, Clem. Tell me, what were you both doing when our unwanted guest managed to board the ship?"

Clem tried to answer, he opened his mouth, but no words came out. Luka, on the other hand, didn't bother trying to answer. He knew anything he had to say the captain wouldn't want to hear it. Luka had a black cloth draped over one eye and tied at the back of his head like an eye patch. He was tall and thin with long black hair that he kept in a man bun. He also had three gold teeth that could blind a man when he smiled. Clem, on the other hand, was the complete opposite. He was neither tall nor thin but short and plumpy and had no hair to put in a bun but had a large scruffy beard and one gold hoop dangling from his ear. Luka was the best carpenter on the ship; there was nothing he didn't know how to build or repair. And Clem was an amazing cook. He sometimes even clashed with the chef on board because the men preferred his cooking.

"I can't hear you," said the captain, still waiting for an answer. "You ever embarrass me again," she said, disgusted. "Everybody listen up!" she shouted. The crew immediately stopped what they were doing to listen to the captain. "For punishment for Clem and Luka's reckless behaviour, all the rum barrels will be locked for a week."

Chaos. With raised voices, the men blamed Clem and Luka for what they saw as the worst punishment yet. To them, it was worse than death. Some of the men hanging from the ratlines jumped down just to take a swing at them.

"You only have yourselves to blame. You all should have been aware trespassers were boarding the ship. How you missed them is beyond me. If it happened once, it could happen again. And I promise you this, the next time I won't be so forgiving. Now get back to work!"

The men did as they were told, moaning, and mumbling away, all giving shifty looks to poor Clem and Luka. "Ah. Not so fast," said the captain. "I'm not finished with you two just yet. I want you both to scrub every skull on the sides of this ship until I can see my reflection in them. Understood!"

They both nodded with their eyes gazing down at their dirty boots. They watched the captain finally walk off until she was out of sight. Clem saw this as an opportunity and discreetly pulled out a little bottle of rum he secretly kept in his pocket. Both he and Luka snorted with laughter until Feroz caught them chuckling behind the captain's back and gave them the look of death. Putting a stop to their childish behaviour. They both froze on the spot with fear, each taking a large gulp, praying that he hadn't seen the bottle of rum they were sneakily hiding.

Drew and Igor ran to the edge of the ship to get a better view of the ocean, looking up at the seagulls fluttering in the sky. Grazox gazed into the distance with a look of regret.

"Uncle?" said Tobin, placing his hand on his shoulder, sensing something was bothering him.

"The Lords of Oro City aren't going to know what hit them." With a far-off look in his eyes, he continued to gaze out towards the sea.

"Set the sails," the captain yelled. With the bright sun shining down on her, she stood behind the helm with an ambitious look in her bright emerald eyes. "To the City of Gold," she smirked with her hands clasped behind her back with Siyah standing beside her.

COLD MOUNTAIN
CHAPTER SIXTEEN

Snow flurries sprinkled down from the grey cloudy sky like specks of fairy dust. One frosty snowflake silently landed, melting on Ruya's nose. Dripping all the way down, it froze into a little icicle at the tip. The cold sent shivers down her spine. When she sneezed loudly, the icicle shattered into pieces all over poor Potion, who was deeply snuggled, tucked away into her arms for warmth.

"Brrrrr... I hate the snow," Kruze complained, viciously rubbing his hands together as they journeyed closer towards Cold Mountain. The home of frost folk, mostly known as the Vorst, who lived in a small town that rested deep in a gorge between large snowy cliffs, surrounded by icy rivers and mountains. Where the weather was always miserable with heavy snowfalls and strong gusty winds. The weather conditions were unbearable. No one could ever survive the harsh cold except for the Vorst, for winter was in their blood. They were the only people who could navigate and venture off into the cold mountains and return to tell their stories.

With his bushy beard and eyebrows frosting up, Tibbot, high above on his Skyrider, glared down at the snowy village. "How could anyone live here?" he said, nodding his head disapprovingly.

"Says the man who lives in a city where it never stops raining," Kruze chuckled, shivering in his boots with his Skyrider hovering side by side with Tibbot's.

"Rain and snow are two completely different things, pretty boy," Tibbot responded with a chuckle.

"I'm just grateful we were able to find our Skyriders in time, and we didn't have to travel all this way by foot," Zyron butted in.

"We should probably set up camp," Zyra yelled across. The flurries came down hard, getting stronger and stronger by the second. The harsh wind blew into their, already, pink sore faces and stung their eyes to the point it was difficult to keep them open.

"You're right. We'll set up camp over there," Tibbot shouted, pointing towards a snowy cliff.

"Why can't we just fly down to the village already?" said Ruya, feeling cold and exhausted from all the travelling. At this point, she wondered how she even managed to keep her eyes open, feeling so cold, tired, and hungry. With her arms tightly wrapped around Tibbot's large waist, the left side of her cheek pressed against his back slowly began to freeze from the cold. Her skin began to sting. She quickly pulled her face back before it stuck to his clothing even more, leaving the whole side of her left cheek red and sore.

"A storm is coming. Best we let the Skyriders have some rest. If we go now without the riders, it will take us at least a day to get down there by foot. We'll wait out the storm then be on the move again when it's clear enough to fly. We don't want another incident like last time. We might not be so lucky where we land with the next harsh wind we encounter," Tibbot replied. "Better safe than sorry, ay."

They finally landed their riders safely on the edge of a cliff, near an entrance that looked like a cave that they hoped would protect them from the cold storm that was heading their way. "This will have to do," Tibbot huffed. "We'll rest here for tonight, then leave first thing in the morning."

Finally settled, it had gotten dark, and the sky lit up like magic. The aurora lights filled the sky with a wave of green, purple, blue, yellow, and pink lights that shimmered, swiftly floating by as the stars twinkled brightly around it like dancing fairies gathered around a rainbow. It was a peaceful night, and thankfully there was no sign of a blizzard.

"So much for that storm ay, must have calculated it wrong. Oh well, we're all settled now, might as well have some grub and get some kip," said Tibbot, shrugging his shoulders, clapping his large hands together and getting ready to fill his empty belly with some food.

"Thank god the wind didn't blow away our food supplies," Kruze laughed.

After they made the fire, some time had passed. Ruya, with a blanket wrapped around her body and over her head like a cloak, sat by the crackling fire. Lost in deep thought, she gazed at the embers with her eyes blazing, burning bright. Feeling low-spirited, she gently sighed, resting her pale face on her arms, not listening to a word Tibbot was saying. Kneeling down while feeding the fire some more, Tibbot couldn't help but notice. He felt the gloom lingering off her like a dark cloud.

"You okay there, lass?" he said, feeling a little concerned for the girl.

"Just thinking about Drew. Wondering where she is and how she's doing. Or if she's even alive. I just hope she's okay," Ruya quietly sighed, taking Potion into her arms, sharing her blanket with the little bunny to make sure she was nice and warm.

"Trust me, lass, nobody knows Grazox better than I do. He will not let any harm come to her as I wouldn't with you. She's in safe hands. Don't you worry your pretty little head about a thing. You will see her again." He smiled, gently patting her on the head as if she was one of his daughters. Being a loving father, comforting those in their early years came quite naturally to him.

Ruya sat in silence for a while, then decided to speak again. "When you found me in the woods, you said that I was your responsibility and priority. You're the main person we need to keep safe, you said. I'm guessing you know what I am."

He smiled. "Of course I do."

"So much for keeping the secret. We were told no one outside of Grazia would know about us."

"I'm not just some stranger, Ruya. Me and Grazox go way back, we're practically brothers. And as for keeping your secret safe, well, you can trust me. Abner knows me well enough; there was even a time when he wanted me to join the House of Grazia and become a Protector."

"Really, why didn't you?" she said, curiously.

"My son was just born, and my only duties were being a good father and husband." Tibbot paused when he caught Ruya daydreaming into the fire once again with sadness.

"Even if I wasn't told about you and Drew, I still would have worked it out for myself."

"How?" she said, shifting her gaze away from the fire and into his eyes.

"Because you both glow with such purity." He smiled once again. He then took her face into his hands. "She going to be okay. You both are," he softly whispered.

Her eyes welled up, sending tears drizzling down her pale cheeks. She reached out her arms and cuddled Tibbot as tight as she could while he cradled her in his large arms.

"I'm more concerned about Fen," Kruze interrupted, ruining a sweet and tender moment, clumsily walking over, wobbling about with more firewood in his arms. "Hope the poor boy made it out of those woods alive and didn't end up in some pie on Madame's table," he continued, warming his hands by the fire with a blanket wrapped around him like a big baby, then toasted up a large loaf of bread all for himself.

"God, you don't think that would have happened, do you?" Ruya gasped, wiping her tears, sitting up with her back straight like she had just been struck by a bolt of lightning. She felt terribly worried for Fen and Gustav, even Lucinda.

"Don't listen to him," said Tibbot. "Of course they made it out safe. Fen, Froggy and the wee blonde lass probably made it out of those woods way before we did."

"But how do you know?" she said.

"I have an instinct for these things," he winked. "Now eat up. You're going to need all your strength for the morning."

Ruya took a loaf of bread from his hands and toasted it by the fire. Zyra handed everybody another warm blanket that Martha had packed for them along with hand-knitted mittens.

"What in god's name are these?" said an unimpressed Berwin, holding the mittens that Martha had kindly knitted close to his face, analysing them carefully.

"Mittens," replied Zyra.

"Mittens!" he moaned. "What good are these supposed to do? I'm freezing my boots off, and all we have are blankets and stupid hand-knitted mittens!" he continued, furiously throwing them to the ground, sulking like a little child.

"You watch your mouth there, Berwin," said Tibbot, lowering his loaf of bread away from his mouth just as he was about to take a bite. "My Martha made these for us out of the goodness of her heart. Now I put up with your constant moaning and rudeness, but I won't have you bad-mouthing my wife. We didn't have any time to prepare when we were attacked, you know that. We had to quickly grab whatever we could and escape from the Screamers. Just be grateful for whatever little we have, ay."

"Hmmff," he huffed, cosying up into his blanket. "Grateful, he says. What's there to be grateful about? I never asked for any of this. I should be at home, safe and warm, not here surrounded by danger. This isn't my fight."

Tibbot paused before taking a large bite out of his bread and gently placing the loaf onto his lap. "You're absolutely right, Berwin; you should be safe at home. But you're wrong in thinking this isn't your fight too."

"Wrong! Of course this isn't my fight," the old gnome snapped angrily with flaming red cheeks.

"If you ever want to return to that safe, warm home of yours, I'm afraid it is. We're all fighting for the same thing here, Berwin. You don't think I don't want to return home to my family? Of course I do. But there is no point returning if the queens win this war by spreading their vile darkness and destroying everyone we love. There will no longer be a safe home for any of us to return to ever again. So I guess this does make it your war after all, and anyone else for that matter who wants a safer world to live in."

Tibbot, taking the loaf from his lap, finally took a large bite. Chewing very loudly, he gave Berwin a little friendly wink to show no hard feelings. Berwin knew that Tibbot's words were true; he just hated to admit it. Gnomes would rather have their beards cut off than admit that they were wrong.

"Here you go," said Zyron, handing Ruya a small wooden bowl filled with mushroom soup. "Better eat it while it's hot," he continued kindly, handing everybody else a bowl each.

"Is there any other soup?" said Kruze. "It's just, mushrooms really give me the creeps."

"What?" Zyron coughed with confusion. "Since when?" he chuckled.

"Erm, since forever. Mushrooms have always been a phobia of mine. You knew that... didn't you?" It suddenly dawned on him that he had never actually shared his phobia with another living soul. The silence was immediately broken with laughter. The loudest was Tibbot, who almost choked on his bread.

"Afraid of mushrooms, Bahahaha," Berwin chuckled underneath his blanket.

"Yes, alright. It's really not that funny," Kruze huffed with blushing cheeks. Feeling slightly embarrassed, he pulled out his pocket mirror and began fixing his lush, thick hair, trying to play it cool in front of the others. It was because of that exact reaction that he had never told anyone about his phobia of mushrooms, worried he might be made fun of. After all, it wasn't the best image for the greatest swordsman to ever live.

"How did you expect to make it once we reach Shroom Forest?" Tibbot laughed.

"Shroom forest?" he responded, wide-eyed, immediately freezing, stopping the comb gliding through his black hair with one raised eyebrow. "You never mentioned... Shroom Forest before," he said with a heavy gulp.

"It's Grazox's job to find allies, and it's my job to find the Wise Shroom. Grazox did mention it back at Vine City. Said he may have answers that could end the war and finish the Evil Queens once and for all. Finding him is our main mission and, of course, convincing the Vorst to fight with us. That is why we're here after all," said Tibbot, slurping down his bowl of mushroom soup.

After their warm meal, everybody settled down bundled up tightly into their blankets. The night was harsh and bitterly cold, but somehow they managed to make it through the frosty night.

THE VORST
CHAPTER SEVENTEEN

Morning had come, and there was no need for a wake-up call, for the harsh snowy wind had already woke them all from their sleep. "I hate this. Thought you said it was going to be clear in the morning?" Berwin moaned, shivering with his blanket wrapped tightly around his entire body, almost resembling a cocoon. He was so tucked away all you could see were his beady eyes and his large nose poking through a tiny gap.

"I must have misread the weather," Tibbot replied, with frustration in his voice. "But we can't stay here for another night," he sighed. "We must move now before the blizzard gets any worse."

Without wasting another second standing around in the bitter cold, they packed up their belongings and hopped onto their riders once again and headed towards Cold Mountain.

"Do you think the Vorst will help us?" Zyron yelled, with his hands clasped around his mouth while his eyes flickered constantly like a burning candle, struggling to keep them open from the cold stabs of the snowflakes.

The wind blew hard, getting stronger and more violent by the second. "Fingers crossed, lad... fingers crossed," Tibbot yelled. The Skyrider slowed down as they lowered towards the ground; the cold icy wind harshly blew Ruya and the others off their riders into the snow. Zyron reached out a helping hand and pulled Ruya back up on her feet.

"HELP!" Berwin yelled in distress. Kruze reached out his hand, rescuing Berwin, who was completely helpless, stuck face down with his scrawny little legs poking out of a large pile of snow.

"Where is everyone?" said Zyra, shifting her eyes suspiciously from side to side, slowly reaching for her weapon.

"Something's not right here," said Kruze. The small village of Cold Mountain seemed lifeless. There wasn't a single soul to be seen.

"Excuse me!" Tibbot yelled, raising his hand, spotting a little old woman cloaked all in black, slowly strolling by holding a basket full of frozen fish.

"Excuse me, ma'am, where is everyone?"

"Hiding," the old woman answered with a dry cough.

"Hiding… from what?"

"We were attacked a few days ago by the Akulls," she continued, with a rusty croak in her voice.

"The Akulls… Lumi's men?" he said, raising an eyebrow.

"Yes," the old woman nodded. "Folk haven't left their homes since the Cold Queen's army ambushed our town, not even for food."

"Is there anyone in charge here, someone I could talk to?"

"Our leader," she said, pointing her crooked wrinkly finger towards the misty village. "You'll find him in the Golden Eagle."

"Thank you." Tibbot smiled with gratitude.

The old woman returned a friendly nod, then slowly limped away carrying her basket of fish under her arm, then mysteriously vanishing into the blizzard, fading away like a ghost into the mist. They searched the entire village until they stopped at a cosy tavern. Looking up, they saw a sign half covered in snow and ice, swinging back and forth creaking in the wind that read: The Golden Eagle.

"This is It," said Tibbot, placing his sore red hand on the door. Tibbot was the first to enter, letting half the blizzard in with him as a gust of wind came swirling into the tavern. As he stood in the doorway stomping his large snowy boots, the others followed behind. With the door slamming shut behind them as they continued to shake off the snow, oblivious to the cold silence and the staring eyes, Tibbot and the others hadn't realised they were being watched.

"Why is snow so difficult to get off—" Kruze awkwardly paused as he looked up, too embarrassed to continue to talk. The room had come to a standstill. All you could hear was the odd creaking chair and a dry cough in the back of the room.

Looking up from their puddles of melted ice, breaking the awkward silence, Tibbot finally spoke. "Who's in charge here?" he said in a loud and clear tone, taking a big step forward.

Nobody answered. The tavern was silent until the sound of heavy boots came stomping into the room. Everybody turned their heads and respectfully made way for the approaching figure.

"You wish to speak with me?" the man spoke with a serious tone to his voice. A rather tall man with a strong build stood in front of Tibbot. He had a bushy silvery grey beard that grew down his broad chest, wide shoulders, gigantic feet, and strong ginormous hands that could crush a skull.

"Yes," Tibbot sternly answered. "There are matters that we need to discuss. Matters that concern you and your people."

The large man paused. He grabbed hold of his beard, gently grooming his fingers through the knots all the way down and twirling at the tip. He raised his left hand unbothered and clicked his chunky fingers loudly. One of the men that stood beside him handed him a scroll of some sort. He unravelled the scroll then violently slammed the mysterious paper onto one of the tables where a couple of serious-looking locals were sat, making their pints of ale wobble about and spill, dripping all the way down the sides onto the creaking floorboards.

"There's a bounty on your head. You're wanted men," said the man, furiously scrunching his eyebrows with his stare angrily fixated on Tibbot. Irritated, Tibbot roughly grabbed the scroll from the table.

"What is it?" said Zyron.

Tibbot sighed, passing it over to the others to take a look.

"Wanted. Dead or alive?" Kruze gasped irritably, grabbing the poster from Zyron's hand.

"What for?" Berwin spat angrily.

"Who would do this?" said Ruya, suddenly feeling very anxious.

"The Lords of Oro City. It's stamped with a gold seal," Tibbot huffed.

"But why would they do this?" she replied, feeling confused.

"Who knows what the lords are up to."

"Do you think Grazox and the others know about this?" said Zyra, furiously gritting her teeth.

"If he doesn't, he will soon enough."

"The Vorst do not deal with fugitives," the man spoke once again, interrupting the gang's conversation.

"I suppose you better turn us in then," said Tibbot, puffing out his chest in a manly manner, showing everyone in the room he wasn't afraid.

The room filled with an uncomfortable silence; the men intimidatingly moved slightly closer towards them. Tibbot and the Protectors reached for their weapons, ready for what was about to occur, while Ruya slowly stood back. The gigantic leader and Tibbot had come face to face. Suddenly the silence was broken. The large man had burst into hysterics, laughing so hard his face turned pink. The men standing behind laughed along with their leader like a bunch of children.

"What is going on here?" said Zyra, confused as to why he was laughing so much. *What could possibly be so funny at such a serious moment*, she thought.

"Friends," he continued to laugh. "We have absolutely no intention of turning you in. We do not take orders from Oro City; any enemy of the lords is always welcome here," he smiled, placing his hand on his chest.

Everybody in the room untensed, gently lowering their weapons. Ruya sighed in relief. *Thank god it didn't end in violence*, she thought, wiping her sweaty forehead.

"Ginger," he yelled to the bar man. "Get our friends here a drink. They call me Beast," he said, reaching out his ginormous hand.

"Tibbot. And these are my friends," he replied, taking his hand roughly.

"Please, my friends, come in, make yourselves at home," he said, patting him on the back and pulling him further in.

"Go on, ask him," said a giggly voice hiding in a corner.

"No, you ask him," laughed another.

A couple of local girls pulled out a Wanted poster. They continued whispering into each other's ears as they giddily giggled their way over to Kruze. The young ladies blushed as they approached the famous hero. "Excuse me," one of the girls said, blushing. "Could you sign this?" she said, holding out the Wanted poster.

With a big confident smile, Kruze took the scroll and quill from the girl's hand and happily signed it. "There you go, ladies," he grinned with a smoulder followed by a little wink.

"Thank you." The girls giggled like a couple of little nervous children, then finally skipped away, excitedly showing their friends, who were hiding in a corner too shy to walk over themselves.

"Honestly," Zyra huffed, rolling her eyes.

"What? I can't help it if I have fans. Not easy being famous, you know."

With the fire crackling, they followed Beast over to a cosy little wooden booth in the corner of the room where they sat by a window. The view was misty and white, Ruya tried to see if she could get a good look at the mountains in the far distance, but the blizzard was so intense she couldn't see a thing.

"What happened here?" said Tibbot.

"We were attacked by the Cold Queen's men. They came in the middle of the night and murdered some of the villagers. Men, women… children," he sighed, lowering his head, ashamed he couldn't do more to save his people.

"There were too many to fight off. The Akulls do not fight like regular men; they're not like you and me. A sickly coldness runs through their pale blue veins. They're soulless creatures with no honour and no mercy. They're cold monsters with no hearts." He raised his large pint of beer and chugged it down, then slammed the empty mug onto the table. "Their strength was unnerving, and we simply didn't have enough men to fight them off."

"You are aware they attacked because their queen will be returning," said Tibbot.

"Yes. I've heard a few whispers in town. Something about a Star?"

Tibbot discreetly shifted his eyes over to Ruya, who looked slightly nervous hiding behind Zyra.

"It was strange," said Beast.

"What was?" said Tibbot.

"They practically slaughtered half the town but took most of our young girls as prisoners. Why not take the rest of us? Something evil is brewing. I can feel it."

"Indeed, my friend, something very dark has finally returned. That is why we are here. There is a huge war coming, and we may need the help of the Vorst to join us. We will be—"

Beast raised his right hand in the air cutting Tibbot's sentence short. "There is no need for a big speech. You don't need to convince us to fight by your side. We will do everything in our power to help you win this war. Together we will defeat the enemy and take back what they have stolen."

Tibbot stood, kicking back his chair. He reached out his hand. "Well then. We better get started."

Beast grinned and roughly grabbed hold of Tibbot's hand.

"Where do we start?"

HUXLEY THE BRAVE
CHAPTER EIGHTEEN

There are many races of Giants settled in the corners of the realm; that's not to say they are all the same. Others may hide in fear as they camouflage into the earth or the rocky mountains and trees. But not War Giants. They didn't believe in hiding like cowards. The only thing they believed in was their strength and courage and their ability to win battles. They live and breathe war; that is what they were born for. Unlike most Giants that roamed the lands by themselves, War Giants kept close to their families and moved in large groups. War Giants were all about honour and family; nothing else mattered to them; nothing else was important.

***

Back at Vine City, Ludlow sighed, pressing his chin into his large hands, watching the rain come down hard from beneath a gigantic toadstool that sheltered him from the terrible weather.

"What's wrong, love?" said Martha.

"I should be out there helping Grazox and the others," he huffed. "I'm useless here," he sighed, once again feeling rather gloomy and depressed.

"But you are helping, love," Martha smiled, trying to reassure the giant. "You're protecting me and my children. My husband will forever be in your dept. Believe me, you are contributing so much to this cause whether you realise it or not, dear."

"To be fair," Celia interrupted with a sweet loaf in her hand, chewing very loudly. "He could be doing so much more... you know, as a War Giant and all."

"CELIA!" Martha snapped furiously at her rude daughter.

"*What?*" Celia chuckled, nudging her shoulders, taking another large bite.

"That was not called for."

"No, no. She's right. I'm useless," he sighed, hiding his face in his large hands with shame and embarrassment.

"Now look what you've gone and done," said Martha, feeling bad for the hopeless giant.

"Mum... Mum!" Greta yelled in the distance.

"What is it?' Oh, for heaven's sake." Martha grunted, making her way over to help Greta, who was being put in a rough headlock by one of her sisters.

"Ida, let your sister go right now!" As Martha's voice faded away as she walked off, Huxley thought this would be a good time to approach the giant.

"Hey there," he smiled, bashfully scratching the back of his head. "We haven't really met properly. I'm Huxley."

"Ludlow," answered the giant.

Huxley awkwardly sat by Ludlow, he tried to make conversation, but every time he tried, no words would come out.

"So—"

"What do I do now?" said Ludlow, cutting off Huxley, desperate for some advice.

"What do you mean?" the boy answered.

"Well, I'm useless here. I'm no good to anyone sitting around. There's going to be a war, and I've done nothing to try and prevent it."

"That's not true," said Huxley. "I'm sure you've done something; I mean you've stayed with me and my family just in case any more Screamers come back. You're protecting us. That's doing something."

"I stayed because I was too big to join my friends. There is no way a giant could have flown on a Mini Skyrider."

They both paused and sat in dismal silence. "Well... aren't there others like you?" said Huxley, finally breaking the gloomy atmosphere.

"Others?"

"Yeah, you know...War Giants."

"The only War Giants I know are my own family," Ludlow answered.

"Great, can't we get them to fight with us? From what I've heard, War Giants live for this sort of thing, fighting in battles and stuff."

"I suppose," said Ludlow, taking a moment to deeply think about it. "But I haven't seen my family in years, not since I left to join the Protectors. They've probably disowned me; a War Giant never turns his back on his family. It's unforgivable."

"Why did you leave, by the way?" said Huxley, with great curiosity.

"It was many things," Ludlow sighed. "I guess I wasn't strong or tough or fearless enough to be a member of my family. I was an embarrassment to them all. You have no idea what it's like being the scrawny one out of so many siblings."

In that moment, Huxley turned his head, shifting his gaze over to his mother, who was still struggling to separate her daughters from fighting. "Oh, believe me. I think I do," he sighed, resting his face in the palms of his hands.

As they both sighed pathetically, suddenly Huxley had a gleam in his eye. He had come up with a plan to help the giant regain his confidence. "Why don't we find them?" he said.

"Who?"

"Your family. Let's go get them and bring them back to fight in the war. That would be doing something to help your friends. I mean, aren't they doing the same thing right now, recruiting more allies for the cause."

"But... I haven't been home in years, not since I left. What if they turn me away?" said the giant with great anxiety.

"Well, there's only one way to find out. And you're not going to by sitting around here feeling sorry for yourself. You need to do something to help your friends, which, may I remind you, include my father. And I would very much like to see him again."

Ludlow carefully listened to what young Huxley had to say. As he sat up with pride, he placed his large hand onto the boy's shoulders. "You're right. What are we waiting for? At a time like this, one must put away one's pride."

"Come on, my loves, chin up." Martha clapped positively, followed by her four plumpy daughters. "We need to get to Grazia," she continued.

"We're not going to Grazia," said Huxley. "We're going to find Ludlow's family instead, to fight against the Evil Queens' armies."

"War Giants!" Matilda jumped with excitement.

"I've always wanted to meet a War Giant; they're brutal in battle," said Ida.

"I am a War Giant," Ludlow huffed.

"Yeah… but I mean a proper War Giant. No offence."

"You mean, leave Vine City?" said Greta. "But we've never left home before. Father would be furious with us."

"She's right," said Celia. "Stormville is the safest place. We can't just up and go."

"Funny because the Screamers managed to enter our city just fine. Clearly, it's not that safe," Huxley snapped.

They all stood back in shock.

"What's got into you?" Ida chuckled, surprised that her brother spoke back so forcefully; it looked like he was going to pop. Their brother barely spoke more than three words to them sometimes, so this was something very new to them.

"Your brother's right," said Martha. "Your father is out there trying to make a difference, risking his life, as are so many others. We can't just sit back and do nothing. We didn't raise our children to hide when things got tough. We have to fight for what's ours."

"I knew you would agree, Mum," said Huxley, jumping up and tightly grabbing hold of his mother by wrapping his arms around her waist.

"Your sister's right," she laughed, running her fingers through her son's soft hair. "What's got into you, ay?"

"Ludlow helped me realise something. No matter how small you may feel, you could always make a difference, and that's what I want to do, make a difference. Even if it's by doing the smallest thing. I've always thought of myself as weak and useless, felt like I've never belonged in this family. But if a War Giant can feel small and useless, then it really is all just in the mind. And no matter who you are, small or big if you think strong, you become strong. Size and strength have nothing to do with it. It's what's in here that counts," he said, placing his hand on his mother's chest.

Martha held her son's face close in her hands and gave him a soft motherly kiss on his forehead. "That's my boy," she whispered, with a tear streaming down her cheek. "Your father would be so proud to hear these words coming out of your mouth."

"Sorry I didn't speak them sooner, and I'm sorry it's taken me this long to realise what you both have been trying to teach me all this time."

With tears in their eyes, Celia, Greta, Ida, and Matilda ran towards their scrawny brother and squeezed him to the point he had no air to breathe.

"Girls, girls, calm down," he laughed, embracing his sisters with laughter, trying to catch his breath.

"You have a good son there, Martha. You should be very proud," said Ludlow.

"I am. Those kids are my world. They're my greatest treasure." She smiled, wiping a tear from her eye. "Now," she said, clapping her hands together, trying not to let her emotions get the best of her. "Where do we find this family of yours?"

The giant stood on his two large feet and stared off into the rainy distance with worry and regret. "Skala."

THE GLASS CASTLE
CHAPTER NINETEEN

"Please… I need to take a break. We've been walking for ages; I have a bad leg, and I need a rest." Lucinda dragged her feet, her arms flopping by her side along the forest path, finally collapsing to the ground. She was hungry and exhausted and was feeling rather frustrated that they had been walking for so long, yet they had not found any food or shelter or any sign of hope.

"Oh come on, Goldie," Susie chuckled, throwing a pinecone high up in the air with her left hand and catching it in her right.

"Don't come on me," Lucinda snapped with frustration, rubbing her leg. "How are you not exhausted? We've been walking for days."

"It's only been two days; there's not that long to go now. Just hang in there a little longer." Fen smiled, placing his hand gently on Lucinda's shoulder. "How's your leg doing, by the way?" he continued, kneeling down, showing some concern for her wellbeing.

"Not that long?" She slapped away his hand. "We don't even know where we are or where we're going," she yelled, once again losing her temper.

"She's right," Gustav sighed. "We should have at least passed a village or small town by now. We're doomed," he gasped, dramatically flinging the back of his hand against his forehead.

"I'm doing my best. At least we're far away from that psycho Madame Balina," Fen huffed, snapping a couple of twigs in his hands like a fed-up little schoolboy always being picked on.

"I've got it!" He jumped up. "I'll just climb up one of the trees and see if I could spot a town or something."

"Great plan," Lucinda sarcastically sighed beneath her breath, picking the dirt from her worn-down nails.

Fen placed his foot on the lowest branch; pushing himself up with a little boost, he grabbed hold of another branch and then another until he finally climbed his way to the top. Reaching the top, he poked his little head up from the rough branches. He was so high he could see the whole forest, but there was no sign of a village or town, only a never-ending sea of tall pine trees and a flock of birds in the distance.

"Well... do you see anything!" Susie yelled up.

"No. I don't see a thi—" Fen paused. He caught a glimpse of bright light that almost blinded him. "Susie, I think I see something. Quick, pass me the little spyglass in Grazox's satchel," he yelled, squinting his eyes and shielding them with one hand.

Susie climbed her way up to Fen. "What is it? What did you see?" she asked, picking twigs from out her hair, finally reaching the top.

"I'm not sure yet," he said, grabbing the spyglass from her hand. "But I'm pretty sure I saw something... I know I did." A few seconds passed, and nothing. Until once again, a bright light mysteriously appeared.

"Over there... see," Fen squeaked, pointing in the direction of the light. With one eye, he peeped through the spyglass and was stunned to see a castle with a dome-shaped roof in the distance that sparkled like diamonds every time the sun's rays reflected onto it.

"I think I found us shelter." Fen smiled.

"Really?" Susie sighed with relief.

"Finally, a bit of luck," he laughed. "But we better hurry, looks like it's going to rain."

The bright sun slowly vanished into the dark smoky clouds, then the sound of a small roar of thunder rumbled in the distance. The wind whistled, making the tops of the tree's dance from side to side. With their hair roughly blowing in the wind, Fen and Susie quickly climbed back down to tell the others the good news.

"Guys, we found shelter," said Fen, looking very pleased.

"Thank heavens," Gustav sighed, wiping his forehead with the back of his hand.

"Where?" said Lucinda, who still sat on the floor, sulking about the whole situation.

"Looks like a castle not too far from here. If we keep moving straight will find it. But we better move fast. I think it's going to rain."

Lucinda paused, feeling a little unsure of this new shelter Fen had found. "A castle?" she said. "In the middle of the woods?"

"Yes." Fen smiled, nodding, grabbing the satchel from Susie, ready to carry on with their journey.

"I'm not sure about this. How do we know it's safe?"

"If you would rather stay out here in the middle of the woods, be our guest," said Susie.

"I wasn't talking to you," Lucinda snapped, feeling annoyed every time Susie gave her opinion.

"Remind me again why *she* had to come along."

"Because *she* saved our lives," Fen answered. "Now hurry up."

Even though she had saved their lives from the Madame's monstrous appetite, Lucinda found it extremely difficult to like Susie. There was something about her that got under her skin. "Can't we try and find another shelter?"

"What shelter? You said it yourself we've been lost out here for two whole days. There is no other shelter. I'm just thankful we've managed to survive this long without having another encounter with Screamers or anything worse that might be lurking around out there."

"But—"

"Lucinda," Fen sighed, turning around. "We don't really have any other choice. We either try our luck or stay in the woods, and I know what I would rather do." Not wanting to hear another word of her complainants, Fen, Susie, and Gustav finally walked off without her. Hoping to find the castle before the weather got any worse, they moved straight forward just like Fen had told them to. The rain gently began to spit from the sky as the clouds darkened even more.

"Great. This is all I needed," Lucinda huffed, slowly strutting behind the others with her hands over her head, feeling rather gloomy and irritable. After some time walking, they finally found themselves at the doors of the mysterious castle. The castle was made purely from glass and had a large round dome on top in-between two tall towers. Fen knocked on the brightly polished doors four times. But there was no answer.

"Hello! Anyone home?"

"Maybe we should just leave," said Lucinda, feeling rather uneasy, trying to shield herself even more from the rain that came pelting down.

"We can't just leave. We need shelter," Gustav argued. "And I, for one, am not willing to spend another night in these ghastly woods sleeping on the rough, filthy ground," he huffed, rolling his great big bulgy eyes.

"Fen," Susie whispered, "look, the door is open."

"Well, what are we waiting for?" said Gustav. They entered the castle; Lucinda was the last. There was something about this place that made her uneasy. She didn't feel right.

"Hello. Anybody home?" Fen yelled. As he continued to call out, his voice rebounded off the walls and echoed through the empty castle halls.

"Where is everybody?" said Susie.

"Fen, I really do think we should leave. I have a bad feeling. Something isn't right, I just know it."

"Would you just hush," snapped Gustav.

"He's right, Lucinda. There's nothing to be worried about," said Fen.

"Guys, over here. Take a look at this," Susie yelled, calling them over to look at a large, old painted portrait hung on the wall.

"Who do you think they are?" said Fen.

"Who cares?" Lucinda tutted with both arms folded like a child. It was a portrait of a well-dressed, very serious and uptight-looking wealthy couple. In-between them sat a grumpy little girl with her arms folded angrily with such a horrible frown that even Lucinda thought she looked spoilt. She wore a huge pink frilly frock that took up half the portrait. Her brown hair was in the shape of two extremely large doughnut rings on each side, decorated with little gems and pearls that twinkled like stars.

"They must be who live here," said Susie.

"Well, at least we know a nice normal family lives here and not some bloodthirsty cannibal," said Gustav, feeling slightly relieved.

"Very nice family, I just adore their friendly smiles," Lucinda smirked sarcastically.

"You just watch that sharp tongue of yours. We're guests here, and I will not have you ruin my chances of sleeping in a warm bed tonight. Got it!" Gustav snapped once again.

"Blah, blah, blah," said Lucinda, rolling her eyes and gesturing with her hand.

As they moved further down to the next portrait, the uptight couple seemed to get older and older, withering away with each painting they passed, yet the young girl seemed to be the only one who hadn't changed in age. On the final portrait, the couple were gone, and the young child was all alone, looking profoundly angrier than ever.

The rain seemed to get heavier by the minute as it tapped loudly onto the sides of the glass castle. Lightning struck, flashing its blinding light onto the strange portrait, highlighting the young girl's unfriendly face, followed by an eerie boom of thunder.

"Strange paintings," said Fen, scratching the back of his head. "Come on," he continued, "let's see if we can find them."

As they searched about the castle, there was still no sign of anybody living there.

"Maybe it's abandoned," said Fen.

"Then why is there still furniture here in perfect condition. If it were abandoned, most of this stuff would be covered in cobwebs. I hate to say this, but I think Goldie's right, something is off here," said Susie.

"Finally," Lucinda huffed. "Can we please leave now?"

"And spend the night in the rain. Are you insane? We're staying put," Gustav argued, stamping his webbed foot to the ground.

"Look here. Do what you want, but I will certainly not take orders from a stupid frog," she snapped, losing her patience even more.

"Stupid frog! How dare you!" Gustav gasped in shock.

As they argued, Fen wedged his way between them, trying to calm down the situation. Through all the madness and raised voices, he hadn't noticed Susie secretly slipping away.

"Fen!" she yelled, calling him over with her hand. Immediately Fen ran over to her side, leaving Gustav and Lucinda alone to squabble.

"What, what is it? Are you hurt?"

"No," she giggled. "Look what I found." She pushed open a thick squeaky door that led them into a huge hall with a giant queen-size bed in the centre of the room, smothered with plumpy pillows. A large canopy hovered above the bed's gold frame that draped its way down to the floors. The room was completely flooded with mountains of toys. Everything a child could only dream of was stuffed all into one room. Wooden doll's houses, jack in the box, rocking horses, teddies, puppets, and dolls. Continuing to argue like little children, Fen and Susie could hear Gustav and Lucinda's voices getting louder as they approached the room.

"Don't you dare call me that, how dare yo—" Gustav immediately stopped. Choking on his last word, he found himself completely speechless and astounded as he entered. Lucinda, not far behind, continued to argue, following him into the room.

"I'll call you whatever I like, you slimly little—" Like Gustav, she too couldn't finish her sentence as she walked through the doors. They were both stunned at the mere sight of so many toys, but Gustav was even more stunned when his eyes clasped onto a large bed smothered with tempting, heavenly, soft bouncy pillows. It had been so long since he slept in a bed that he couldn't quite remember what it felt like.

"What is this place?" said Lucinda, slowly walking further into the room with curiosity.

"This is the place you had such a *bad* feeling about," Fen chuckled. "See," he said, winding up a jack in a box. "Toys. There is nothing friendlier than toys. You were just being paranoid, which is understandable considering everything we've been through."

"Well, I still don't feel right. You're telling me this doesn't seem odd to you?" she said, unconvinced that everything seemed kosher.

"This does seem a little weird," Susie agreed, analysing one of the dolls with her mouth sewn shut. "Is it me or... do some of these toys look sad to you?"

"Who cares?" Lucinda huffed. "But keep agreeing with me, Susie, and I might consider actually liking you," she continued.

"Yippie," Susie sarcastically smirked, placing the doll back where she had found it.

"What are you both talking about? There is nothing wrong with this place," Fen argued.

"Look around you. Can you honestly say you don't find this all just a bit weird?" said Lucinda.

"Gustav, back me up here... Gustav?" Fen turned his head to Gustav, who looked completely lost in thought. Gustav, not interested in anyone's opinion, had happily made his way over to the large queen-sized bed without even thinking twice about it. The bed was so huge and high that he had to use the fancy golden steps coming out of the side of the bed just to climb on.

"Gustav. What are you doing?" said Fen.

"I haven't had a good night's sleep in forever. I'm taking a nap," he answered without a care in the world.

"A nap? Are you insane!" Lucinda shrieked. "We don't even know who lives here. You can't just fall asleep in a stranger's bed. They could be back any minute."

"Look around you, I see no one living here but toys, and I'm sure they wouldn't mind."

"Gustav is right. Maybe we should have a little rest. We've got a long way ahead of us after all," said Fen, joining Gustav as he climbed up onto the bed that was almost the size of a ship.

"Susie?" Lucinda pleaded, hoping that maybe she would have a little more sense.

"Sorry, Goldie, but they're right. We might not get another chance like this one, might as well make the most of it."

"Well, that's just terrific!" Lucinda yelled, flinging her hands up in the air. "Go ahead and sleep. I'll just stay watch as a guard, shall I? You know just in case whoever lives here finally decides to show up."

The others once again ignored Lucinda like most of the times she complained. Exhausted, Gustav, with his arms by his side, fell face down on his belly into a bunch of feathered pillows and immediately fell into a deep sleep, almost as if a spell had been cursed upon him.

"Listen to him snore," Fen yawned, stretching out his scrawny arms, drifting off into a deep sleep himself. He slowly disappeared into a bundle of plumped pillows that were so soft they could have easily been mistaken for clouds, sucking him in like quicksand.

"How about that," Susie whispered, catching his yawn. She, too, slowly fell victim to the power of the softness of the heavenly pillows that surrounded them, vanishing her into a deep lazy snooze.

Suddenly, Lucinda found herself alone, the only one to remain awake.

"Idiots, just listen to them snore like pigs. Well, not me, not this time. I will certainly not allow myself to fall into another trap, that's for sure." Lucinda refused to sit on the bed but instead sat on the floor at the very end of the bed's backboard.

With her arms crossed tightly and her legs stretched out straight, she leaned back and watched her feet tapping together, trying her utmost to stay awake. "Fools," she tutted. As she continued to tap her feet, their snores seemed to get louder and louder. "I'll show them," she yawned. Feeling slightly drowsy, her eyes slowly closed. Luckily she managed to quickly snap them back open every time they shut, blinking repeatedly, trying her best to stay awake. But it was no use, for the sounds of their snores brought a certain laziness to her that she couldn't control until eventually she too dozed off into a deep slumber. With her neck losing grip, her head fell into her tightly folded arms that slowly loosened up once she fell asleep. She managed to out-snore Fen, Susie and Gustav all put together. With them all in a deep slumber, the glass castle remained still and silent with only the sounds of their snores and the rain beating down against the glass walls.

SPELLENBORG
CHAPTER TWENTY

Magic bounced from one wall to another in Spellenborg, home of the Spellborns. The entire air was filled with enchantment. No mortal had ever stepped foot through the magic gates before; it belonged only to those who believed in magic and the wonders that surrounded them. It was a city like no other. Unlike the mortals, the Spellborns welcomed any creature to live among them, for magic did not belong only to those born of blue blood. It was a place where the unusual was the norm. A place where dreams were made to come true. A place where being different was praised and not frowned upon. Spellenborg was one of the largest and most diverse cities ever known, made up of four districts. Each district practised magic and contributed to the city's needs. North, East, South, and West of the city worked together like one big family, and each brought something different to the table.

The Northern folk worked hard making weapons sculpted from the ice mountains of Spellenborg. Even in the blazing sun, their weapons did not melt, for they were enchanted by powerful magic. In the East of the city, the forest spread out like the ocean. Forest folk lived high in the trees, some even underground beneath large roots where they studied strange herbs and plants that only grew in Spellenborg. From the rare magic that grew from beneath their soil that so many tried to steal, they made medicine that could cure any sickness. The Spellborns wasted no time, they were prepared for any disaster that may or may not accrue in their city. The safety and wellbeing of the Spellborns were the lords' number one priority.

Deep in the South district of Spellenborg in a desert city lived some of the world's greatest blacksmiths ever born. The local residents were cloaked in the finest fabrics, selling fruit and jewellery made from magic gems on their tented stools. Unlike the rest of Spellenborg, the sun was blazing in the south. But that did not distract the blacksmiths from doing their job. They made shields and armour so strong even a giant's blade would snap at the tip as it would barely pierce through. The Spellborn soldiers had won many battles thanks to their blue-blooded brothers, who had dedicated their lives up North and down South to making strong weapons and armour.

And finally, the West of the city, Spellenborg, the capital of all districts. It was the birthplace of magic and all Spellborns. It was there where they had trained and taught young Spellborns the rules of sorcery. The city was chaotic like no other. Foreigners would travel from across the world just to see the wonders for themselves. Parents would send their children to attend only the best magic schools in the realm. And the sick would fall to their knees at the city's gates in hopes of getting their hands on the medicines being grown in the East District.

With a loud thunderous bang, a huge puff of smoke appeared outside the gates of Spellenborg.

"I knew we couldn't trust the mortals," said Sir Arkin, straightening out his long black beard.

"We had no choice; we need all the men we can to build a strong army," said Oba.

"I just hope the Spellborns will not be so blinded by hate like the foolish mortals," said Abner, tightly gripping his sceptre, watching the light dim from the gem.

"My Spellborn brothers do not let hate poison their minds. They know what has to be done for the greater good, even if that means joining the mortals. The lords of Spellenborg are nothing like Genzo and his corrupt council."

"You speak wisely, my old friend," Sir Abner huffed, feeling a little queasy.

"Sir?" Oba spoke with concern as she watched Abner fragilely tilt to one side.

"I'm fine," he coughed, raising his hand in the air. "I haven't teleported this much in one day for a long time. Truth be told, I didn't know the old girl still had it in her," he smirked, addressing his very old sceptre. As they stood outside the gates of Spellenborg, a man posted in a watchtower dressed in blue armour called out.

"Who goes there?" the man yelled.

"It is I, Sir Arkin." Without another word, the gates immediately opened.

"Shall we?" said Arkin, kindly reaching out his arm for the others to go first. As they entered through the gates, they were greeted by two extremely tall thin identical figures that kindly approached them. With a big friendly grin that stretched out from one ear to the other, one of the men reached out his arms to embrace Sir Arkin.

"Our brother has finally returned home." He smiled, tightly wrapping his arms around him. "Been a long time since you've been home. After you joined the Protectors all those years ago, we thought we would never see you again."

"Indeed, it's been far too long," Sir Arkin laughed.

"Welcome back, my old friend," said the other with his hands clasped behind his back, gracefully bowing in his presence.

Lord Stava and Lord Urok were named rulers of the magic city after the death of their beloved King Saiyan. They were twins, and each wore long identical robes the colour of indigo, periwinkle and orchid that sparkled like an aurora in the night sky, leaving a long train of velvet trailing behind them, along with large funny-looking hats that flopped to one side. Both lords had bright green eyes that gleamed like emeralds. Their beards were the colour of blue, and each wore their hair in a plait so long it almost touched the floor. It was impossible to tell them apart.

"We knew you would be coming," said Lord Stava. "Darkness is not very far behind," he murmured discreetly.

"How did you know?" said Abner.

"The earth beneath us cries, as do the stars above," said Lord Urok.

"Unlike the mortals, us magic folk feel everything that surrounds us. We feel the pain of those who suffer," said Lord Stava. "Something a mortal will never understand," he continued to tut, rolling his eyes.

"Then you know what we have come to ask of you," said Sir Abner.

"Indeed, but best we continue this discussion somewhere more private. Follow us," said the twins.

Following behind the two lords, Sir Arkin took in his surroundings with a happy gleam in his eyes. For too long he had been away from the place he once called home. As he gracefully strolled through the city of magic, he took the opportunity to reminisce about the past, retracing the footsteps he once walked as a young wizard. Not much had changed from what he could remember, except the old wonky clock tower that stood in the middle of the city square that was now being run by Brownies. Brownies were hard mechanical workers and took their jobs extremely seriously. The clock tower was encrusted with blue, purple, green and red glowing gems. As they walked further into the city, two black silky horses with wings came swooping down from the sky, landing a large golden carriage holding 12 people at the drop point.

"Heading to the North District!" yelled the whistle-blower in a high-pitched tone. A group of people bundled up in thick fur coats and luggage climbed on board. The horses once again took to the sky as another carriage landed, heading to the East District. As the carriages flew back and forth from the drop point, Sir Arkin remembered his first carriage ride as a young boy when he and his mother travelled to the East. His heart was filled with such joy, just as it once did all those years ago. Strolling past a long line of stools and tents of bubbling, brewing cauldrons and mini, colourful explosions, a cloaked man with a tiny pointed hat and little round spectacles hovered by with his nose buried inside a book of spells. With his feet in the air, he swiftly passed by, leaving a large amount of bubbles behind that mysteriously came from beneath his sparkling cloak that made bubbling popping sounds all the way down the path until he was out of sight.

"Oh, how I have missed this place," Sir Arkin sighed. It had been a very long time since Sir Arkin had shown anyone his tender side. Being extremely serious all the time, he almost thought he had forgotten how to smile. At last they came to the doors of two tall emerald towers that were so high, they made their way up into the clouds. Entering the large, marbled halls, Lord Urok walked over to a table made from enchanted vines.

"Make our guests a drink." The vines without any further instructions twirled and wrapped its way around a pointy gold lid to a large glass bottle filled with mermaid tears, a very sweet and famous beverage only made in Spellenborg. Pouring the tears into four golden goblets, the magic table reached out its green vines and kindly handed everybody in a room a goblet each.

"Now," said Lord Stava taking a sip of his tasty beverage. "Let's discuss why you have come to Spellenborg."

"Well, I think you already know why we have come," said Sir Abner. "We are on the brink of war, and we must protect the Star."

"Ah yes, the Star." Lord Urok smiled. "And how are the girls doing?"

"The girls?" said Oba.

"Yes, the girls. Or have you completely forgotten we were there the day the witches banished the queens and hid the Star? If my memory serves me correctly, it was us Spellborns that also shared a helping hand in that little endeavour."

"Of course I haven't forgotten," said Oba. "We will forever be grateful to the Spellborns, and not only for helping hide the

Star, but also for your discretion. Something many could not manage."

"Of course, anything to help." Lord Stava smiled.

"And what news of the mortals?" said Lord Urok.

"Useless and selfish as always," Abner answered with a huff.

"They will not join their forces with our own," said Sir Arkin.

"Well, what did you expect from that pompous fool Genzo? The man has always and forever will be an enemy of the Spellborns. Why on earth would he want to join forces?"

"But why can't he see the real threat that is coming," Abner yelled furiously. "The queens will show no mercy. In order to stand strong, we must stand together. Are the mortals really that ignorant to make the same mistakes as the kings once did?"

"For years the mortals have tried to erase our kind from the face of the earth. When the time finally comes for war they will be sorry," said Lord Stava.

"I say let the mortals fight for themselves. They don't deserve our help," said Lord Urok.

"Yes, but you forget not all mortals are the same. I'm sure there are some out there worth protecting. Why should their good names be tarnished because of the selfish acts made on behalf of their leaders?" Oba argued.

"Oba speaks wisely," said Sir Abner.

"And why should we help those who mean us harm?" said Lord Stava.

"Because we are Protectors, and we protect, no matter who or where you come from," Abner sternly replied.

Lord Urok and Lord Stava both paused, each taking a sip of wine, they exchanged a look of agreement.

"Very well," said the lords. "We will assemble an army. And if the mortals decide to join, then we will proudly stand with them, like we once did so many years ago."

"I knew I could count on the brotherhood of the Spellborns." Sir Arkin proudly bowed.

"But the Star?" said the lords.

"The girls are in safe hands, do not fret," said Arkin.

"Well, now that we have begun assembling an army, what now, sir?" said Oba, shifting her eyes over to Abner.

He paused, taking a large sip of mermaid tears, and rolled his eyes over to a large window overlooking the city. "Now... we wait for war to begin."

LADY OCTAVIA
CHAPTER TWENTY-ONE

Deep in the forest, the rain continued to beat down hard against the glass castle walls. Fen and the others were still fast asleep with absolutely no intention of waking up. Letting out a huge satisfying yawn, Gustav stretched out his scrawny arms as wide as he could. He gently rolled off his side and onto his back, reaching out for a soft feathery pillow to place above his face. He couldn't remember the last time he had felt this happy and content, now all he needed was a good meal. Falling back into a deep sleep, his tympanums vibrated with the sounds of whispers. He assumed it was the others, maybe they had finally woken up, so he decided just to ignore it and continue to sleep. Growing more irritated as the vague whispers continued, he finally snapped.

"Keep it down, please, still trying to sleep over here," he moaned with a muffled voice from beneath his quilted pillow. But the whispering voices continued to mutter.

"*Who are they?*" one voice said, rising above the rest.

"I said, would you please keep it down? I'm trying to—" Gustav angrily removed the feathered pillow from his face and was aghast as he looked up only to see a bunch of large googly eyes circling him.

"Aaahh!" Gustav jumped in shock, making the toys flee in fear.

"What! What!" Fen yelled, jumping out from beneath a pile of pillows.

"What's wrong?" Susie cried, being the third to finally wake up.

"The toys! They're alive!" Gustav jumped up and down, pointing his webbed hand towards the edge of the bed. The room was suddenly silent, followed by a bang of thunder. Fen crawled to the edge of the bed and looked down. He saw a couple of quivering, scrawny little legs poking from beneath the thick duvet.

"It's okay," he calmly spoke. "Please don't be afraid; we're not going to hurt you."

"Fen, what are you doing?" said Susie, grabbing him by the shoulder and gently pulling him away.

"Just keep back," he whispered, patiently waiting for the toys to emerge once again. After a few seconds went by, the toys cautiously came out of their hiding places. A little wooded puppet crawled out from beneath the bed, followed by a battered rag doll. In the corner of the large room, the lid of a toy chest slowly lifted, a plumpy teddy bear with one button eye missing surfaced from the chest. From behind the curtains, a couple of wooden soldiers appeared, cautiously making their way to the centre of the room. The third drawer of a large chest of drawers slowly squeaked open with a bunch of clown dolls clumsily falling out, landing on top of each other. As more toys emerged from their hiding places, they all gathered around the bed. Some of them took an interest in an oblivious Lucinda, who was still very much fast asleep, unaware of the situation taking place around her.

Curious, one of the clown dolls decided to get a closer look and hopped on her lap but immediately ran off as she let out a huge snort-like snore, scaring the poor clown away.

With the last toy coming out from its hiding place, joining the crowd, a jack in the box hopped his way over. The room was now silent as they all stared intently, looking up towards Fen, Susie, and Gustav. Speechless, Fen cleared his throat and finally spoke.

"What are you?" he gasped.

"Toys," answered the jack in the box with his head swaying back and forth.

"No, I know what you are. But how are you all alive?"

At first the toys were extremely tight-lipped, almost too afraid to speak. But one of the wooden puppets, irritated, pushed his way through the crowd.

"You mean you don't know!" the puppet yelled, looking up angrily towards Fen.

"Know what?" said Fen, feeling slightly confused. "We only just arrived. We got lost in the woods and luckily found this place by chance."

The toys gasped in horror, whispering among themselves. "You should take your friends and leave," said the rag doll.

"Why?" said Susie with great concern.

"BECAUSE IT'S NOT SAFE!" one of the toys in the back yelled.

"Not safe? What on earth are you talking about. This place seems perfectly harmless to me," Gustav argued, snuggling up to one of the pillows.

"You idiot. This place is the opposite of harmless. Just take a look around," the grumpy puppet continued to moan.

"All we see is toys," said Fen.

"Then you're blind. And if you know what's good for you, you best get your friends and leave this place before it's too late."

"But you still haven't told us why?" said Susie.

Once again, the toys decided to whisper among themselves discussing their current situation, deciding whether they should tell them or not. After their intense discussion, they all looked to the puppet to take charge. Lowering his head, he finally spoke. "The Mistress of this castle," the puppet sighed with sadness.

"What about her? Fen coughed curiously.

"She is incredibly cruel and insane. She is the reason we're all here in this... mess," the puppet huffed, lowering his head.

"You mean that family we saw in the portrait?"

"Yes," he answered.

"That's great," Fen chuckled, turning his head towards his friends. "We would like to speak to them. We've been lost in the woods for a few days now. Maybe they would be kind enough to let us stay for a couple of nights then point us in the right direction."

"Good luck with that. They both died years ago," said the puppet.

"But… you just said the mistress—"

"Yes, the little girl in the portrait, she's the mistress. When her parents died, everything was left to her."

"Well, I guess that explains all the toys, makes sense now. This room belongs to a sweet little girl," said Susie.

"Little, yes, sweet… you're sadly mistaken," said the puppet. "Lady Octavia is insane, she did this to us, and she'll do the same to you if you don't leave now."

"Did what?" whispered Susie with a frightened expression.

"Let's just say… we didn't always look like this," the puppet sighed with great sorrow in his voice.

"What do you mean?" said Gustav.

The puppet opened his mouth to answer but was suddenly interrupted by a loud bang.

"I'M BORED!" cried a voice furiously echoing in the distance.

"She's coming!" cried the jack in a box swaying from side to side, then quickly popping himself back into his box for shelter.

"HIDE! HIDE!" the toys cried in fear as they immediately scattered back to their hiding places.

"Who's coming?" said Susie. Leaning over the edge of the bed on her hands and knees, she watched the poor toys panicky bumping into each other as they ran for their lives.

"Lady Octavia!" one of the clowns shivered with a heavy gulp before hiding behind the curtains.

"Fen, what do we do?" said Susie.

"I guess we hide." He shrugged, still feeling a little confused as to what was going on.

As the toys were safely tucked away in the darkest corners of the room, Fen and Susie slipped beneath the bed with some of the others as they cowered, clinging onto one another for dear life.

"This is insane," Gustav argued, being the only one left out in the open.

"Listen to them, Gustav. They wouldn't be this afraid for nothing," Susie whispered from beneath the bed while he stubbornly stayed put on top with the comfy pillows.

"I'm not hiding! This is absolutely ridiculou—"

"I SAID I'M BORED!" the voice aggressively cried once again as the doors burst open. Luckily, just in time, Gustav had managed to hide, diving into the pillows for safety.

A ten-year-old girl came rushing into the room with such rage she shoved and knocked over everything in sight, followed by a group of quivering servants falling at her feet.

"I NEVER GET WHAT I WANT!" she cried, jumping onto her bed, lying flat down on her belly and kicking and screaming like a spoilt brat.

"But, my lady," gulped one of the servants. "You have almost everything a child could possibly dream of."

"IT'S NOT ENOUGH! I WANT MORE!" she continued to cry. As she furiously kicked and pounded onto the pillows piled up on her large bed, Gustav desperately tried his best to stay hidden. He carefully watched the young girl through a tiny gap beneath the pillows, trying his utmost not to breathe or make a sound that could give him away.

"What was that?" Octavia gasped, curiously shooting her head back up as tears drizzled down her plump cheeks.

"What was what, my lady?" said the servant, nervously twiddling his fingers.

"I can hear breathing," she said, raising one eyebrow curiously.

Gustav, in fear, quickly slung both hands across his mouth and over his nose.

"I don't hear a thing, my lady," said the servant.

"Shhh. Listen."

Zzzz… Zzzz.

"There it goes again," she said, moving away from the pile of pillows Gustav was hiding under. Gustav rolled his eyes with great relief and removed both hands from his mouth, wiping his sweaty forehead as he watched the young girl move away.

"Oh no," Fen silently gasped with wide eyes.

"What?" Susie whispered.

"We forgot Lucinda," he cried in horror, biting down hard on his fingernails.

Listening to the mysterious snores, Lady Octavia made her way down from her large bed and walked around over to the headboard, where she saw Lucinda fast asleep like a little lamb. As the young girl approached, the shadow of her large doughnut rings on each side of her head loomed over Lucinda. Octavia reached out her foot and gently tapped Lucinda on the Leg. But still, Lucinda continued to snore even louder. Losing her patience, the girl roughly kicked her for the second time. Lucinda's eyes shot open, jumping out of her sleep.

"OUCH!" she cried. "WHY YOU LITTL—"

Silence.

Both girls were completely still as they stared at each other. Octavia continued to stare with great curiosity. On the other hand, Lucinda felt slightly confused, just waking up and all. Feeling nervous, she had nothing to say and waited uncomfortably for the child to speak first. "Who are you?" Octavia finally spoke, breaking the awkward silence.

"Lucinda Dowling. Who are you?"

"*Who am I?*" the girl sneered. "*I* am the Lady of this castle."

Lucinda suddenly remembered the miserable child in the painted portrait she and the others had found earlier.

"How did you manage to enter my domain?" Octavia suspiciously asked, pressing her little finger against her pink cheek, tapping her glossy heels onto the floorboards, impatiently waiting for an answer.

"We got lost in the woods and found your castle. It was raining and the door was open, so we just let ourselves in. We thought the place was abandoned, honest."

"We?" the girl said with wide eyes, loosening her arms and lowering her finger away from her cheek.

"Yes, me and my..." Lucinda hesitated, for she had never used such a word in her life. "Friends," she continued to mumble, rolling her eyes.

"Friends?" Octavia jumped excitedly. "You mean... there are more of you?" she giggled, immediately stopping her glossy heel from tapping on the floorboard.

"And where are these friends now?" she asked curiously.

"I'm not sure," Lucinda huffed, folding her arms crossly together. "They were here when I was awake."

Lucinda felt extremely betrayed, angry, and very upset that they had left her behind like that. She was so furious; all sorts of nasty thoughts were going through her head.

"How could they just leave me like this," she tutted to herself.

"You see, Basil, my plan worked perfectly. Didn't I say leaving the front door open would attract new toys?" Octavia grinned.

"Yes, my lady. Once again, you have proven to be a genius." The servant smiled.

"What did she say?" Fen muttered beneath his breath.

"New toys?" Susie whispered, feeling slightly confused and a bit horrified.

"What do you think she meant by that?" He shivered.

Hiding with them, a rag doll with her mouth sewn shut reached out her little hand and placed it above Susie's with a look of deep sadness.

"Fen," Susie gasped with a tear in her eye. "I think these toys used to be people."

Hiding beneath the bed, Fen and Susie jumped in fear when they heard Lady Octavia lose her patience with Lucinda. Her intimidating yells clashed with the mighty sound of thunder, for the rain seemed to get heavier by the second.

"I'M NOT GOING TO ASK YOU AGAIN! WHERE ARE YOUR FRIENDS!" the young child screamed, violently stomping her foot to the ground.

"I don't know, I don't know," Lucinda cried, feeling the pressure eating away at her. With sweat dripping down her forehead, she suddenly shifted her eyes to the right. That's when she saw Fen secretly poking his pale face out from beneath the bed. Shifting his eyes towards the door, he carefully made hand gestures, encouraging her to make a run for it.

"THERE!" Lucinda yelled, pointing her finger towards Fen, who quickly ducked his head back under the bed.

"BASIL! CATCH THEM!" Lady Octavia screamed in outrage.

Basil and the rest of Octavia's workers surrounded the bed like human shields. There was no way out; they were completely blocked in. The toys cowered in their hiding places with fear as they watched Fen and Susie being ambushed.

"Fen, what do we do," Susie stressfully sighed, shifting her eyes to each corner of the bed in panic.

"Here's the plan, we just simpl—" Unfortunately, Susie never got to hear the rest of his plan, for he was taken by the legs and brutally dragged out from beneath the bed. The ragdoll gave Susie one last look of sorrow before Susie herself was dragged away.

INVASION
CHAPTER TWENTY-TWO

"Ah, I can smell the gold already," the captain laughed with the wind blowing loose strands of her hair as they sailed closer and closer to Oro City.

"Remember your promise," said Grazox. "After you get what you want, you're going to take us to Zehir Island."

"I make no promises. If my men and I are satisfied with what treasures we find, then and only then will I make up my mind about taking you."

"Captain!" one of the men yelled, pulling her attention away from Grazox.

"Impossible woman," Grazox huffed, gritting his teeth furiously, balling his hand into a fist as she walked away from him.

"I did warn you," said Igor. "Pirates cannot be trusted. You should have known better than asking for their help."

"What's going to happen if she doesn't take us to the island?" said Drew.

"Let's pray that she does," Grazox responded irritably.

***

"Mmmm, hmmff," Helix mumbled with a mouth full of food, enjoying a large feast all to himself.

"Enjoying yourself, are we? Everything to your satisfaction, I hope?" said Lord Genzo, who sat impatiently at the other end of a long dining table, tapping his fingers against the polished wood, watching the potion maker make a pig of himself.

"Mmhmm," he mumbled, finally swallowing the food that was preventing him from speaking. "Could do with some more gravy, mind you, the chicken's a little dry."

Genzo snapped his fingers to one of the servants who stood close by with a gold gravy boat in hand, pouring the old gnome some more.

"Enough, enough!" Helix snapped. "What you trying to do, drown me in it? Go away!" he yelled, shooing the poor servant away like a fly.

"Helix, you've been with us for a few days now, and still you have not spoken of the Star. Remember, the only thing keeping you from being imprisoned at Black Rock is your cooperation. Now about the Star?"

"It's a girl," Helix mumbled, ripping into a turkey leg.

"Yes, we've already established that the Star hides in the form of a human. But where is she?"

"How in the name of Zivot am I supposed to know that? Grazox brought a girl to my potion shop, and that's when I saw it."

"Saw what?"

"Her blood. The girl bleeds starlight."

"The blood of the Gods," Genzo whispered. "This is just amazing," he smirked, biting his lower lip. Leaning back into his chair, he placed his thumb onto his chin and his finger pressed against his thin lips, falling into a deep daze with a wicked grin.

"What are you thinking?" said Helix before slurping down a bowl of soup that drizzled down his beard.

"I was just thinking how wonderful our little rendezvous has been. But sadly it has come to an end." Genzo clicked his fingers and two guards in gold armour stepped forwards, each forcefully grabbing Helix by the arms, dragging him away from his soup bowl that crashed to the ground shattering into pieces.

"Wha-what's going on here. I thought we had a deal," Helix yelled in his croaky voice.

"If you think I make deals with traitors, you're sadly mistaken," Genzo smirked. "You see, if I let you go, what's to say you won't betray me?"

"But I won't. You have my word," promised Helix.

"HA! Your word," he laughed. "Once a traitor, always a traitor. Take him away."

With Helix kicking and yelling, cursing the guards, they carried him away until his moans and cries could no longer be heard.

"Have fun at Black Rock, Potion Maker," Genzo wickedly grinned as the doors slammed shut behind the guards.

"Captain, there it is. The City of Gold," Feroz yelled, pointing towards Oro City as they sailed closer, finally reaching their destination.

"Good. Raise the flag," yelled the captain.

"My Lord! My lord!" cried one of the servants bursting through the doors to the great hall.

"Yes, yes, what is it?" answered Genzo.

"My lord, there seems to be a foreign ship approaching the city."

"Are you positive it's not one of ours?"

"Look at the sails, my lord."

Genzo immediately hurried over to the balcony and grabbed a fancy gold spyglass from the servant's hand.

"Pirates!" he gasped angrily.

"What do we do, my lord?" said Hickman

"Sound the alarm. I want more guards protecting the main gate. They mustn't get through the city," Genzo yelled furiously, grabbing the poor servant by the throat.

"Yes, my lord," the servant croaked, releasing himself from Genzo's tight grip, rushing off in a panic.

As the captain's ship approached, people fled in terror when they heard the sound of warning spreading through the Golden City. A large shiny bell that sat in a tall tower was rung by one of Genzo's guards. As it vibrated through the whole of Oro City, the people ran around in chaos.

DONG! DONG! DONG!

"PIRATES! PIRATES ARE COMING."

"Do you hear that?" The captain smiled at her men, listening to the people's screams beyond the golden wall. "Remember, take as much as you can carry, but only things that are worth carrying. Do not waste time with unnecessary junk. Now go. Raid!" the captain ordered, pointing her sword in the direction of the gates.

Reaching the shore with their weapons in hand, the pirates fearlessly jumped off the ship and chaotically ran towards the great gates.

"How do you think you are going to get past all those guards with only 60 men?" said Grazox with great concern.

"You lack faith," said the captain. "Me and my 60 men have won many battles when we were completely outnumbered. Sometimes greater things are achieved in smaller numbers. Don't underestimate us."

The pirates flung large, rusted hooks shaped as claws high up into the air, that clung onto the other side of the wall as they climbed higher and higher until they reached the top. The guards tried to stop them with arrows but failed miserably each time they shot. Although they managed to pierce a few pirates, it still didn't stop them. The more wounds the pirates got, the more fearless they became.

"IDIOTS!" Lord Genzo hollered with great anger as he watched his useless guards through his spyglass from a safe distance. He stressfully watched his men try and fight off the pirates, but the guards that tried to stop them just became victims, falling to their knees from the agonising pain of the pirates' swords. Genzo's men were fully trained fighters, and yet they were no match for Iona's men. Unlike the guards, pirates have and always will be their own master. They had no training but had taught themselves how to survive in the unknown like many other free fighters in the land. Before any more guards came rushing over, the pirates had already made it over the wall and quickly opened the great gates to the city by unleashing a very large lever.

"Shall we?" said the captain, gracefully reaching out her hand.

"After you," Grazox answered. His nephew followed behind. "No," said Grazox, placing his hand on his chest. "You three stay here where its safe."

"Fine with me," said Igor.

"But, Uncle, I want to fight with you," Tobin pleaded.

"You need to stay here and protect Drew. You know how important she is. We can't let any harm come to her."

"Okay," Tobin agreed, nodding his head. He knew not to argue with his uncle, especially when it came to matters that could jeopardise the future.

"Stay safe." Drew smiled, feeling slightly worried for Grazox, for she had started to grow quite fond of him. Grazox reached out his hand and gently gave her a little pat on the head, turned to his nephew and roughly did the same on his shoulder.

"Igor, keep an eye on these two. Won't be long," he said before jumping off the ship and following the captain through the gates to Oro City. Drew, Igor, and Tobin waited on the ship with Clem, Luka, and the captain's panther, Siyah.

"It's even better than you described," the captain laughed, strolling through the gates while some of the townspeople quickly ran by in fear.

"How the other half live, ha."

"Just take what you want, and let's go," said Grazox, frustrated by the amount of time he was losing. He was on a tight schedule that Sir Abner had given him and the others of what to do before the queens' awakening. They didn't have much time before the final star fell out of line. Following the captain, his eyes quickly caught a glimpse of a scroll that was pinned against a wall. It was a Wanted poster of himself and the others. He tore down the poster and furiously scrunched it in his large bulky hand with anger.

"You men, with me. I want the others down here protecting the ship. Make sure the gates stay open ready for when we leave," the captain instructed the other half of her crew.

"My lord. The pirates have made it through the city gates. And they are heading this way," cried one of the servants, chaotically waving his arms high up in the air.

"DAMN!... Hickman!" Genzo yelled out to his most trusted servant. "Are the doors heavily barricaded?"

"There are guards posted at every door, my lord."

"Good, make sure all the entrances are thoroughly blocked."

"My lord," one of the other lords calmly called out. "There is no need to worry."

"No need to worry?" said Genzo. "These are pirates we're talking about, brutal savages. If they get through, who knows what they—"

"Trust me," the lord laughed. "They are no match for our personal bodyguards that have been highly trained from only the best fighters in the city. We'll be absolutely fine—"

The lord's sentence was cut short with a look of terror. The sounds of their bodyguards' cries and screams beyond the large doors left their bottom lips quivering in fear. Suddenly, the cries and screams came to a stop. There wasn't a single sound to be heard. All was silent in the great hall.

"Did we stop them?" said one of the lords.

"Did we win?" said another. Suddenly the silence was corrupted by a large boom that made the lords jump out of their gem-covered robes.

"They're breaking in! Do something!" Genzo yelled to some of the guards posted by his side. The doors finally burst open, and the pirates, with no fear of what was waiting for them on the other side, came rushing into the hall like beasts. One of the guards quickly shot an arrow towards Feroz, but his reflexes were far quicker as he shielded himself with a large axe, breaking the arrow in half. He immediately pulled out a dagger and flung it towards the bodyguard at the speed of lightning and sent him crashing down to the ground. It was in that moment the other guards realised they were no match for the wrath of the pirates. Surrendering, they all dropped their weapons to the ground and fell to their knees.

"You cowards!" Genzo sneered with embarrassment. "Get up, you fools! Get up!" he yelled angrily with his cheeks burning. As the guards surrendered, Genzo tried to sneakily get away.

"Who's in charge here?" said the captain.

The lords sat high in their chairs refused to answer.

"You, are you in charge?" she said, pointing her dagger towards one of the lords on ground level. Biting his tongue in fear, he didn't answer.

"Listen carefully," she said, shouting up towards the lords so everybody in the room could hear her nice and clearly. "I just wanted to let whoever is in charge here know that I will not be leaving this city empty-handed, and I will be taking as much gold as my ship will allow me to carry. And there is nothing you can do to stop me. But if you wish me to leave the city peacefully, then I'm willing to negotiate with whoever is in charge."

Once again the room was dead silent; you could hear a pin drop. No one dared to breathe until the lords began to whisper among themselves. "Him," said one of the lords hesitantly, sat in his highchair and pointing down towards Genzo, who tried his best to hide in a small crowd of servants.

"Bring him to me," said the captain.

The lords and some of the servants grabbed Genzo by the arms, nudging him to step forward.

"Traitors," Genzo sneered. "I'll have all your heads for this," he yelled, addressing everybody in the room.

"So you're in charge of this wonderful city?" said the captain.

"Yes," he answered with hatred in his voice.

The captain slowly walked over to Genzo, placed her dagger beneath a beautiful sparking chain he had around his neck, and raised it higher so she could get a better look.

"Pretty," she said, not breaking any eye contact with him as she intimidatingly moved closer. "Shame it's around such an ugly neck. Maybe it should go to a more suitable owner. Someone more worthy. All I need to do is remove your head, and it's all mine."

"How dare you," Lord Genzo's advisor gasped with disgust as he stepped forwards, confronting the pirates head-on. "Have you no respect? Don't you know who you are talking to? You should apologise at onc—"

Before the advisor could finish preaching about respect to the pirates, which was a terrible idea, one of Iona's men headbutted the man so severely that he passed out. Fear struck through their hearts. The lords sat back in their chairs not daring to speak. They didn't want to end up like Genzo's advisor... or worse.

"Here's what's going to happen," said the captain. "We are going to take whatever treasures we please, and you're going to tell your men to stand down while we sail out of here."

"Ha, ha, ha," Genzo chuckled sarcastically. His laugh echoed through the great hall, triggering the other lords to bravely laugh along with him. "And what in god's name makes you think I'm going to agree to that?"

In that moment, more of Genzo's guards came rushing into the hall with large shields and swords. This had given the lords the impression they had won, and the pirates would leave with their tails between their legs.

"You'll never walk out of here alive. You're outnumbered, pirate. Now I'll have all your heads for this." He grinned.

"Well, well. It does seem we're outnumbered, boys," Iona sighed with a touch of defeat, lowering her head. "But" she childishly smirked, "luckily, you're my backup plan." She laughed once again, lifting her head back up, forcefully grabbing him by the arm and placing a dagger beneath his chin, pressing against his wrinkly fragile neck.

"Wha... what are you doing?" Genzo cried.

"I suggest you tell your men to back off... unless you want me to kill you here and now for everybody to see. Do not test me, Lord. I will take your life without a second thought. We are, after all, nothing but savages," said the captain, finally losing her patience.

The captain's words had struck fear into Genzo, so much so that he immediately demanded his men lower their weapons and let the pirates take what they wanted.

"Good. See, that wasn't very hard, now was it?" the captain whispered into the frightened lord's ear, still holding the dagger very close to his Adam's apple, reminding him she was in charge.

"You got what you wanted. Now let me go."

"Of course. Once we get to the ship."

"What?"

"Oh, didn't I mention you're coming with us? Silly me," the captain chuckled.

"That isn't what we negotiated. You said you would leave peacefully."

"First thing you should know, pirates never stick to negotiations, and they certainly do not leave peacefully."

With Genzo's guards obeying his strict orders, they stood to one side as they watched the careless pirates happily making it back to their ship carrying large treasure boxes and wheeling gold crates filled with gems and other unimaginable riches. One of the captain's men had stolen an emerald silk gown and a little tiara ornamented with sparkling diamonds. The pirate laughed at Genzo's men as he strutted by wearing the gown, mockingly skipping by them with a childish grin as he made fun of their pitiful defeat. Before boarding the ship, the captain had warned Genzo and his posse, threatening she would be back with others and burn Oro City to the ground if his men decided to follow them. Genzo, among many others, knew the sea was infested with revenge-seeking pirates, even if it wasn't their fight to avenge. Genzo was an extremely important man to the Golden City. But still, the lords could not take that risk. As Genzo was being roughly manhandled by Iona's men forcing him to board the ship, he looked back at one of the other lords who stood at the gates. He had made a small gesture with his hand, indicating to Genzo they would send help and bring him back home.

In return, Genzo gave a slight nod.

"What do we do now. We need him?" said one of the lords.

"Do we?" said another, lowering his hand by his side.

"My lord?"

"With Genzo out the way, we could expand Oro City and make it even more powerful."

"How?" said the second lord with great curiosity.

"That fool Genzo was far too obsessed with going to war with the Spellborns. His mind was clouded with too much hate to even think about the city's future. War costs money, and that old fool would have spent every last dime to be rid of the Spellborns. But with him gone, we can forget about going to war but instead raise the taxes in all the lands. Even lands we do not own."

"But how, my lord?"

"When folk cannot pay, we will buy the lands or take it by force. We have the power to do so. Who's going to stop us? We will take every small village, city, and farm for ourselves and expand our city. Out with the old and in with the new. We will not only be known as the City of Gold but the Land of Gold. The Golden Empire."

"Genius, my lord. Seems like the pirates came as a blessing in disguise."

"Indeed," he laughed.

"But what of Genzo? Are we not going to send for help?"

"he's the pirate's problem now," the lord spoke, sneeringly watching the pirates' ship sail away in hopes of their leader never returning.

THE LONER IN THE MOUNTAINS
CHAPTER TWENTY-THREE

"So, my friends, what's the plan. When do we attack?" Beast coughed, taking a large gulp of ale. Necking it all the way back, he slammed his large empty wooden mug onto the table, eager to take the next step for action.

"It's not that simple, my friend. We won't be attacking Lumi's men but doing something far greater. Something that could end the war before it even begins," said Tibbot.

"We're not going to fight?" Beast huffed, slamming his balled fist onto the table, making his jug wobble off the edge, feeling extremely frustrated at the thought.

Once again, Tibbot spoke. "Believe me, there will be plenty of fighting. But for now, me and my friends are recruiting as many as possible to join our army. And we must find the Wise Shroom. He has the answers to everything."

As they continued their discussion of war, Ruya, not interested, sat by one of the windows and watched the icy blizzard dancing to the sound of the wind, singing its cold lonely sorrows in a dismal gloom.

"Here," said Zyron handing her a cup of piping hot soup.

"What's in this?" she curiously asked, taking a small whiff, gagging in disgust.

"Fish. Seems like that's all the Vorst eats around here," he laughed.

"Fish soup? I think I'll pass." She smiled, politely pushing the cup to one side.

"Don't blame you," he chuckled. "Mind if I..."

"No, please take a seat," she said with a smile.

"How you holding up. You okay?" he asked as he sat opposite her.

"Yes."

"It's okay if you're not. It's scary times, and you're allowed to be afraid, you know. All this talk of war can be a bit much sometimes. Believe me, I know. I've been fighting since I was a kid. *Child of War,* remember."

"Were you ever afraid?" she asked curiously.

"Of course I was, I still am. But when you're fighting for the greater good of the future, you have no time to think or be afraid. Sometimes you just have to put your fear to one side and keep fighting to your very last breath. But I see where you're coming from. This is all new to you, I understand your fear."

"That's just it." She turned away from the window. "I don't fear for myself, but for the others. I can't stop thinking about Drew and Miss Mabel and all the other girls at Lakeshore. Not to mention all the people murdered here in this town and the young girls the Cold Queen's men kidnapped, thinking one of them could possibly be the Star. I can't help but feel responsible for their deaths... I feel so guilty."

"You can't do that. You can't blame yourself for something you had no control over," said Zyron, reaching out his hand and squeezing her forearm, reassuring her that none of it was her fault.

"I know, but I can't help thinking this way," she sighed, continuing to watch the harsh blizzard with sadness.

"Hang in there. Soon this will all be over, you'll see. You're a lot stronger than you think," he said with a smile.

"Drew's the strong one, not me," she sighed, once again lowering her head.

"You're forgetting you both share the same heart, so if she's strong, so are you. Remember that the next time you doubt yourself." He gave her one last smile before joining the others in discussion across the room.

His comforting words left her feeling slightly less gloomy. Smiling to herself, she reached over for the bowl of soup and took a small gulp but immediately spat it back out, grimacing at the unpleasant taste it left in her mouth.

"I SAY WE FIND THEM AND KILL THEM ALL!" one of the men yelled, followed by an uproar of the Vorst yelling with approval, clanking their beer mugs together.

"We have to be smart about this," said Tibbot. "We can't just barge into the queen's lair without knowing what to expect. You said it yourself that her men's strength was unnerving."

"But the queens have not yet returned from their slumbers. So why not destroy their armies now! Get them while they are weak," Beast yelled, once again slamming his fist.

"Because we have no idea how big their armies are. You forget we'll not only be fighting the Cold Queen's men, But Queen Ates's too, and the Swamp Queen. There are enemies all around us."

"What's going on?" said Ruya with concern, barely able to hear herself speak over the men's raised voices and tension in the room.

"The Vorst want to attack Lumi's men," said Zyra, standing in the shadows with her arms folded and her back pressed against the wall with one leg up bent at the knee. "Typical men, only thinking with their fists," she huffed.

"Would that be a bad idea?" said Ruya, watching over the crowd of angry men.

"A very bad idea," Zyra answered.

After the bickering calmed down, Tibbot spoke once again. "I understand your frustration, my friends, believe me, I do. The queen's men attacked your hometown. Murdered those you love. Kidnapped your sisters and daughters. And I can see why you would want revenge, but we must be careful. Even war has its rules. My friend Grazox has gone to recruit strong allies to join us, and we must do the same. Not only will we gather the strongest fighters in the land, but we will go on a journey to find the Wise Shroom."

"The Wise Shroom is a myth!" one of the men yelled at the back.

"I can assure you, my friend, the Wise Shroom is no myth. And he will give us answers that will be the queens' undoing. But before we go on that journey, there is another we must seek."

"Who?" said Beast.

Tibbot paused. "Kartal."

The men gasped, lowering their mugs. One man intensely gulped his ale. The room that was filled with such loud roars suddenly went as silent as a graveyard. There wasn't a single peep from any of the men.

The only sound was the cold crying wind in the distance, gently tapping against the windows along with the burning fire that crackled and spat out of control.

"The loner in the mountains?" Beast finally spoke, breaking the silence.

"Yes," Tibbot answered.

"They say she fights like a demon," said one of the men.

"I heard she lives among the Giant Snow Eagles," said another.

"They say she has wings of her very own," the third man spoke.

"The mountain people died out many, many years ago. What's to say she's still alive?" said Beast.

Tibbot could tell by the men's reactions they had absolutely no desire to find Kartal or enter her mountains. For no man had ever dared to try.

"They didn't name her the loner in the mountains for nothing. Unlike other mountain folk, she is strong... she's a survivor. So many battles have been won from the edge of her sword. She is a warrior, probably one of the greatest living warriors this world has ever known. Not to mention she has an army of Giant Eagles. It could make a great difference if we had someone like her on our side. That's also why we came to you for help. No one knows these mountains like the Vorst... So, my friends, will you help us?"

Once again, the room was silent. The cold wind whistled even more viciously as the storm grew stronger.

"Ginger!" Beast yelled over to the barman. "Get our friends here some proper clothing. You can't go up into the mountains dressed like that; you'll never survive the cold."

As they prepared for their journey, Zyra, with a soft grin, made her way over to her twin brother, who sat on the other side of the room, squeezing into large furry boots.

"Perfect fit," she said

"not at all," said Zyron. "They're a little too big."

"Not the boots," she sighed seriously

"what are you talking about?" he answered with confusion

"you and Ruya," she continued.

"What on earth are you talking about?" he repeated.

"I saw that earlier," she said

"saw what? I was just comforting her, she was afraid," he argued.

"Ok, if you say so. But you can't hide your feelings from me, I'm your twin sister, I know you. Just don't go getting too emotionally involved, could be dangerous and lead to your downfall."

"Zyra I'm a little too busy right now to be hearing this," he irately responded, binding the thick lace around his large fury boots.

"Pretty boy, what on earth are you doing?" said Tibbot as he walked over to Kruze, who seemed to be struggling with the clothing the Vorst had kindly given him.

"They don't actually expect us to wear this, do they?" said Kruze.

"Why, what's wrong with it?" said Tibbot.

"This is something that would fit a giant. Look at the size of it," he moaned, holding the coat up for Tibbot to get a better look.

"There's nothing wrong with it. Stop your whinging," Tibbot huffed.

"Easy for you to say," Kruze mumbled beneath his breath.

"What was that?" said Tibbot.

"All I'm saying is, it's easier for men who are stocky to wear this type of clothing, no offence. The size of the hood alone is going to destroy my hair."

"One of these days, lad, when you're fast asleep... I'm going to cut that precious hair of yours. Then you won't have anything to whinge about."

"You wouldn't dare," Kruze gasped, taking a small step back.

"Lad, we're going up into the mountains. This isn't some fancy gown parade. Do you want to freeze to death up there?"

"Of course not."

"Then stop acting like a pretty boy and get dressed. We have a job to do."

Ruya, all finally warm and dressed, took Potion into her arms. "Now, no wandering off, do you hear me? We're going up into the mountains where it's very dangerous, so stay close." The work bunny twitched her little nose and blinked her round beady eyes as if to say she understood.

"Help! God damn it," came a muffled voice in distress on the other side of the room.

"You okay there, little one?" said Beast.

"NO, YOU FOOL. HELP ME OUT!" Berwin angrily snapped.

Beast reached out a helping hand and pulled out the old gnome, who was lost beneath one of the fur coats. With one hand, he held Berwin high up in the air and watched him dangle and squabble about with amusement.

"Unhand me, you clod!"

"Woah, easy there. I was just trying to help," said Beast.

"I said unhand me, you great big oaf!" Berwin yelled once again, throwing a punch in the air with one arm.

"You're a feisty little fellow, aren't you," Beast laughed.

Finally everyone in the inn was all dressed and ready to go.

"How you feeling, Ruya?" said Tibbot placing his large hand on her shoulder.

"A little scared, but I think I'll be okay." She smiled with confidence.

"Good girl." He smiled, gently patting her on the head.

Brushing past the men, Beast stood by the door to the inn and raised his hand for silence.

"My friends," he spoke, looking over a crowd of men. "We have a very long, tiresome odyssey ahead of us. But the Vorst never give up, and we will journey on to our very last breath. As we go on this quest with our new friends, some of us may not make it back. So for any man that has any doubts, please raise your hand." The room was silent as Beast shifted his eyes from side to side, waiting for someone to raise their hand. But no one did.

"My fellow Vorst," said Beast, placing his hand against his broad chest. "You all make me proud to be your leader." The men all respectfully bowed their heads in response.

"Now," said Beast, unlatching the door to the brutal blizzard that awaited them.

"Let's go and make the enemy pay."

TEA PARTY
CHAPTER TWENTY-FOUR

Gustav quivered beneath the pillows, watching his friends through a small gap. With his hands tightly gripped over his trembling lip, h sneakily watched lady Octavia, who continuously questioned the others in a rather unpleasant manner.

"I'M NOT GOING TO ASK AGAIN... ARE THERE MORE OF YOU!" she screamed, over and over again, stamping her foot in rage and waiting for an answer.

"For the last time... NO!" Susie snapped, annoyed at being spoken down to like a little child by someone half her size.

"She's telling the truth, honest," Fen squeaked.

"YOU!" Lady Octavia yelled, pointing her little finger in Lucinda's direction. "You look like someone who would do just about anything to save herself. Tell me, are there any more of you hiding in my castle? Think carefully now because, unlike your friends, if you speak the truth, you'll be free to go."

"She's lying," Susie spat.

Octavia irritably coxed her head over to her servant with wide eyes. "Basil, would you be so kind," she tutted, rolling her eyes furiously.

"Come here, you," said the servant, roughly grabbing Susie by the arms, gagging her with a cloth tied around her mouth.

"Get your hands off her. Leave her alone," Fen argued in a small fit of rage wriggling about helplessly. But there wasn't much he could do to help his friend. One of the servants held him tight by the arms.

"What's it going to be, blondie?" Octavia smirked. "Are there any more of you hiding in my castle?"

Before answering, Lucinda's eyes slowly shifted over towards Gustav's direction. *Why shouldn't I tell?* she thought. She tried to convince herself they probably would have given her away in a heartbeat if the shoe was on the other foot in order to save themselves. It's not like they were her friends.

"WELL!" Lady Octavia impatiently snapped, once again stamping her heels to the ground.

But after a few good seconds of thinking about it, Lucinda shook her head. "No, there are no others," she said with a heavy gulp. Both Fen and Susie rolled their eyes in relief. For a minute there, they were both certain Lucinda would have given him up.

"Well then, now we've established that. It's time for some fun." Octavia viciously turned her head to one of the servants. "Basil!" she screamed. "Send a message to the gypsy. I want her here right away."

Basil, Lady Octavia's most trusted servant, pulled out a little note and passed it along to another. "Send out a crow with this message. It must reach the gypsy by noon."

The servant immediately did as he was told and scurried out of the room.

Who was this Gypsy she spoke of, and why did she need her? they wondered.

"I've been awfully bored lately and was growing quite tired of my old toys," Octavia continued to speak, with a spiteful tone in her voice. "Thank heavens you found your way to me." She had a grin so wicked it sent chills down their spines, making them all feel extremely anxious about what was going to happen next. What on earth was she planning on doing to them, and who was this gypsy? They had no idea how they were going to get out of this one. Gustav was their only hope now.

Octavia happily skipped out of the room, followed by a group of servants nudging Susie, Fen and Lucinda out the door. But before they left, Fen managed to discreetly signal over to Gustav, shifting his eyes towards Grazox's satchel he left behind beneath the duvet. As they left the room, their voices faded away, with the large doors slamming shut behind them. Gustav found himself all alone in the bedroom. He slowly emerged from beneath the pillows and grabbed the satchel safely in his arms.

"You there," he said to one of the puppets hiding behind a tall toy shelf. "Where are they taking my friends?"

"To the Pink Hall," the puppet answered, quickly ducking his head back behind the shelf.

"The Pink Hall?" Gustav repeated, raising one eyebrow.

"Yes," said one of the dolls. "That's where she hosts her tea parties. You must save them before the gypsy arrives, or else…" the doll hesitated to continue.

"Or else what?" Gustav gasped.

"Or else it's too late. And you're all stuck here forever, like the rest of us."

Gustav, with the satchel tightly in his arms, glanced around the room at all the toys. "My goodness," he whispered. "You were all people… weren't you?" The toys said nothing, they didn't need to. The answer was clearly shown through all their sad, tortured faces.

"You better hurry," said the doll.

Gustav hopped over towards the door, but before he left the room, he gave one final glance over his shoulder. "I'm sorry." He smiled softly with sadness.

The toys returned a smile. "Hurry! Don't worry about us," they yelled.

And just like that, Gustav was out the door heading towards the notorious Pink Hall, ready to save his friends from becoming a child's plaything. The hall was brightly polished with shiny, pink cotton candy marbled floors and large matching pillars on each corner of the room. In the centre of the hall was an enormous round table that could fit 20 people. The table was spread with sugar cakes, lemon, and strawberry tarts, along with a bowl filled with sugar cubes next to jugs of cream and milk, and in the centre was a large cream cake. Sat around the table was Lady Octavia, Lucinda, Fen and Susie with some of the rag dolls, teddies, and puppets they met earlier.

"Drink up, everybody," Octavia giggled, raising her little pinkie in the air as she took an elegant sip from a tiny pink teacup. "Please eat." She kindly smiled, gesturing at the colourful, sprinkled desserts, perfectly laid out. "Please, don't be shy, eat." She smiled once again. "EAT!" she yelled furiously, startling everybody to quickly pick up their napkins, fastening them to their collars.

Susie, still bound and gagged, shifted her eyes towards Gustav, who hid behind one of the large doors. She tried not to make it obvious and continued to stare straight ahead, watching Lady Octavia stuff her face with mini cakes.

"Hand over a raspberry tart," she said to one of the servants, not bothering to reach out for it herself, although it was at a reachable distance. Disgusted, she furiously spat the tart out of her mouth. "I said raspberry, this is lemon! Does this look like raspberry to you... well, does it!" she continued to scream, holding the lemon tart closely to the servant's face.

"N-n... no, my lady," the servant stuttered, terrified of angering her any further.

"GUARDS. TAKE HIM AWAY!"

Fen and the others watched the poor servant being dragged away with horrified expressions, listening to the large doors slam shut behind them.

As the time passed, the rain got heavier by the minute, drizzling down the glass walls. They could see the whole forest from where they were sitting. Tall pine trees surrounded the glass castle like a shield. "What miserable weather," Octavia hissed, with fresh cream smudged around her mouth, picking a cherry from the top of a cupcake. "I SAID WHAT HORRIBLE WEATHER!" she roared furiously at the others, waiting for them to agree.

"Disgusting," Fen gulped, while the others all quickly shook their heads in fear.

"Wonder what it feels like?" Octavia sighed depressingly, shifting her eyes towards the grey storm, watching the rain beating down on the glass, continuing to pick at the glossy red cherry from her creamy cupcake.

"What, the rain?" said Fen.

"Yes," Octavia answered with a huff.

"You mean, you've never felt the rain?" he continued to make conversation.

"Not for a very long time," she answered, taking a small sip of tea.

"So, why don't you?" he said, confused.

Lady Octavia stood, kicking back her chair. She walked over to one of the glass walls and stared out. With her eyes glazing as she watched the trees dance to the wind, she pressed her hand against the glass and finally spoke. "A long, long time ago, there once was a wealthy couple. They had everything a person could dream of. Their wealth was far and beyond anyone's imagination. One cold, stormy day, quite like this, there was a knock at the castle door. An old gypsy woman and her young daughter stood outside in the pouring rain. She asked the couple if they could be so kind as to spare a horse, so they could get back to their family, who were waiting for them on the other side of the woods. The couple turned the old gypsy and her daughter away. The gypsy begged one last time. 'Please, my daughter is sick, and I must get her back home,' the old woman continued to cry. But still, the couple showed no remorse and slammed the door in her face. The gypsy, feeling angry and degraded, knocked on the door one last time. The couple opened the door once again to shoo the old woman away for good. But before they could, the gypsy woman spoke first.

'*May the one you love most, stand still in time,*
while you wither away, your beloved will stay behind.
Forever lonely, trapped inside these walls,
for when you are gone, nobody will hear her calls.'"

Lady Octavia continued to stare out into the distance as her story came to an end.

"I don't understand?" said Fen.

"My parents were the ones who turned the old gypsy away. Because they refused to help her daughter, she cursed theirs. You see, I'm doomed to live my life as an outcast. Forever trapped, bound, and cursed to stay hidden inside these treacherous glass walls. Forbidden to ever leave, caged like an animal. I'm damned to never leave this castle; I have no knowledge of the outside world. My parents perished years ago, and I stayed the same."

"But, your servants, surely they are free to leave anytime?" said Fen.

"After my parents realised what the old gypsy had done, they sent out for another. They paid her handsomely to use the same curse that was used upon me on all the other servants in the castle, so they too could be bound inside these walls never to leave, never to age… forever trapped in time itself. They were very caring people, my parents; they didn't want me to be lonely, you see."

"I understand," Fen gulped. "They were just doing what any other good parent would have done." He looked over to Susie with an expression of terror. Without a sound, he gently moved his lips. "We've got to get out of here," he secretly mimed.

"You see," Octavia continued. "I get very bored. Well, a hundred years stuck in a castle can do that sometimes," she chuckled. "And I get so fed up of my old toys, that when new ones find their way to me, it makes me so happy. I'm always on the hunt for new playthings, and you and your friends are perfect. And once the gypsy arrives, you'll be my playthings forever."

"What's that's supposed to mean?" Lucinda coughed, choking on a strawberry tart.

"Well, if I'm trapped here forever, I need to be entertained. And if I can't leave…" She dramatically turned away from the window facing the others. "Neither can you."

Susie bound and gagged, wiggled about in panic. Lucinda dropped her strawberry tart into her tea out of shock, and Fen almost choked on his own spit, taking a large gulp.

"Now." Octavia grinned maliciously. "I'm bored. Entertain me."

Gustav, shocked at what he had just heard, trembled with fear. He had to do something, and he had to do something quick to save his friends before the gypsy arrived.

"Lady Octavia," said Basil, entering the Pink Hall. "We just got word; the gypsy is on her way and expects triple pay this time. She wasn't happy with the payment she received the last time she used the captivity curse."

"Yes, yes, fine," Octavia huffed, seating herself back at the table. "Now go away, I'm trying to have a tea party with my new friends."

Gustav quickly scurried out the way and hid behind another door when he saw Basil approaching as he left the hall.

"Now," the young girl giggled, clapping her tiny hands together. "The question is, what toys should I have you all turned into? I have too many dolls, and they can get quite boring after some time." Octavia reached out for a sugar cake and dipped it in her milky tea. "Any suggestions?" she smirked, looking up at them and waiting for an answer.

Everybody around the table had nothing to say. All so terrified, they didn't utter a single word.

"Come on now, don't be shy," she giggled. "Surely you have some suggestions for me. After all, it's how you'll be living the rest of your days for all eternity." Octavia carefully observed everyone sat around the table individually. With her finger pressed against her chin, she thought long and hard.

"You would be perfect as a wooden soldier, wouldn't you agree?" she smirked.

Again, Fen said nothing but clenched in fear.

"Unless you all want to be turned into spinning tops and spend the rest of your pathetic days spinning hours on end, I suggest you all start talking."

"Ma... maybe we could keep you company as we are?" Lucinda hesitantly suggested.

Wide-eyed, the toys around the table gasped, followed by an uncomfortable silence.

Calmly lowering her teacup away from her lips, Lady Octavia's eyes glared with fury. Never has anyone gone against her wishes with such insolence. Even her parents knew better.

"How dare you," Octavia muttered, gritting her teeth tightly together. "*Stay as we are*? Don't you know to whom you speak?"

"It was just a suggestion," Lucinda gulped. "I mean… you did say to give suggestions."

Once again, Lucinda had made things worse for herself. Octavia from beneath the table kicked as hard as she could, making all the silverware and teacups jump, silencing her. "Do you have any idea what it is like, being cursed to watch the world from the inside. Seeing the trees sway to the wind, the rain falling down, the sun rising?"

Lucinda gulped, nodding her head.

"I will never get to enjoy the fruits of nature for as long as I'm cursed. So, I'll have my fun in any way I choose." Rising from her chair, she intimidatingly made her way over to Lucinda and leaned over her. "Have a cupcake." She grinned, pulling the plate closer towards her with a sickeningly sweet smile. Lucinda, terrified, took the creamy cupcake from her little hand and ate the whole thing. "Have another," she smiled once again. Lucinda, far too horrified to disobey, did as she was told. Two cupcakes turned into three and so on. Twelves cupcakes later, Lucinda felt her belly in great discomfort from all the sweetness. "Please," she begged. "I can't eat another; I'm going to be sick."

"You'll eat whatever I give you!" Octavia viscously growled. "Now open wide."

Octavia reached out for another cake and forcefully held it up to Lucinda's mouth.

"No, no… please," Lucinda cried.

"My lady," said Basil, entering the hall once again.

"WHAT!" Octavia snapped. "How many times have I told you. When I'm hosting a tea party, do NOT interrupt."

"Yes, of course, my lady. I do apologise, but the gypsy has arrived."

"Well, don't just stand there, you idiot, send her in," Octavia yelled angrily, releasing Lucinda from her rough grip.

"My lady, she refuses to come in unless she speaks directly to you. She said she wants to discuss payment."

"Bloody Gypsies," Octavia grunted, aggressively throwing the tea towel onto the table. "I'll be right back, my little pretties," she smirked at the others. "And remember, there are guards posted outside every door, so if you try to run... I'll have you all killed," she continued to giggle, then happily skipped her way out of the hall with her large pink frilly frock swaying from side to side.

Finally, Fen moved closer to Susie and ungagged her.

"Ah, that feels better," she sighed in relief. "Quick, untie my hands."

"You okay?" he said, quickly unravelling the rope tied tightly around her wrists.

"Just great," Susie sighed. "I escaped one madhouse to end up in another."

"Well, what do we do?" Lucinda gasped, grabbing a little fancy tea towel to clean the cream from her face.

"We?" Susie chuckled angrily. "You sold us out. Its thanks to you we're stuck in this mess."

"Oh please, you would have done the same thing to me," Lucinda snapped back.

"What!" Susie laughed with frustration.

"You all left me sleeping. This is all your fault. I told you something wasn't right about this place and that we should have left while we had the chance. I knew something bad was going to happen, just like I did back at Lakeshore before we were attacked by Screamers. But you idiots didn't listen to me. Now look at us, drinking tea with a hundred-year-old psycho trapped inside a ten-year-old body, about to be turned into toys!"

"That's no excuse," Susie argued. "Don't you see, we would have had a better chance if you were the only one taken. We would have saved you. Now the odds of us leaving this circus are very slim, thanks to you. We have absolutely no plan, except for Gustav. And the chances of him saving the day are very unlikely."

The girls squabbled even more.

"Girls, girls... please," Fen pleaded. "Stop arguing for the love of god."

But the girls didn't listen. Fen picked up two slices of cream cake and slung them towards the girls' faces.

"Why you little—"

"Lucinda, I'm sorry I had to do that, but you really need to stop fighting and think of a way we're going to escape."

"Well, I did see Gustav earlier," said Susie, wiping the cream off her face.

"You did. Where?"

"He was by the door," she answered.

"Did he have the satchel with him?"

"Yeah, I think so. Why?"

"There's something in that satchel that would be of great use to us," said Fen.

Lucinda, feeling itchy, scratched the side of her thigh until she felt a little lump. She reached down in her pocket and found the love potion she stole from Healer Higgles potion shop back at Healers Town.

"Guys," she squeaked. "Look!"

"What's that?" said Fen.

"A love potion, I stole it from that old croak, Helix," she continued.

"But Helix said it was missing a few ingredients; it could be lethal."

In that moment, they all raised their heads, staring at each other with mischief.

Meanwhile, Octavia found herself finally coming to an agreement of payment with the old gypsy.

"Hurry," Fen gasped. "Just pour it all in."

Susie emptied the whole bottle into Lady Octavia's teacup. Suddenly, the sound of loud mumbling voices approached the hall.

"Quick, she's coming back."

Susie rushed back to her seat and pretended she was still tied at the hands, and quickly tied the cloth back over her mouth. Lady Octavia entered the Pink Hall followed by her servants, Basil and the old gypsy woman cloaked in back rags by her side.

"Is this them?" said the old woman in a foreign accent.

"Yes!" Octavia jumped with excitement.

"When shall I begin?" said the gypsy.

Octavia reached for her teacup and moved it closer towards her lips. "Oh, immediately," she giggled. "Can't wait another second to play with my new toys." She jumped again, spilling some of her tea onto her fancy frock. Lucinda, Fen and Susie watched with great anticipation every time she moved the cup closer towards her mouth. As she was about to take a sip, intense, they all sat back in their chairs and watched.

"STOP!"

Everybody in the room turned their heads to the other side of the hall. Gustav stood in one of the doorways. "Unhand my friends, you scum!"

"What on earth is that?" Octavia gasped, once again lowering the teacup away from her lips.

"It's a frog, my lady," Basil answered, confused, wondering how he could have possibly slipped past the guards.

"I don't care what it is, it looks fun, and I want it. Bring it to me!" she demanded. "Looks like it's your lucky day," Octavia smirked to the old gypsy. "More gold coins for you," she laughed, gulping down her tea with her pinkie in the air. Finishing her tea, she placed the cup onto the table and gave another order. The others carefully watched her, waiting for some kind of reaction. But nothing happened. "BASIL! WILL YOU HURRY AND BRING THAT THING OVER TO ME—"

Octavia's legs caved in. She coughed so hard she leaned over the table for support with one hand clenched around her throat.

"My lady?" Basil, rushed over to her side, placed his hand on her shoulder and roughly patted her back with the other.

Octavia, with watery eyes, stood back up and took a deep breath. Gustav, unfortunately for him, was the first face she saw.

"My love," she sighed, throwing her hands against her chest with wide watery eyes that glistened like diamonds.

"Uh, oh," Fen, Susie and Lucinda whispered, sharing an expression of regret.

"My lady... are you okay?" said Basil with concern.

"Bring that little green thing to me, but be careful not to harm its little head, for it is far too precious and beautiful to be manhandled," she sighed once more, completely, and madly in love.

"If that is what my lady orders," Basil spoke with confusion, suspiciously raising one eyebrow.

The guards, followed by a group of servants, tried to block Gustav in so he'd have nowhere to hop. But luckily, he pulled out a small object from Grazox's satchel.

"STAND BACK, YOU FIENDS!" Gustav pulled out the stormball and held it in his hands, although he hadn't the foggiest idea what it actually did.

Everybody stood back and laughed at the poor frog.

"Oh, look," Basil chuckled. "Everybody stand back. He has a snow globe."

Again, everybody in the hall laughed and giggled with amusement. Their laughs echoed through the hall, bouncing off the walls.

"GUSTAV, NOW!" Fen cried loudly.

"Wait, what does it do?" Gustav yelled back, unsure of what exactly he was holding in his hands.

"JUST DO IT!"

"But is it dangerous?" he continued.

"DO IT!" the girls angrily yelled, loosing their patients with him.

Gustav tightly gripped the stormball in his hand and, with the other, nervously slid off the lid until it came off entirely. A sweeping sound filled the hall, a twirling white storm twisted its way out of the bottle like a hurricane. Violent wind forced everybody in the room to fall to their knees, shielding their eyes from the sharp stabs of little specks of ice and snow swirling out of control. The glass walls immediately frosted up, and the once pink varnished floors were now ice blue. Fen grabbed the girls on each arm and headed towards the exit.

"GUSTAV, HURRY," he yelled.

Gustav couldn't hold onto the stormball any longer. He let go and skidded across the icy floors, almost making it to the others. But unfortunately, Lady Octavia grabbed his webbed foot before he could make it out the exit.

"And where do you think you're going, my sweet. You belong to me now."

"I say, let go of me at once, you silly girl. Let go!"

Gustav pulled and kicked, desperately trying to break free from Octavia's deadly grip. Clonked over the head with a rattle, Octavia finally let go of Gustav. The toys bravely gathered together, restraining her, holding her down so she couldn't move.

"Quick, leave why you have the chance," said the wooden puppet.

"but... what about you?" Gustav sniffled.

"I'm afraid it's far too late for us now. But you can still save yourself. Now hurry!"

"Thank you, my friends. I'll never forget this," Gustav yelled, waving behind him with deep gratitude and sadness for leaving them behind.

"QUICK, YOU IDIOTS. THEY'RE GETTING AWAY, AND THEY'RE TAKING MY LOVE AS A HOSTAGE!" Octavia screamed furiously. Breaking free from the toys' hold, she furiously got back up on her little feet and brutally kicked the toys to one side. Shielding her eyes from the cold stormy blizzard, she tried to follow behind Gustav but could barely take another step, for the cold began to take its toll. She crackled with each step, slowly freezing her entire body. With her arm stretched out and her finger pointing towards Gustav, she froze like a statue.

From a distance, the dome above the glass castle resembled a giant snow globe, enchanting, capturing one's complete attention as if by magic.

"Hurry," Fen called out to the others.

Looks like luck was on their side once more as they safely made it to the front doors. The doors that they wished they had never entered.

"Quick, over there," said Fen. Grabbing a large piece of wood, they tried to bolt the doors so the others wouldn't come rushing out behind them.

"Hurry up and do it," Lucinda squeaked, watching Fen and Gustav do all the work while chomping on her nails.

"Guys," Susie huffed, watching the others try and bolt the doors shut in a panic. But no one listened until she yelled again. "GUYS!"

The others finally stopped what they were doing and turned their heads to Susie.

"They're cursed, remember? They can't leave the castle, so you're wasting your time."

They all stood back with relief. How on earth did they manage to forget something as insane as that.

"Come here, you." Susie grabbed Gustav into her arms and kissed him repeatedly, thanking him for saving their lives and apologising for thinking he couldn't.

Fen gave him a big pat on the back. "Thank you, if it wasn't for you, I would have spent the rest of my days as a fluffy teddy trapped with that lunatic and these two," he laughed.

"Oi," Susie chuckled.

Gustav was so proud of himself; he was finally starting to feel like a real hero. If only he could have freed the poor toys that saved his life.

"What do we do now?" Lucinda cried, tired, and fed up.

"Now, we need to be careful not to fall into any more traps," Fen answered with a sigh.

"Let's go," said Susie.

Susie trotted off ahead with Gustav while Fen took his time at the back with Lucinda.

"So, who was the love potion for?" he asked curiously with blushing cheeks.

"None of your business," Lucinda coughed. "But, if you must know, it was for Tobin." She smiled giddily to herself.

"Of course it was," Fen mumbled beneath his breath.

"Come on, you two, we got to keep moving," Susie yelled, way ahead of them continuing with their journey.

STOWAWAY
CHAPTER TWENTY-FIVE

The pirates celebrated their small but glorious victory by singing songs and getting drunk beneath the bright burning stars. The captain had made a small exception on this occasion and had allowed her men to open one of the rum barrels. Dizzy with fatigue, Igor felt uneasy. He wasn't drunk, although the fumes of liquor were in his head streaming through his brain cells. Hobgoblins' sense of smell was powerful and could be somewhat frustrating at times. The scent of rum combined with the salty sea air and the pirates' torturous endless songs left him feeling queasy. With his knees wobbling about like jelly, he stood.

"Seasick are we?" Grazox laughed, viciously ripping into a turkey leg.

"I think I need to lie down. All this singing is making me nauseous," sighed the hobgoblin with irritation in his gruff voice, widening his eyes as he gazed over to the pirates dancing arm-in-arm in circles. Rubbing his large round belly in a circular motion, he headed below deck towards the sleeping quarters.

"Poor Igor," said Drew, watching her friend walk away, wobbling about from one side of the deck to the other.

The sea at night was eerily dark, almost black. But as long as the stars and moon shined their bright light, Drew felt safe. The pirates had lit a bunch of lanterns that brightened up the deck as they danced and drank the night away, enjoying a great feast.

"So... do you think the captain will take us to this island now she got what she wanted?" said Drew.

She stared at the captain from a distance, she was sat in her throne made from carved wood, petting her panther. Iona laughed, watching her men idiotically dance around with jewels wrapped around their necks and dangling from the palms of their hands. Some of the pirates wore gold crowns while the others drank from large shiny gold goblets, mocking the Lords of Oro City.

"I'll take care of it in the morning. Tonight let's just eat and get some rest," said Grazox, handing her a bunch of juicy purple grapes.

"You!" yelled one of the drunk pirates.

"Me?" Tobin responded, pressing his hand against his chest.

"Yes, you. Come, come, and drink with us," he said, waving him over with his grimy hand.

Tobin, not wanting to offend the couple of drunk pirates, joined them and hesitantly sat by their side.

"I am Clem. And this bag of bones is Luka."

"Tobin," the boy replied as he awkwardly sat between the two rum-stinking pirates.

"You like her, yes," said Luka.

"Who?" Tobin confusingly answered, shifting his eyes around the ship.

"The girl." Luka laughed, pointing his rum bottle over to Drew, who sat on the other side of the deck alongside Grazox, eating food the pirates stole from Oro City.

"What makes you say that?" said Tobin, awkwardly trying to hide his blushing cheeks.

"You can't keep your eyes off her, boy," Clem chuckled.

Tobin, too proud to admit he had any feelings for Drew, sat up aggressively, not wanting to hear another word the drunk pirates had to say. Embarrassed, he tried to walk away.

"Just admit it, boy," Luka laughed, raising his bottle of rum into the air with a silly grin.

"Yeah, tell the girl how you really feel," Clem hiccupped, patting his bottle above his mouth, desperately trying to get the last drop of rum to drip out.

Tobin wanted so badly to tell Drew how he felt about her but was too afraid to admit it to himself. After the death of his beloved parents, he swore he would never allow himself to love again.

"TELL HER!" the pirates laughed as they continuously insisted the boy speak the truth.

"Tell her what?" came a voice.

Tobin, in panic, turned to his uncle, who stood behind him with a handful of grapes. He couldn't help but be curious about the conversation his nephew had struck up with the drunken pirates.

"Nothing, Uncle," Tobin coughed, suddenly feeling his nerves shoot up and down with anxiety.

"The boy's in love," Clem whispered with a chuckle, followed by a squeaky hiccup right before passing out and crashing onto his back like a drunken slob.

"Fool," Luka laughed, tilting his head back and taking a large sip of rum.

"What?" Grazox smirked. "With who?" He smiled, interested in who the lucky girl was who had managed to steal his nephew's heart. For so long, he had prayed for his nephew to find peace and love in his heart once again and become the young man he once was. The young man who wasn't riddled with so much hate and anger. Whose mind wasn't clouded with darkness and revenge. The young man who he used to be when his parents were still alive.

"Her," said Luka, effortlessly pointing over to Drew, who still sat on the other side of the deck, stuffing her face with a great feast. Shifting his gaze away from the girl, Grazox's soft smile suddenly turned into a bitter frown. "Can I have a moment alone with my nephew?"

"Of course, of course," Luka slurred. As he got up, his knees caved in, almost making him crash to the ground alongside Clem, who was still very much passed out on his back. "Oops. Sorry, my friend," Luka laughed, pressing his hands onto Clem's fat bouncy belly, using it to find his balance by pushing himself back up. He was so drunk he didn't know which way to go. Grazox and Tobin impatiently watched the pirate wobble about, trying to regain his balance. As Luka finally stumbled away, Grazox was all alone to talk freely with his nephew.

"Is it true?" said Grazox with a furious look in his eyes.

"What?" his nephew timidly answered, shifting his eyes from side to side, not daring to look directly into his uncle's face.

"Are you in love with her?"

"With who?"

"DREW!" Grazox snapped, losing his patience as he waited for a straightforward answer.

Feeling trapped inside one of his nightmares, Tobin opened his mouth to defend himself, but every time he opened it, no words came out. Until eventually he finally found the courage to speak. "Of course not, Uncle," he answered with an awkward smirk. "How could you ask such a thing. Why on earth would I be in love with her."

Grazox knew his nephew far too well to know when he was lying and when he spoke the truth. He always had this look, a look of someone whose heart was heavy with great sadness. Grazox paused tensely, staring at the boy.

"Your mouth says no... but your eyes are saying something else... You are in love with her, aren't you?"

Tobin stood in silence; there was no point in trying to deny it. His uncle stared into his dark brown eyes like he could see straight through him, sensing all the feelings he had kept locked away for so long. "Uncle, I—"

"No," said Grazox raising his hand. "Listen to me and listen to me carefully. You cannot fall in love with her, do you understand? We are on a mission here, trying to save our world from destruction. You cannot allow yourself to fall in love with the very reason we are going to war."

"I understand, Uncle," the boy sighed. "I'm sorry, I don't know what's wrong with me. I can't control the way I feel." He paused, staring off into the distance then spoke again. "I fell in love the second I laid eyes on her. From the very moment we were introduced, I've been fighting my feelings, and it's eating me up inside. I've never felt this way before. I don't like it. And I don't know why this is happening."

Grazox placed his hand onto his nephew's shoulder with a sympathetic look in his eyes. "You're just longing for love like the rest of us. It's natural to search for light, especially in the darkest of times. Believe me, son, I know what it's like to fall so madly in love that it fills your heart with every emotion you could think of. Emotions you thought were impossible to feel, emotions you thought never existed until you met the right person. There's not a second of the day when I don't tell my wife I love her." Grazox's eyes welled up with the mention of his wife, but in a time when one must be strong, he sucked it all in and continued to warn his nephew of the dangers he would endure if he let his emotions get the better of him.

"But you cannot fall in love with Drew. She's a Star, the daughter of a God. She's far too important. She and Ruya are our only hope of our world surviving the darkness the queens will bring with them when they return. As a Protector, we have a job to do, *you* have a job to do, and that's keeping the Star safe from harm. Do not let your feelings for her get in the way of that. You can get too emotionally involved, and that could cloud your judgment which will lead to disaster. Believe me, I've seen it happen before, and I don't want that for you. If you truly love her, then do what was asked of you and protect her, that's all." Grazox, once again placed his hand onto the boy's shoulder.

Tobin lowered his head, staring at the floor. "I understand, Uncle," he softly spoke, placing his hand above his uncle's.

"I love you like a son. You're my brother's child, the only family I have left in this horrible world, and I'm just looking out for you. We have no idea how this is all going to end. We have no idea what fate awaits us. Especially those girls. And at the end of it all... I don't want your heart broken." Placing his hands on each side of Tobin's cheeks, Grazox cupped the boy's face into his palms and looked him dead in the eye. "You can never tell her how you feel. Do your job as a Protector and Protect, and if we see the light at the end of all this, then you're free to speak the truth and let the girl know how you feel."

Both uncle and nephew exchanged one final look of secrecy before finally departing.

"Well, look who's back. How you feeling?" Drew had a wooden bowl in her lap filled with fresh fruit. Back from his short nap, Igor had joined her after regaining his strength.

"Better now the singing has stopped," he answered, reaching for a shiny red apple.

"Well, don't get too happy. I think they're just taking a break," she laughed, gripping onto a dagger, trying to slice the thick skin off a mango.

"Ouch!" Drew cried, dropping the mango to the ground, accidentally piercing her thumb with the dagger's sharp blade.

"My lady, are you okay?" The hobgoblin jumped with concern.

"I'm fine, Igor, thank you… bloody thing," she sighed with irritation, sucking on her wound in pain.

The mango rolled across the wooden deck but was suddenly stopped by a black boot. The captain roughly grabbed hold of Drew's wrist. She stared at the girl's glowing silvery blood dripping down her thumb like the tear of an angel. Drew, too shocked, didn't even try to pull her arm away. She felt tense and slightly intimidated by Iona as she continued to curiously stare at the starlight leaving her body.

"Feroz!" yelled the captain to her right-hand man.

"Yes, Captain," he answered, rushing to her aid.

Drew took a large gulp, expecting the worst now that the captain had learnt the truth.

"Bring me a clean cloth."

"Right away, Captain."

The captain once again paused, intensely staring at Drew. "You should be more careful. There are many out there hunting someone with your… special ways."

"Here you are, Captain," said Feroz, handing Iona a little white cloth.

"Leave us," she said, taking the cloth from his hand.

"If I bled the way you do, I wouldn't be so careless with a dagger in hand around strangers."

"It's not what you think… I—"

"I know what you are," said the captain.

"You do?" Drew whispered in fear. Horrified, she had a vision of the captain ordering her men to attack Grazox and the others and take her for herself.

"Yes," said the captain, "but do not fret; your secret's safe with me." She handed Drew the little cloth to hide and clean up her wound.

Drew was suddenly lost for words. "You mean, you're not going to—"

"In the future, little one, be more careful. Next time you might not be so lucky whose eyes gaze upon that glowing light." Iona looked down at Drew's thumb, referring to the blood that shone brighter than any star in the galaxy.

Drew took in Iona's words and suddenly gained some respect for the captain, grateful to her that she hadn't told her men or tried to take her for her own selfish intentions.

"Please don't tell Grazox. He will be furious with me for being so careless," she pleaded, tightly wrapping the cloth around her sore thumb.

Before walking away, Iona gave her a little side smile and tilted her head, reassuring her that her secret would stay only between them.

"You really should be more careful, my lady. You know there are those out there that mean you harm. People are searching for the Star, and if the wrong person had seen that, god knows what would have happened," Igor spoke with great concern.

"I know, I know," Drew tutted, rolling her eyes. "I'm sorry, it really was an accident. I promise in the future I'll be more careful. Just promise you'll keep this between us. Last thing I need is to hear Grazox's trap." Once again, Drew took the mango in her hand. About to take a bite, she was suddenly interrupted. A loud commotion broke out among the men. But it wasn't the sound of singing or being drunk; it was a surge of violent anger. The men had found something. What was a pleasant, joyful night had been interrupted by an intruder.

"Captain!" one of the pirates hollered, showing his crooked, discoloured teeth.

"What is going on here? What's all this noise?" Iona approached her crew, who stood around in a large crowd. She roughly barged her way through, pushing some of the crew members to one side, and saw one of her men, Driss, who was still wearing the emerald gown he had stolen from Oro City, holding a scrawny man by the arms.

"Who is this?" said the captain.

"A stowaway, he was hiding in the barrels," Driss spat, roughly throwing the defenceless man to the ground like a ragdoll as the rest of the crew yelled and growled with rage.

Petrified, the stowaway stayed on his knees with his face pressed down onto the ground, not daring to look up.

"What is your name?" said the captain.

He waited a few seconds before answering her. "Hic—"

"Look at me when I'm talking to you!" said the captain, raising her voice.

The man, out of fear, took his time before raising his head from the ground.

"Good. Now what is your name?" the captain asked again.

"Hickman," he answered with a quivery lip.

"Tell me, Hickman, how did you board my ship?"

"I hid among your men while they were loading it up with treasures they had stolen from the city."

"And why would you risk your life doing a thing like that?" said the captain curiously.

Lowering his head, he didn't answer her question. Taking a glimpse of his clothes, she knew right away he wasn't a lord, but a servant.

"Oh, I see," the captain laughed. "You're here to save your master. Are the lords that scared and pathetic they send a servant to save one of their own," the captain continued to laugh, triggering off her men to laugh along with her. The husky laughter of the pirates got louder and louder like a wave going around the deck in a circular motion, tormenting the poor man.

"NO!" Hickman snapped. Finally having enough, he raised his voice very loudly.

The laughter stopped, and the deck was silent.

"Excuse me?" the captain sneered, angrily raising her weapon towards the servant's face.

"I did not board your ship to save him... but myself," he sighed, lowering his head with deep sorrow once again.

"What do you mean?" said Drew, curiously pushing and shoving her way through the crowd of men, making her way towards Hickman, who was slouched down on his knees in the centre of a circle of intimidating pirates.

"Yes," said the captain, "what exactly do you mean?"

"I saw it as my only opportunity to escape the city and finally break free from my chains. I couldn't breathe; I was suffocating. I no longer wish to live out my days obeying another, quivering with every demand. For centuries my family have served the lords. They have all suffered from the hands of those in power, and I, for one, will no longer stand for it and be a slave for anyone... especially those that call themselves Ruler of the Golden City. I no longer want to live the life of a servant. Never again do I wish to lay eyes on anything gold or sparkly. I was born in Oro City, the richest city of them all, but that does not mean I got to taste the fruits of its splendour. I was born as a servant; I don't want to die as one.

"I've never been beyond the golden walls, and I want to explore the world and be surrounded by the real riches the land has to offer. Go on adventures and live my life as a free man and not somebody's slave. I just want... to be free." As he lowered his head into the palms of his hands, everyone on deck stood still in silence.

The captain gazed down at Hickman with a strange look on her face, conflicted by her feelings. She wasn't sure if she felt sorry for him or if she wanted to feed him to the sharks for sneaking onto her ship. "Liar! It's probably a trick. Take him to the dungeon," the captain finally ordered.

"Wait!" Drew yelled.

Everybody turned around and stared at her.

"What are you doing?" Tobin whispered, awkwardly watching the pirates that surrounded them.

"I don't know," she quietly answered, brushing by the pirates, making her way over to the poor servant.

"I believe him," she stuttered.

"What!" the captain snapped.

"I mean… look at him. He doesn't look like a man who's lying. I felt every word he said. There was a point in my life when I thought I was going to die in Lakeshore and never adventure off beyond the school gates. Now, I'm not saying I've had it as bad as living like a servant, but I know a thing or two about what it feels like to be trapped and belittled by others in a position of power.

"You wouldn't understand that because you obey no one and take no orders. Everyone should live a free life and have the chance to see what's beyond the school gate… or golden wall." She smiled, turning her head to Hickman. "I mean… you're a pirate, a free soul. What would you do if you had your freedom taken away from you?"

"I would make the world and everybody in it pay," the captain answered with great anger. The men roared in the background, clanging their weapons in response to the captain's answer.

"So why not give this man a chance, let him go and enjoy his freedom." Drew hoped maybe somehow she was actually getting through to her, and the captain for once would see sense.

"You're right," the captain sighed, lowering her weapon. "Everybody does deserve to have a taste of freedom."

Drew took a deep breath and rolled her eyes in relief.

"But not when they sneak onto *my* ship! take him away."

The pirates aggressively grabbed the servant by the arms and dragged him away like he was nothing.

"But—"

"Drew," said Grazox, stopping her from following them. "Know your place. We're guests on this ship." Placing his hand on her shoulder, he gently pulled her back. "The captain is a stubborn person; she listens to no one, best you don't anger her by interfering with her affairs. You did your best. It was kind of you to even speak up; not many would have."

"I don't know... I kinda felt bad for him. I related to some of what he was saying."

"Don't worry, I'm sure everything will work out fine." He smiled with confidence, patting her left cheek. But he knew all too well what happened when you angered the captain. There was no turning back. After he had left her alone, Drew felt a sudden sadness come over her.

"Uncle's right, best you don't anger her or she will never take us to the island."

Drew turned around and came eye to eye with Tobin while Aero sat on his right shoulder, fluttering his brown wings.

"Open your eyes, for god's sake!" Drew snapped. "She has no intention of taking us to that island; she never did."

"You don't know that" said Tobin.

"Oh, come on, does she look like someone who keeps their word? She got what she wanted, and that's all that matters. Now we're stuck out here wasting time." Drew stormed off to the other side of the deck and sat on the ground, wrapping her arms around her legs, hiding her face between her knees like a helpless child.

"Drew?" Tobin softly spoke, following behind her. "I didn't mean to upset you." He kneeled down beside her and hesitantly placed his hand on her shoulder. "It's going to be okay," he whispered softly.

After a minute or so, with tears streaming down her face, she lifted her head and caught Tobin staring up at the stars. "No, Tobin, it's not going to be okay," she said, putting an end to his stargazing as he focused his eyes back onto her.

"You heard your uncle; we don't have much time left. There's a reason why we needed to get to that island. Like I've heard so many times, the queens will be returning soon. We have no idea when that last star will shift out of line. It could happen any day now, any minute, any second and we're not prepared, then what are we gonna do."

"I understand, Drew, but try not to worry."

"How can I not worry when I know Ruya is out there. She could be hurt for all I know."

"She's not hurt," Tobin coughed with confidence, tilting his head back, staring at the stars once again and cupping both arms around his knees.

"Oh yeah," Drew huffed, wiping her wet cheek. "How do you know?"

"I don't... but you will."

"I don't understand."

"You're both one and the same person. You share a heart, giving you both a connection, so if she was hurt, I think deep down you would know. Somehow you would feel it."

Drew paused, staring at her sore thumb, then lifted her head back up and smiled.

"Really, you think so?"

"I know so," he smirked.

Drew took a moment to appreciate this tender moment with Tobin. This was the first time she thought she could actually grow to like him.

"Thanks, Tobin. You know you're not that bad after all." She smiled playfully, nudging her shoulder against his. As he desperately tried to hide his blushing cheeks, he returned a smile and gently nudged her back, enjoying the rest of the night stargazing together.

ONWARDS
CHAPTER TWENTY-SIX

The whipping wind sent icy tingles down the men's backs. Ruya felt more of a cold stabbing sensation coursing through her pale, fragile body, shivering repeatedly in her fur coat. Beast led the men high up into the dangerous snow-capped mountains surrounded by steep, slopy sides and sharp pillars that could kill a man instantly with one fatal slip.

"Ruya, stay close to me," Tibbot yelled through the harsh snowy blizzard.

Ruya didn't answer; she couldn't. She tried to nod her head, but even that took an effort. Her feet were numb from the cold, and her eyebrows frosted up along with the tip of her nose. But still she managed to keep Potion safely tucked away in her coat as she had throughout her entire journey.

"There must be a safer way up; it's too dangerous to continue," Zyra yelled over to Tibbot.

"You want to reach Kartal. I'm afraid this is the only way to her. Trust us, we know what we're doing," Beast interrupted.

Without another word, the men continued to climb deeper and deeper into the mountains until they reached the legendary warrior.

***

Some of the men's snores viciously crept their way into Drew's ear. But still, the sound of their thunderous snores didn't wake her, for she was an extremely deep sleeper. Some of the crew slept in wooden bunks neatly aligned, while others slept in swinging hammocks slung from the deck overhead.

"My lady. My lady, wake up," Igor whispered quietly, trying not to wake the men. Igor nudged and pulled anxiously until she opened her eyes.

"Igor? What is it?" Drew yawned irately. Drew hated many things but being woken up from a good dream was the worst.

"You better get up; I think something is happening," said the hobgoblin.

"But it's not sunrise yet; it's too early to wake up now," she moaned, slowly turning to her side once again, hoping to fall back into her dream.

"My lady, get up!" he yelled.

"Jeez, okay. Didn't know hobgoblins were so pushy. What's so important you had to wake me up?" she huffed.

"I think the pirates are getting ready."

"Getting ready for what?" she coughed curiously.

"I heard a couple of the men speak of an execution."

"Oh no," Drew gasped. "Hickman."

The pirates stomped around deck carrying large gold crates of jewels and leftover food from last night's celebration. Drew spotted Tobin across the deck and immediately rushed over to his side.

"What's happening?" she said.

"I'm not sure, but it's not good," he answered, taking a small piece of meat, moving it closer towards Aero's beak, who was clutched around his arm. "I think they're preparing an execution for the prisoners," he continued, stroking the tip of his finger onto his pet eagle's head.

"If only there was a way I could speak to him."

"Who?" said Tobin.

"That poor servant guy from last night," she sighed. Drew had strangely developed compassion for Hickman. She was always sympathetic and concerned herself over those who had bad misfortune and suffered at the hands of those in higher positions.

From the side of his eye, Tobin caught Clem and Luka sneakily trying to open one of the rum barrels. "Hurry, the captain will be up shortly," said Clem, twiddling his chubby fingers with anticipation.

"I'm trying, you fool," Luka snapped with sweat drizzling down his dark tan.

"Thirsty, are we, boys?" said Tobin sneaking up behind them.

Clem and Luka immediately stopped what they were doing and quickly carried on scrubbing the deck.

"We don't know what you're talking about," said Luka, splashing his cloth filled with bubbles onto the dirty wooden deck.

"Rum barrels still locked up; I see. I could help you know," Tobin continued.

Clem and Luka glanced over at each other and laughed, scrubbing the deck on their hands and knees. "What can you help us with, boy?" Clem chuckled.

Tobin reached into his pocket and sneakily pulled out a little bottle of rum he had stashed there for safekeeping. When the captain gave the order to lock up the barrels, he saw it as an opportunity and managed to steal a bottle when no one was looking. He knew it would come in handy for a moment like this. Pirates were predictable and would happily sell their right arm just for a drop of liquor. As he dangled the bottle above them, Clem and Luka bolted up onto their feet quicker than lightning.

"HA," Clem laughed, holding onto his fat round belly. "See, didn't I say the boy was a good one."

"Hand it over, boy," Luka twitched, reaching out his filthy hand.

"I don't think so," Tobin chuckled, safely placing the bottle back into his pocket. "First, there's something you need to do for me."

***

"Beast!" one of the Vorst yelled over to their leader. "There's a steep drop ahead; what do we do?"

They all looked to the leader for an answer. "We'll have to walk across the edge. It's the only way."

"But that's too dangerous," Zyra voiced her concern once again.

"You want to waste another day and walk around, be our guest," Beasts answered sternly.

Placing his hand on Zyra's shoulder, Tibbot stopped her from speaking another word against the leader of the Vorst. "I understand your frustration, but we need them if we're going to reach Kartal. Remember why we're here."

"It's too dangerous. He'll be leading his men to their deaths if we continue," Zyra said angrily.

"We can't waste another day and go around, that will take too much time." He smiled and placed his hand on her shoulder once again. "Have faith."

Beast was the first to walk across the thin icy edge. With his large furry boots, he gently slid his feet across in turn, gripping his hooks into the icy rocks for support. Without any trouble, he managed to make it across safely. "Okay, who's next?" he yelled across from the other side.

"Ruya and Berwin should go next," said Zyron.

"I don't need anybody holding my hand," complained the grumpy old gnome. "I'll be fine to walk across on my own."

"Suit yourself," Tibbot coughed, with no energy to argue.

Berwin took the first step onto the thin edge and glanced below him, which was a huge mistake. The deep drop made him feel dizzy and paralysed him with fear.

"You okay there, Berwin?" Tibbot yelled over.

"Erm, maybe I should have someone come along with me after all." Berwin shivered in fear.

"Okay, Ruya, remember, whatever you do, don't look down and keep using your hooks for a steady balance," said Tibbot, tightening the ropes around her waist for extra safety.

"Okay," she gulped with shaky hands.

"I believe in you; you've got this," said Zyron.

Ruya made sure Potion was tucked away in her coat nice and safe before she took her first step. She followed behind Berwin, who was sweating in fear. Heights were never his strongest point. Step by step, with their bellies pressed against the rocks and their heels dangling off the edge, they gently made it halfway. They were almost there when Berwin decided to look down once again. Sharp rocks and ice, shaped like dragon's teeth, rested below them. In a panic, Berwin rushed across the thin edge, hoping to make it safely to the other side.

"BERWIN, NO!" Ruya gasped in horror. His rope that was attached to her own snapped, and Berwin slipped. Ruya had managed to grab the gnome's little hand just in time. She tried to pull him back up, but with her hands frozen, they were far too weak, which made him seem even heavier than he was.

"RUYA!" Tibbot yelled, rushing towards her.

"No, let me," said Zyron, "I'm much lighter than you. It won't be able to hold the three of you at once."

"Okay," Tibbot nodded. "Hurry and be careful, lad."

Zyron had successfully made his way over to Ruya and pulled Berwin back up.

"Zyron, thank you." Ruya nervously laughed with great gratitude, shakily wiping the sweat from her forehead.

"Don't thank me just yet. We still haven't made it to the other side," he laughed. But thankfully they did. As Ruya leapt to safety, a thin layer of ice cracked. Zyron managed to grab her in his arms just in time. They just stared at each other.

"Thanks again." Ruya blushed, gripping tightly to his arm.

He returned an awkward smile. "No worries."

"Ahem," Berwin coughed, eyeing up the pair grumpily, feeling rather annoyed for he almost lost his life. Immediately they parted. Zyron awkwardly fixed his belt while Ruya, blushing, quickly straightened out her messy hair. Next to walk across was Zyra, followed by Kruze. Now was Tibbot's turn, followed by the other men. Everything seemed to be going well, but unfortunately things took a turn for the worse. The ground beneath them rumbled, the snow rushed down from the rocks.

"AVALANCHE!" Tibbot yelled with his large hands cupped around his mouth.

A mass of snow, ice and rocks descended rapidly down the mountainside.

"RUN! RUN!" Beast yelled. But it was too late.

***

"I'm not sure about this," said Clem, trying to unlock the doors to the dungeon where the prisoners were being held.

"Do you want this or not?" said Tobin, taking the small bottle of rum from his pocket once again, reminding them why they agreed in the first place.

"Faster," Luka quietly yelled, pressuring Clem to unlock the door.

As they stood aside and waited for the pirates to unlock the door, Tobin noticed Drew looking a little taken aback with a strange look on her face.

"What's wrong?" he said.

"Nothing... I suddenly feel very cold." Drew, feeling a little bizarre, wrapped her arms around her body and shivered.

"That's strange. I feel just fine," Tobin answered, watching the pirates finally unlock the door.

"You have five minutes," the pirates warned. "If the captain finds us down here, they won't be the only ones being executed." Luka reached out his hand and snapped his fingers impatiently, waiting for his reward. Tobin rolled his eyes and reached for the rum in his pocket. And just like that, Clem and Luka were gone.

"Alright, you heard what they said; you have five minutes." Tobin gently nudged Drew further into the dungeon. "I'll be out here if you need me."

"Thanks, Tobin, means a lot that you did this." She gave him a small peck on the cheek then walked off before she could see him blush. With his hand pressed against his cheek, he softly smiled to himself then left the room.

"Who's there?" said the prisoner, clasping his hands around the iron bars of his cell.

"It's only me, don't worry," said Drew.

"You're the girl who tried to save me?"

Drew smiled. "I just wanted to see how you were holding up."

"I'm fine. To be honest, I'm just glad to be away from Oro City. That place could be a nightmare." He paused, then spoke again. "Thank you, by the way, for speaking up for me. In all my years, no one has ever done anything quite like that for me before. You truly are an angel."

"Well, I don't know about that," she laughed, scratching the back of her scruffy hair. "All I know is if I were ever in your position, I would have wanted someone to speak up for me. It's not fair you're being punished for wanting a better life. I know what it's like to be stuck somewhere people mistreat you."

"Is this the place you spoke of before… Lakeshore, was it?"

"Yes. It is… *was*, a school for girls."

"Sounds awful," Hickman gasped.

"It was," Drew laughed. In the very small amount of time she got to speak to the prisoner, she managed to tell him all about Lakeshore, Miss Gumberg, Lucinda, and the night they were attacked. Of course, she had left out the part that she was a Star.

"I'm sure Lord Genzo and that dreadful woman Gumberg would have got along splendidly," Hickman shrugged.

"It's strange," Drew sighed. "Despite the fact that she was a horrible wretch, I often think about her and Lakeshore. Seems like a lifetime ago. And the idea of not knowing what happened to them haunts me. She treated me badly, but I still never wished any harm on her."

"That's because you have a good heart." Hickman smiled. "No matter how bad someone treats you, people like you always find a way to forgive. And that takes a lot of courage."

"Nah, I think Ruya is more of the forgiving type," Drew smirked, scratching the back of her head once again.

"I need to speak with the prisoner!" came a loud voice.

Tobin burst through the door. "Quick, Grazox and the captain are coming."

"You must leave, hurry."

"Don't worry, I promise I'll find a way to save you," said Drew, quickly rushing towards the exit. Luckily they had managed to escape the dungeon before anyone saw them.

"Where's Genzo?" said Grazox, entering the gaol.

"I kept him locked away in another room," said the captain.

"Take me to him."

Entering the next room where Lord Genzo was being kept, Grazox aggressively bolted towards him and held up the Wanted poster, slamming it against the iron bars of his cell. "Why are you after me and my men?" Grazox demanded an answer.

Genzo, not giving Grazox any eye contact, didn't utter a word. He just sniffed his nose and looked away in a snide manner.

"ANSWER ME!" Grazox growled in rage.

"Why so angry?" the captain smirked. "You should have known a man like this will not talk."

"I should have known a pirate wouldn't keep their word neither, but here we are," Grazox huffed with frustration. "You had no intention of ever taking us to the island, did you?"

The captain raised her eyebrows and said nothing.

"Why did you take me for a fool?" said Grazox.

"I needed you to show me the way to the Golden City," the captain answered without a care. "You and your friends can take a few pieces of gold and jewels as a reward for showing me and my men the way."

"I don't want any gold... I want you to take us to Zehir Island like you promised."

"I'm afraid I cannot do that. We will be taking the prisoners to our city Azul for a proper execution. You may find someone there willing to sail you to the island. But for now, I will hear no more about it. Unless you want you and your friends to be fed to the sharks."

Grazox, in rage, stormed out of the dungeon.

"Ha," Lord Genzo smirked beneath his breath.

"That's right," smiled the captain. "Laugh while you can, for you won't be laughing for much longer."

"My men are coming for me." Lord Genzo smirked with confidence.

The captain paused, then sarcastically looked around the room, mocking the lord. "That's funny, it's going on to two days now. I mean it's been a while. Wouldn't they have come for you already? If it was me in your place, my men would have burned down your city by now. Maybe your people don't think you're worthy enough to save."

Lord Genzo paused in deep thought. "They're coming for me; you'll see."

Captain Iona smiled. "You keep telling yourself that. Soon we'll reach Azul. There you'll be executed, and even if your men decide to show up, it will be too late. No one can save you now."

Genzo sneered as he looked up at the captain with great hatred.

"Get some rest, Lord. We will be reaching our destination very soon." Iona laughed, slowly closing the creaking door behind her.

Above deck, Drew paced up and down, trying to figure out a way to save Hickman.

"Give it up, my lady," Igor sighed. "Sometimes you just have to accept we can't save everyone."

"I know I can save him; I just know I can," Drew argued, gnawing away at her nails, desperately trying to come up with a quick solution.

"Captain, what's the plan?" said Feroz.

The captain, with a gleam in her eyes, took a large breath and inhaled the salty sea air. She placed her hand above Siyah's head and smiled. "We're going home."

Grazox and Drew exchanged a look of desperation. How were they going to get to the island now and stop the queen's men before their awakening?

The pirates raised the sails, and Iona took one more glance out to sea. "Onwards, my brothers."

Epilogue

Deep in the murky, shadowy lands of Sombra, an army of Great Beasts, Gors and Screamers gathered outside a large fortress made from the bones of the Fire Queen's enemies.

Large, spiked doors opened, letting in a gust of cold wind. The firelit torches against the black stone walls danced chaotically. A scrawny, pale, skeletal-like man with a hunch back and a fearsome squint in his left eye crept down the dungeon stairs. His long, black, hooded cloak flickered in the candlelight, fluttering behind him, leaving a trail of darkness.

Approaching the dungeon, the old man raised his lantern to get a clearer look, each prisoner quivered with fear as he passed by. Stopping at the very last cell, the old man moved his lantern closer between the bars.

"It is almost time for the return of our queen," the old man sneered with a whispery voice.

The prisoner didn't answer and remained in the shadows.

"Soon, darkness will be upon us, and you'll have no choice but to tell us where the Star is hiding."

Still, the prisoner refused to speak. The only sound that came from the cell was the echo of dripping water that leaked from a black hole above into a small puddle in the corner.

"You have nowhere to run to this time, Princess. If you speak now, the queen may let you die with dignity."

Finally, the prisoner confidently stepped out of the shadows of her cell.

"You will never have the Star, nor will your queen," she bravely spoke.

The old man raised his long, pointy, skinny finger towards the woman. And with a vile smirk, raised one eyebrow. "You will be the first to perish in Her Majesty's flames if you refuse to speak of the Star." Lowering his hand, he gave her one last smile, and with his hunched back, limped his way back up the dungeon stairs. Sneering behind his bony shoulder, he looked back with an evil gleam in his bright yellow eyes. "When the queen returns, I suggest you tell her all she wishes to know. You don't want to die the same way your father did." The old man harshly slammed the dungeon doors behind him.

With tears in her eyes, Miss Mabel clutched onto the black iron bars of her cell with a look of worry and defeat.

"Girls, wherever you may be, I pray you're safe. For I fear the worst is yet to come."

MUSHRO
SLEEPY MEADOW
SKALA
BLACK ROCK
THE SWAMPS
GOBLIN VILLE

OREST
ZEHIR ISLAND
AZUL
SAND LAND
THE GYPSY LANDS
HE WASTE LANDS

CPSIA information can be obtained
at www.ICGtesting.com
Printed in the USA
LVHW101935100622
720908LV00003B/20